"You should have come directly to me."

Augusta narrowed her eyes. "What would have been the point? You would have lectured me and made a most unpleasant scene, just as you are doing now."

"I would have taken care of the matter for you," Harry said grimly. "And you would not have put your neck and your reputation at risk as you did tonight."

"It seems to me, my lord, that both of our necks and our reputations were at risk tonight." Augusta tried a tentative smile of appeasement. "And I must say, you were most impressive. I am very glad you turned up when you did, sir. It seems to me it all turned out for the best and we should both be thankful the thing is over."

"Do you really believe I am going to let the matter rest there?"

Augusta drew herself up proudly. "I will, of course, understand completely if you feel my actions tonight have put me beyond the pale. If you feel you cannot possibly tolerate the notion of marrying me, I shall be quite willing to cry off and free you from this engagement."

"Free me, Augusta?" Harry reached out to catch hold of her wrist. "I fear that is impossible now. I have come to the conclusion that I shall never be free of you. You are going to bedevil me for the rest of my life and if that is to be my fate, I may as well take what consolation I can for what I shall be obliged to endure."

Before Augusta had time to realize what he intended, Harry had yanked her across the short distance between them. An instant later she found herself lying across his strong thighs, as his mouth came down on hers. . . .

Rendezvous

BANTAM BOOKS BY AMANDA QUICK

Seduction

Surrender

Scandal

Rendezvous

Rendezvous

AMANDA QUICK

BANTAM BOOKS
NEW YORK • TORONTO • LONDON • SYDNEY • AUCKLAND

RENDEZVOUS
A BANTAM BOOK / NOVEMBER 1991

ISBN 0-553-29325-7

Published simultaneously in the United States and Canada

Bantam Books are published by Bantam Books, a division of Bantam Doubleday Dell Publishing Group, Inc. Its trademark, consisting of the words "Bantam Books" and the portrayal of a rooster, is Registered in U.S. Patent and Trademark Office and in other countries. Marca Registrada. Bantam Books, 666 Fifth Avenue, New York, New York 10103.

PRINTED IN THE UNITED STATES OF AMERICA

RAD   0 9 8 7 6 5 4 3

FOR TWO VALUED EDITORS:

*Coleen O'Shea, who took a chance
on the first Amanda Quick books*

AND

*Rebecca Cabaza, who edits them now
with understanding and perception.*

MY THANKS

PROLOGUE

The war was over.

The man once known as Nemesis stood at the window of his study and listened to the clamor in the streets. All London was celebrating the final defeat of Napoléon at Waterloo as only Londoners could celebrate. Fireworks, music, and the roar of thousands of exuberant people filled the city.

It was over, but as far as Nemesis was concerned it was not finished. Now it appeared it would never be finished, at least not to his satisfaction. The identity of the traitor who had called himself Spider was still a mystery. The final puzzle must go unsolved. There would be no justice for those who had died at the Spider's hands.

As for Nemesis, he knew it was time to get on with his own life. He had duties and responsibilities to fulfill, not the least of which was the matter of finding himself a suitable bride. He would approach the task as he approached everything else, with logic and intellectual precision. He would make up a list of candidates and he would choose one from the list.

He knew exactly what he wanted in a wife. For the sake of his name and title, she must be a woman of virtue. For the sake of his soul she must be a woman he could trust, a woman who understood the meaning of loyalty.

Nemesis had lived too long in the shadows. He had learned the true value of trust and loyalty and he knew they were priceless.

He listened to the noise in the streets. *It was over*. No man was more grateful for an end to the appalling waste of war than the man who had been called Nemesis.

But a part of him would always regret that there had been no final rendezvous between himself and the bloody traitor known as Spider.

1

There was no sound as the library door was opened, but the slight draft created caused the candle flame to flicker. Crouched in the shadows at the opposite end of the long room, Augusta Ballinger froze in the act of trying to insert a hairpin into the lock of her host's desk.

From her damning position on her knees behind the massive oak desk she stared in stunned shock at the single candle she had allowed herself for illumination. The flame sputtered once more as the door was closed very softly. With a gathering sense of dread, Augusta peered over the edge of the desk and gazed down the length of the darkened room.

The man who had entered the library stood quietly in the inky depths near the door. He was tall and appeared to be wearing a black dressing gown. She could not see his face in the gloom. Nevertheless, as she crouched there holding her breath, Augusta was aware of a deep, disturbing sense of awareness.

Only one man had this effect on Augusta's senses. She

did not need to see him clearly in order to hazard a guess as to who lounged there like a large beast of prey in the shadows. She was almost certain it was Graystone.

He was not sounding an alarm, however, which was an enormous relief. It was strange how at ease he appeared to be in the darkness, as if it were his natural environment. Then again, Augusta thought optimistically, perhaps he saw nothing out of the ordinary. Perhaps he had only come downstairs to look for a book and assumed the candle had been carelessly left behind by someone who had come down before him.

For an instant Augusta even dared to hope he had not noticed her peering anxiously at him over the top of the desk. Perhaps he had failed to observe her there at the other end of the big room. If she was very careful she might still get out of this mess with her reputation intact. She ducked her head behind the edge of the heavily carved oak.

She heard no footfalls on the thick Persian carpet, but a moment later the man spoke from no more than a few feet away.

"Good evening, Miss Ballinger. I trust you have found something suitably edifying to read down there behind Enfield's desk? But surely the light is rather poor in that location."

Augusta recognized the terrifyingly calm, unemotional male voice at once and groaned silently as her worst fears were confirmed. It *was* Graystone.

Just her bad luck that of all the guests who were inhabiting Lord Enfield's country house this weekend, her discoverer was her uncle's good friend. Harry Fleming, Earl of Graystone, was the one man in the house who probably would not believe any of the glib tales she had carefully prepared.

Graystone made Augusta uneasy for several reasons, one of which was that he had a disconcerting manner of looking straight into her eyes as if he would look into her very soul and demand the truth. Another reason she was wary around him was that he was simply too bloody damned clever.

Frantically Augusta began sorting among the various stories she had planned to use in just such an eventuality as this. It would have to be a very clever story. Graystone was no fool. He was gravely dignified, chillingly correct, and at times solemnly pompous as far as Augusta was concerned, but he was no fool.

Augusta decided she had no choice but to brazen out the embarrassing situation. She forced herself to smile very brightly as she looked up with a feigned little start of surprise.

"Oh, hello, my lord. I did not expect to encounter anyone here in the library at this hour. I was just searching for a hairpin. I seem to have dropped one."

"There appears to be a hairpin stuck in the lock of the desk."

Augusta managed another amazed start and jumped to her feet. "Good heavens. So there is. What a very odd place for it to have landed." Her fingers trembled as she snatched the pin out of the lock and dropped it into the pocket of her chintz wrapper. "I came downstairs to look for something to read because I could not sleep and the next thing I knew, I had lost my hairpin."

Graystone solemnly considered her bright smile in the pale glow of the candle flame. "I am surprised you could not sleep, Miss Ballinger. You certainly had plenty of exercise today. I believe you participated in the archery contest organized for the ladies this afternoon, and then there was the long walk to the old Roman ruins and the picnic. All topped off by a great deal of dancing and whist this evening. One would have thought you'd have been quite exhausted."

"Yes, well, I expect the unfamiliarity of my surroundings is to blame. You know how it is, my lord, when one sleeps in a strange bed."

His cool gray eyes, which always made Augusta think of

a cold winter sea, gleamed faintly. "What an interesting observation. Do you sleep in a lot of strange beds, Miss Ballinger?"

Augusta stared at him, uncertain how to take the question. A part of her was very nearly inclined to believe there might have been a deliberate sexual innuendo in Graystone's seemingly polite remark. But that was impossible, she quickly decided. This was *Graystone,* after all. He would never do or say anything the least improper in the presence of a lady. Of course, he might not consider her a lady, she reminded herself bleakly.

"No, my lord, I do not have much opportunity to travel and therefore have not grown accustomed to the notion of changing beds frequently. Now, if you will excuse me, I had best be getting back upstairs. My cousin might awaken and notice I am gone. She would worry."

"Ah, yes. The lovely Claudia. We certainly would not want the Angel to become concerned about her hoyden of a cousin, would we?"

Augusta winced. It was obvious she had sunk quite low in the earl's estimation. Graystone clearly considered her an ill-mannered baggage. She could only hope he did not also think her a thief.

"No, my lord, I would not want to worry Claudia. Good evening, sir." Head high, she made to step around him. He did not move and she was forced to halt directly in front of him. He was extremely large, she noticed. Standing this close, she felt overwhelmed by the solid, unyielding strength in him. Augusta gathered her courage.

"Surely you do not intend to keep me from returning to my bedchamber, my lord?"

Graystone's brows rose slightly. "I would not want you to go back upstairs without that which you came for."

Augusta's mouth went dry. *He could not possibly know about Rosalind Morrissey's journal.* "As it happens, I feel quite sleepy now, my lord. I do not think I shall need anything to read, after all."

"Not even the item you hoped to find in Enfield's desk?"

Augusta took refuge in high dudgeon. "How dare you imply I was attempting to get into Lord Enfield's desk? I told you, my hairpin simply happened to land in the lock when it fell."

"Allow me, Miss Ballinger." Graystone removed a length of wire from his dressing gown pocket and slid it gently into the desk lock. There was a faint but quite distinct *snick*.

Augusta watched in astonishment as he eased open the top drawer and studied the contents. Then he waved a casual hand, inviting her to search for what she wanted.

Augusta eyed the earl warily, chewed on her lower lip for a few tense seconds, and then hastily leaned down and began pawing through the drawer. She found the small leather-bound volume beneath several sheets of foolscap. She snatched it up at once.

"My lord, I do not know what to say." Augusta clutched the journal and looked up to meet Graystone's eyes.

The earl's harsh features appeared even more grim than usual in the flickering candlelight. He was not a handsome man by any measure, but Augusta had found him strangely compelling since the moment her uncle had introduced her to him at the start of The Season.

There was something in those aloof gray eyes of his that made her want to reach out to him, even though she knew he probably would not thank her for it. Part of the attraction, she knew, must have been nothing more than sheer feminine curiosity. She sensed a closed door deep inside the man and she longed to open it. She did not know why.

He was really not her type at all. By rights she ought to have found Graystone extremely dull. Instead, she found him a dangerously disturbing enigma.

Graystone's thick, dark hair was flecked with silver. He was in his mid-thirties but he could easily have passed for forty, not because of any softness in his face or form; rather the opposite. There was a hard, somber quality about him that spoke of too much experience and too much knowledge. It was an odd mien for a classical scholar, she realized. Another part of the enigma.

Dressed as he was for his bedchamber, it was clear the breadth of Graystone's shoulders and the lean, solid lines of his body were natural and owed nothing to his tailor. There was a sleek, heavy, predatory grace about him that sent strange sensations down Augusta's spine. She had never met a man who had the effect on her that Graystone had.

She did not understand why she found herself attracted to him. They were complete opposites in temperament and manner. In any event, the effect was quite wasted, she was sure. The sensual thrill, the shiver of excitement that vibrated deep within her whenever the earl was close, the feelings of anxiety and wistful longing she experienced when she spoke to him, all meant nothing.

Her deep conviction that Graystone had known loss, just as she had, and the knowledge that he needed love and laughter to overcome the bleak, cold shadows in his eyes did not matter in the slightest. It was well known Graystone was hunting a bride, but Augusta knew he would not consider a woman who might overset his carefully regulated life. No, he would select another sort of female entirely.

She had heard the gossip and knew what the earl required in a wife. Rumor had it that, being the methodical type he was, Graystone had a list and that he had set his standards very high. Any woman who wished to get herself added to his list, it was said, must be a model of the female virtues. She must be a paragon: serious of mind and temperament, dignified of manner and bearing, and totally unsullied by even a hint of gossip. In short, Graystone's bride would be a pattern of propriety.

The sort of female who would never dream of rifling through her host's desk in the middle of the night.

"I would imagine," the earl murmured, eying the small

volume in Augusta's hand, "that the less said, the better. The owner of that journal is a close friend of yours, I assume?"

Augusta sighed. There was little to lose now. Further protests of innocence were useless. Graystone obviously knew far more than he ought about this night's adventures.

"Yes, my lord, she is." Augusta lifted her chin. "My friend made the foolish mistake of writing down certain matters of the heart in her journal. She later came to regret those emotions when she discovered that the man involved was not equally sincere in his feelings."

"That man being Enfield?"

Augusta's mouth tightened grimly. "The answer to that is obvious. The journal is here in his desk, is it not? Lord Enfield may be accepted in the most important drawing rooms because of his title and his heroic actions during the war, but I fear he is a despicable cad when it comes to dealing with women. My friend's journal was stolen immediately after she told him she was no longer in love with him. We believe a maid was bribed."

"We?" Graystone repeated softly.

Augusta ignored the veiled inquiry. She certainly was not going to tell him everything. Most especially she was not going to enlighten him on the matter of how she had arranged to be here at Enfield's estate this weekend. "Enfield told my friend he intended to demand her hand in marriage and that he would use the contents of her journal to ensure that she accepted."

"Why would Enfield bother to blackmail your friend into marriage? He is exceedingly popular with the ladies these days. They all appear to be quite enthralled by his account of his own actions at Waterloo."

"My friend is the heiress to a great fortune, my lord." Augusta shrugged. "Gossip has it that Enfield has gambled away a great deal of his own inheritance since returning from the continent. He and his mother have apparently decided he must marry money."

"I see. I had not realized word of Enfield's recent losses had spread so quickly among the fair sex. He and his mother have both worked very hard to keep the matter quiet. This large house party is evidence of that."

Augusta smiled very pointedly. "Yes, well, you know how it is when a man begins hunting for a very particular sort of bride, my lord. The rumors of his intentions precede him and the more intelligent of the quarry take note."

"Are you implying something about my own intentions, by any chance, Miss Ballinger?"

Augusta felt the heat in her cheeks but refused to back down before his cool, disapproving gaze. After all, Graystone invariably looked disapproving when he was talking to her.

"Since you ask, my lord," Augusta said firmly, "I may as well tell you that it is well known you are looking for a very specific sort of female to marry. It is even said you have a list."

"Fascinating. And do they say who is on my list?"

She glowered at him. "No. One hears only that it is a very short list. But I suppose that is understandable when one considers your requirements, which are said to be extremely strict and exacting."

"This grows more intriguing by the moment. What, precisely, are my requirements in a wife, Miss Ballinger?"

Augusta wished she had kept her mouth shut. But prudence had never been one of the stronger suits of the Ballingers who descended from the Northumberland side of the family. She plunged on recklessly. "Rumor has it that, like Caesar's wife, your bride must be above suspicion in every way. A serious-minded female of excessively refined sensibilities. A pattern of propriety. In short, my lord, you are looking for perfection. I wish you luck."

"From your rather scathing tone, I have the impression you think a truly virtuous woman is not going to be easy to find."

"That depends upon how you define virtuous," she

retorted crossly. "From what I have heard, your definition is unduly strict. Few women are true paragons. It is very boring being a paragon, you know. Indeed, sir, you would have a somewhat longer list of candidates from which to select if you were searching for an heiress, as Lord Enfield is. And we all know how short in supply heiresses are."

"Unfortunately, or fortunately, depending on one's view of the situation, I do not happen to be in need of an heiress. I can, therefore, set other standards of suitability. Your information concerning my personal affairs amazes me, however, Miss Ballinger. You seem very well informed. May I ask how you came to have so many details?"

She certainly was not going to tell him about Pompeia's, the ladies' club which she had helped form and which was a bottomless well of rumors and information. "There is never a shortage of gossip in town, my lord."

"Very true." Graystone's gaze narrowed speculatively. "Gossip is as common as the mud on London's streets, is it not? You are quite correct when you assume I would prefer a wife who will come to me without a great deal of it sticking to her."

"As I said, my lord. I wish you luck." It was very depressing hearing Graystone confirm everything she had heard about his infamous list, Augusta thought. "I only hope you do not regret setting your standards so very high." She tightened her grip on Rosalind Morrissey's journal. "If you will excuse me, I would like to return to my bedchamber."

"By all means." Graystone inclined his head, gravely polite as he stepped aside and allowed her to pass between him and Enfield's desk.

Relieved at the promise of escape, Augusta stepped quickly around from behind the huge desk and rushed past the earl. She was all too well aware of the intimacy of their situation. Graystone dressed for riding or a formal ball was impressive enough to capture all her attention. Graystone dressed for bed was simply too much for her unruly senses.

She was halfway down the length of the room when she remembered something very important. She stopped and swung around to face him. "Sir, I must ask you a question."

"Yes?"

"Will you feel obliged to mention any of this unpleasant business to Lord Enfield?"

"What would you do if you were in my place, Miss Ballinger?" he asked dryly.

"Oh, I would definitely maintain a gentlemanly silence on the subject," she assured him quickly. "After all, a lady's reputation is at stake."

"How true. And not just that of your friend. Yours is just as much at risk tonight, is it not, Miss Ballinger? You have played fast and loose with the most valuable jewel in a woman's crown, her reputation."

Damn the man. He really was an arrogant beast. Too pompous, by half. "It is quite true I have taken some risks tonight, my lord," she said in her most chilling tones. "You must remember that I am descended from the Northumberland Ballingers, not the Hampshire Ballingers. The women of my side of the family do not care a great deal for Society's rules."

"You do not consider that many of those strictures are designed for your own protection?"

"Not in the least. Those rules are designed for the convenience of men and nothing more."

"I beg to differ with you, Miss Ballinger. There are times when Society's rules are extremely inconvenient for a man. I can promise you that this is one of those occasions."

She frowned uncertainly and then decided to let that enigmatic comment pass. "Sir, I realize you are on the best of terms with my uncle and I would not have us be enemies."

"I quite agree. I assure you I have no wish to be your enemy, Miss Ballinger."

"Thank you. Nevertheless, I must tell you frankly that you and I have very little in common. We are completely opposite in terms of temperament and inclination, as I am sure you will acknowledge. You are a man who will always be bound by the dictates of honor and correct behavior and all those pesky little rules that govern Society."

"And you, Miss Ballinger? What will bind you?"

"Nothing at all, my lord," she said candidly. "I intend to live life to the fullest. I am, after all, the last of the Northumberland Ballingers. And a Northumberland Ballinger would sooner take a few risks than bury herself beneath the weight of a lot of very dull virtues."

"Come, Miss Ballinger, you disappoint me. Have you not heard that virtue is its own reward?"

She scowled at him again, vaguely suspicious that he might just possibly be teasing her. Then she assured herself that was very unlikely. "I have seen very little evidence of that fact. Now, please answer my question. Will you feel obliged to tell Lord Enfield about my presence here in his library this evening?"

He watched her with hooded eyes, his hands shoved deep into the pockets of his dressing gown. "What do you think, Miss Ballinger?"

She touched the top of her tongue to her lower lip and then smiled slowly. "I think, my lord, that you are well and truly tangled up in the snare of your own rules. You cannot tell Enfield about this night's work without violating your own code of behavior, can you?"

"You are quite right. I will not say a word to Enfield. But I have my own reasons for keeping silent, Miss Ballinger. And as you are not privy to those reasons, you would be well advised not to make assumptions."

She tipped her head to one side, considering that carefully. "The reason for your silence is the obligation you feel toward my uncle, is it not? You are his friend and you would not want to see him embarrassed because of my actions this evening."

"That is a little closer to the truth, but it is not the whole of it, by any means."

"Well, whatever the reason, I am grateful." Augusta grinned suddenly as she realized she was safe and so was her friend Rosalind Morrissey. Then it suddenly struck her that there was still one very large question that remained unanswered. "How did you know what I had planned here tonight, my lord?"

It was Graystone's turn to smile. He did so with a curious twist to his mouth that sent a chill of alarm through Augusta.

"With any luck that question should keep you awake for a while tonight, Miss Ballinger. Consider it well. Perhaps it will do you good to ponder the fact that a lady's secrets are always prey to gossip and rumor. A wise young woman should, therefore, take care not to take the sort of risks you took tonight."

Augusta wrinkled her nose in dismay. "I should have known better than to ask you such a question. It is obvious someone of your high-minded temperament cannot refrain from issuing reproving lectures at every opportunity. But I forgive you this time because I am grateful for both your help and your silence tonight."

"I trust you will continue to feel grateful."

"I am certain I shall." On impulse Augusta hurried back toward the desk and came to a halt directly in front of him. She stood on tiptoe and kissed him lightly, fleetingly on the edge of his hard jaw. Graystone stood like stone beneath the soft caress. She knew she had probably shocked him to the core and she could not resist a wicked little chuckle. "Good night, my lord."

Thrilled by her own boldness and by the success of her foray to the library, she whirled around and dashed toward the door.

"Miss Ballinger?"

"Yes, my lord?" She halted and turned back to face him once more, hoping that in the shadows he could not see that her face was flaming.

"You have neglected to take your taper with you. You

will need it to climb the stairs." He picked up the candle and held it out to her.

Augusta hesitated and then went back to where he stood waiting for her. She snatched the candle from his hand without a word and hastened out of the library.

She was glad she was not on his list of prospective wives, she told herself fiercely as she flew up the stairs and down the hall to her bedchamber. A Northumberland Ballinger female could not possibly chain herself to such an old-fashioned, unbending man.

Aside from the marked differences in their temperaments, they had few interests in common. Graystone was an accomplished linguist and a student of the classics, just as was her uncle, Sir Thomas Ballinger. The earl devoted himself to the study of the ancient Greeks and Romans and ~~_____~~ imposing books and treatises that were well received by people who knew about that sort of thing.

If Graystone had been one of the exciting new poets whose burning prose and smoldering eyes were currently all the rage, Augusta would have understood her own fascination for him. But he was not that sort of writer at all. Instead he penned dull works with titles such as *A Discussion of Some Elements in the Histories of Tacitus* and *A Discourse on Certain Selections from Plutarch's Lives*. Both of which had been recently published to critical acclaim.

Both of which Augusta had, for some unknown reason, read from beginning to end.

Augusta extinguished the candle and let herself quietly into the bedchamber she was sharing with Claudia. She tiptoed over to the bed and took off her dressing gown. A shaft of moonlight seeping in through a crack in the heavy drapes revealed her cousin's sleeping form.

Claudia had the pale golden hair of the Hampshire branch of the Ballinger family. Her lovely face with its patrician nose and chin was turned to the side on the pillow. The long sweep of her lashes hid her soft blue eyes. She deserved the title of the Angel which had been bestowed upon her by the admiring gentlemen of the *haute ton*.

Augusta took personal pride in her cousin's recent social success. It was Augusta, after all, who, at four-and-twenty, had undertaken to launch the younger Claudia into the world of the *ton*. Augusta had decided it was the least she could do to repay her uncle and her cousin for taking her into their home after her brother's death two years ago.

Sir Thomas, being a Hampshire Ballinger and therefore quite wealthy, had the blunt to pay for his daughter's launch and he was generous enough to underwrite Augusta's expenses as well. Being a widower, however, he lacked the female contacts to manage a successful Season. He also lacked any knowledge of style and dash. That was, of course, where Augusta could contribute mightily to the project.

The Hampshire Ballingers might have the money in the family, but the Northumberland Ballingers had gotten all the style and dash.

Augusta was very fond of her cousin, but the two of them were as different as night and day in many ways. Claudia would never have dreamed of sneaking downstairs after midnight to break into her host's library desk. Claudia had no interest in joining Pompeia's. Claudia would have been appalled at the notion of standing around in one's wrapper at midnight chatting with a distinguished scholar such as the Earl of Graystone. Claudia had a very nice sense of the proprieties.

It occurred to Augusta that Claudia was probably on Graystone's list of prospective wives.

Downstairs in the library Harry stood for a long while in the darkness and stared out the window at his host's moonlit gardens. He had not wanted to accept the invitation to Enfield's weekend house party. Normally he avoided such events whenever possible. They tended to be boring in the extreme and an utter waste of his time, as were most of Society's frivolous affairs. But he was hunting a wife this Season and his quarry had a disconcerting habit of appearing in unpredictable locations.

Not that he had been bored this evening, Harry reminded himself wryly. The task of keeping his future bride out of trouble had certainly enlivened this little jaunt into the countryside. He wondered how many more such midnight rendezvous he would be obliged to endure before he had her securely wed.

She was such a maddening little baggage. She ought to have been married off to a strong-willed husband years ago. She needed a man who could keep her firmly in hand. One could only hope it was not too late to control her rash ways.

Augusta Ballinger was twenty-four years old and still unwed due to a variety of reasons. Among them had been a series of deaths in the family. Sir Thomas, her uncle, had explained that Augusta had lost her parents the year she turned eighteen. The pair had been killed in a carriage accident. Augusta's father had been driving in a wild, neck-or-nothing race at the time. His wife had insisted on accompanying him. Such recklessness was, Sir Thomas admitted, unfortunately typical of the Northumberland side of the family.

There had been very little money left for Augusta and her older brother, Richard. Apparently a certain devil-may-care attitude toward economy and financial matters also characterized the Northumberland Ballingers.

Richard had sold off all his small inheritance except for a cottage in which he and Augusta lived. He used the money to buy himself a commission. And then he had been killed, not in battle on the continent, but by a highwayman on a country lane not far from the cottage. He had been on leave at the time and had been riding home from London to see his sister.

Augusta, according to Sir Thomas, had been devastated by Richard Ballinger's death. She was alone in the world.

Sir Thomas had insisted she had come to live with himself
and his daughter. Augusta had eventually agreed. For
months she had appeared sunk in a deep melancholy that
nothing could lift. All the fire and dazzle that characterized
the Northumberland side of the family appeared to have
been extinguished.

And then Sir Thomas had had his brainstorm. He had
asked Augusta to undertake the task of giving his daughter
a Season. Claudia, a lovely bluestocking, was twenty years
old already and had never had her opportunity in town
because her own mother had died two years previously.
Time was running out, Sir Thomas had gravely explained to
Augusta. Claudia deserved a Season. But being from the
intellectual side of the family she had no knowledge of how
to go on in Society. Augusta had the skills and instincts
and—through her new friendship with Sally, Lady Arbuthnott—the contacts to show her cousin the ropes.

Augusta had been reluctant at first but she had soon
plunged into the business with true Northumberland
Ballinger enthusiasm. She had worked night and day to
make Claudia a great success. The results had been spectacular and somewhat unexpected. Not only was the
demure, well-behaved bluestocking Claudia immediately
hailed as the Angel, but Augusta herself had proved just as
successful.

Sir Thomas had confided to Harry that he was quite
pleased and expected both young ladies to form suitable
alliances.

Harry had known it was not going to be quite that
simple. He strongly suspected that Augusta, at least, had
very little intention of finding herself a suitable husband.
She was having too much fun.

With that lustrous chestnut brown hair of hers and those
lively, mischievous topaz eyes, Miss Augusta Ballinger
could have had a dozen husbands by now had she truly
desired marriage. The earl was very sure of that.

His own, undeniable interest in her amazed him. On the

face of it, she was definitely not what he required in a wife, but he could not seem to ignore her or put her out of his mind. From the moment his old friend Lady Arbuthnott had suggested that Augusta be added to Harry's list of prospective brides, he had been fascinated by her.

He had even established a personal friendship with Sir Thomas in order to get closer to his prospective wife. Not that Augusta was aware of the reason behind the new association between her uncle and Harry. Few people were ever aware of Harry's subtle plots or the reasons behind them until he chose to reveal himself.

Through his conversations with Sir Thomas and Lady Arbuthnott, Harry had learned that, as strong-willed and reckless as Augusta was, she nevertheless had a steadfast loyalty to family and friends. Harry had learned long ago that loyalty was as priceless as virtue. Indeed, in his mind it was synonymous with virtue.

One could even overlook the occasional harebrained escapade such as the one that had taken place tonight, if one knew the lady could be trusted. Not that Harry intended to allow that sort of nonsense to continue after he had Augusta safely wed.

During the past few weeks Harry had come to the conclusion that, although he might have moments of dire regret, he was going to marry Augusta. Intellectually, he could not resist. She would never bore him. In addition to her capacity for intense loyalty, she was intriguing and unpredictable. Harry, who had always been compelled by puzzles, had found her impossible to ignore.

As a final seal on his fate, there was the undeniable fact that he was fiercely attracted to Augusta. His whole body tightened with awareness whenever she was near.

There was a feminine energy about Augusta that captured his sense. The image of her had begun to haunt him when he was alone at night. When he was near her he would find his gaze lingering on the curve of her breasts, which were far too prominently displayed in the scandalously low-cut gowns she wore with such natural grace. Her small waist and sweetly flaring hips teased and tantalized as she moved about with a subtle swaying motion that never failed to make the muscles of his lower body clench.

Yet she was not beautiful, he told himself for the hundredth time—at least not in the much-admired classical style. He conceded, however, that there was an undeniable charm and vivacity about her faintly slanting eyes, tilted nose, and laughing mouth. Lately he had grown increasingly hungry for a taste of that mouth.

Harry stifled an oath. It was very much as Plutarch had once written about Cleopatra. Her beauty was not remarkable in itself, but her charm and presence were irresistible, even bewitching.

He was no doubt mad to be plotting to wed Augusta. He had set out looking for another sort of woman entirely. Someone serene, serious, and refined. Someone who would be a good mother to his only child, Meredith. Someone who would devote herself to hearth and home. Most importantly, he had intended to marry a woman who was completely free of any taint of gossip.

Previous Graystone brides had brought disaster and scandal to the title and had left a legacy of unhappiness that stretched back for generations. Harry had no intention of marrying a female who would continue that sad tradition. The next Graystone bride must be above reproach. And above suspicion.

Like Caesar's wife.

He had set out to find that treasure which intelligent men had always considered more valuable than rubies: a virtuous woman.

Instead he had found himself a reckless, headstrong, extremely volatile creature named Augusta who had the potential to make his life a living hell.

Unfortunately, Harry realized, he seemed to have lost interest in all the other females on his list.

2

*A*ugusta arrived at the door of Lady Arbuthnott's imposing town house shortly after three on the day following her return to London. She had Rosalind Morrissey's
journal safely tucked into her reticule and she could hardly
wait to tell her father that all was well.

"I shall not be staying long today, Betsy," she said to her
young maid as they went up the steps. "We must hurry
home to help Claudia prepare for the Burnett soiree. This is
a very important evening for her. The most eligible males
in Town will no doubt be there and we want her to look her
best."

"Yes, ma'am. Miss Claudia always looks like an angel
when she goes out, though. I don't expect tonight will be
any different."

Augusta grinned. "How very true."

The door was opened just as Betsy was preparing to
knock. Scruggs, Lady Arbuthnott's elderly, stoop-shouldered
butler, glared at the newcomers as he saw two other young
women out the door.

Augusta recognized Belinda Renfrew and Felicity Oatley
as they came down the steps. They were both regular
visitors to Lady Arbuthnott's home, as were several other
well-bred ladies, all of whom came and went on a regular
basis. The ailing Lady Arbuthnott, the neighbors frequently noted, was never short of visitors.

"Good afternoon, Augusta," Felicity said cheerfully.
"You are looking well this afternoon."

"Yes, indeed," Belinda murmured, her eyes speculative
as she took in the sight of Augusta dressed in a fashionable
dark blue pelisse over a sky blue gown. "I am delighted you
are here. Lady Arbuthnott has been most anxiously awaiting your arrival."

"I would not dream of disappointing her," Augusta said
as she went past with a laughing smile. "Or Miss Norgrove,
either." Belinda Renfrew, Augusta knew, had wagered
Daphne Norgrove ten pounds that the journal would not be
returned to its owner.

Belinda gave her another sharp glance. "All went well at
the Enfield house party?"

"Of course. I do hope I shall see you later this evening,
Belinda."

Belinda's answering smile was wry. "You most certainly
shall, Augusta. And so will Miss Norgrove. Good afternoon."

"Good afternoon. Oh, hello, Scruggs." Augusta turned
her smile on the glowering, bewhiskered butler as the door
was closed behind her.

"Miss Ballinger. Lady Arbuthnott is expecting you, of
course."

"Of course." Augusta refused to be intimidated by the
irascible old man who guarded the Arbuthnott front door.

Scruggs was the only male member of the Arbuthnott
household and held the high honor of being the only man
Lady Arbuthnott had hired in ten years. He was new to her
staff this season and in the beginning no one had understood quite why Sally had taken him on. It was obviously

a gesture of kindness on her part because the aging butler was clearly unable to cope physically with many of his duties. There were entire days and evenings when he did not appear at the door at all due to his rheumatism and other assorted complaints.

Complaining was one of the few things Scruggs apparently enjoyed. He complained of everything: his painful joints, the weather, his duties in the household, the lack of assistance he received in carrying out those duties, and the low wages he claimed Lady Arbuthnott paid.

But somewhere along the line the ladies who visited here so regularly had concluded that Scruggs was the finishing touch they had been needing all along. He was eccentric, original, and vastly entertaining. They had adopted him wholeheartedly and now counted him as a valuable addition to the premises.

"How is your rheumatism today, Scruggs?" Augusta asked as she untied her new feather-trimmed bonnet.

"What was that?" Scruggs glared at her. "Speak up if you want to ask a question. Don't understand why ladies are always mumbling. Think they could learn to speak up."

"I said, how is your rheumatism today, Scruggs?"

"Extremely painful, thank you, Miss Ballinger. Rarely been worse." Scruggs always spoke in a deep, raspy voice that sounded like gravel being ground under a carriage wheel. "And it don't help none having to answer the door fifteen times in one hour, I'll tell you that much. All the comings and goings around here are enough to drive a sane man straight into Bedlam, if you ask me. Don't understand why you females can't stay put for more than five minutes."

Augusta clucked sympathetically as she reached into her reticule and drew out a small bottle. "I have brought along a remedy you might wish to try. It was my mother's recipe. She used to make it up for my grandfather, who found it very effective."

"Is that right? What happened to your grandfather, Miss

Ballinger?" Scruggs took the bottle with a wary expression and examined it closely.

"He died some years ago."

"From the effects of this medicine, I daresay."

"He was eighty-five, Scruggs. Legend has it that he was found dead in bed with one of the housemaids."

"Is that a fact?" Scruggs eyed the bottle with renewed interest. "I shall try it straightaway, in that case."

"Do that. I only wish I had something equally useful to give to Lady Arbuthnott. How is she today, Scruggs?"

Scruggs's bushy white brows rose and fell. There was a gleam of sadness in his blue eyes. Augusta was always fascinated by those beautiful aqua-colored eyes. They struck her as surprisingly sharp and disconcertingly youthful in his heavily lined and whiskered face.

"This is turning out to be one of her good days, Miss. I believe you will find she is anticipating your arrival with great enthusiasm."

"Then I shall not keep her waiting." Augusta glanced at her maid. "Go and have a cup of tea with your friends in the kitchen, Betsy. I shall have Scruggs summon you when I am ready to leave."

"Yes, ma'am."

Betsy bobbed a curtsy and hurried off to join the other maids and footmen who had accompanied their mistresses on the afternoon visits. There was never a lack of companionship in the Arbuthnott kitchens.

Scruggs moved toward the entrance of the drawing room with a painfully slow, crablike gait. He opened the door, wincing broadly at the discomfort the action gave him. Augusta went through the doorway and stepped into another world.

It was a world where she could experience, at least for a few hours each day, a sense of belonging. She had longed for that feeling since her brother had been killed.

Augusta knew Sir Thomas and Claudia had tried very hard to make her feel at home and she, in turn, had tried equally hard to make them believe she did feel a part of their family. But the truth was she felt like an outsider. With their serious, intellectual ways and their sober, thoughtful airs, so typical of the Hampshire branch of the family, Sir Thomas and Claudia would never be able to fully understand Augusta.

But here on the other side of Lady Arbuthnott's drawing room door, Augusta felt that, if she had not quite found a true home, she was at least among her own kind.

She was inside Pompeia's, one of the newest, most unusual, most exclusive clubs in all of London. Membership was, of course, by invitation only and nonmembers had no real notion of just what went on in Lady Arbuthnott's drawing room.

Outsiders assumed Lady Arbuthnott amused herself by conducting one of the many fashionable salons that appealed to the ladies of London society. But Pompeia's was much more than that. It was a club, patterned along the lines of a gentlemen's club, that catered to modern-thinking females of the *ton* who shared a certain unconventional outlook.

At Augusta's suggestion the club had been named Pompeia's after Caesar's wife, the one he had divorced because she had not been completely above suspicion. The name suited its membership. The ladies of Pompeia's were all well bred and quite socially acceptable, but they were generally considered to be Originals, to say the least.

Pompeia's had been carefully designed to emulate the fashionable gentlemen's clubs in several respects. But the furnishings and decor had been given a decidedly feminine twist.

The warm yellow walls were covered with paintings of famous classical women. There was a nicely done portrait of Panthia, the healer, at one end of the room. Beside it was a beautifully rendered picture of Eurydice, mother of Philip II of Macedon. She was portrayed in the act of dedicating a monument to education.

A depiction of Sappho composing her poems with a lyre hung over the fireplace. Cleopatra on the throne of Egypt graced the opposite end of the long room. Other paintings and statues illustrated the goddesses Artemis, Demeter, and Iris in a variety of graceful poses.

The furniture was all in the classical style and an assortment of judiciously placed pedestals, urns, and columns had been artfully scattered about to give the drawing room the look of an ancient Greek temple.

The club offered its patrons many of the amenities offered in White's, Brooks's, and Watier's. There was a coffee room in one alcove and a card room in another. Late in the evenings club members with a taste for whist or macao could frequently be found at the green baize tables, still elegantly garbed in the gowns they had worn earlier to a ball.

High-stakes playing was strongly discouraged by the management, however. Lady Arbuthnott made it clear she did not want any enraged husbands knocking on her door to make inquiries about their ladies' recent heavy losses in her drawing room.

A variety of daily newspapers and journals including the *Times* and the *Morning Post* were always available in the club, as were a cold buffet, tea, sherry, and ratafia.

Augusta swept into the room and was immediately enveloped in the pleasant, relaxed atmosphere. A plump, fair-haired woman seated at the writing desk glanced up and Augusta nodded to her as she went past.

"How is your poetry going, Lucinda?" Augusta inquired. Lately it seemed that every club member's burning ambition was to write. Augusta alone had escaped the call of the muse. She was quite content to read the latest novels.

"Very well, thank you. You are looking in fine form this morning. Can we assume good news?" Lucinda gave her a knowing smile.

"Thank you, Lucinda. Yes, you may assume the best.

'Tis positively amazing what a weekend in the country can do for one's spirits."

"Or one's reputation."

"Precisely."

Augusta sailed on down the length of the room to where two women were enjoying tea in front of the fire.

Lady Arbuthnott, patronness of Pompeia's and known to every member of the club as Sally, was wearing a warm India shawl over her elegant, long-sleeved, rust-colored gown. She was ensconced in the chair closest to the flames. From that vantage point she commanded a view of the entire room. Her posture was, as always, elegantly graceful and her hair was piled high in a fashionable coiffure. Lady Arbuthnott's charms had once been the toast of Society.

A wealthy woman who had been widowed shortly after her marriage to a notorious viscount thirty years earlier, Sally could afford to spend a fortune on her clothes and did so. But all the fine silks and muslins in the world could not disguise the underlying weariness and the painful thinness caused by the wasting disease that was slowly destroying her.

Augusta was finding Sally's illness almost as hard to endure as Sally herself was finding it. Augusta knew that losing Sally was going to be like losing her mother all over again.

The two women had first met at a bookshop where they had both been perusing volumes on historical subjects. They had struck up an immediate friendship which had deepened quickly over the months. Although separated by years, their shared interests, eccentricities, and sense of adventure had drawn them close. For Augusta, Sally became a replacement for the mother she had lost. And for Sally, Augusta was the daughter she had never had.

Sally had assumed the role of mentor in many ways, not the least of which was in opening the doors of the *ton*'s most exclusive drawing rooms. Sally's contacts in the social world were legion. She had enthusiastically whisked Augusta into

the whirl of Society. Augusta's natural social abilities had
secured her position in that Society.

For months the two women had enjoyed themselves
immensely dashing about London. And then Sally had
begun to tire easily. In a short while it became evident that
she was seriously ill. She had retreated to her own home and
Augusta had created Pompeia's to entertain her.

In spite of the ravages of her illness, Sally's sense of
humor and acute intelligence were still very much intact.
Her eyes sharpened with pleased amusement as she turned
her head and saw Augusta.

The young woman seated next to Lady Arbuthnott
glanced up also, her pretty dark eyes filled with anxiety.
Rosalind Morrissey was not only the heiress to a considerable fortune, she was also enchantingly attractive with her
tawny brown hair and full-bosomed figure.

"Ah, my dear Augusta," Sally said with deep satisfaction
as Augusta bent down and kissed her affectionately on the
cheek. "Something tells me you have met with success,
hmmm? Poor Rosalind here has been quite overset for the
past few days. You must put her out of her misery."

"With pleasure. Here is your journal, Rosalind. Not
exactly with Lord Enfield's compliments, but what does
that signify?" Augusta held out the small leather-bound
volume.

"*You found it.*" Rosalind leaped to her feet and grabbed
the journal. "I can hardly believe it." She threw her arms
around Augusta and gave her a quick hug. "What an
enormous relief. How can I possibly thank you? Was there
any problem? Any danger? Does Enfield know you took it?"

"Well, matters did not go precisely according to plan,"
Augusta admitted as she sat down across from Sally. "And
we should probably discuss the business immediately."

"What went wrong?" Sally asked with interest. "Were
you discovered?"

Augusta wrinkled her nose. "I was interrupted in the
very act of retrieving the journal by Lord Graystone, of all

people. Who would have imagined that he would have been wandering around at that hour? One would think he would have been busy writing another treatise on some moldering old Greek if he was even awake. But no, there he was, sauntering into the library, cool as you please while I was on my knees behind Enfield's desk."

"*Graystone*." Rosalind sank back down into her chair with a horrified expression. "That high stickler? He saw you? He saw my journal?"

Augusta shook her head reassuringly. "Don't worry, Rosalind. He did not know it was yours, but yes, he did discover me in the library." She turned to frown seriously at Sally. "I must say, it was all very mysterious. He apparently knew that I would be there and he even knew I wanted something out of the desk. In fact, he even produced a length of wire and picked the lock. But he refused to tell me his source of information."

Rosalind put a hand to her mouth and her dark eyes widened in alarm. "Dear heaven, we must have a spy in our midst."

Sally made soothing noises. "I am quite certain there is nothing to worry about. I have known the man for years. Graystone's town house is just at the other end of the street, you see. I can tell you from experience that he is almost always possessed of the most unusual information."

"He gave me his word he would not tell a soul about the incident and I am inclined to believe him," Augusta said slowly. "He has become a close friend of my uncle's in recent months, you know, and I believe he thought he was doing Sir Thomas a favor by keeping an eye on me at Enfield's."

"That's another thing about Graystone," Sally said smoothly. "He can be trusted to keep a secret."

"Are you certain?" Rosalind looked at her anxiously.

"Absolutely positive." Sally raised her teacup to her pale lips, took a sip, and set the cup and saucer firmly on the end table. "Now, then, my bold young friends. We have managed to brush through this unfortunate affair safely enough, thanks to Augusta's daring and my own ability to secure invitations for acquaintances on short notice. Lady Enfield did owe me a few favors, after all. However, I feel I should take this opportunity to make a point."

"I believe I know what you are going to say," Augusta murmured, pouring herself a cup of tea. "But it is entirely unnecessary. Not only did Lord Graystone see fit to read me a boring lecture, I can assure you, I have learned a lesson from poor Rosalind's sad plight. I, for one, will never, ever, put anything down in writing that can possibly come back to haunt me."

"Nor will I, ever again." Rosalind Morrissey clutched the journal very close to her breast. "What a beast that man is."

"Who? Enfield?" Sally smiled grimly. "Yes, he is most definitely a bastard when it comes to his dealings with women. Always has been. But there is no denying he fought bravely enough during the war."

"I do not know what I ever saw in him," Rosalind stated. "I much prefer the company of someone like Lord Lovejoy. What do you know of him, Sally? Your information is always the most current, even though you rarely leave the comforts of your own home."

"I have no need to go abroad for the latest *on dit*." Sally smiled. "Sooner or later it all flows through the front door of Pompeia's. As for Lovejoy, I have only recently begun hearing of his charms. They are many and varied, I am told." She glanced at Augusta. "You can testify to that, can you not, Augusta?"

"I danced with him at the Lofenburys' ball last week," Augusta said, remembering the laughing, red-haired baron with the brilliant green eyes. "I must admit it is quite exciting to dance the waltz with him. And he is rather mysterious, I understand. No one seems to know much about him."

"He is the last of his line, I believe. There was

something said about estates in Norfolk." Sally pursed her lips. "But I have no notion of how prosperous his lands are. Best take care that you are not becoming enamored of another fortune hunter, Rosalind."

Rosalind groaned. "Why is it that all the most interesting men have a serious character flaw of one sort or another?"

"Sometimes it is just the reverse," Augusta said with a sigh. "Sometimes the most interesting male around perceives a serious character flaw in a certain female who happens to be quite attracted to him."

"We are discussing Graystone again?" Sally gave Augusta a shrewd glance.

"I fear so," Augusta admitted. "Do you know he all but admitted he has a list of suitable candidates he is reviewing for the position of Countess of Graystone?"

Rosalind nodded soberly. "I have heard about that list. Whoever is on it will find it difficult to live up to the standards set by his first wife, Catherine. She died in childbirth the first year of her marriage. But in that single year she apparently managed to leave behind a lasting impression on Graystone."

"She was a paragon, I presume?" Augusta queried.

"A model of womanly virtue, or so it is said," Rosalind explained wryly. "Just ask anyone. My mother knew the family and frequently held Catherine up to me as an example. I met her once or twice when I was younger and I must confess I found her a prig. Quite beautiful, however. She looked like a Madonna in one of those Italian paintings."

"It is said a virtuous woman is worth more than rubies," Sally murmured. "But I believe many men discover the hard way that virtue, like beauty, is often in the eye of the beholder. It is quite possible that Graystone does not seek another paragon."

"Oh, he definitely wants a paragon," Augusta assured her. "And in my more rational moments, I realize he would

make a perfectly obnoxious, quite intolerable husband for a
woman of my spontaneous and uninhibited temperament."

"And in your more irrational moments?" Sally pressed
gently.

Augusta grimaced. "In my darkest hours I have actually
considered taking up the serious study of Herodotus and
Tacitus, throwing away all my tracts on the rights of
women, and ordering up a whole new wardrobe of unfash-
ionable gowns with very high necklines. But I have found
that if I have a cup of tea and rest for a few minutes such
madness passes quickly. I soon return to my normal self."

"Good heavens, one would certainly hope so. I cannot
see you in the role of a paragon of female behavior." Sally
broke out in uproarious laughter and the sound caused
everyone in the room to turned toward the threesome seated
near the fire. The ladies of Pompeia's smiled knowingly at
each other. It was good to see their patronness enjoying
herself.

Scruggs, who had opened the drawing room door at that
moment, apparently heard the laughter, too. Augusta
happened to glance up and saw him watching his mistress
from beneath his thick, beetled brows. She thought there
was something oddly wistful in his expression.

Then his startling blue eyes met Augusta's and he
bobbed his head once before turning away. She realized
with a start of surprise that he was thanking her silently for
giving Sally the gift of laughter.

A few minutes later on her way out of the club, Augusta
paused to glance at the latest entries in the betting book
that was enshrined on an Ionic pedestal near the window.

She saw that a certain Miss L.C. had wagered a Miss
D.P. the sum of ten pounds that Lord Graystone would ask
for the hand of "the Angel" before the month was out.

Augusta felt quite irritable for the next two hours.

•   •   •

"I swear, Harry, there is a wager on it in Pompeia's betting book. Most amusing." Peter Sheldrake lounged with languid ease in the leather chair and eyed Graystone over his glass of port.

"I am glad you find it amusing. I do not." Harry put down his quill pen and picked up his own glass.

"Well, you wouldn't, would you?" Peter grinned. "After all, there is very little you seem to find amusing about this business of getting yourself a wife. There are wagers in the betting books of every club in town. Hardly surprising there's one in Pompeia's. Sally's collection of dashing female friends work frightfully hard to ape the men's clubs, you know. Is it true?"

"Is what true?" Harry scowled at the younger man. Peter Sheldrake was suffering from a serious case of ennui. It was not an uncommon problem among the men of the *ton,* especially those who, like Peter, had spent the past few years on the continent playing Napoléon's dangerous war games.

"Don't fence with me, Graystone. Are you going to ask Sir Thomas's permission to pay court to his daughter?" Peter repeated patiently. "Come, now, Harry. Give me a hint so that I can take advantage of the situation. You know me, I like a good wager as well as the next man." He paused to grin briefly again. "Or lady, for that matter."

Harry considered the matter. "Do you think Claudia Ballinger would make a suitable countess?"

"Good God, no, man. We're talking about the Angel. She is a model of propriety. A paragon. To be perfectly blunt, she is too much like you. The pair of you will only reinforce each other's worst traits. You will both find yourselves bored to the teeth within a month of the wedding. Ask Sally, if you do not believe me. She happens to agree."

Harry raised his brows. "Unlike you, Peter, I do not require constant adventure. And I most certainly do not want an adventurous sort of wife."

"Now, that is where you are going wrong in your analysis of the situation. I have given this considerable thought and I believe a lively, adventurous wife is precisely what you do need." Peter got to his feet with a restless movement and went to stand at the window.

The fading sunlight gleamed on Peter's artfully styled blond curls and emphasized his handsome profile. He was, as usual, dressed in the first style of fashion. His elegantly tied cravat and crisply pleated shirt were a perfect complement to his faultlessly cut coat and snug trousers.

"It is you who craves action and excitement, Sheldrake," Harry observed quietly. "You have been bored since you returned to London. You spend too much time on your clothes, you have begun to drink too much, and you gamble too heavily."

"While you bury yourself in your study of a lot of old Greeks and Romans. Come, now, Harry, be honest. Admit you, too, miss the life we lived on the continent."

"Not in the least. I happen to be quite fond of my old Greeks and Romans. In any event, Napoléon is finally out of the way at last and I have duties and responsibilities here in England now."

"Yes, I know. You must see to your estates and titles, honor your responsibilities. You must get married and produce an heir." Peter gulped down a long swallow of his wine.

"I am not the only one who must see to his responsibilities," Harry said meaningfully.

Peter ignored that. "For God's sake, man, you were one of Wellington's key intelligence officers. You controlled dozens of agents such as myself who collected the information you wanted. You developed the ciphers that broke several of the most important secret codes the French had. You risked your neck and mine to get the maps that were needed for some of the most crucial battles in the Peninsula. Do not tell me you don't miss all that excitement."

"I much prefer deciphering Latin and Greek to poring

over military dispatches written in sympathetic ink and secret codes. I assure you I find the histories of Tacitus far more stimulating than pondering the workings of the minds of certain French agents."

"But think of the thrill, the danger you lived with on a daily basis for the past several years. Think of the deadly games you played with your opposite number, the one we called Spider. How could you not miss all that?"

Harry shrugged. "My only regret regarding Spider was that we never succeeded in unmasking him and bringing him to justice. As for the excitement, I never sought it out in the first place. The tasks I assumed were more or less thrust upon me."

"But you carried them out brilliantly."

"I discharged my duties to the best of my ability and now the war is over. And none too soon, as far as I'm concerned. You're the one who still seeks out unhealthy thrills, Sheldrake. And I must say, you are finding them in the oddest places. Do you like being a butler?"

Peter grimaced. His blue eyes were bright with wry humor as he turned to face his host. "The role of Scruggs certainly lacks the thrill of seducing a French officer's wife or stealing secret documents, but it has its moments. And it is worth a great deal to see Sally enjoying herself. I fear she will not be with us too much longer, Harry."

"I know. She is indeed a gallant woman. The information she was able to glean from certain parties here in England during the war was invaluable. She took grave risks for her country."

Peter nodded, his gaze thoughtful. "Sally has always loved intrigues. Just as I do. She and I have much in common and it pleases me to guard the portals of her precious club. Pompeia's is the most important thing in her life these days. It gives her much pleasure. You can thank your little hoyden friend for that, you know."

Harry's mouth curved ruefully. "Sally explained that the harebrained notion of a ladies' club modeled after a gentlemen's club was all Augusta Ballinger's idea. Somehow it does not surprise me."

"Hah. It would not surprise anyone who knows Augusta Ballinger. Things have a way of happening around her, if you know what I mean."

"Unfortunately, I believe I do."

"I am convinced Miss Ballinger came up with the idea of the club solely as a way to amuse Sally." Peter hesitated, looking thoughtful. "Miss Ballinger is rather kind. Even to staff. She gave me some medicine for my rheumatism today. Few ladies of the *ton* would have bothered to think of a servant long enough to worry about his rheumatism."

"I did not know you suffered from rheumatism," Harry said dryly.

"I don't. Scruggs does."

"Just see that you guard Pompeia's well, Sheldrake. I do not want Miss Ballinger to come to social grief because of that ridiculous club."

Peter quirked a brow. "You're concerned about her reputation because of your friendship with her uncle?"

"Not entirely." Harry toyed absently with the quill pen on his desk and then added softly, "I have another reason to want her kept safe from scandal."

"*Ah-hah*. I knew it." Peter leaped toward the desk and slammed his empty glass down on the polished surface with explosive triumph. "You're going to take Sally's and my advice and add her to your list, aren't you? Admit it. Augusta Ballinger is going on your infamous list of eligible candidates for the role of Countess of Graystone."

"It defeats me why all of London is suddenly concerned with my marital prospects."

"Because of the way you are going about the business of selecting a wife, of course. Everyone's heard about your list. I told you, there are bets all over town on it."

"Yes, you told me." Harry studied his wine. "What, precisely, was the wager in Pompeia's betting book?"

"Ten pounds that you would ask for the Angel's hand by the end of the month."

"As a matter of fact, I intend to ask for Miss Ballinger's hand this very afternoon."

"Damnation, man," Peter was clearly appalled. "Not Claudia. I know you have the impression she would make you a very proper sort of countess, but a lady who wears wings and a halo is not really what you want. You need a different sort of female altogether. And the Angel needs a different sort of man. Do not be a fool, Harry."

Harry raised his brows. "Have you ever known me to play the fool?"

Peter's eyes narrowed. Then he grinned slowly. "No, my lord, I have not. So that's the way of it, eh? Excellent. *Excellent*. You will not be sorry."

"I am not so certain of that," Harry said ruefully.

"Let me put it this way. At least you will not be bored. You will propose to Augusta this afternoon, then, eh?"

"Good God, no. I do not intend to propose to Augusta at all. This afternoon I am going to ask her uncle for his permission to wed his niece."

Peter looked momentarily blank. "But what about Augusta? Surely you will have to ask her personally first? She is four-and-twenty, Graystone, not a schoolroom miss."

"We both agreed I am not a fool, Sheldrake. I am not about to put an important decision such as this in the hands of the Northumberland side of the Ballinger family."

Peter continued to appear blank for a moment longer and then comprehension set in. He roared with laughter. "I understand completely. Good luck to you, man. Now then, if you will excuse me, I believe I shall make a quick trip to a couple of my own clubs. I wish to place a few wagers in the betting books. Nothing like having a bit of secret intelligence, is there?"

"No," Harry agreed, thinking of how many times his life and the lives of others had depended on such intelligence.

Unlike his restless friend, he was very glad those days were behind him.

At three o'clock that afternoon, Harry was shown into the library of Sir Thomas Ballinger.

Sir Thomas was still a vigorous man. A lifetime of devotion to the classics had not softened his sturdy, broad-shouldered frame. His once-blond hair was silvered now and quite thin on top. His well-trimmed whiskers were gray. He had on a pair of spectacles which he removed as he glanced up to see his visitor. He beamed at the sight of Harry coming toward him.

"Graystone. Good to see you. Have a seat. I have been meaning to call on you. I have come across a most intriguing translation of a French work on Caesar which I think you will enjoy."

Harry smiled and took one of the chairs on the other side of the fire. "I am certain I shall find it fascinating. But we shall have to discuss it some other time. I have come upon another sort of errand today, Sir Thomas."

"Is that so?" Sir Thomas eyed him with indulgent attention as he poured two glasses of brandy. "And what would that be, sir?"

Harry took the brandy and sat back in his chair. He studied his host for a long moment. "You and I, sir, are rather old-fashioned in some respects. Or so I have been told."

"There is much to be said for the old ways, if you ask me. Here's to ancient Greeks and amusing Romans." Sir Thomas raised his glass in a toast.

"To ancient Greeks and amusing Romans." Harry obediently took a swallow of the brandy and set the glass down. "I have come to ask for Miss Ballinger's hand in marriage, Sir Thomas."

Sir Thomas's thick brows rose. A thoughtful expression

appeared in his eyes. "I see. And does she know you are making this request?"

"No, sir. I have not yet discussed the matter with her. As I said, I am old-fashioned in many respects. I wanted your approval before I proceeded further."

"But of course, my lord. Quite right. Rest assured I am delighted to grant my approval to the match. Claudia is an intelligent, serious-minded young female, if I do say so myself. Very well mannered. Takes after her mother, you know. Even attempting to write a book, just as my wife did. My wife wrote books designed for young ladies in the schoolroom, you know. Quite successful at it, I'm pleased to say."

"I am aware of Lady Ballinger's excellent educational works, Sir Thomas. They are in my own daughter's schoolroom. However—"

"Yes, I feel certain Claudia will make you an admirable countess and I shall be most gratified to have you in the family."

"Thank you, Sir Thomas, but it was not Claudia's hand I intended to request, delightful though your daughter is."

Sir Thomas stared at him. "Not Claudia, my lord? Surely you don't mean . . . you can't mean—"

"I have every intention of marrying Augusta if she will have me."

"*Augusta?*" Sir Thomas's eyes widened. He gulped his brandy and promptly choked on it. His face turned a deep, dark shade of crimson as he coughed and sputtered and flailed about with his hand. He appeared torn between stunned amazement and laughter.

Harry calmly rose from his chair and went over to pound his host between the shoulder blades. "I know what you mean, Sir Thomas. It is a somewhat unnerving notion, is it not? I myself had a similar reaction when I first contemplated it. But now I have grown quite accustomed to the idea."

"*Augusta?*"

"Yes, Sir Thomas, Augusta. You are going to give me your permission, are you not?"

"Certainly, sir," Sir Thomas said immediately. "God knows she won't get a better offer, not at her age."

"Precisely," Harry agreed. "Now, then, it occurs to me that as we are dealing with Augusta rather than Claudia, we must assume her response to an offer of marriage might be somewhat, shall we say, unpredictable."

"Damned unpredictable." Sir Thomas looked glum. "Unpredictability runs in the Northumberland side of the family, Graystone. Most unfortunate trait, but there you have it."

"I understand. Given that lamentable characteristic, perhaps it would be more efficient if we simply made this entire event a fait accompli for Augusta. It might be easier on her if we take the decision out of her hands, if you see what I mean."

Sir Thomas gave Harry a shrewd glance from beneath his thick brows. "Are you by any chance suggesting I fire the notices off to the papers before you ask my niece for her hand?"

Harry nodded. "As I said, Sir Thomas. It will be more efficient if Augusta is not called upon to actually make a decision."

"Bloody clever," said Sir Thomas, clearly awed. "Brilliant notion, Graystone. Absolutely brilliant."

"Thank you. But I have a hunch this is only the beginning, Sir Thomas. Something tells me that staying one step ahead of Augusta is going to take a great deal of cleverness and an even greater amount of fortitude."

3

"You sent the notices off to the papers? Uncle Thomas, I do not believe it. This is a disaster. 'Tis obvious a terrible mistake has been made."

Still reeling from the stunning blow of her uncle's offhanded announcement that he had accepted an offer of marriage on her behalf, Augusta paced the library. She was ablaze with a furious energy and she scowled fiercely as she tried to think her way clear of the dreadful situation.

She had just come in from an afternoon ride in the park and was still wearing a dashing new ruby-colored riding habit trimmed in gold braid *à la militaire*. The matching confection of a hat with its perky red feather was still perched on her hair and she was still wearing her gray leather boots. A servant had told her that Sir Thomas had a message for her and she had breezed straight into the library.

Only to be met with the shock of her life.

"How could you have done such a thing, Uncle Thomas? How could you have made such a mistake?"

"Don't think there was any mistake," Sir Thomas said vaguely. Having delivered his announcement from his armchair, he had immediately plunged back into the book he had been reading before Augusta had arrived. "Graystone appeared to know exactly what he was doing."

"But there must have been a mistake. Graystone would never offer for me." Augusta pondered the problem furiously as she paced back and forth. "'Tis obvious what happened. He offered for Claudia and you misunderstood."

"Don't believe so." Sir Thomas buried himself deeper in his book.

"Come, now, Uncle Thomas. You know you get quite absentminded on occasion. You have frequently confused Claudia's name with mine, especially when you are working on one of your books, as you are now."

"What do you expect? You were both named after Roman emperors," Sir Thomas said by way of excuse. "Bound to be the occasional mistake."

Augusta groaned. She knew her uncle. When he was concentrating on old Greeks and Romans it was impossible to get his full attention. He had no doubt been just as preoccupied earlier when Graystone had called. No wonder matters had gotten confused. "I cannot believe you have done something that will affect my future so drastically without even consulting me."

"He'll make you a sound husband, Augusta."

"I do not want a *sound* husband. I do not particularly want any sort of husband at all, least of all a *sound* one. What the devil does that mean, anyway? *Sound.* A horse is *sound.*"

"The thing is, my girl, you are not likely to get a better offer."

"Very likely not. But don't you see, Uncle Thomas, the offer was not for me. I am quite certain of it." Augusta whirled about, the ruby skirts of her habit pooling around her boots. "Oh, Uncle Thomas, I do not mean to be short with you. Heaven knows you have been all that is kind and generous to me and I shall be forever grateful, you must know that."

"Just as I am grateful to you, my dear, for all you have done for Claudia this Season. You have brought her out of her shell and turned her from a shy little mouse into a sensation. Her mother would have been proud."

"'Twas nothing, Uncle Thomas. Claudia is a beautiful, accomplished woman. She merely needed advice on her clothes and on the proper ways of conducting herself in Society."

"All of which you could provide."

Augusta shrugged. "A legacy from my mother. She entertained frequently and taught me much. I have also had the assistance of Lady Arbuthnott, who knows everyone. So you must not hand me all the credit. I am well aware you gave me the task of launching Claudia as a remedy for my melancholy. And it was kind of you. Truly it was."

Sir Thomas grunted in surprise. "As I recall, I merely asked you to accompany Claudia to a soiree one evening. You took charge from there. You made her one of your projects. And whenever you are involved in a project, my dear, things have a way of happening."

"Thank you, Uncle Thomas. But about Graystone. I must insist—"

"Now, don't you worry about Graystone. As I said, he'll make you a sound husband. Man's solid as a rock. Got brains and a fortune. What more could a woman want?"

"Uncle Thomas, you don't understand."

"You're just feeling a bit emotional at the moment, that's all. The Northumberland side of the family always was emotional."

Augusta stared at her uncle in seething frustration and then she rushed from the room before she burst into tears.

Augusta was still simmering with frustration later that evening as she dressed for the night's array of soirees and parties. But at least she was no longer on the point of tears, she told herself with pride. This was a crisis that called for action, not emotion.

Claudia studied Augusta's scowl with gentle concern. Then, with a naturally graceful gesture, she poured two cups of tea and offered one to her cousin with a soothing smile. "Calm yourself, Augusta. All will be well."

"How the devil can all be well when such a dreadful mistake has been made? Dear God, Claudia, don't you understand? Disaster is upon us. Uncle Thomas got so excited he went ahead and sent the notices off to the papers. By tomorrow morning Graystone and I shall be officially engaged. There will be no honorable way for him to get out of the arrangement once the news is in print."

"I understand."

"Then how can you sit there pouring tea as if nothing has happened?" Augusta slammed her cup and saucer down and shot to her feet. She whirled about and began striding back and forth across the width of her bedchamber. Her dark brows were drawn together above her narrowed eyes.

For once Augusta was hardly aware of what she was wearing. Her mind had been in such turmoil that she had been unable to concentrate on the usually pleasant task of choosing her attire. Her maid Betsy had selected the rose-colored evening gown with its daringly cut neckline edged with tiny satin roses. It was Betsy who had chosen the matching satin slippers and elbow-length gloves. And it was Betsy who had decided to dress Augusta's dark chestnut brown hair in the Grecian style. The cascading ringlets bobbed about wildly as Augusta stalked back and forth.

"I fail to see the problem," Claudia murmured. "I had the impression you were growing rather fond of Graystone."

"That is simply not true."

"Come, now, Augusta. Even Papa noticed your interest in the earl and remarked upon it just the other day."

"I asked to read a copy of one of Graystone's recent treatises on some moldering old Roman, that's all. You can hardly call that a sign of deep fondness."

"Well, be that as it may, I am not surprised Papa went ahead and accepted Graystone's offer on your behalf. He assumed you would be delighted, as indeed you should be. It is a wonderful match, Augusta. You cannot deny it."

Augusta stopped pacing long enough to give her cousin an anguished glance. "But don't you see, Claudia? 'Tis all a *mistake*. Graystone would never have asked for my hand in marriage. Never in a million years. He thinks me a terrible hoyden, an unruly scapegrace who is always one step away from falling into a scandal broth. To him I am an ungovernable little baggage. In his eyes I would make a most unsuitable countess. And he is quite right."

"Nonsense. You would make a lovely countess," Claudia said loyally.

"Thank you." Augusta groaned in frustrated annoyance. "But you are quite wrong. Graystone has already been married to a most suitable female, from what I have heard, and I have no desire to try to live up to my predecessor's standards."

"Oh, yes. He was married to Catherine Montrose, was he not? I seem to recall Mother talking about her. Mrs. Montrose was a great believer in the value of Mother's books for young ladies. She raised Catherine on them, I believe. And Mother always claimed Catherine Montrose was a fine example of the efficacy of her instructional techniques."

"What a jolly notion." Augusta went to the window and stood gazing forlornly down into the gardens behind the town house. "Graystone and I have absolutely nothing in common. We are violently opposed on all the modern questions. He does not care for free-thinking females, you know. He has made that quite clear. And he does not even know the half of it. He would no doubt have a fit of the vapors if he realized some of the things I have done."

"I cannot envision Lord Graystone having a fit of the

vapors under any circumstances, and in any event I do not think you behave so very poorly, Augusta."

Augusta winced. "You are too generous by half. Believe me, Claudia, Graystone cannot possibly want me for his bride."

"Then why did he ask for your hand?"

"I do not believe he did," Augusta announced grimly. "In fact, I am certain he did not. As I told you, it was all a ghastly error. He no doubt thought he was asking for your hand."

"Mine?" Claudia's cup clattered in the saucer. "Good heavens. That is impossible."

"Not at all." Augusta frowned intently. "I have been thinking about it and I can see precisely how the mistake occurred. Graystone no doubt arrived here this afternoon and asked for the hand of a *Miss Ballinger*. Uncle Thomas persuaded himself the earl meant me because I am the eldest. But of course he did not. He meant you."

"Really, Augusta. I doubt Papa would have made a mistake of that magnitude."

"No, no, it is entirely possible. Uncle Thomas is always mixing us up. You know that. Only think of all the times he calls one of us by the other's name. He gets so involved in his studies that he frequently forgets us altogether."

"It does not happen all that often, Augusta."

"But you must agree it has happened," Augusta insisted. "And in this situation where he no doubt wanted to convince himself he was going to get me married off at last, it is easy to see how the mistake occurred. Poor Graystone."

"Poor Graystone? I hear he is quite wealthy. Estates in Dorset, I believe."

"I am not talking about his financial situation," Augusta said impatiently. "The thing is, he will be quite horrified when he sees the notice in the papers tomorrow. Horrified and trapped. I have got to do something immediately."

"What on earth can you possibly do? It is nearly nine

o'clock. We shall be leaving for the Bentleys' soiree in a few minutes."

Augusta set her jaw with grim determination. "I must pay a brief call on Lady Arbuthnott this evening."

"You are going to Pompeia's again this evening?" Claudia's gentle voice held a hint of reproof.

"Yes. Would you like to come with me?" It was not the first time Augusta had made the offer and she already knew what Claudia's answer would be.

"Heavens no. The name alone must give one pause. *Pompeia's*. All those rather nasty connotations about unvirtuous behavior. Really, Augusta, I do believe you spend entirely too much time visiting that club."

"Claudia, please. Not tonight."

"I know how much you enjoy the place and I know you are fond of Lady Arbuthnott. Nevertheless, I do wonder if Pompeia's might not be encouraging certain characteristics in you that are known to be latent in the blood of the Northumberland branch of the family. You should be working to restrain and control those streaks of impulsiveness and recklessness. Especially now that you are about to become a countess."

Augusta narrowed her eyes at her lovely cousin. There were times when Claudia bore a striking resemblance to her mother, the renowned Lady Prudence Ballinger.

Augusta's Aunt Prudence had been the author of several volumes for the schoolroom. The books had titles such as *Instructions on Behavior and Deportment for Young Ladies* and *A Guide to the Improvement of the Mind for Young Ladies*. Claudia was intent on following in the illustrious footsteps of her mother and was hard at work on a manuscript tentatively titled *A Guide to Useful Knowledge for Young Ladies*.

"Tell me something, Claudia," Augusta said slowly. "If I get this horrid tangle straightened out in time, will you be happy to marry Graystone?"

"There is no mistake." Claudia rose and walked sedately toward the door. Dressed for the evening in a gown selected by Augusta to accentuate her image, she appeared angelic indeed. The elegantly cut pale blue silk gown she was wearing swung gently around her slippered feet. Her blond hair had been parted in the center and dressed in the fashionable Madonna style. The coiffure was accented with a small diamond comb.

"But if there *has* been a mistake, Claudia?"

"I shall do as Papa wishes, of course. I have always tried to be a good daughter. But I truly feel you will discover there has been no mistake. You have been giving me excellent advice all Season, Augusta. Now let me offer some to you. Endeavor to please Graystone in all things. Work hard to conduct yourself in a manner befitting a countess and I believe the earl will treat you tolerably well. You might want to reread one or two of Mother's volumes before your wedding day."

Augusta stifled an oath as her cousin walked out of the bedchamber and closed the door behind her. Living in a household populated by members of the Hampshire branch of the family could be extremely trying at times.

No doubt about it, Claudia would make Graystone a perfect countess. Augusta could just hear her cousin now as she sat across the breakfast table from the earl and discussed the proposed schedule of the day. *I shall do as my lord wishes, of course.* The pair would no doubt bore each other to death in a fortnight.

But that was their problem, Augusta told herself as she paused in front of her looking glass. She frowned at her own reflection, aware that she had not yet selected any jewelry to complement the rose gown.

She opened the small gilt box on her dressing table. Inside were her two most valuable possessions, a carefully folded sheet of paper and a necklace. The folded paper, marked with ominous brown stains, contained a rather unpleasant little poem Augusta's brother had penned shortly before his death.

The necklace had been the property of the Northumberland Ballinger women for three generations. Most recently it had belonged to Augusta's mother. It was composed of a strand of blood-red rubies interspersed with tiny diamonds. In the center hung a single large ruby.

Augusta clasped the necklace carefully around her throat. She wore the piece often. It was all she had left of her mother's. Everything else had been sold to buy Richard his precious commission.

When the necklace was in place, the large ruby nestled just above the valley between her breasts, Augusta turned back to the window and feverishly began making her plans.

Harry arrived home from his club shortly after midnight, sent his staff to bed, and headed for the sanctuary of his library. His daughter's latest letter detailing the progress of her studies and the weather in Dorset lay on the desk.

Harry poured himself a glass of brandy and sat down to reread the painstakingly penned letter. He smiled to himself. Meredith was nine years old and he was extremely proud of her. She was proving to be a serious and diligent student, anxious to please her father and to perform well.

Harry had personally designed Meredith's curriculum and supervised each stage carefully. Frivolous elements such as watercolor painting and the reading of novels had been ruthlessly expunged from the program. As far as Harry was concerned such things were much to blame for the general flightiness and romantical inclinations that characterized so much of the female population. He did not want Meredith exposed to them.

The day-to-day instruction was carried out by Meredith's governess, Clarissa Fleming. Clarissa was an impoverished Fleming relation whom Harry felt extremely fortunate to have available in his household. A serious bluestocking in her own right, Aunt Clarissa shared his views on education. She was fully qualified to teach the subjects Harry wanted Meredith to learn.

Harry put down the letter, took another sip of his brandy, and contemplated what would happen to his strictly regulated household once he put Augusta in charge of it.

Perhaps he truly had lost his wits.

Something shifted in the shadows outside the window. Frowning, Harry glanced up and saw nothing but darkness. Then he heard a faint scratching noise.

Harry sighed and reached out for the handsome black ebony walking stick that was never far from his side. London was not the continent and the war was over, but the world was never a completely peaceful place. His experience of human nature told him it probably never would be.

He got up, cane in hand, and put out the lamp. Then he went to stand to one side of the window.

As soon as the room went dark, the scratching noise increased. It had a frantic quality now, Harry decided. Someone was hurrying through the bushes alongside the house.

A moment later there was an urgent tapping on the window. Harry looked down and saw a figure in a hooded cloak peering through the glass. Moonlight revealed the small hand raised to rap again.

There was something familiar about that hand.

"Bloody hell." Harry stepped away from the wall and put the ebony stick on the desk. He opened the window with a brusque, angry motion, planted both hands on the sill, and leaned out.

"Thank goodness you are still here, my lord." Augusta threw back the hood of her cloak. The pale moon revealed the relief in her face. "I saw that the light was on and I knew you were in there and then quite suddenly the lamp went out and I was afraid you had left the room. What a disaster if I had missed you tonight. I have been waiting for over an hour at Lady Arbuthnott's for your return."

"If I had realized there was a lady waiting for me, I would have made it a point to return much sooner."

Augusta wrinkled her nose. "Oh, dear. You are angry, aren't you?"

"Whatever gave you that notion?" Harry reached down, grasped her arms through the fabric of the cloak, and hauled her bodily in through the window. It was then he saw the other figure crouching in the bushes. "Who the devil is that?"

"That is Scruggs, my lord. Lady Arbuthnott's butler," Augusta said breathlessly. She righted herself as he released her and straightened her cloak. "Lady Arbuthnott insisted he accompany me."

"Scruggs. I see. Wait here, Augusta." Harry swung one leg over the windowsill and then the other. He dropped down onto the moist earth and beckoned to the stooped figure in the bushes. "Come here, my good man."

"Yes, your lordship?" Scruggs came forward with an awkward, limping gait. His eyes glinted with laughter in the shadows. "May I be of service, sir?"

"I think you have already done quite enough for one night, Scruggs," Harry said through his teeth. Aware of Augusta hovering in the open window, he lowered his voice as he confronted Peter Sheldrake. "And if you ever assist the lady in another adventure of this sort, I shall personally straighten out that extremely poor posture of yours. Permanently. Do you understand me?"

"Yes, sir. Most definitely, your lordship. Quite clear, sir." Scruggs bobbed his head in a servile bow and edged backward, cowering pathetically. "I'll just wait out here in the cold for Miss Ballinger, sir. Never mind that the night air brings out the rheumatism in these old bones. Don't concern yourself with my joints, my lord."

"I do not intend to concern myself with your joints unless I find it necessary to take them apart one by one. Go on back to Sally's. I'll take care of Miss Ballinger."

"Sally is planning to send her home in her carriage with a couple of other members of Pompeia's," Peter said softly in his own voice. "Do not fret, Harry. No one except Sally and myself knows what is going on here. I'll wait for Augusta in Sally's garden. She'll be safe enough once you get her back there."

"You cannot know how that knowledge relieves my mind, Sheldrake."

Peter grinned through his false whiskers. "This was not my idea, you know. Miss Ballinger came up with it all on her own."

"Unfortunately, I can believe that."

"There was no stopping her. She asked Sally to let her sneak through the gardens and down the lane to your house and Sally very wisely insisted I come along. Wasn't much else we could do except make certain she did not come to harm in the process of getting to you."

"Be off, Sheldrake. Your excuses are too lame to interest me."

Peter grinned again and faded into the shadows. Harry went back to the open window where Augusta stood peering down into the darkness.

"Where is Scruggs going?" she demanded.

"Back to his employer's house." Harry climbed back into the library and closed the window.

"Oh, good. That was very kind of you to send him back." Augusta smiled. "It is very cold out there and I would not want him standing around in the damp air. He suffers from rheumatism, you know."

"That is not all he will be suffering from if he tries anything like this again," Harry muttered as he relit the lamp.

"Please, you must not blame Scruggs for my appearance here tonight. It was all my idea."

"So I understand. Allow me to tell you it was a distinctly unsound notion, Miss Ballinger. An addlepated, idiotic, entirely reprehensible idea. But as you are here now, perhaps you will explain exactly why you felt it necessary to risk your neck and your reputation to see me in such a fashion?"

Augusta gave a small, frustrated exclamation. "This is going to be extremely difficult to explain, my lord."

"No doubt."

She turned to face what was left of the fire, allowing her cloak to fall open as she stood in front of the glowing embers. The large red gem above her breasts glowed with the reflection of the flames.

Harry caught a glimpse of the sweet curves revealed by the low neckline of Augusta's gown and stared. *Good lord, he could almost see her nipples peeping out from behind a couple of strategically placed satin roses.* His imagination soared, providing a vivid image of those barely concealed buds. Firm and ripe, they would be made for a man's mouth.

Harry blinked, suddenly aware that he was already half aroused. He fought for his normal, unshakable self-control.

"I suggest you start the explanations, whatever they may be, immediately. It's getting late." Harry propped himself against the edge of his desk. He folded his arms across his chest and contented himself with an expression of severe reproof. It was hard to maintain the scowl when what he really wanted to do was pull Augusta down onto the carpet and make love to her. He sighed inwardly. The woman had bewitched him.

"I came here tonight to warn you that a disaster is imminent."

"May I inquire as to the nature of this disaster, Miss Ballinger?"

She turned her head to give him an unhappy look. "There has been a dreadful mistake, my lord. You apparently paid a visit to my uncle this afternoon?"

"I did." Surely she had not pulled this stunt just to tell him she was going to reject his proposal, Harry thought, seriously alarmed for the first time.

"Uncle Thomas misunderstood you, sir. You see, he thought you were offering for me, rather than my cousin. Wishful thinking on his part, no doubt. He has been fretting about my spinster status for ages. Feels he has a duty to see me wed. In any event, I fear he has already sent the notices off to the papers. I regret to inform you that the announcement of our betrothal will be all over town tomorrow morning."

Harry jerked his gaze away from the satin roses and glanced down at the highly polished toes of his Hessians. In spite of the growing heaviness in his groin he managed to keep his voice free of any inflection. "I see."

"Please believe me, my lord, it was an honest mistake on my uncle's part. I questioned him carefully and he was quite certain you meant to offer for me. You know how he is. He lives in a different world most of the time. He can remember the name of every one of his ancient Greeks and Romans but he can be distressingly vague about the names of the members of his own household. I expect you can understand that."

"Hmmm."

"Yes, I thought you would. You no doubt suffer the same problem. Now, then." Augusta swung around, her cloak sweeping out behind her like a dark velvet sail. "All is not lost. It will be difficult for both of us tomorrow when the news bursts upon the world, but never fear, I have a plan."

"God help us," Harry said under his breath.

"I beg your pardon?" She pinned him with a glare.

"'Twas nothing, Miss Ballinger. You said something about a plan?"

"Precisely. Listen closely, now. I know you have not had much experience with schemes and such due to your interest in scholarly matters, so you must pay strict attention."

"I assume you have had experience with this sort of thing?"

"Well, not this sort of thing precisely," she admitted, "but with schemes in general, if you see what I mean. There is a knack to carrying out a good scheme. One must be bold. One must act as if nothing at all is out of the ordinary. One must be calm at all times. Do you comprehend me, my lord?"

"I believe so. Why don't you go over your plan briefly so that I can get the general outline of it?"

"Very well." She frowned intently and studied a map of Europe that hung on the wall. "The thing is, once the notice of our betrothal is in the papers, you cannot honorably withdraw your offer."

"True," he allowed. "I would not think of doing so."

"Yes, you are quite trapped. But I, on the other hand, can exercise a lady's privilege and cry off. And that is what I shall do."

"Miss Ballinger—"

"Oh, I know there will be a lot of gossip and I shall be called a jilt, among other things. I may have to leave town for a time, but that is neither here nor there. In the end you will be free. You will have everyone's sympathy, in fact. When the storm has died down, you may ask for my cousin's hand, as you had originally intended." Augusta looked at him expectantly.

"That is the whole of your scheme, Miss Ballinger?" Harry asked after a moment's thought.

"I fear so," she said in a worried tone. "Does it seem a bit too simple, do you think? Perhaps we could elaborate on it somewhat and make it more clever. But on the whole, I am inclined to believe that the simpler a scheme is, the easier it will be to carry it out."

"Your instincts in such matters are no doubt better than mine," Harry murmured. "Are you so very anxious, then, to get yourself unbetrothed?"

She flushed a telltale shade of red and her eyes slid away from his. "That is not the point, sir. The point is, you did not intend to get yourself engaged to me. You were asking for Claudia's hand in marriage. And who could blame you? I understand completely. Although I must warn you I am not certain it will be a good match. You are both too much alike, if you see what I mean."

Harry held up a palm to halt the flow of words. "Perhaps I should clarify something before we go any further with your scheme."

"What is that?"

He gave her a slight, quizzical smile, decidedly curious to find out what would happen next. "Your uncle did not make a mistake. It was your hand in marriage I requested, Miss Ballinger."

"*Mine?*"

"Yes."

"My hand? You asked for *my hand* in marriage, my lord?" She gazed at him with dazed eyes.

Harry could not stand it any longer. He straightened away from the desk and deliberately closed the short distance between them. He came to a halt in front of her and caught hold of one of her fluttering hands. He brought it to his lips and kissed it gently. "Your hand, Augusta."

Augusta's fingers were quite cold, he realized. He became aware of the fact that she was trembling. Without a word he drew her slowly into his arms. She was surprisingly delicate to the touch, he thought. Her spine was elegantly curved and he could feel the soft shape of her hips through the rose-colored gown she was wearing.

"My lord, I do not understand," she breathed.

"That much is obvious. Perhaps this will make things clear to you."

Harry bent his head and kissed her. It was the first time he had actually embraced her. He certainly did not count the little peck on the cheek she had given him the other night in Enfield's library.

He gave her the kiss he had been contemplating for the past several nights as he lay awake alone in his bed.

Harry took his time with the matter, brushing his mouth lightly, fleetingly across Augusta's parted lips. He was aware of her tension and also of her deep, feminine curiosity and uncertainty. The range of her emotions simultaneously excited him and made him feel fiercely protective. He longed to ravish her even as he ached to keep her safe. The unholy combination of powerful desires made his head whirl.

Very gently he guided Augusta's small hand up to his shoulder. Her fingers clutched at him. Harry deepened the kiss, lingering on her luscious mouth.

The taste of her was indescribable. Sweet, spicy, profoundly female, it tugged at all his senses. Before he quite realized what he was doing, Harry was sliding his tongue into the intimate depths of her mouth. His hands tightened around her small waist, crushing the rose-colored silk. He could feel the satin roses pressing against his shirt. Beneath the fabric, he felt the taut little nipples.

Augusta gave a soft cry and abruptly raised both arms to twine around his neck. Her cloak fell back over her shoulders, exposing the upper curves of her breasts. Harry was intensely, blindingly aware of the scent of her and of the perfume she was wearing. His whole body suddenly clenched in anticipation.

He caught hold of one tiny sleeve of Augusta's gown and eased it down over her shoulder. Her left breast, small but beautifully shaped, spilled out of the almost nonexistent bodice. Harry cupped the firm fruit in his palm. He had been right about her nipples. The one he was touching with his fingertip was as inviting as a red, ripe berry.

"Oh, my goodness. *Harry.* I mean, my lord."

"Harry will do nicely." He let his thumb glide over the budding nipple again and felt Augusta's instant tremor of response.

The glow from the hearth danced on the red stones in the glittering necklace. Harry looked down at the beautiful sight of Augusta shimmering in firelight and blood-red gems. He saw the awakening sensuality in her gaze and his brain conjured up haunting images of legendary queens of antiquity. "My own Cleopatra," he muttered thickly.

Augusta stiffened and started to draw away. Harry

touched her nipple again, lightly, coaxingly. He kissed the curve of her throat.

"*Harry.*" Augusta gasped, then shivered and sagged heavily against him. Her arms tightened violently around his neck. "Oh, Harry. I have been wondering what it would be like. . . ." She kissed his throat and clung to him.

The sudden flare of passion in her confirmed all his masculine instincts. Harry realized that something in him had known all along that she would respond to him like this. What he had not considered or expected was the reaction that response would have on him. The reality of her flowering desire swamped his senses.

Keeping her breast cradled in one palm, Harry eased Augusta down to the carpet. She clutched at his shoulders, gazing up at him through her lashes. Her beautiful topaz eyes were filled with longing and wonder and something that might have been fear.

Harry groaned as he stretched out beside her and reached for the hem of her gown.

"My lord—" The words were a bare whisper on her lips.

"Harry," he corrected again, kissing the rosy nipple he had been caressing with his thumb. Slowly he drew the rose silk up the length of her legs to her knees, revealing her delicately striped stockings.

"Harry, please, I must tell you something. Something important. I would not have you wed me and then feel yourself deceived."

He went very still as an icy fire seized his gut. "What is it you would have me know, Augusta? Have you lain with some other man?"

She blinked, uncomprehending for an instant. And then her cheeks were suffused with a warm blush. "Good heavens, no, my lord. That is not what I wanted to talk about at all."

"Excellent." Harry smiled faintly as relief and exultation shot through him. Of course she had not been with anyone else. All his instincts had told him that weeks ago. Still, it was good to have it confirmed. One less problem to concern him, he thought, not without some satisfaction. There was no lover from the past with which to contend. Augusta would belong to him completely.

"The thing is, Harry," Augusta continued very earnestly, "I fear I will make you a very bad wife. I tried to explain to you the other night when you found me in Enfield's library that I do not consider myself bound by the normal strictures of Society. You must remember I am a Northumberland Ballinger. I am not at all angelic in the manner of my cousin. I care not for the proprieties and you have made it quite clear that you want a very proper sort of wife."

Harry inched the hem of her gown up a little higher on her legs. His fingers found the incredible softness of her inner thighs. "I think that with a little instruction you will make me a very proper sort of wife."

"I am not at all certain of that, sir," she said, sounding desperate. "It is very hard to change one's temperament, you know."

"I am not asking you to do that."

"You are not?" she searched his face anxiously. "You actually like me the way I am?"

"Very much." He kissed her shoulder. "There are, perhaps, one or two areas of concern to be addressed. But I am convinced that everything will work out and that you will make me an excellent countess."

"I see." She bit her lip and clamped her legs together. "Harry, do you love me?"

He sighed and stilled the movement of his hand on the inside of her thigh. "Augusta, I am aware that many modern young ladies such as yourself believe love is some mystical, unique sensation that descends like magic without any rational process or explanation. But I hold a different opinion entirely."

"Of course." The disappointment in her eyes was clear. "I expect you do not believe in love at all, do you, my lord?

You are a scholar, after all. A student of Aristotle and Plato and all those other terribly logical types. I must warn you, sir, that too much rational, logical thinking can seriously rot the brain."

"I shall bear that in mind." He kissed her breast, delighting in the texture of her skin. God, she felt good. He could not remember the last time he had wanted a woman the way he wanted this one tonight.

He was impatient now. His body was throbbing with desire and the faint, pungent scent of Augusta's arousal was enthralling him. *She wanted him.* Deliberately he urged her legs apart again and eased his fingers into her damp heat.

Augusta cried out in shock and clutched at him. Her eyes widened with amazement. "*Harry.*"

"Do you like that, Augusta?" He trailed small kisses over her breast as he stroked his fingers across the soft plump petals that guarded her most intimate secrets.

"I am not sure," she managed on a strangled gasp. "It feels quite strange. I do not know if—"

The tall clock in the corner chimed the hour. It was as if someone had thrown a bucket of cold water over Harry. He came to his senses with a sudden start.

"Good God. What the devil am I doing?" Harry sat up abruptly and yanked Augusta's gown down to her ankles. "Look at the time. Lady Arbuthnott and your friend Scruggs will be waiting for you. There is no telling what they will be thinking by now."

Augusta smiled uncertainly as he tugged her to her feet and straightened her clothing. "There is no call for alarm, my lord. Lady Arbuthnott is a very modern sort of female, just as I am. And Scruggs is her butler. He will not say anything."

"The hell he won't," Harry muttered as he struggled to adjust the satin roses around her bodice and pull her cloak over her shoulders. "Damn this gown. You are practically falling out of it. Allow me to tell you that one of the first things you will do after we are married is arrange for a new wardrobe."

"Harry—"

"Hurry, Augusta." He took her hand and hauled her over to the window. "We must get you back to Lady Arbuthnott's without further delay. The last thing I want is gossip about you."

"Indeed, my lord." There was a hint of frost in her tone now.

Harry ignored her irritation. He climbed through the window and reached up to help Augusta down onto the grass. She felt supple and warm in his hands and he groaned. He was still painfully aroused. He thought briefly of carrying her straight upstairs to his bedchamber rather than taking her back to Sally's. But that was quite impossible tonight.

Soon, he promised himself as he took her hand and led her through the gardens toward the gate. This marriage would have to take place quite soon. He would not survive this kind of torture for long.

Good lord, what had the woman done to him?

"Harry, if you are so concerned about gossip and if you do not believe you love me, why on earth do you wish to marry me?" Augusta wrapped her cloak securely around herself and skipped to keep up with him.

The question surprised him. It also annoyed him, although he knew he should have been expecting it. Augusta was not the type to let a subject drop easily.

"There are any number of sound, logical reasons," he told her brusquely as he paused at the gate to check that the lane was empty. "None of which I have time to go into tonight." Cold moonlight revealed the cobbled pavement quite plainly. The windows of Sally's house glowed warmly at the far end of the narrow lane. There was no one in sight. "Pull your hood up over your head, Augusta."

"Yes, my lord. We certainly would not want to risk anyone seeing me out here with you, would we?"

He heard the prim, offended note in her voice and winced. "Forgive me for not being as romantic as you might wish, Augusta, but I am in somewhat of a hurry."

"That is obvious."

"You may not care about your reputation, Miss Ballinger, but I do." He concentrated on getting her safely down the lane to the back entrance of Lady Arbuthnott's garden. The gate was unlocked. Harry urged Augusta inside. He saw a shadow detach itself from the house and start forward with a crablike motion. Scruggs was still in full costume, he noted wryly.

Harry looked down at his new fiancée. He tried to see her expression but found it impossible because her face was hidden by the hood. He was very aware of the fact that he was probably not behaving like every maiden's dream of a romantic husband.

"Augusta?"

"Yes, my lord?"

"We do have an understanding, do we not? You are not going to try to cry off tomorrow, are you? Because if so, I must warn you—"

"Heavens, no, my lord." She lifted her chin. "If you are content with the notion of marrying a frivolous female who wears her gowns cut much too low, then I expect I can tolerate a stuffy, sober-minded, unromantic scholar. At my age, I rather suspect I should be grateful for what I can get. But there is one condition, my lord."

"What the devil is that?"

"I must insist on a long engagement."

"How long?" he demanded, suddenly wary.

"A year?" She eyed him with an assessing gleam in her eye.

"Good God. I do not intend to waste a year on this engagement, Miss Ballinger. It should take no more than three months to prepare for the wedding."

"Six."

"Bloody hell. Four months and that's my final offer."

Augusta lifted her chin. "So very generous of you, my lord," she said acidly.

"Yes, it is. Too generous by half. Go on into the house, Miss Ballinger, before I regret my generosity and do something quite drastic for which we will both no doubt be extremely sorry."

Harry turned and stalked out of the garden and back down the lane. He seethed every step of the way over the fact that he had just bargained like a fishmonger over the length of his own engagement. He wondered if this was how Antony had felt when dealing with Cleopatra.

Harry was inclined to be more sympathetic with Antony tonight than he had been in the past. Previously he had always considered the Roman a victim of his own unbridled lust. But Harry was beginning to understand how a woman could undermine a man's self-control.

It was a disturbing realization and Harry knew he would have to be on his guard. Augusta was displaying a talent for being able to push him to the edge.

Hours later, safe in her bed, Augusta lay wide awake and stared at the ceiling. She could still feel the commanding warmth of Harry's mouth on hers. Her body remembered every place he had touched her. She ached with a strange new longing to which she could not put a name. A heat seemed to be flowing in her veins, pooling in her lower body.

She realized with a shiver of awareness that she wished Harry were here with her now to finish whatever it was he had started there on the floor of his library.

This was what was meant by passion, she thought. This was the stuff of epic poems and romantic novels.

For all her vivid imagination, she had not truly understood how enthralling it would be, nor how dangerous. A woman could lose herself to this kind of glittering, compelling excitement.

And Harry was intent on marriage.

Augusta felt a wave of panic rise up inside her. Marriage? To Harry? It was impossible. It would never work. It would be a terrible mistake. She had to find a way to end this engagement, for both their sakes. Augusta watched the shadows on the ceiling and warned herself that she would have to be very careful and very clever.

4

*H*arry propped one shoulder against the ballroom wall and sipped meditatively at a glass of champagne as he watched his fiancée step into the arms of yet another man.

Augusta, glowing in a gossamer silk gown of dark coral, was smiling with pleasure as her tall, handsome, red-haired partner swept her into a dashing waltz. There was no denying the couple made an attractive sight on the crowded dance floor.

"What do you know of Lovejoy?" Harry asked Peter, who was lounging beside him with a bored expression on his handsome face.

"You'd do better to ask that question of one of the ladies." Peter's gaze wandered restlessly across the crowded ballroom. "I understand he's got quite a reputation among the fairer sex."

"Obviously. He's danced with every eligible female in the room tonight. Not one of them has turned him down yet."

Peter's mouth twisted briefly. "I know. Not even the

Angel." His eyes lingered briefly on Augusta's demure, golden-haired cousin who was dancing with an elderly baron.

"I don't care if he dances with Claudia Ballinger, but I may have to put a stop to his waltzing with Augusta."

Peter's brow rose mockingly. "You think you can accomplish that feat? Augusta Ballinger has a mind of her own, as you should know by now."

"Be that as it may, she is engaged to me. It's time she learned to behave with a bit more propriety."

Peter grinned. "So now that you've selected your bride you intend to turn her into the sort of wife you think you want, is that it? This should prove interesting. Bear in mind that Miss Augusta Ballinger comes from the wild branch of the Ballinger family. From what I have heard that lot never could do anything with propriety. Augusta's parents scandalized Society by making a runaway marriage, Sally tells me."

"That is an old piece of business and need not concern anyone now."

"Well, then, how about more current news?" Peter said, beginning to show some interest in the conversation. "There's the rather mysterious manner in which Miss Ballinger's brother was killed two years ago."

"He was shot dead by a highwayman on the way home from London."

"That's the official story. Things were hushed up, but according to Sally there was some speculation at the time that the young man was involved in highly questionable activities."

Harry scowled. "Bound to be some speculation and gossip when a young rakehell is cut down by violence. Everyone knows Richard Ballinger was a hotheaded, neck-or-nothing sort, just like his father before him."

"Yes, well, speaking of the father," Peter murmured with relish, "have you pondered the reputation the man had for fighting duels because of his wife's penchant for drawing the wrong sort of attention? Aren't you afraid that sort of problem might continue in the current generation? Some say Augusta is very much like her mother."

Harry set his jaw, aware that Peter was deliberately baiting him. "Ballinger was a reckless idiot. From what Sir Thomas has told me, the man exercised no control over his wife. He allowed her to run wild. I do not intend to permit Augusta to get into the sort of trouble that will oblige me to go about making dawn appointments. Only a fool finds himself fighting a duel over a woman."

"Pity. I think you'd be rather good at them. Duels, I mean. There have been times when I have actually believed you had ice instead of blood in your veins, Harry. And everyone knows cold-blooded men do better than hot-blooded ones on the dueling field."

"That is a theory I do not intend to test personally." Harry frowned as he watched Lovejoy whirl Augusta around in a particularly uninhibited turn on the dance floor. "If you will excuse me, I believe I shall claim a dance with my fiancée."

"Do that. You can entertain her with some elevating lectures on propriety." Peter levered himself away from the wall. "In the meantime, I believe I shall ruin the Angel's evening by requesting a dance. Five to one she turns me down flat."

"Try talking to her about the book she is writing," Harry suggested absently as he set down his glass on a passing tray.

"What book is that?"

"I believe Sir Thomas said the title was *A Guide to Useful Knowledge for Young Ladies.*"

"Good God." Peter looked suitably appalled. "Is every woman in London writing a book?"

"It would appear so. Cheer up," Harry advised. "You might learn something useful."

He moved off into the crowd, forging a path through the colorful throng. His progress was halted on several occa-

sions by acquaintances who insisted on detaining him long
enough to offer congratulations on the engagement.

During the past two days, in fact, ever since the notices
had appeared in the papers, Harry had become well aware
that most of Society was quite intrigued by the announcement of the unexpected alliance.

Lady Willoughby, a stout matron dressed in pink,
rapped her fan on the black sleeve of Harry's evening coat as
he went past. "So it's Miss Augusta Ballinger who made it
to the top of your list, eh, my lord? Never would have
guessed the two of you would make a match of it. But then,
you've always been a deep one, haven't you, Graystone?"

"I assume you are congratulating me on my engagement," Harry said coolly.

"But of course, sir. All of Society is happy to congratulate you. We are expecting the entire affair to provide us
with considerable entertainment this Season, you see."

Harry narrowed his eyes. "No, madam, I do not see."

"Come, now, my lord, you must admit this is all bound
to be wonderfully amusing. You and Augusta Ballinger are
such an unlikely pair, are you not? It will be vastly
interesting to see if you can get her to the altar without
being obliged to fight any duels or without requesting her
uncle to ship her off to the country. She's a Northumberland
Ballinger, you know. Troublesome lot, that branch of the
family."

"My fiancée is a lady," Harry said very quietly. He held
the woman's gaze for a chilling instant, allowing no
emotion to cross his face. "I expect that when people speak
of her, they will keep that fact in mind. You will remember
that, will you not, madam?"

Lady Willoughby blinked uncertainly and turned a dull
red. "Well, of course, my lord. I meant no offense. I was
merely teasing you. Our Augusta is a lively young woman,
but we are all fond of her and wish her the best."

"Thank you. I shall convey that information to her."
Harry inclined his head with icy politeness and turned

away. Inwardly he groaned. No doubt about it, Augusta's enthusiastic approached to life had endowed her with an unfortunate reputation for recklessness. He was going to have to rein her in before she got into trouble.

He finally cornered her on the far side of the ballroom, where she stood chatting and laughing with Lovejoy. As if she sensed his close proximity, she broke off in the middle of a sentence and turned her head to meet Harry's gaze. A speculative gleam appeared in her eyes and she unfurled her fan with languid grace.

"I wondered when you would show up tonight, my lord," Augusta said. "Have you made the acquaintance of Lord Lovejoy?"

"We've met." Harry nodded brusquely at the other man. He did not like the slyly amused expression in Lovejoy's face. Nor did he care for the way the man was standing so close to Augusta.

"Yes, of course. Belong to some of the same clubs, don't we, Graystone?" Lovejoy turned to Augusta and caught her gloved hand in a gallant gesture. "I suppose I must relinquish you to your future lord and master, my dear," he said as he brought her fingers to his lips. "I realize now that all is lost as far as I am concerned. I can only hope that you will feel some pity in your heart for the devastating blow you have delivered to me by getting yourself engaged to Graystone, here."

"I am sure you will recover quickly, sir." Augusta retrieved her fingers and dismissed Lovejoy with a smile. She turned to Harry as the baron disappeared into the crowd.

Her eyes held a certain challenging glitter and she looked flushed. It struck Harry that Augusta had had that oddly heightened color in her face on each of the two short occasions he had seen her since the engagement had been announced.

He thought he knew the reason for the blush. Every time Augusta looked at him she was obviously remembering their midnight rendezvous when she had wound up lying in his arms on the floor of his library. It was clear that Miss Ballinger, in spite of being descended of the Northumberland branch of the family, was horribly embarrassed by the memory. It was a good sign, Harry decided. It indicated the lady had some notion of propriety, after all.

"Are you too warm, Augusta?" Harry asked with polite concern.

She shook her head quickly. "No, no, I am fine, my lord. Now, then, have you come over here to ask me to dance, sir? Or to lecture me on some fine point of behavior?"

"The latter." Harry took her hand and led her out through the open windows into the garden.

"I was afraid of that." Augusta toyed with her fan as they crossed the terrace. Then she snapped it closed. "I have been doing a great deal of thinking, my lord."

"So have I." Harry drew her to a halt near a stone bench. "Sit down, my dear. I believe we should talk."

"Oh, dear. I knew it would be like this. *I just knew it.*" She scowled up at him as she sank gracefully down onto the bench. "My lord, this is never going to work out. We may as well face it and be done with it."

"What is never going to work out?" Harry put one booted foot on the end of the bench and rested an elbow on his knee. He studied Augusta's earnest face as she confronted him in the shadows. "Are you referring to our engagement, by any chance?"

"I most certainly am. I have been going over this matter again and again and I cannot help but believe you truly are making a grave mistake. I want you to know that I am extremely honored by your offer, but I really feel that for both our sakes it would be best if I cried off."

"I would rather you did not do that, Augusta," Harry said.

"But, my lord, surely now that you have had time to

consider the matter you see that an alliance between us simply will not work."

"I think it can be made to work."

Augusta's mouth tightened. She leaped to her feet. "What you mean, sir, is that you think you can force me to conform to your notions of proper female behavior."

"Do not put words in my mouth, Augusta." Harry took her arm and forced her gently back down onto the bench. "What I meant was that I think that, with a little adjustment here and there, we shall deal very well together."

"And which one of us do you envision making the *adjustments,* my lord?"

Harry sighed and directed his gaze thoughtfully toward the massive hedge behind Augusta. "Both of us will no doubt make the slight changes that are required by marriage."

"I see. Let us try being more specific here. Just what particular modifications do you see me having to make, sir?"

"To begin with, I think it would be best if you did not dance the waltz with Lovejoy again. There is something I do not quite like about that man. And I noticed tonight that he has begun paying you a great deal of attention."

"*How dare you, sir.*" Augusta shot to her feet again, incensed. "I shall dance the waltz with whomever I wish and you may as well know right now that I would never allow my husband or any other man to dictate my choice of dancing partners. I am sorry if that sort of behavior is too unrefined for your taste, sir, but I vow it is only a hint of the sort of impropriety of which I am capable."

"I see. I am, of course, deeply alarmed to hear this."

"Are you laughing at me, Graystone?" Augusta's eyes blazed with fury.

"No, my dear, I am not. Sit down, if you please."

"It does not please me in the least. I have no intention of sitting down. I am going straight back into that ballroom, find my cousin, and go home. And when I get there, I intend to tell my uncle that I am ending the engagement immediately."

"You cannot do that, Augusta."

"Why not, pray tell?"

Harry took her arm again and once more gently but firmly urged her down onto the stone bench. "Because I believe you to be an honorable young woman, in spite of your hotheaded nature. A woman who would not, under any circumstances, bestow certain favors upon a man and then jilt him."

"Certain favors?" Augusta's eyes widened in shock. "What are you talking about?"

It was time, Harry decided, for a few gentle threats, perhaps even a spot of blackmail. Augusta needed to be prodded in the appropriate direction. She was obviously resisting the notion of marriage. "I think you know the answer to that. Or have you conveniently forgotten what transpired on the floor of my library two nights ago?"

"*The floor of your library.* Good grief." Augusta sat frozen on the bench, staring at him. "My lord, you cannot possibly mean that simply because I allowed you to kiss me that I am therefore honor bound to remain engaged to you."

"We enjoyed considerably more than a kiss, Augusta, and I think you are well aware of that."

"Yes, well, I admit things went a trifle too far." She began to look desperate.

"A trifle? You were half undressed before it was over," Harry reminded her with calculated ruthlessness. "And if the clock had not struck when it did, I fear we would have gone very far indeed. I know you pride yourself on your modern ways, Augusta, but surely you are not cruel."

"Cruel? There was nothing cruel about it," she snapped. "Not on my part, at any rate. You took advantage of me, sir."

Harry shrugged. "I believed us to be engaged. Your uncle had accepted my offer and you were paying me a visit in the middle of the night. What was I to think? Some would say you invited my attentions and were more than generous with your favors."

"I don't believe this. The entire sequence of events is getting muddled. Once and for all, I did not bestow any favors on you, Graystone."

"You underestimate yourself, my dear." He smiled whimsically. "I considered them very great favors indeed. I shall never forget the feel of your lovely breast cupped in my hand. Soft and firm and full. And it was crowned with a perfect rosebud that flowered beneath my fingers."

Augusta gave a horrified squeak of dismay. "*My lord.*"

"Do you really believe I could forget the elegant form of your thighs?" Harry continued, well aware of what this intimate recitation was doing to Augusta's composure. He told himself it was past time the lady received a sharp lesson. "Round and finely shaped like those on a Grecian statue. I will treasure forever the great privilege you allowed me when you let me touch your beautiful thighs, my sweet."

"But I did not allow you to touch them," Augusta protested. "You just went ahead and did it."

"You did not lift a finger to stop me. Indeed, you kissed me with a great deal of very warm, one might even say very willing passion, did you not?"

"No, I did not, sir." She looked slightly frantic now.

Harry's brows rose. "You felt nothing when you kissed me? I am deeply hurt. And sadly disappointed to think that you gave me so much and felt nothing in return. For me, it was a rendezvous with passion. I shall never forget it."

"I did not say I felt nothing. I only meant that what I felt was not precisely a warm and willing passion. I was taken by surprise, that is all. My lord, you are misreading the situation. You should not have placed such a serious significance on those events."

"Does that mean you find yourself at that sort of

midnight rendezvous so frequently that you no longer take such intimate encounters seriously?"

"I meant nothing of the kind." Completely flustered now, Augusta glared at him in mounting dismay. "You are deliberately trying to make me feel that I ought to stay engaged to you merely because we got a little carried away on the floor of your library."

"I feel that certain promises were made that night," Harry said.

"I made no promises."

"I disagree. I felt that you very definitely made binding promises when you allowed me the intimate privileges of an engaged man. What was I to think when you gave every indication that you would welcome me as a lover and as a husband?"

"I did not give any such indication," she retorted weakly.

"I beg your pardon, Miss Ballinger. I cannot bring myself to believe that you were merely amusing yourself with me that night. Nor can you convince me that you have sunk so low as to make a habit of toying with a man's affections on the floor of his library. You may be reckless and rash by nature, but I refuse to believe that you are heartless, cruel, or completely without regard for your honor as a woman."

"Of course, I am not without regard for my own honor," she said through gritted teeth. "We Northumberland Ballingers care a great deal for our honor. We would fight to the death for it."

"Then the engagement stands. We are both committed now. We have gone too far to turn back."

There was a sharp cracking sound and Augusta looked down at her fan. She had been clutching it so tightly she had snapped the fragile sticks. "Oh, bloody hell."

Harry smiled and reached down to catch her chin on the edge of his hand. Her long lashes swept up, revealing her deeply troubled, hunted gaze. He bent his head and brushed a kiss against her parted lips. "Trust me, Augusta. We shall do very well together."

"I am not at all certain of that, my lord. I have given this much thought and I can only conclude we are making a grave mistake."

"There is no mistake." Harry listened to the first strains of a waltz drifting through the open windows. "Will you honor me with this dance, my dear?"

"I suppose so," Augusta said ungraciously as she jumped to her feet. "I do not see that I have a great deal of choice in the matter. If I refuse, you will no doubt tell me that propriety demands I dance the waltz with you simply because we are engaged."

"You know me," Harry murmured as he took her arm. "I am a stickler for the proprieties."

He was aware that Augusta was still gritting her teeth as he led her back into the brilliantly lit ballroom.

Much later that evening Harry got out of his carriage in St. James Street and walked up the steps of a certain dignified establishment. The door was opened immediately and he stepped at once into the uniquely comfortable, solidly masculine warmth afforded only by a properly managed gentlemen's club.

There was nothing else quite like it, Harry reflected as he took a seat near the fire and poured himself a glass of brandy. No wonder Augusta had come up with the notion of entertaining Sally and her friends with a parody of a St. James Street club. A man's club was a bastion against the world, a refuge, a home away from home where one could either be alone or find companionship, according to one's personal whim.

In a club a man could relax with friends, win or lose a fortune at the tables, or conduct the most private of business, Harry reflected. He himself had certainly done enough of the last during the past few years.

Although he had been forced to spend much of his time on the continent during the war, he had always made it a point to drop in on his clubs whenever he had been in London. And when he had been unable to keep tabs in person he had made certain to ensure that one or two of his agents had memberships at the more important establishments. The sort of secret intelligence one could glean in this environment never ceased to astound Harry.

He had once learned the name of a man who had been responsible for the death of one of his most valued intelligence officers here in this very club. The killer had suffered an unfortunate accident a short while later.

In another, equally dignified establishment farther along St. James, Harry had contracted to buy the very private journal of a certain courtesan. He had been told the lady enjoyed entertaining the many French spies who, disguised as émigrés, had been sprinkled about London during the war.

It was in the course of deciphering the childishly simple code in which the lady had written her memoirs that Harry had first come across the name *Spider*. The woman had been killed before Harry had had a chance to talk to her. Her maid had tearfully explained that one of the courtesan's lovers had stabbed her mistress in a jealous rage. And, no, the distraught maid had absolutely no idea which of her employer's many lovers had done the deed.

The code name *Spider* had haunted Harry for the duration of his work for the Crown. Men had died in dark alleys with the word on their lips. Letters from French agents referring to the mysterious Spider had been discovered on the persons of secret couriers. Records of troop movements and maps thought to have been meant for the Spider had been intercepted.

But in the end the identity of the man Harry had early on learned to think of as his personal opponent on the great chessboard of war had remained a mystery. It was unfortunate that he had a difficult time tolerating unsolved puzzles, Harry told himself. He would have given a great deal to have learned the truth about the Spider.

His instincts had assured him from the start that the man had been English, not French. It annoyed Harry that the traitor had escaped detection. Too many good agents and too many honest soldiers had died because of the Spider.

"Trying to read your future in the flames, Graystone? I doubt you'll find any answers there."

Harry glanced up as Lovejoy's drawling voice interrupted his quiet contemplation. "I rather thought you might be along sooner or later, Lovejoy. I wanted to have a word with you."

"Is that so?" Lovejoy helped himself to brandy and then leaned negligently against the mantel. He swirled the golden liquid in his glass and his green eyes gleamed malevolently. "First you must allow me to offer you my congratulations on your engagement."

"Thank you." Harry waited.

"Miss Ballinger does not seem your type at all. I fear she has inherited the family inclination toward recklessness and mischief. 'Twill be an odd match, if you don't mind my saying so."

"But I do. Mind, that is." Harry smiled coldly. "I also object to your dancing the waltz with my fiancée."

Lovejoy's expression was one of malicious expectation. "Miss Ballinger is rather fond of the waltz. She tells me she finds me a skilled partner."

Harry went back to contemplating the fire. "It would be best for all concerned if you found someone else to impress with your dancing skills."

"And if I do not?" Lovejoy taunted softly.

Harry sighed deeply as he got up from his chair. "If you do not, then you will oblige me to take other measures to protect my fiancée from your attentions."

"Do you really believe you can do that?"

"Yes," said Harry. "I believe I can. And I will." He

picked up his unfinished brandy and swallowed what was
left in the glass. Then, without a word, he turned and
walked toward the door.

So much for rash statements about not getting into duels
over women, Harry thought ruefully. He knew he had just
come very close to issuing a challenge a moment ago. If
Lovejoy did not take a hint, it might very well come to
something irritatingly melodramatic such as pistols at
dawn.

Harry shook his head. He had only been engaged for two
days and already Augusta was having an extremely unsettling effect on his quiet, orderly existence. It certainly made
one wonder what life was going to be like after he married
the woman.

Augusta sat curled in the blue armchair near the library
window and frowned down at the novel in her lap. She had
been attempting to read the page in front of her for at least
five minutes. But every time she got halfway through the
first paragraph she lost her concentration and had to start
over again.

It was impossible to think about any subject other than
Harry lately. She could not believe the swift, headlong rush
of events that had led her to the situation in which she
found herself.

Above all, she could not understand her own reaction to
those events. From the moments she had found herself on
the floor of Harry's library, swept away by her first taste of
passion, she had been going about in a dazed state of mind.

Every time she closed her eyes, she relived the excitement of Harry's kiss. The heat of his mouth still seared her.
The memory of his shockingly intimate touch still had the
power to make her weak.

And Harry was still insisting on marriage.

When the door opened she looked up with relief.

"There you are, Augusta. I have been looking for you."

Claudia smiled as she came into the room. "What are you reading? Another novel, I suppose?"

"*The Antiquary.*" Augusta closed the book. "Very entertaining, with lots of adventure and a lost heir and plenty of narrow escapes."

"Oh, yes. The new Waverley novel. I should have known. Still trying to work out the identity of the author?"

"It must be Walter Scott. I am absolutely convinced of it."

"And so are any number of other people, apparently. I vow the fact that the author is keeping his identity a secret is probably contributing greatly to the sale of his books."

"I do not think so. They are vastly enjoyable stories. They sell for the same reason Byron's epic poems sell. They are fun to read. One cannot resist turning the pages to see what happens next."

Claudia gave her a gently reproving look. "Do you not think that, as you are now an engaged woman, you ought to be reading something a bit more elevating in nature? Perhaps one of Mother's books would be more suited to a lady who is about to become the wife of a serious-minded, well-educated man. You will not want to embarrass the earl with uninformed conversation."

"If you ask me, Graystone could do with a bit of uninformed conversation," Augusta muttered. "The man is too straitlaced by half. Do you know he actually told me I should not dance the waltz with Lovejoy?"

"Did he really?" Claudia sat down across from her cousin and poured herself a cup of tea from the pot on the end table.

"Practically ordered me not to do so."

Claudia considered that. "Perhaps that is not such bad advice. Lovejoy is very dashing, I'll grant you that much, but one cannot help but believe he might not be above taking advantage of a lady who allowed him too many liberties."

Augusta raised her eyes toward heaven and prayed for

patience. "Lovejoy is perfectly manageable and very much a gentleman." She bit her lip. "Claudia, would you mind very much if I asked you a delicate question? I would like a little advice concerning the proprieties and, frankly, I cannot think of anyone who could give me more accurate information on that sort of thing than you."

Claudia straightened her already rigid spine and looked gravely attentive. "I shall try to guide you as best I can, Augusta. What is troubling you?"

Augusta abruptly wished she had not started this. But it was too late now. She plunged into the matter that had disturbed her sleep so badly after last night's ball. "Do you think 'tis true that a gentleman has the right to feel certain promises are made or implied by a lady simply because she allows him to kiss her?"

Claudia frowned, considering the matter closely. "Obviously a lady should not allow anyone except her fiancé or her husband to take such liberties. Mother made that very clear in her *Instructions on Behavior and Deportment for Young Ladies*."

"Yes, I know," Augusta said, growing impatient. "But let us be realistic about this. It happens. People do steal the occasional kiss out in the garden. We all know that. And as long as they are discreet about it nobody feels they have to announce an engagement afterward."

"We are speaking hypothetically, I assume?" Claudia said with a sudden, sharp glance.

"Absolutely." Augusta waved a hand airily. "The issue arose during a discussion with some, uh, friends of mine at Pompeia's and we are all trying to form a proper conclusion as to what is expected of the woman in such a situation."

"It would no doubt be best if you refrained from being drawn into that sort of discussion, Augusta."

Augusta ground her teeth. "No doubt. But do you have an answer to the question?"

"Well, I suppose one could say that allowing a man to kiss one is an example of deplorable behavior but not precisely beyond the pale, if you see what I mean. One could wish the lady had a nicer notion of propriety, but one would not condemn her completely for a stolen kiss. At least, I would not do so."

"Yes, that is exactly my feeling on the matter," Augusta said eagerly. "And certainly the gentleman involved has no right to think the lady in question had promised to marry him merely because he was such a cad as to steal a kiss."

"Well . . ."

"Lord knows, I have wandered out into the garden during a ball and seen any number of gentlemen and ladies embracing. And they did not all rush back into the ballroom and announce their engagements."

Claudia nodded slowly. "No, I do not think it would be fair of a gentleman to think the lady had made a firm commitment merely on account of a kiss being exchanged."

Augusta smiled, pleased and relieved. "Not fair in the least. Just what I concluded, Claudia. I am so glad you agree with me."

"Of course," Claudia continued thoughtfully, "if there were a bit more than a kiss involved, that would put an entirely different light on the matter."

Augusta felt suddenly sick. "It would?"

"Yes, definitely." Claudia took a sip of tea as she pondered the nuances of the hypothetical situation. "Most definitely. If the lady in question responded to such behavior on the part of the gentleman with any degree of warmth at all—that is, if she allowed further intimacies, for example, or encouraged him in any way . . ."

"Yes?" Augusta prompted, dreading the direction in which this was going.

"Then I think that it would be quite fair of the gentleman in question to assume the lady did indeed return his affections. He would have every reason to believe she was plighting her troth by such actions."

"I see." Augusta stared glumly down at the novel in her lap. Her mind was suddenly filled with visions of herself lying in disgraceful abandon in Graystone's arms on the floor of his library. She could feel the heat in her own cheeks and could only pray her cousin would not notice and remark upon it. "What if the gentleman had been a bit too warm in his advances?" she finally ventured cautiously. "What if he had more or less coaxed her into allowing intimacies she had not initially even considered allowing?"

"A lady is responsible for her own reputation," Claudia said with a lofty certainty that reminded Augusta a great deal of Aunt Prudence. "She must always exercise great care to behave with such perfect propriety that unfortunate situations do not arise in the first place."

Augusta wrinkled her nose and said nothing.

"And, of course," Claudia continued gravely, "if the gentleman in question happened to be a man of excellent breeding and possessed of an unimpeachable reputation for honor and propriety, that would make the case even more clear."

"It would?"

"Oh, yes. One could certainly see why he would have been led to believe certain promises had been made. And a gentleman of such dignity and refined sensibilities would naturally expect the lady's implied promises to be kept. Her own honor would demand it."

"That is one of the things I have always admired about you, Claudia. You are four full years younger than I, but you have such clear-sighted notions of what is proper." Augusta opened her novel and gave her cousin a tight smile. "Tell me, do you sometimes find that a life filled with such perfect propriety tends to be a trifle dull?"

Claudia smiled warmly. "Life has not been the least bit dull since you came to live with us, Augusta. Something of interest seems to be always occurring in your vicinity. Now, I have a question to put to you."

"What is that?"

"I would like your opinion of Peter Sheldrake."

Augusta looked at her in surprise. "But you know my

opinion of him. I arranged to have him introduced to you. I like him very much. Reminds me a bit of my brother Richard."

"That is one of the things that worries me," Claudia admitted. "He does have a certain reckless, devil-may-care air about him. And he has become increasingly attentive lately. I am not quite certain I ought to encourage him."

"There is nothing wrong with Sheldrake. He is heir to a viscountcy and a nice fortune. Even better, he has a sense of humor, which is more than I can say of his friend Graystone."

5

"**I** don't believe I mentioned the fact that I had the privilege of meeting your brother a few months before he died, Miss Ballinger." Lovejoy smiled from the other side of the card table as he dealt another hand.

"Richard? You knew my brother?" Augusta, who had been telling herself that it was time to leave the card room and rejoin the crowd in Lady Leebrook's elegant ballroom, looked up, stunned. All thought of cards and strategy went out of her head in an instant.

Her stomach clenched as she waited to see what Lovejoy would say next. As always, when her brother's name was mentioned, she was immediately on the defensive, ready to do battle should anyone happen to question Richard's honor.

She was the only Ballinger left who could fight for Richard's name and memory and whenever the subject arose, she gave her all to the task.

She had been playing cards with Lovejoy for half an hour now, not because she was a particularly enthusiastic player but because she had rather hoped Graystone might wander into the ballroom and come in search of her. She knew he would be irritated, perhaps even mildly shocked by the somewhat dubious propriety of a lady engaging in a card game with a gentleman in such a formal setting.

It was not exactly improper. There were, after all, several other card games in progress in the same room. A few of the ladies involved had been known to lose sums equal to those their husbands occasionally lost in the clubs. But the high-sticklers in the *ton,* of which Graystone was surely one, did not approve of such goings-on. And Augusta was fairly certain that when he found her playing with Lovejoy, of all people, the earl would be genuinely annoyed.

It was a small vengeance for his high-handed treatment of her in the garden the other evening when he had insisted her honor demanded she remain engaged, but it was all she was likely to get. She had the arguments in her own defense already thoroughly prepared. Indeed, she looked forward to delivering them with relish.

When Graystone took her to task for playing cards with Lovejoy, Augusta planned to point out that he could hardly complain, as he had only forbidden her to dance the waltz with the baron. There had been no stipulations regarding cards. Graystone was a man who prided himself on his logic. He could just choke on it this time.

And if he found the offense of card playing simply too grave to tolerate, he could release her from her *implied* promises and allow her to cry off the engagement.

But Graystone had apparently elected not to attend the Leebrooks' elegant affair tonight and the entire attempt to challenge him had been wasted. Augusta had tired of the card game, even though she was winning. Lovejoy was pleasant enough company, but all she could think about was the fact that Graystone was absent.

The notion of ending the game and returning to the ballroom came to a crashing halt, however, at the mention of Richard's name.

"I did not know your brother well, you understand," Lovejoy said easily as he casually dealt the cards. "But he seemed quite likable. I believe I met him at a race meeting. He won a considerable sum on a horse I had been certain would lose."

Augusta smiled sadly. "Richard was very fond of attending sporting events of all types." She picked up her cards and glanced at them with unseeing eyes. She could not concentrate on what she held. Her mind was totally riveted on Richard. *He had been innocent.*

"So I gathered. Took after his father, I believe?"

"Yes. Mother always claimed they were both cut from the same cloth. True Northumberland Ballingers. Always eager for adventure and ready for any sort of excitement." With any luck Lovejoy would not have any inkling of the rumors that had circulated for a time after her brother had been killed on that lonely country lane. The baron had, after all, spent most of the past few years with his regiment on the continent.

"I was sorry to learn of your brother's untimely death two years ago," Lovejoy continued, frowning thoughtfully down at the cards he held. "My belated condolences, Miss Ballinger."

"Thank you." Augusta pretended to study her own cards as she waited to see if Lovejoy would say anything else. All the old memories of Richard's laughter and warmth returned with a rush, blotting out the hum of conversation in the room. The muttered accusations had been so grossly unfair. One only had to know Richard to realize he would never have betrayed his country.

A silence descended on the card table. Lost in her memories of Richard and her bitterness over the unfair accusations that had been lodged against him, Augusta could not begin to concentrate on her hand. She lost for the first time that evening.

"It seems my luck has turned, sir." She started to rise from her chair as she realized that Lovejoy had just won back in one round most of the ten pounds she had succeeded in taking from him.

"I doubt it." Lovejoy smiled, gathered up the cards, and shuffled again.

"I believe we are about even, my lord," Augusta said. "I suggest we call it a draw and return to the dancing."

"There were certain unfortunate rumors surrounding the events of your brother's death, were there not?"

"*Lies*. All lies, my lord." Augusta sank slowly back down into her chair. Her fingers trembled as she reached up to touch her mother's ruby necklace.

"Of course. I never believed them for a moment." Lovejoy gave her a gravely reassuring look. "You may depend upon that, Miss Ballinger."

"Thank you." Augusta's stomach started to unclench. At least Lovejoy did not believe the worst, she thought.

Another silence descended, during which she did not know what else to say. She stared down at the fresh hand of cards she had just been dealt and automatically picked them up with unsteady fingers.

"I heard that certain documents were apparently found on his body at the time of his death." Lovejoy frowned over his hand. "Documents of a military intelligence nature."

Augusta froze. "I believe they were deliberately placed in his pockets to make him look guilty of treason. Someday I shall find a way to prove it, my lord."

"A noble goal. But how will you go about doing that?"

"I do not know," Augusta admitted tightly. "But if there is any justice in this world, I shall find a way."

"Ah, my dear Miss Ballinger. Have you not yet learned that there is very little justice in this world?"

"I cannot believe that, sir."

"Such an innocent. Perhaps you would care to tell me more about the situation. I have some experience in these matters, you see."

Augusta looked up, startled. "You do?"

Lovejoy smiled indulgently. "When I served on the

continent I was occasionally assigned the task of investigating occurrences of a criminal nature that cropped up in the
regiment. You know, the odd knifing in the alley of a
strange town or an officer suspected of selling information
to the enemy. Unpleasant as they are, such things happen
in war, Miss Ballinger. And investigations into them must
be conducted with absolute discretion. The honor of the
regiment is always at stake, you see."

"Yes, I do see." Augusta felt a flare of hope unfurl within
her. "Did you have much success in conducting that sort of
investigation, my lord?"

"Considerable success."

"It is a great deal to ask, but would you by any chance
be interested in helping me prove my brother's innocence?"
she asked, hardly daring to breathe.

Lovejoy frowned as he gathered up the cards and dealt
another hand. "I'm not sure if I could be of much assistance,
Miss Ballinger. Your brother was killed shortly before
Napoléon abdicated in 1814, was he not?"

"Yes, that's right."

"It would be very difficult to start tracing his contacts
and associations now. I doubt that there would be any clues
left." Lovejoy paused and gave her an inquiring glance.
"Unless you have some notion of where to begin."

"No. None at all. I suppose it is hopeless." Augusta's
brief stir of hope faltered and died.

She gazed down at the green baize forlornly, thinking of
the poem that lay tucked into the jewel box on her dressing
table. The strange verse written on paper that was stained
with Richard's own blood was all she had left of her brother.
It was certainly no clue. It did not even make any sense, as
far as she had ever been able to tell. There was no point even
mentioning it. She had kept it because it was the last thing
Richard had given to her.

Lovejoy smiled consolingly. "Nevertheless, why don't
you tell me what little you do know and I will see if there
is anything that comes to mind."

Augusta began to talk as the card game continued. She made a fierce effort to answer the various questions Lovejoy idly tossed out. She tried to recall the names of all her brother's friends and acquaintances and where he had spent his time during the few months preceding his death.

But Lovejoy apparently saw no significance in any of it. Nevertheless, he kept asking questions and as he gently interrogated her, he continued to deal the cards. Augusta automatically played each hand she was dealt, one after another, giving no thought to her game. Her focus was entirely on the questions Lovejoy asked about Richard.

When she finally ran out of information, Augusta looked down at the pad of paper on which Lovejoy had been keeping score and realized she owed him a thousand pounds.

A thousand pounds.

"Dear God." She clapped her hand to her mouth in horror. "My lord, I fear I do not have such an amount readily available." *Or even unreadily available.* There was no way on earth she could come up with that large a sum.

The thought of going to her uncle to ask him to cover her debts was too awful to contemplate. Sir Thomas had been astonishingly generous since she had gone to live in his household. She could not possibly repay his kindness by asking him to cover a gaming debt of a thousand pounds. It would be unthinkable. Her honor would not allow it.

"Pray do not concern yourself, Miss Ballinger." Lovejoy calmly collected the cards. "There is no great rush. If you will merely give me your vowels tonight, I shall be happy to wait until such time as it is more convenient for you to settle your debt. I am certain we shall be able to come to terms."

Wordlessly, her heart pounding with the enormity of what she had done, Augusta wrote out an IOU for a thousand pounds and signed her name. Then she got to her feet, aware that she was shaking so badly she might actually humiliate herself by collapsing.

"If you will excuse me, sir," she managed with creditable calm, "I must return to the ballroom. My cousin will wonder where I am."

"Of course. Let me know when you are prepared to deal with your debt. We shall work out an arrangement that is mutually agreeable." Lovejoy smiled a slow, insinuating smile.

Augusta wondered why she had never before noticed the unpleasant gleam in his fox-green eyes. She steeled herself to ask a favor. "Will you give me your word, sir, as a gentleman, not the mention this incident to anyone? I would not want my uncle or . . . or certain other parties to hear of it."

"Certain other parties such as your fiancé? I can understand your concern. Graystone would not be inclined to be indulgent about a lady's gaming debts, would he? Such a stickler for the proprieties as he is would probably not approve of ladies playing cards in the first place."

Augusta's heart sank even farther. What a mess this was going to be. And it was all her own fault. "No, I imagine not."

"You may rest assured I will keep silent." Lovejoy inclined his head with mocking gallantry. "You have my word on it."

"Thank you."

Augusta turned away and fled toward the bright lights and laughter of the ballroom. Her mind was reeling with the knowledge that she had been a fool.

Quite naturally the first person she saw when she left the card room was Harry. He had spotted her and was making his way toward her through the glittering crowd. Augusta took one look at him and was filled with an overwhelming desire to throw herself into his arms, confess all, and beg for advice.

Dressed in his austere evening attire with an immaculately folded white cravat around his strong throat, Graystone looked formidable enough to take on two or three

Lovejoys and dispatch them all with ease. There was something reassuringly strong and solid about her fiancé, Augusta realized. This was a man one could depend upon, if one had not gotten oneself into a situation through sheer stupidity.

Unfortunately, Graystone had no patience with stupidity.

Augusta straightened her shoulders. The problem was of her own making and she was obliged to find a way to pay her own debts. She could not possibly involve Harry in this fiasco. A Northumberland Ballinger took care of her own honor.

Augusta watched wistfully as Harry forged a path through the throng in her direction. She saw with dismay that he appeared displeased. His hooded gaze flickered briefly over her shoulder to the entrance to the card room and then raked her face.

"Are you all right, Augusta?" he asked sharply.

"Yes, quite all right. I vow it is rather warm in here, is it not?" She unfurled her fan and employed it industriously. Frantically she sought for a topic of conversation that might deflect his attention from the card room. "I wondered if you'd put in an appearance tonight. Have you been here long, my lord?"

"I arrived a few minutes ago." His gaze narrowed thoughtfully as he studied her flushed face. "I believe they have opened the doors for a late supper. Would you care for something to eat?"

"That would be wonderful. I should like to sit down for a few minutes." The truth was she wanted to sit down before she fell down. When Harry offered her his arm, she clung to it as though it were a lifeline in a raging sea.

It was while she was munching on a lobster pattie and gulping chilled punch which Harry procured for her that Augusta finally calmed herself sufficiently enough to start thinking clearly. There was really only one solution to her dilemma: her mother's ruby necklace.

The thought of parting with it made the tears burn in Augusta's eyes, but she told herself she deserved the anguish. She had been a fool and now she must pay the price.

"Augusta, are you quite certain there is nothing wrong?" Harry asked again.

"Quite certain, my lord." The lobster pattie tasted like sawdust, she noticed.

Harry's brow rose slightly. "You would, of course, feel free to tell me if anything serious was troubling you, would you not, my dear?"

"That would depend, my lord."

"On what?" There was an unexpected hint of steel in Harry's normally unemotional voice.

Augusta shifted restlessly in her chair. "On whether or not I thought you might be inclined to respond in a kind, understanding, and helpful manner."

"I see. And if you feared I would not respond in such a manner?"

"Then I would no doubt refrain from telling you a single blasted thing, sir."

Harry's eyes narrowed slightly. "Need I remind you we are engaged, Augusta?"

"You do not need to remind me of that fact, my lord. I assure you it is usually at the forefront of my mind these days."

There was only one place to go for advice on how to proceed with the business of pawning a valuable necklace. The day after the shocking disaster in the card room, Augusta went straight to Pompeia's.

The door was opened by a grouchy Scruggs, who peered at her from beneath his bushy brows.

"It's you, is it, Miss Ballinger? I suppose you know the members are all busy settling the wagers they made regarding your engagement."

"I am glad to hear that someone is gaining something out of it," Augusta muttered as she went past him. She paused in the hall, recalling the medicine she had brought him a few days earlier. "I almost forgot. Did the tonic help your rheumatism, Scruggs?"

"The tonic worked miracles after I followed it with a bottle of Lady Arbuthnott's best brandy. Unfortunately, I could not induce any of the housemaids to assist me in testing the remainder of the cure."

Augusta smiled briefly in spite of her low mood. "I am glad to hear that."

"This way, Miss Ballinger. Madam will be pleased to see you, as usual." Scruggs opened the doors to Pompeia's.

There were a handful of ladies in the club, most busy reading the newspapers or scribbling away at the writing tables. The gossip concerning the scandalous love lives of both Byron and Shelley had only fueled the determination of the club's aspiring writers to get themselves published.

It was odd how virtue, or the lack thereof, could affect one, Augusta reflected. Byron's or Shelley's distinctly unvirtuous romantic liaisons might very well produce just the inspiration needed by one of Pompeia's members to get her own work into print.

Augusta swept through the room, heading straight for the hearth. There was a cheerful blaze going, as usual, although the day was pleasant. Sally seemed to always be cold these days. She was in her chair near the fire and, fortunately for Augusta, she was temporarily without company. A book lay open on her lap.

"Hello, Augusta. How are you today?"

"Perfectly miserable. Sally, I have gotten myself into a terrible situation and I have come to beg your advice." Augusta sat down close to the older woman and leaned over to whisper. "I want you to tell me how one goes about pawning a necklace."

"Oh, dear, this does sound serious." Sally closed her

book and gazed inquiringly at Augusta. "Perhaps you had better tell me everything right from the beginning."

"I have been a perfect idiot."

"Yes, well, we all are, sooner or later. Now, why don't you tell me the tale? I confess I have been a trifle bored this afternoon."

Augusta took a deep breath and explained the disaster in all its unpleasant detail. Sally listened attentively and then nodded in complete understanding.

"Of course you must settle the debt, my dear," she said. "It is a matter of honor."

"Yes, precisely. I have no choice."

"And your mother's necklace is the only thing of value you have to pawn?"

"I fear so. All my other jewelry has been given to me by Uncle Thomas and I would not feel right selling it."

"You do not feel you could go to your uncle and request his assistance in this?"

"No. Uncle Thomas would be vastly overset by this entire mess and I could not blame him. He would be extremely disappointed in me. A thousand pounds is a great deal of money. He has been far too generous already."

"He will be getting a considerable sum in marriage settlements from Graystone," Sally pointed out dryly.

Augusta blinked in surprise. "He will?"

"I believe so."

"I did not know that." Augusta scowled. "Why is it that men never discuss that sort of thing with the women involved? They treat us as if we were feebleminded. No doubt doing so makes them feel superior to us."

Sally smiled. "That may be part of it, but I think there is more to it than that. I believe, at least in the case of men such as your fiancé and your uncle, that they act the way they do because they feel protective."

"Rubbish. But be that as it may, the settlements, whatever they are, will not be made for another four months. I cannot wait that long. I have the distinct impression that Lovejoy will begin hounding me for repayment very soon."

"I see. And you do not feel you could take this matter to Graystone?"

Augusta stared at her, utterly aghast. It took her several seconds to close her mouth. "Tell Graystone I lost a thousand pounds to Lovejoy? Are you mad? Have you any notion of how he would react to such information? I cannot even bear to contemplate the explosion that would take place if I were to confess this to him."

"You may have a point. He would not be pleased, would he?"

"I could probably tolerate his displeasure," Augusta said slowly. "Who knows? It might even convince him to let me cry off the engagement. But I could never in a million years endure the humiliation of having to explain to him that in my desire to teach him a lesson I made a complete fool of myself."

"Yes, I can fully comprehend that. A woman has her pride. Let me consider this for a moment." Sally idly tapped the leather binding of the book in her lap. "I believe the simplest way to handle this is for you to bring the necklace to me."

"To you? But I must pawn it, Sally."

"And so you shall. But it is very difficult for a lady to pawn an expensive item without the business going unnoticed by someone. If you bring the necklace to me, on the other hand, I can send Scruggs to the pawnbroker's for you. He will keep his silence."

"Oh, I see what you mean." Augusta leaned back in her chair, somewhat relieved. "Yes, that would work. It is very kind of you to assist me in this, Sally. How can I ever repay you?"

Sally smiled and for a moment her fine-boned features held a hint of the radiant beauty that had once made her the toast of London. "It is I who am happy to be able to repay you in some small way for all you have done for me,

Augusta. Now run along and fetch your mother's necklace. You shall have your thousand pounds by nightfall."

"Thank you." Augusta paused and gave her friend a searching glance. "Tell me, Sally, do you think it is possible that Lord Lovejoy used the conversation about investigating my brother's death to lure me into deep play? I am not trying to excuse myself, but one cannot help but wonder . . ."

"I think it entirely possible. Some men are extremely unscrupulous. He probably sensed your weakness and used it to distract you."

"He never meant a word of his promise to help me prove Richard was not a traitor, did he?"

"I think it highly unlikely. How could he? Augusta, you must be realistic about the matter. Nothing will bring back Richard and there is no way you can ever clear his name except in your own heart. You know he was innocent and you must be satisfied with that inner knowledge."

Augusta's hand tightened into a small fist in her lap. "There must be a way."

"It has been my experience that in matters such as this, the best solution is silence."

"But it is not fair," Augusta protested.

"Much of life is not, my dear. On your way out, Augusta, would you please ask Scruggs to have one of the maids bring me my tonic?"

Quite suddenly Augusta's own problems faded into the background. A deep, helpless anguish gripped her. Sally's tonic was brewed from the juice of the opium poppy. The fact that she was calling for it this early in the day meant that the pain was getting worse.

Augusta reached out and took hold of one of Sally's frail hands. She held it very tightly for a while. Neither woman spoke.

After a time Augusta rose and went to tell Scruggs to fetch the tonic.

• • •

"I ought to paddle her backside so hard she could not sit a horse for a week. She should be locked up and not allowed out except under guard. The woman is a menace. She is going to make my life a living hell." Harry stalked across Sally's small library, found himself blocked by a bookcase, swung around, and stalked back in the other direction.

"She is going to make your life interesting." Sally sipped her sherry and did not bother to conceal an amused smiled. "Things have a way of happening around Augusta. Quite fascinating, actually."

Harry slammed his hand down on the gray marble mantel over the fireplace. "Quite infuriating, you mean."

"Now, do calm down, Harry. I only told you about the incident because you were demanding to know what was going on and I was afraid you would start making inquiries. When you make inquiries, you generally get answers. So I cut the process short by supplying you with the answers."

"Augusta is going to be my wife. I have a perfect right to know what the devil she's up to at any given time, damn it."

"Yes, well, now you know and you must let that be the end of it. You are not to interfere in this, do you understand? This is a matter of honor for Augusta and she would be most upset if you stepped in and resolved the issue for her."

"Honor? What has honor got to do with this? She was willfully defying me by flirting with Lovejoy and she got herself into serious trouble."

"Augusta is well aware she behaved somewhat recklessly. She does not need any lectures from you. This is a gaming debt, Harry. It must be settled. Allow her to do so in her own way. You would not want to injure her pride, would you?"

"This is intolerable." Harry came to a halt and stood

glowering down at his old friend. "I cannot stand by and do nothing. I will deal with Lovejoy myself."

"No."

"A man is responsible for his wife's debts," Harry reminded her.

"Augusta is not yet your wife. Let her handle this. It should be over quite soon and I assure you she has learned her lesson."

"If only I could believe that," Harry muttered. "Damn Lovejoy. He knew what he was doing."

Sally considered that briefly. "Yes, I rather believe he did. And Augusta reasoned that out for herself, by the bye. She is no fool. It was no coincidence that he brought up the subject of her brother just as she was getting ready to quit the table and return to the ballroom. If there was one thing guaranteed to distract her attention, it was the matter of Richard Ballinger's innocence."

Harry drove his fingers through his hair in a distracted motion. "She was apparently quite close to that damned rakehell brother of hers."

"He was all she had left after their parents were killed in the carriage accident. She adored him. She has never stopped believing him innocent of selling his country's secrets and she would give anything to clear the stain on his reputation."

"From all accounts Ballinger was wild and reckless, just like his father." Harry stopped pacing and went to stand in front of the window. It was after midnight and it was raining. He wondered if Augusta was even now paying her gaming debt. "It is entirely possible he got involved in something serious simply because of the promise of adventure. Perhaps he was not aware of the nature of his actions."

"That branch of the Ballinger family has always been a bit reckless, but no one has ever accused any Ballinger of being a traitor. Indeed, Ballingers have always guarded their honor quite fiercely."

"Certain documents were found on his body, I believe?"

"So it is said." Sally paused." 'Twas Augusta who found him, you know. She heard the shot. Sound carries a long distance in the country. She went rushing out into the lane. Richard died in her arms."

"Christ."

"The documents were discovered by the local magistrate who was called in to investigate. Once everyone realized what had been found, Sir Thomas exerted every ounce of influence he had to get the facts suppressed. Obviously he did not have quite enough influence to stop all the rumors. But it has been two years now and most people have forgotten the incident."

"That son of a bitch."

"Who? Lovejoy?" As usual, Sally had no trouble following Harry's chain of thought. "Yes, he is, is he not? There are many like him in Society, Harry. They prey on vulnerable young women. You know that. But Augusta is going to get herself out of this predicament and, as I said, she has most definitely learned her lesson."

"Not bloody likely," Harry said with a resigned sigh. But he had made his decision. "Very well, I shall allow Augusta to repay her debt, collect her vowels, and keep her pride intact."

Sally cocked a brow. "And then?"

"And then I shall have a little chat with Lovejoy myself."

"I rather thought you would. By the way, there is one thing you might like to do for Augusta."

Harry looked at her. "What is that?"

Sally smiled and picked up the velvet pouch that sat on a table beside her chair. She loosened the thong that bound the pouch and allowed the necklace inside to spill out into her hand. Red stones sparkled in her palm. "You might like to retrieve her mother's necklace from pawn."

"You still have the necklace? I thought you sent it out to a jeweler's."

"Augusta does not know it, but I acted as her moneylender." Sally shrugged. "It was the only thing I could do under the circumstances."

"Because you could not bear for her to have to part with the necklace?"

"No, because the thing is not worth a thousand pounds," Sally said bluntly. "It is paste."

"Paste? Are you certain?" Harry crossed the room and plucked the necklace from Sally's hand. He held it up to the light, examining it closely. Sally was right. The red stones sparked attractively but there was no fire in their depths.

"Quite certain. I know jewels, Harry. Poor Augusta thinks the stones in that necklace are real, however, and I would not want her to learn the truth. The thing has great sentimental value to her."

"I know." Harry dropped the necklace back into the pouch. He frowned thoughtfully. "I suppose her brother pawned the real rubies when he bought his commission."

"Not necessarily. The workmanship on those stones is excellent and very old-fashioned. It was probably done many years ago. I suspect the real rubies were sold sometime in the family's past, perhaps two or three generations back. The Northumberland Ballingers have a long history of living on their wits and not much else."

"I see." Harry's hand tightened around the pouch. "So now I owe you a thousand pounds for a string of false rubies and fake diamonds, is that it?"

"Exactly." Sally chuckled. "Oh, Harry, this is all so very delightful. I am enjoying myself immensely."

"I am glad someone is."

6

Augusta, dressed in an emerald green gown with long, matching green gloves and a green plume in her hair, stood frozen in the theater lobby. She stared up at Lovejoy, whom she had just succeeded in cornering. She could not believe what he had just said to her.

"Not allow me to pay my debt? You cannot be serious. I pawned my mother's necklace in order to repay you. It was all I had of hers."

Lovejoy smiled without any warmth. "I did not say I would not allow you to repay the debt, my dear Augusta. I agree it must be paid. It is, after all, a debt of honor. I merely said I could not take your money. It would be unconscionable under the circumstances. Your mother's necklace, no less. Good lord, I simply cannot do it and continue to live with myself."

Augusta shook her head, completely at a loss. She had gone to Pompeia's earlier to collect the money Scruggs had received when he had pawned the necklace late that afternoon. Then she had rushed off to the theater fully intending to make arrangements to pay off Lovejoy.

Now he was refusing to take the money.

"I do not understand what you are talking about," Augusta hissed softly, anxious not to be overheard in the crowded lobby.

"'Tis quite simple. After due consideration I realize I could not possibly take your thousand pounds, my dear Miss Ballinger."

Augusta eyed him warily. "That is very kind of you, sir, but I must insist."

"In that case, we must arrange to discuss the matter in a more private atmosphere." Lovejoy glanced meaningfully around at the throng that filled the lobby. "This is surely not the appropriate time or place."

"But I have a draft for the amount with me."

"I have just told you I cannot take your money."

"Sir, I demand that you allow me to settle this debt." Augusta was beginning to feel frustrated and quite desperate. "You must return my marker for the thousand pounds."

"You want your marker back very badly, do you?"

"Well, of course I do. Please, my lord, this is very awkward."

Lovejoy's eyes glittered with amused malice as he appeared to consider her demand. "Very well, I think we can make arrangements. You shall have your vowels back if you care to call on me two nights hence. Say around eleven o'clock in the evening? Come alone, Miss Ballinger, and we will settle the debt."

Augusta was suddenly chilled from head to toe as she realized what he was saying. She moistened dry lips and tried to keep her voice calm. It sounded unnaturally thin, even to her own ears. "I cannot possibly call on you alone at eleven o'clock at night. You know that very well, my lord."

"Do not concern yourself with the little matter of your

reputation, Miss Ballinger. I assure you, I will mention your visit to no one. Least of all to your fiancé."

"You cannot force me to do this," she whispered.

"Come, now, Miss Ballinger. Where is that adventurous spirit and thirst for recklessness which everyone says is a family trait? Surely you are not too timid to risk a little late-night rendezvous at the home of a friend."

"My lord, be reasonable."

"Oh, I shall be, my dear. Most reasonable. I shall expect you at eleven, evening after next. Do not disappoint me, or I shall be obliged to make public the fact that the last of the Northumberland Ballingers does not pay her gaming debts. Think of the humiliation, Augusta. And so easily avoided by a short visit."

Lovejoy turned and walked off into the crowd.

Augusta stared after him, her stomach churning.

"Oh, there you are, Augusta," Claudia said as she came up behind her cousin. "Shall we join the Haywoods in their box now? It is almost time for the performance to begin and we are expected."

"Yes. Yes, of course."

Edmund Kean was as compelling on stage as always, but Augusta did not hear one word of the play. She spent the entire time trying to deal with the new twist in the disaster that had befallen her.

No matter how she viewed the situation, there was no way around the horrible fact that a note saying she owed Lovejoy a thousand pounds was in the odious man's possession and he had no intention of returning it unless she compromised herself.

Augusta was reckless, but she was far from naive. She did not believe for one minute that Lovejoy intended her late-night visit to be a social call. The man was clearly going to demand much more of her than a little conversation.

It was clear that Lord Lovejoy was no gentleman. There was no telling what he would do with her vowels should she fail to show two nights hence. But she had seen the chilling promise in his eyes. Sooner or later he would use her note against her in some malicious manner.

Perhaps he would go to Graystone with her marker. Augusta closed her eyes and shuddered at the thought. Harry would be furious with her. The evidence of her foolishness would confirm all his darkest suspicions concerning her character.

It would be humiliating, but she could tell Harry the whole story now. He would be thoroughly displeased, even disgusted with her behavior. This incident would no doubt be just the impetus he needed to finally agree to allow her to call off the engagement.

That thought should have brought her a giddy sense of relief, but for some reason it did not. Augusta forced herself to examine the reason why. Surely she did not actually want the engagement to stand. She had resisted the notion right from the start.

No, she decided firmly, it was not that she still believed that marriage to Harry was a sound idea, it was simply that she did not wish to be embarrassed and humiliated in front of him.

She had her pride, after all. She was the last of the proud, daring, neck-or-nothing branch of the Ballinger clan. She would look after her own honor.

On the way home in the Haywoods' carriage, Augusta came to a grim conclusion. She had to find a way to retrieve the incriminating gaming voucher before Lovejoy found a way to embarrass and humiliate her with it.

"Where the devil have you been, Graystone? I've gone to every damn ball and soiree in town tonight looking for you. You've got a bloody disaster on your hands and here you sit, calm as you please, drinking claret at your club." Peter Sheldrake dropped into the chair across from Harry and continued to mutter darkly as he reached for the bottle. "I should have tried here first."

"Yes, you should have." Harry looked up from the notes he was making for a book on Caesar's military campaigns. "I decided to come here for a few hands of cards before retiring for the evening. What seems to be the problem, Sheldrake? I have not seen you this agitated since the night you nearly got caught with that French officer's wife."

"The problem is not mine." Peter's eyes sparkled with satisfaction. "It is yours."

Harry groaned, sensing the worst. "Are we by any chance about to discuss Augusta?"

"I fear so. Sally sent me to find you when it transpired that you were not conveniently at home. Your lady has taken up a new profession, Graystone. She is about to become a cracksman."

Harry went cold. "The devil she is. What are you talking about, Sheldrake?"

"According to Sally, your fiancée is even now on her way to break into the house Lovejoy has leased for The Season. It seems she tried to repay her debt but Lovejoy refused to take the money. Nor would he return her marker unless she collected it in person. At his place. At eleven o'clock tomorrow evening, to be precise. She was instructed to come alone. One can imagine what he had in mind."

"That son of a bitch."

"Yes, I fear he is playing some rather dangerous games with your Miss Ballinger. However, never fear. Your intrepid and ever resourceful fiancée has decided to take matters into her own hands. She has gone to fetch her marker herself tonight while Lovejoy is out on the town."

"This time I really will beat her." Harry got to his feet, ignoring Peter's wicked grin as he headed for the door. *And afterward I will deal with Lovejoy.*

Dressed for the occasion in a pair of trousers and a shirt that had once belonged to her brother, Augusta crouched beneath Lovejoy's garden window and surveyed the situation.

The window of Lovejoy's small library had opened easily enough. She had been afraid she might have to smash one of the small panes of glass in order to force her way inside. But one of the servants had apparently failed to lock the window earlier in the day.

Augusta breathed a sigh of relief and took one more look around the little garden to make certain she was still unobserved. All was quiet and the windows of the floor above were still dark. Lovejoy's small staff was either abed or out for the evening. Lovejoy himself, Sally had managed to ascertain, was at the Beltons' soiree and would no doubt stay out until dawn.

Convinced the entire business was going to be very simple and straightforward, Augusta hopped up onto the windowsill, swung her legs over the edge, and dropped soundlessly to the carpeted floor.

She stood still for a moment, attempting to get her bearings in the dark room. The silence was oppressive. There was no sound at all from anywhere in the house. She could hear the distant clatter of carriages out in the street and the whisper of rustling leaves through the open window, but nothing else.

There was enough moonlight filtering in through the window to reveal Lovejoy's desk and some of the furniture. A large wing chair was placed near the hearth. Two bookcases loomed in the shadows, but there was only a handful of volumes on the shelves. A large globe on a heavy wooden base stood in the corner.

Augusta glanced across the small chamber and assured herself the door was closed.

Her observations of the male sex had informed her years ago that gentlemen were strongly inclined to keep their most valuable papers locked in their library desks. Her father, brother, and uncle had all followed that policy. It was that observation that had enabled her to guess the location of Rosalind Morrissey's stolen journal. Augusta was certain she would find her marker in Lovejoy's desk tonight.

It was unfortunate that she had been unable to ask Harry to come along on this venture, she thought as she went over the desk and crouched behind it. His knowledge of how to use a bit of wire to open locks would have come in handy. She wondered where he had picked up the skill.

Augusta gently tugged on the drawer, which was most definitely locked shut. She wrinkled her nose as she studied the desk. She could just imagine Harry's reaction if she had requested his help tonight. The man had no sense of adventure.

The lock of Lovejoy's desk was difficult to see in the shadows. Augusta toyed with the notion of lighting the taper. If she closed the drapes no one would be likely to spot the light coming from the library window.

She rose to her feet and started to search for a light source. Her back was to the open window and she was just reaching for what appeared to be a candle holder on a high shelf when she sensed a presence. *Someone else is in the library. I have been discovered.*

Shock and fear vibrated through Augusta. A cry of raw panic rose in her throat, threatening to choke her. But before she could whirl around or even utter a scream, a strong hand closed forcefully over her mouth.

"This is getting to be a most unpleasant habit," Harry growled in her ear.

"*Graystone.*" Augusta went limp with relief as his hand dropped away from her lips. "Dear God, you gave me an awful start. I thought it was Lovejoy."

"You little fool. It easily could have been. Indeed, you may wish it had been by the time I have finished with you."

She turned to face him and found him looming tall and dark in the shadows. He was dressed entirely in black, including black leather boots and a long, black greatcoat which concealed his clothing. He carried his ebony cane, she noticed, but saw that for once he was not wearing a crisp white cravat. It was the first time she had ever seen him without one. Dressed in this fashion the earl blended perfectly into the darkness.

"What on earth are you doing here?" she demanded softly.

"I would have thought it obvious. I am attempting to keep my future wife out of Newgate Prison. Have you found what you came for?"

"No, I just got here. The desk is locked. I was searching for a taper when you snuck up behind me." Augusta scowled as a thought occurred to her. "How did you know I was here?"

"That is not important at the moment."

"Sir, you have the most unsettling way of always knowing what I am about. One would almost believe you can read minds."

"No great feat, I assure you. Why, if you try very hard, I'll wager you could even read mine tonight. For example, what do you believe I am thinking at this very moment, Augusta?" Harry went back to the window and closed it softly. Then he moved to the desk.

"I suspect you are rather annoyed with me, my lord," Augusta ventured as she followed him across the room. "But I can explain everything."

"Your explanations can come later, although I doubt that I will find them much of an excuse for this nonsense." Harry went down on one knee behind the desk and fished a familiar-looking length of wire out of his pocket. "But first let us finish this business and be gone."

"Excellent notion, my lord." Augusta crouched beside him, peering intently at what he was doing. "Do you not need a taper to see what you are doing?"

"No. This is not the first desk I have opened by touch. If you will recall I had some practice on Enfield's."

"Yes, so you did. Which reminds me, Harry, wherever did you learn—"

There was a faint click from the small keyhole. The desk was unlocked.

"Ah," said Harry very softly.

Augusta was filled with admiration. "Where did you learn how to do this so efficiently, my lord? I vow it is a most remarkable skill. I practiced on Uncle Thomas's desk with one of my hairpins, but I never acquired this degree of talent."

Harry slanted her a repressive glance as he pulled open the desk drawer. "The ability to pry open someone else's desk is not an admirable skill. I do not consider it the sort of accomplishment a young lady should learn."

"No, you would not, would you, Graystone? You think it is only men who should get to do the exciting things in this world." Augusta peered into the desk drawer. She saw nothing that even remotely resembled her IOU among the neatly arranged papers. She reached out to sift through the small assortment of items in the drawer.

Harry's hand closed over hers. "Wait. I will do the searching."

Augusta sighed. "I assume this means you know what I am searching for, my lord?"

"Your note to Lovejoy for the thousand pounds you owe him." Harry was sorting rapidly through the contents of the center drawer. When he found nothing, he closed it and started opening other drawers in the desk.

It was obvious Harry knew everything. Augusta decided to get an early start on her explanations. "The thing is, Graystone, it was all a mistake."

"On that we agree. A very stupid mistake." He finished going through the last of the drawers and straightened, frowning intently. "But we now have an even larger problem on our hands. I see no sign of your vowels."

"Oh, no. I was certain he would keep them in here. Every man I have ever known keeps his valuable papers in his library desk."

"You have either not known a great many men or you

were not privy to all of their secrets. Many men keep their valuables in a safe." Harry started around the desk toward the bookcases.

"A safe. Yes, of course. Why didn't I think of that? Do you suppose Lovejoy has one?"

"No doubt." Harry shifted some volumes on the shelves of the bookcases. He hauled out a few of the larger ones and opened them. When they proved to contain only pages, he put them back on the shelves in exactly the same positions in which he had found them.

Seeing what he was doing, Augusta started working on another row of books. She found nothing. Alarmed that they might not find her vowels after all, she swung around in agitation and nearly stumbled into the globe. She reached out hastily to brace herself.

"Good grief, this is heavy," she muttered.

Harry turned, his gaze riveted on the globe. "Of course. It is just the right size."

"What are you talking about?" Augusta watched in amazement as he moved over to the globe and knelt beside it. She suddenly realized what he was thinking. "How very clever of you, my lord. Do you think this is Lovejoy's safe?"

"I think it is a possibility." Harry was already working on the mechanism that held the globe in its wooden frame. His fingers slid over the wood with a lover's touch, testing and probing. Then he paused. "Ah, yes. There we are."

A moment later some hidden spring gave way and the top half of the globe opened to reveal a hollow interior. A shaft of moonlight revealed a few papers and a small jeweler's box inside.

"*Harry.* There it is. There's my note." Augusta reached inside to pluck out her IOU. "I have it."

"Right. Let's be off, then." Harry closed the globe. "Damnation."

He went absolutely still at the faint sound of the front door of the house opening and closing. There were booted footsteps in the hall.

"Lovejoy has come home." Augusta's eyes met Harry's as she spoke. "Quick. The window."

"No time. He is coming this way."

Harry was on his feet. He grabbed his cane and her wrist and yanked Augusta toward the sofa at the far end of the room. Pushing her down behind it, he hunkered beside her, the cane in his hand.

She swallowed heavily and did not move so much as a fraction of an inch.

The footsteps paused outside the door of the library. Augusta held her breath, fiercely glad that Harry was here beside her.

The door opened and someone came into the library. Augusta stopped breathing altogether. *Dear God, what a mess. And it is all my fault. I might very well succeed in plunging that paragon of propriety, the Earl of Graystone, into a scandal broth tonight. He would never forgive me.*

Next to her, Harry did not stir. If he was unduly alarmed about the prospect of impending humiliation and social disaster, he did not show it. He seemed unnaturally calm, even detached as the situation reached a crisis point.

The footsteps crossed the carpet. Glass clinked as someone picked up the brandy decanter near the wing chair. Whoever it was would turn and light a lamp now, Augusta thought in horror.

But a moment later the footsteps retreated back to the door. The door closed softly and the footsteps went on down the hall.

Augusta and Harry were once more alone in the library.

Harry waited a few heartbeats and then surged to his feet, tugging Augusta up beside him. He gave her a small shove. "The window. Hurry."

Augusta hastened to the window and opened it. Harry grasped her around the waist and lifted her up onto the sill.

"Where the devil did you get yourself a pair of trousers?" he muttered.

"They belonged to my brother."

"Have you no notion of propriety at all?"

"Very little, my lord." Augusta dropped down onto the grass and turned to watch him come through the window.

"There is a carriage waiting in a lane down the street." Harry closed the window behind him and took her arm. "Move."

Augusta glanced back over her shoulder and saw a light appear in the upstairs window. Lovejoy was preparing for bed. It had been a near thing and it was not over yet. If he chanced to glance out of his window and look down into the small garden, he might easily see two shadowy figures racing toward the gate.

But there was no angry shout or cry of alarm as Harry and Augusta let themselves out of the garden.

Augusta could feel Harry's fingers clenched like a manacle around her upper arm as he led her quickly down the street.

A hackney carriage went past and then a gig carrying two obviously inebriated young dandies clattered down the street. But no one paid any attention to the man in the black greatcoat or his companion.

Halfway along the street, Harry jerked Augusta to a halt and turned into a lane that was not much more than an alley. The path was almost completely blocked by a handsome closed carriage that bore a familiar crest.

"That is Lady Arbuthnott's carriage, is it not?" Augusta turned startled eyes toward Harry. "What is she doing here? I know she is your friend, but surely you have not made her come out at such an hour. She is too ill for travel."

"She is not here. She was kind enough to loan me the carriage so that my own crest would not be noticed in this part of town. Get inside. Quickly."

Augusta started to obey and then paused to glance up at the familiar-looking figure who sat on the box. He was draped in a many-tiered cape and a hat was pulled low over his bushy brows, but Augusta recognized him instantly.

"Scruggs, is that you?"

"Yes, Miss Ballinger, I fear it is," Scruggs growled in an aggrieved tone. "Summoned from a warm bed, I was, without so much as a by-your-leave. I pride myself on being a first-class butler but I am not paid to handle the ribbons. I was ordered to ape John Coachman tonight, however, and I'll do my best, though I don't imagine I'll get much of a tip."

"You should not be out in the night air," Augusta said with a frown. "'Tis not good for your rheumatism."

"Aye, that's true enough," Scruggs agreed dourly. "But try telling that to the high and mighty sort who like to run around in the middle of the night."

Harry jerked open the carriage door. "Pray do not concern yourself with Scruggs's rheumatism, Augusta." He seized her lightly around the waist. "It is your own person you need worry about."

"But, Harry—I mean, my lord—ooof." Augusta landed with a thud against the green velvet cushions as Harry tossed her rather negligently inside the dark carriage. She heard him speak to Scruggs as she righted herself.

"Drive until I tell you to return to Lady Arbuthnott's."

"Drive where, man?" Muffled by the carriage, Scruggs's voice sounded different now. The hoarse, rasping tone was gone.

"I do not particularly care," Harry snapped. "Around one of the parks or toward the outskirts of town. It makes no difference. Just see that you do not attract any attention. I have a few things to say to Miss Ballinger and I can think of no other place where I shall have the privacy and leisure in which to say them except inside this carriage."

Scruggs cleared his throat. When he spoke again, his voice still sounded different yet oddly familiar. "Uh, Graystone, perhaps you ought to reconsider this notion of driving aimlessly about tonight. You are not in the best of tempers at the moment."

"When I want your advice, Scruggs, I shall ask for it."

The edge on Harry's voice was as sharp as a knife. "Is that quite clear?"

"Yes, my lord," Scruggs said dryly.

"Excellent." Harry bounded up inside the coach and slammed the door. He reached out and drew the curtains across the glass.

"There was no need to snarl at him," Augusta said reproachfully as Harry dropped down onto the seat across from her. "He is an old man and he suffers a great deal from rheumatism."

"I do not give a damn about Scruggs's rheumatism." Harry spoke much too softly. "It is you who concerns me at the moment, Augusta. Exactly what in hell do you think you were about, breaking into Lovejoy's house tonight?"

It dawned on Augusta just how furious Harry really was. For the first time she began to wish she were safely back in her own bedchamber. "I got the impression you understood what I was doing, my lord. You seemed to know about my vowels being in Lovejoy's possession. I presume you also know how I lost a thousand pounds to him. Did Sally tell you?"

"You must forgive Sally. She was quite concerned."

"Yes, well, I tried to repay the debt, but Lovejoy refused to take the money. I must say, he is no gentleman. I got the distinct impression he had some nasty plans to use my signed note to humiliate me or perhaps you. I thought it best to retrieve it."

"Damnation, Augusta, you had no business getting lured into a game of cards with Lovejoy in the first place."

"Well, looking back on it, I can certainly see it was a mistake. But I must say, I was holding my own, sir. I was winning, in fact, until I got distracted by another matter. We started talking about my brother, you see, and all of a sudden I looked down and saw that I had lost rather heavily."

"Augusta, a lady with any notion of proper behavior would never have gotten herself into such a situation."

"You are no doubt correct, my lord. But I did warn you I was not the sort of lady you should even contemplate marrying, did I not?"

"That is beside the point," Harry said through gritted teeth. "The fact is, we are going to be married, and allow me to tell you here and now, Augusta, that I will not tolerate another incident such as this. Do I make myself plain?"

"Very plain, sir. But for my own part, I would point out that it was my pride and my honor that were involved here. I had to do something."

"You should have come directly to me."

Augusta narrowed her eyes. "No offense, my lord, but I do not think that would have been such a brilliant notion. What would have been the point? You would have lectured me and made a most unpleasant scene, just as you are doing now."

"I would have taken care of the matter for you," Harry said grimly. "And you would not have put your neck and your reputation at risk as you did tonight."

"It seems to me, my lord, that both of our necks and our reputations were at risk tonight." Augusta tried a tentative smile of appeasement. "And I must say, you were most impressive. I am very glad you turned up when you did, sir. I would never have found my marker if you had not suspected the globe was a secret safe. It seems to me it all turned out for the best and we should both be thankful the thing is over."

"Do you really believe I am going to let the matter rest there?"

Augusta drew herself up proudly. "I will, of course, understand completely if you feel my actions tonight have put me beyond the pale. If you feel you cannot possibly tolerate the notion of marrying me, my original offer still stands. I shall be quite willing to cry off and free you from this engagement."

"Free me, Augusta?" Harry reached out to catch hold of her wrist. "I fear that is impossible now. I have come to the conclusion that I shall never be free of you. You are going to bedevil me for the rest of my life and if that is to be my fate, I may as well take what consolation I can for what I shall be obliged to endure."

Before Augusta had time to realize what he intended, Harry had yanked her across the short distance between them. An instant later she found herself lying across his strong thighs. She clung to his shoulders as his mouth came down on hers.

7

"*H*arry."

Augusta's startled cry was stifled under the fierce, exciting pressure of Harry's mouth. He took command of her senses in a single instant. Her stunned amazement dissolved into a shimmering excitement, just as it had that first time on the floor of his library.

Augusta wound her arms slowly around Harry's neck as she recovered from the initial shock. He was demanding entrance into her mouth and she obediently parted her lips. The instant she did so, he was inside, claiming her warmth. Augusta shivered.

Her body was reacting so quickly she could not think clearly. Part of her was aware of the sway and jostle of the vehicle, the rattle of the wheels, and the ring of the horses' hooves on stone. But here in the carriage, locked in Harry's arms, she was in another world.

It was a world to which she had secretly longed to return ever since that first time Harry had held her like this. The hours she had spent reliving those intimacies in her imagination paled now as reality took its place. A euphoric sensation unfolded within her as she realized she was going to have another opportunity to experience the wonder of Harry's kisses.

Obviously he had forgiven her for the unpleasant business involving Lovejoy and her debt, Augusta thought happily. Surely Harry would not be kissing her like this if he were still angry with her. She clutched at him, her fingers sinking deeply into the heavy fabric of his black greatcoat.

"Good God, Augusta." Harry raised his head slightly, his eyes gleaming in the shadows. "You are going to drive me mad. One minute I could cheerfully shake you and the next you make me want to drag you into the nearest bed."

She touched the side of his face and smiled wistfully. "Will you please kiss me again, Harry? I do so like it when you kiss me."

With a muffled oath, Harry's mouth came back down on hers. She was aware of his hand gliding over her shoulder, stroking gently, and she froze for an instant when his fingers touched her breast through the fabric of her shirt. But she did not pull away.

"Do you like that, my reckless little hoyden?" Harry's voice was husky as he began to unfasten her shirt.

"Yes," she breathed. "I want you to kiss me and go on kissing me forever. I vow it is the most fascinating experience, my lord."

"I am very glad you find it so."

Then his hand was sliding inside the open shirt and cupping her bare breast. Augusta closed her eyes and sucked in her breath as Harry's thumb circled her nipple.

"My God," Harry whispered thickly. "Like the sweetest of ripe fruit."

Then he lowered his head to take the rosy bud into his mouth and Augusta moaned in response.

"Hush, love," he muttered, his hand moving down to the fastening of her trousers.

Dimly Augusta realized they were in a carriage some-where on a busy street and that Scruggs was only a few feet away, blissfully unaware of what was happening inside the cab. She knew she should keep silent, but she could not swallow each tiny gasp of surprise. Harry's touch made her body sing with pleasure. An unbearable eagerness was rippling through her, creating a tension that was too new and too strange to deal with in complete silence.

When she felt Harry's fingers inside her open trousers, searching out the warm secrets between her thighs, Augusta caught her breath and cried out softly. "Oh, *Harry.*"

Harry responded with a groan that was half laughter and half oath. "Silence, sweetheart. You must have a care, love."

"I am sorry, but I cannot seem to keep quiet when you touch me like that. It feels so very odd, Harry. I vow I have never felt anything like it."

"Damnation, woman. You do not have an inkling of what you are doing to me, do you?" Harry shifted, changing position quickly. He swung the greatcoat off his shoulders and spread it on the green cushions. Then he moved again, stretching Augusta out on the coat. Her knees were raised because of the close quarters.

When Augusta opened her eyes, Harry was crouched beside her. He bent over her, opening her shirt with feverish impatience to bare her breasts.

Augusta was just growing accustomed to the touch of his hand on her upper body when she became aware of the fact that Harry was jerking off her shoes and tugging her trousers down over her thighs.

"My lord? What are you doing?" She stirred restlessly on the cushion, half lost in the daze of sensual awareness that was enveloping her. Harry's warm hand cupped her softness with shocking intimacy and she trembled.

"Tell me again that you want me," he muttered against her breast.

"I want you. I have never wanted anything so much in

my life." She arched against his hand and heard him groan. All thought of protest faded away once more, to be replaced by a spiraling need. She cried out again and Harry's mouth was suddenly back on hers, silencing her gently.

Augusta shuddered as she felt him shift position once again. He was on his knees between her legs now. She realized he was fumbling quickly with his breeches.

"Harry?"

"Hush, love. Hush."

She gasped as his weight came down on top of her, crushing her into the cushions. He had settled himself between her thighs before she fully realized what he intended.

His fingers slid down between their bodies, stroking her urgently, parting her. "Yes, love. That's it. Yes. Open yourself for me. Just like that. Lord, you are soft. Soft and moist for me. Let me feel you, darling."

The husky, coaxing words spilled over her. Augusta felt something hard and unyielding pushing slowly but steadily against her softness.

Panic flared for an instant. She should stop him, she thought vaguely. He would surely regret this in the morning, perhaps blame her again, just as he had last time. "Harry, I do not think we should do this. You will think me wanton."

"No, love. I will think you very sweet. Very soft."

"You will say I encouraged you." She gasped as he pressed harder. "You will say I made certain promises again."

"The promises have already been made and they will be kept. You belong to me, Augusta. We are engaged. You have nothing to fear by giving yourself to the man who will be your husband."

"Are you certain?"

"Absolutely certain. Put your arms around me, love," Harry muttered against her mouth. "Hold me. Take me fully inside you. Show me that you truly want me."

"Oh, Harry, I do want you. And if you are certain you want me, if you will not think me sadly lacking in virtue—"

"I want you, Augusta. God knows I want you so badly I do not believe I will survive until morning if I do not have you tonight. Nothing has ever felt so right."

"Oh, *Harry*." He wanted her, Augusta thought, dazzled by the realization. He needed her desperately. And she longed to surrender herself to him; she ached to discover what it would feel like to be possessed by him.

Augusta's arms tightened around his neck and she lifted herself tentatively into his strength.

It was all the encouragement Harry needed.

"God, yes, Augusta. *Yes*." His mouth fastened on hers as he thrust heavily into her.

Augusta, poised on the brink of a blazing sensual awareness, felt as if someone had suddenly tossed her into an icy cold pond. The shock of the intimate invasion roared through her. *This was not what she had been expecting.*

She gasped and cried out in surprise and dismay. The protest was no more than a muffled squeak, however, because Harry kept his mouth clamped savagely over hers. He swallowed her small exclamations, soothing her with his kiss. Neither of them moved.

Harry lifted his head cautiously after a moment. The soft light of the carriage lamp revealed the perspiration on his forehead and his tightly clenched jaw.

"Harry?"

"Easy, love, easy. 'Twill be all right in a moment or two. Forgive me, sweet, for rushing matters so." He dropped hot, urgent kisses along her cheeks and down her throat. His hands gripped her tightly. "You have made me drunk with desire and like any drunkard I have blundered about in a clumsy fashion when I should have used more grace and skill."

Augusta did not respond. She was too busy adjusting to the strange sensation of having Harry deep inside her.

For a timeless moment Harry continued to lay absolutely still on top of her. Augusta could feel the rigid tension in him as he held himself in check.

"Augusta?"

"Yes, Harry?"

"Are you all right, love?" he demanded through set teeth. He sounded as though he were exercising every ounce of self-control he possessed.

"Yes. I think so." Augusta frowned as her body slowly grew accustomed to the impossibly tight, impossibly stretched sensation. Nothing had ever felt like this.

At that moment the coach bounced mightily as a wheel struck a hole in the street. Harry was driven even more deeply inside Augusta by the unexpected motion. He groaned. Augusta gasped.

Harry muttered something under his breath and rested his forehead on Augusta's. "It will get better. I give you my word on that, Augusta. You are so sweet, so responsive. Look at me, sweetheart." He cradled her face between his palms. "Damn it, Augusta, open your eyes and look at me. *Tell me you still want me.* The last thing I wanted to do was hurt you."

She obeyed, lifting her lashes to survey his stark face. She realized that even as he fought to hold himself in check, he was chastising himself for having caused her discomfort. She smiled gently, deeply touched by his tender consideration. No wonder she loved him, she thought suddenly.

"Do not fret yourself, Harry. It is not that bad, truly. I doubt any real damage has been done. Not all adventures go smoothly, as we both discovered this evening in Lovejoy's library."

"Good God, Augusta. Whatever am I going to do with you?" Harry buried his face in the curve of her throat and began to move inside her.

Augusta did not particularly care for the new sensation at first, but she was slowly starting to change her mind—

was, in fact, even beginning to find it all quite tolerable—when it was suddenly over.

"*Augusta*." Harry surged into her one last time, arched his back, and went violently rigid. Augusta was fascinated by the taut strength of him and the feral expression of raw masculine power on his hard face. She realized he was gritting his teeth against a hoarse shout and then he groaned and collapsed heavily against her.

For a moment there was only the steady jostling of the carriage and the distant sounds out in the street. Augusta stroked Harry's back soothingly as she listened to him drawing in great, ragged gulps of air. She decided she liked the warm, heavy feel of him lying on top of her, even though he was crushing her into the cushions. She even liked the scent of him. There was something unmistakably and utterly masculine about it.

Most of all, she liked the strange intimacy of the situation. She felt almost a part of Harry now, she realized. It was as if they had both given something of themselves to each other and were now bound in some indefinable way that had nothing to do with the formalities of an engagement.

It took Augusta a few seconds to identify just what she was feeling and then she had it. It was a joyous sense of belonging. She and Harry were together now, as if tonight they had created the foundation of a new family. A family to which she could fully belong.

"Christ," Harry muttered. "I don't believe this."

"Harry," Augusta murmured thoughtfully, "will we do this a great deal during the next four months of our engagement, do you think? If so, we might have to arrange for a different coachman." She giggled softly. "I cannot see Scruggs agreeing to drive us around the city every night, can you? His rheumatism, you know."

Harry went still. His head came up abruptly and there was a distinctly stunned look in his eyes. When he spoke, all trace of a lover's warmth and urgency was gone from his voice. *"Four months.* Damnation. 'Tis impossible."

"What is wrong, my lord?"

He lifted himself away from her, running his fingers through his tousled hair. "Nothing that cannot be remedied. I need a few minutes to think. Sit up, Augusta. Hurry. I am sorry to rush you, but you must get dressed."

Harry's impatient, commanding tone succeeded in squelching much of the lingering sense of intimacy Augusta had been feeling. She winced as she awkwardly levered herself into an upright position and began fumbling with her clothing.

"Really, Harry. I do not understand you. Why are you so angry?" Augusta's fingers stilled on her clothing as a sudden horrible thought struck her. "Are you going to blame me, after all, for what happened a few minutes ago?"

"Damn it to hell, I am not angry with you, Augusta. At least, not about this." He gestured brusquely to indicate the interior of the carriage and all that had taken place within it. "The business of breaking into Lovejoy's house is another matter entirely and I do not intend to let it drop."

He fastened his breeches, straightened his shirt, and then reached out to assist her in getting back into her clothes. His hand stilled briefly on her thigh.

Augusta smiled as she sensed that he was torn between conflicting emotions. "Yes, my lord? Did you want something more?"

"A great deal more." He shook his head grimly as he adjusted her trousers. "And I shall never last another four months before I take it again, that is for certain."

"Then we shall be doing this frequently, my lord?"

He glanced up and there was no mistaking the sensual promise in his eyes. "No doubt. But not in some bloody damn carriage in the middle of London. Here, fix your shirt, Augusta." He started to fasten it for her. "I shall procure a special license as quickly as possible and we shall be married in a day or two."

"*Married*. By special license?" Augusta stared at him. She could not seem to get her thoughts straight. Everything was happening too fast. "Oh, no, Harry. What about our engagement?"

"I am afraid ours is destined to be one of the shorter betrothals on record. Just as short as I can make it, in fact."

"The thing is, I am not at all certain I want it shortened."

"Your feelings on the matter are no longer of any great significance," he told her gently. "I have just made love to you and will no doubt be tempted to do so again in the very near future. We shall therefore get married immediately. I am not going to wait four months to have you again, that much is a certainty. I would not survive the torture."

"But, Harry—"

He held up a hand to silence her. "Enough. Not another word. The matter is settled. This situation is entirely of my own doing and I will do what must be done."

"Well, as to that," Augusta said thoughtfully, "I do not think you can say it was entirely your fault. You have mentioned on several occasions that my own sense of propriety is sadly lacking in many respects and everyone knows I am inclined to be somewhat reckless. This is partly my fault, Harry. In fact," she added in chagrin as she thought of what Claudia's reaction would be to this news, "some people would be of the opinion that it is all my fault."

"I said I did not want to hear another word about it." Harry started to sweep up his greatcoat from the seat of the carriage and paused to stare down at the small, damp stains on it. He drew a deep breath.

"Is something wrong, Harry?"

"My apologies, Augusta." His voice was gruff. "I had no right to take advantage of you tonight. I do not know what happened to my self-control. You deserved a proper bed and all the trappings of a honeymoon for your first experience of lovemaking."

"Do not fret about it, sir. To tell you the truth, this was a rather exciting way to begin the whole business." She pushed aside the curtain that covered the window and gazed out into the street. "I wonder how many of those other carriages out there contain couples doing exactly what we were just doing?"

"One shudders to even contemplate the notion." Harry shoved open the trapdoor in the roof with his ebony walking stick. "Scruggs, take us back to Lady Arbuthnott's immediately."

"About time," Scruggs growled from the box. "Left it a bit late, didn't you, sir?"

Harry did not bother to respond. He let the trap close with a loud crack. Then he sat facing Augusta in silence for a long moment. "I cannot believe I have just made love to my fiancée in a carriage in the middle of a London street."

"Poor Harry." Augusta studied the strange expression on his hard face. "I suppose you will find this very difficult to reconcile with your fine notion of propriety, will you not, my lord?"

"Are you laughing at me, by any chance, Miss Ballinger?"

"No, my lord. I would not dream of doing so." She struggled to conceal the grin that was tugging at her mouth. She wondered why she felt so lighthearted and happy after such an astounding event.

Harry swore softly. "I begin to believe that if I am not extremely careful, you will be an exceedingly bad influence on me, Augusta."

"I shall certainly try my best, sir," she murmured. Then she sobered. "But about this matter of being married by special license, I really do not feel it is necessary to do anything quite so drastic, Harry."

"No?" His brows rose. "Well, I do. And that is all there is to it. I shall notify you tomorrow of the time and place. And I shall speak to your uncle and explain that there is no choice now."

"But that's just it, Harry. There is a choice. I am in no great rush. And marriage is so very permanent, is it not? I want you to be quite certain of what you are doing, my lord."

"You mean you are still having qualms."

She bit her lip. "I did not say that precisely."

"You do not need to say it. You have been dragging your feet about our engagement right from the start. But now matters have gone too far and neither of us has any honorable alternative but to proceed with the wedding as quickly as possible."

A jolt of fear went through Augusta. "I hope you are not going through with this because you feel you must do the right thing, my lord. I realize you are very touchy about matters having to do with respectability and propriety, but there really is no need for such haste."

"Do not be a goose, Augusta. There is every need to hurry along this marriage. You might even now be pregnant."

Her eyes widened. "Dear heaven, I had not thought of that." *Which only goes to show what chaos my mind is in tonight,* she thought. *I might be pregnant. With Harry's baby.* Instinctively she touched her stomach with protective fingers.

Harry's gaze followed her hand. He smiled. "Obviously that possibility had slipped your mind."

"We could wait awhile and be certain," she ventured.

"We are not going to wait a day longer than necessary."

She heard the unyielding note in his voice and knew that further argument was useless. She was not even certain she wanted further discussion. She did not know what she wanted just then.

What would it be like to have Harry's baby?

Augusta sat tense and quiet until the carriage arrived at Lady Arbuthnott's residence.

When they alighted, Augusta turned to Harry one last time. "My lord, it is not too late to reconsider. Pray, do not make any decisions until the morrow. You may feel differently then."

"I shall be too busy arranging for a special license and taking care of certain matters tomorrow to do any reconsidering," he informed her. "Come, I will escort you through the garden to a door at the back of the house. You can change your clothing in one of Sally's bedchambers and then she will send you home in her carriage along with a companion."

"What do you mean, you will be too busy tomorrow?" she demanded as he hurried her toward the back door of the house. "What are you going to do tomorrow besides arrange for the special license?"

"I plan to pay a call on Lovejoy, among other things. Please try to move a little more quickly, Augusta. It makes me very uneasy being out here in the open with you dressed like that."

But Augusta suddenly dug in her booted heels and came to a complete halt. "*Lovejoy?* What the devil do you mean, you're going to pay a call on him?" She reached up and grasped the lapels of his coat. "Harry, you are not going to do something extremely foolish like challenge him to a duel, are you?"

He looked down at her, eyes unreadable in the shadows. "You find that notion foolish?"

"Good lord, yes. Excessively foolish. Out of the question. Unthinkable. Harry, you must not do any such thing. Do you hear me? I will not allow it."

He studied her thoughtfully. "Why not?" he asked at last.

"*Because something dreadful might happen,*" she gasped. "You might be killed. And it would be all my fault. I could not bear that, Graystone. Do you understand? I will not have that on my conscience. The entire matter of the debt was my problem and it is now resolved. There is no need to challenge Lovejoy. Please, Harry, I beg you. Promise me you will not do so."

"From what I have been told, I would hazard a guess that your father or brother, were either still alive, would have made a dawn appointment with Lovejoy," Harry observed softly.

"But it is not the same thing at all. They were very different types of men." Augusta was feeling desperate. "They were reckless and daring sorts, perhaps a bit too much so at times. In any event, I would not want them challenging Lovejoy, either. As I said before, the entire disaster was of my own doing."

"Augusta—"

She gave the lapels of his greatcoat a sharp, admonishing shake. "I do not want someone else risking his neck for what was all my own fault. Please, Harry. Give me your word you will not do so. I could not bear it if something were to happen to you because of me."

"You seem quite certain I would be the one who would lose in such a duel," he said. "I imagine I should feel somewhat offended by your lack of confidence in my skill with a pistol."

"No, no, it is not that." She shook her head frantically, anxious to reassure him lest he be embarrassed. "It is just that some men such as my brother are more inclined by nature toward dangerous activities. You are not. You are a scholar, sir, not a hot-blooded out-and-outer or a Corinthian."

"I begin to believe you actually have some affection for me, Augusta, even if you do not think highly of my dueling skills."

"Well, of course I think highly of you, Harry. I have always thought highly of you. I have even grown somewhat fond of you of late."

"I see."

She felt the heat rise in her cheeks as she heard the soft mockery in his words. She had just allowed this man to make love to her on a carriage cushion and here she was telling him she was somewhat *fond* of him.

He must think her a perfect goose. On the other hand, she could hardly tell him she was wildly in love with him. This was hardly the time or place for such a passionate declaration. Everything was in too much chaos.

"Harry, you have been most helpful to me this evening and I would not want you to suffer because of my actions," Augusta concluded stoutly.

Harry was silent for another long moment. Then he smiled grimly. "I will make you a bargain, Augusta. I will refrain from issuing a challenge to Lovejoy on the morrow if you will give me your word you will not give me any further argument about being married by special license in two days' time."

"But, Harry—"

"Do we have a bargain, my dear?"

She drew a deep breath, knowing she was trapped. "Yes, we have a bargain."

"Excellent."

Augusta narrowed her eyes in sudden suspicion. "Graystone, if I did not know better, I would swear you were an exceedingly cunning and rather clever beast."

"Ah, but you do know me better than to conclude that, do you not, my dear? I am merely a rather dull and plodding classical scholar."

"Who makes love in carriages and who just happens to know how to open locks and secret safes."

"One learns the most amazing facts in books." He kissed the tip of her nose. "Now run along inside and get out of those damn breeches. They are most unsuitable for a lady. I prefer my future countess in proper female attire."

"That does not surprise me, my lord." She turned to leave.

"Augusta?"

She glanced back over her shoulder and saw Harry reach into the pocket of his greatcoat. He drew out a small pouch. "Yes, Harry?"

"I believe this belongs to you. I trust you will not find yourself in a position where you must pawn it again."

"*My necklace.*" She smiled glowingly up at him as she took the pouch from his hand. She stood on tiptoe to brush a soft kiss against his jaw. "Thank you, my lord. You cannot know what this means to me. However did you manage to find it?"

"Your moneylender was more than willing to part with it," Harry said, his voice dry.

"I shall, of course, give you the thousand pounds I got when I pawned it," Augusta said quickly, thrilled to have the necklace safely back in her possession.

"Never mind the thousand pounds. You may consider it a portion of the marriage settlements."

"That is very generous of you, my lord. But I could not possibly allow you to give me such a gift."

"You can and you will," Harry said coolly. "I am your fiancé, if you will recall. It is my privilege to give you the occasional gift. And I shall consider myself amply repaid if you have learned your lesson tonight."

"About Lovejoy? Never fear. I have definitely learned my lesson about him. I shall never play cards with him again." Augusta paused, feeling wonderfully generous herself. "Nor will I even dance with him in future."

"Augusta, you will not even talk to him in future. Is that understood?"

"Yes, Harry."

His face softened slightly as his eyes skimmed over her. The possessiveness in his gaze sent a shiver of awareness through Augusta.

"Run along, my dear," Harry said. "It grows late."

Augusta turned and fled into the house.

Harry was shown into Lovejoy's small library shortly before noon the next morning. He casually surveyed the room and saw that everything was just as it had been last night, including the globe, which was still in its location near the bookcase.

Lovejoy leaned back in his chair behind the desk and eyed his unexpected visitor with seemingly lazy interest. But there was a wary gleam in his green eyes. "Good morning, Graystone. What brings you here today?"

"A personal matter. It will not take long." Harry seated himself in the wing chair near the hearth. Contrary to Augusta's assumption last night, he'd had no intention of challenging Lovejoy this morning. He believed in knowing an enemy well before choosing an appropriate method of dealing with him.

"A personal matter, you say. I must admit I am surprised. I did not think Miss Ballinger would go to you about the little matter of her gaming debts. So she had asked you to pay them, has she?"

Harry lifted an inquiring brow. "Not at all. I am unaware of any such debts, sir. However, one should never make assumptions about Miss Ballinger. My fiancée is not entirely predictable."

"So I am given to understand."

"I, however, am very predictable in my ways. I think you should know that, Lovejoy. If I say I will do something, it generally gets done."

"I see." Lovejoy toyed with a heavily chased silver paperweight. "And just what are you proposing to do?"

"Protect my fiancée from the sort of games you apparently enjoy playing with women."

Lovejoy gave him a deeply offended look. "Graystone, it is not my fault your fiancée enjoys the occasional hand of cards. If you are truly bent on marrying the lady, you would do well to consider her nature. She is inclined toward reckless entertainment. The tendency runs in the family, I hear. At least on the Northumberland side of the clan."

"It is not my fiancée's fondness for cards that concerns me."

"No? I should think it would concern you deeply,

Graystone. Once your fortune is at her disposal, she will no doubt grow even more fond of games of chance." Lovejoy smiled meaningfully.

Harry smiled back quite blandly. "As I said, I am not concerned about her choice of entertainments. It is your teasing her about the matter of her brother's death that has brought me here today."

"She told you about that, did she?"

"I was informed you more or less promised to help her investigate the incident. I seriously doubt you can offer her any useful assistance. Nor do I want the past dug up. It will only succeed in causing my fiancée pain and that I will not tolerate. You are to leave the matter alone, Lovejoy. Do you understand?"

"What makes you so certain I cannot help her get her brother's reputation out from under the cloud of suspicion that hovered over him at the time of his death?"

"We both know there is no way to go back and prove or disprove Ballinger's guilt. It is best that the matter stay buried." Harry held Lovejoy's gaze. "Unless, of course," he said quietly, "you have some special knowledge of the event, in which case you will tell me about it. Do you know anything, Lovejoy?"

"Good lord, no."

"I thought not." Harry got to his feet. "I trust you are telling the truth, because I would be most unhappy to learn otherwise. I will bid you good day. By the bye, although I do not intend to forbid my fiancée the occasional game of cards, I am forbidding her to play with you. You must try your tricks elsewhere, Lovejoy."

"How dull. I quite enjoy Miss Ballinger's company. And there is the little matter of the thousand pounds she owes me. Tell me, Graystone, given the rumor that you are demanding excessively virtuous behavior in your next countess, does it not alarm you that you are engaged to a young woman who tends to play rather deep?"

Harry smiled faintly. "You must be mistaken, Lovejoy.

My fiancée does not owe you any money. Certainly not a thousand pounds."

"Do not be too certain of that." Lovejoy got to his feet, a look of satisfaction in his eyes. "Would you care to see her marker?"

"If you can produce it, I shall, of course, settle the debt here and now. But I doubt you can present any such marker."

"One moment."

Harry watched with interest as Lovejoy crossed the room to the globe and took a key from his pocket. He inserted it in the hidden lock and the top half of the globe sprang open, just as it had last night.

There was an acute silence as Lovejoy stood gazing down into the bottom half of the globe for a long moment. Then he turned slowly around to face Harry. His face was expressionless.

"I appear to have been mistaken," Lovejoy said softly. "I do not have your lady's marker, after all."

"I did not think so. I believe we understand each other very well now, do we not, Lovejoy? Again, I shall bid you good day. You may congratulate me, by the way. I am to be married tomorrow."

"So soon?" Lovejoy could not completely hide his start of surprise. His eyes narrowed. "You amaze me, sir. I would not have thought you so rash. From all accounts anyone who marries Miss Augusta Ballinger must be prepared for a great many adventures."

"It will no doubt make an interesting change for me. I am told I have spent too many years buried in my books. Perhaps it is time I was introduced to a bit of adventure." Without waiting for a reply, Harry opened the door and let himself out of the library. Behind him he heard the lid of the globe safe being slammed shut with sufficient force to echo in the hall.

Lovejoy's choice of Augusta as a target for his obnoxious little games was interesting, Harry thought as he left the house. He decided it was time to make a few inquiries into the man's past. The task would give Peter Sheldrake something more useful to do than play at being Scruggs the butler.

8

Claudia walked into Augusta's bedchamber and stood calmly amid the whirlwind of commotion that was taking place there. She frowned gently at her cousin over a sea of gowns, shoes, hatboxes, trunks, and plumes.

"I do not understand the necessity for all this packing up and dashing about, Augusta. It makes no sense to get married by special license when the plans for your wedding in four months are coming along very nicely. It is not quite the thing to hurry matters like this. Graystone, of all people, should understand that."

"If you have any questions, I suggest you take them directly to Graystone. This is all his idea." Augusta, busy directing the flurry of activity from her command position near the wardrobe, scowled at her maid. "No, no, Betsy, put my ball gowns in the other trunk. The petticoats go in that one. Have my books been packed?"

"Yes, Miss. I packed 'em meself this mornin'."

"Good. I do not want to find myself stuck in Dorset with only the contents of my future husband's library available to me. I imagine it contains a great many volumes on old Greeks and Romans and not a single novel."

Betsy hoisted a mountain of silk and satin out of one trunk and lowered it into another. "Don't know what ye'll be needin' these for in the country, Miss."

"Best to be prepared. Do not forget the matching slippers and gloves for each gown."

"Yes, Miss."

Claudia waded forward through the piles of trunks and hatboxes and forged a path around the bed, which was strewn with petticoats, stockings, and garters. "Augusta, I would like to talk to you."

"Talk away." Augusta turned to call through the open door of the bedchamber. "Nan, is that you? Will you please come in here and give Betsy a hand?"

A housemaid stuck her head in the door. "You want me to help with the packing, Miss?"

"Yes, please. There is a great deal to be done and we are growing short of time. My fiancé has sent word that we are to be on our way tomorrow morning directly after the wedding."

"Oh, dear, Miss. That ain't much time at all, is it?" Nan scurried into the room and began taking instructions from a frazzled Betsy.

"Augusta, please," Claudia said firmly, "we cannot talk amid this confusion. Let us have a cup of tea downstairs in the library."

Augusta straightened her frilled muslin cap and eyed the bedchamber. So much remained to be done and she had a feeling Harry would not be pleased if he were obliged to delay their departure because she had not finished packing. On the other hand, she was badly in need of a strong cup of tea. "Very well, Claudia. I believe things are under control here. Let us go downstairs."

Five minutes later, Augusta sank into an armchair, put her slippered feet up on a stool, and took a long swallow of tea. She set the cup and saucer down with a sigh. "You were right, Claudia. This was an excellent notion. I need this little break. I feel I have been rushing about since dawn. I vow, I shall be exhausted before I even set out for Dorset."

Claudia studied her cousin over the rim of her teacup. "I wish you would tell me why all this haste is necessary. I cannot help feeling that something is not quite right here."

"As I said, you must ask Graystone." Augusta massaged her temples wearily. "Personally, I believe the man has become slightly unhinged, which certainly does not bode well for my future as his wife, does it? I wonder if that sort of thing runs in his family."

"You cannot mean that." Claudia looked genuinely alarmed. "You think he has truly gone mad?"

Augusta groaned. Claudia's branch of the family had a somewhat limited sense of humor. Rather like Graystone, now that she considered the matter. "Good heavens, no. I was being sarcastic. The thing is, Claudia, I myself do not particularly see the need for a special license and all this rushing about, either. I would have much preferred to spend the next four months getting to know Graystone better and allowing him to come to know me."

"Precisely."

Augusta nodded morosely. "I cannot help but think he may be letting himself in for some rude shocks by marrying me. And after the wedding, there will not be much he can do about it, will there? He will be stuck with me."

"I did not think Graystone the precipitous type. Why is he suddenly consumed with a need for this hasty wedding?"

Augusta cleared her throat and studied the toes of her slippers. "I fear that, as usual, it is all my fault, although he gallantly denies it this time."

"Your fault? Augusta, whatever are you saying?"

"Do you recall how we once discussed the problems that can arise when one allows a man a few harmless intimacies?"

Claudia's brows knitted together and a slight flush appeared in her cheeks. "I recall that discussion very well."

"Yes. Well, Claudia, the long and the short of it is that

last night, due to some unforeseen circumstances, I happened to find myself in a darkened carriage alone with Graystone. Suffice it to say that this time I allowed him more than a few kisses. A great deal more."

Claudia paled and then turned a bright pink. "Are you saying you . . . *Augusta,* I cannot believe any such thing. I refuse to believe it."

"I fear I did." Augusta heaved a sigh. "Mind you, if I had it to do over again, I would think twice about the matter. It was not really all that wonderful, although it started out pleasantly enough. But Graystone assures me it will grow more comfortable with time and I shall just have to trust he knows what he is talking about."

"Augusta, are you actually telling me the man made love to you in a carriage?" Claudia's voice was weak with shock.

"I know you must find the whole notion disgusting and thoroughly reprehensible, but it did not actually seem that way at the time. I suppose you had to be there to understand."

"Graystone seduced you?" Claudia demanded, her voice hardening now.

Augusta frowned. "I would not say I was seduced, precisely. As I recall, he began the whole thing by reading me an extremely severe lecture on my general lack of propriety. He was quite annoyed with me. One might say passionately annoyed with me. And one sort of passion led to another, if you see what I mean."

"Good grief. He *attacked* you?"

"Heavens, no, Claudia. I just explained he made love to me. There is a difference, you know." Augusta paused for another sip of tea. "Although I did wonder about that difference myself for a time afterward. I confess I was a bit stiff and somewhat uncomfortable. But I felt much better after a bath this morning. I do not think I shall go riding in the park this afternoon, however."

"This is outrageous."

"I am well aware of that. I suppose there's a moral here

somewhere. Aunt Prudence would no doubt have been able to summarize it for us. Something succinct and pithy, such as, *Never get into a closed carriage with a gentleman or you are likely to find yourself married in haste and repenting at leisure,* perhaps."

"I suppose that under the circumstances you must be grateful Graystone is willing to marry you," Claudia announced primly. "Some men might take the attitude that such loose behavior before marriage on the part of a female implies a grave lack of virtue."

"I fear it is his own behavior which shocked Graystone. Poor man. He is such a stickler for the proprieties, you know. He was extremely annoyed with himself and feels he will surely fall from grace again before the four months of our engagement are out. That is why we are all rushing around this morning preparing for a special license."

"I see." Claudia hesitated. "Are you truly unhappy about the way events have gone, Augusta?"

"Not entirely, but I will confess I am extremely anxious about the whole thing," Augusta admitted. "I wish I had the next four months to be certain of what I am about. I do not know if Graystone loves me, you see. He never said a word about love last night, not even—" She broke off, her face growing warm.

Claudia's eyes widened. "Graystone does not love you?"

"I have my doubts. He professes not to be concerned with such nonsense, you see. And the thing is, Claudia, I am not certain I can teach him to love me. That is what is so frightening about this business of rushing the marriage." Augusta gazed glumly out the window. "I do so wish he loved me. It would be very reassuring."

"As long as he is a good husband to you, I hardly think you have grounds for complaint," Claudia said crisply.

"I knew a Hampshire Ballinger would say that."

"Very few people in our circles marry for love. Mutual respect and some degree of affection are all that one can ask.

Many couples do not even have that much. You know that, Augusta."

"Yes. But I suppose I had allowed myself some foolish dreams over the years. I wanted a marriage like that of my parents. Full of love and laughter and warmth. I am not quite certain what I shall be getting into with Graystone. I have realized recently that there is a part of him that is hidden from me."

"What an odd thing to say."

"I cannot fully explain, Claudia. I only know that much of Graystone lies deep in shadow. Lately I have begun to wonder just how much darkness there may be in him."

"Yet you are drawn to him, are you not?"

"From the first," Augusta agreed. "Which does not, I suppose, speak well for my intelligence." She set down her teacup with a clatter. "And then there is the matter of his daughter. I have never even met her and I cannot help wondering if she will like me."

"Everyone likes you, Augusta."

Augusta blinked. "That is very nice of you to say." She smiled bravely. "But enough of that morbid conversation. I am to be married on the morrow and that is all there is to it. I shall just have to make the best of matters, shall I not?"

Claudia hesitated and then leaned forward to speak in a soft rush. "Augusta, if you are genuinely alarmed by the notion of marrying Graystone, perhaps you should speak to Papa. You know he cares for you very much and he would not want to force you into this marriage against your will."

"I doubt that even Uncle Thomas could convince Graystone to hold off on the wedding now. The man has made up his mind and he is quite strong-willed." Augusta shook her head ruefully. "In any event, I am afraid it is much too late for me to back out. I am soiled goods, you know. A fallen woman. I can only be grateful the gentleman who assisted me in my fall from virtue is willing to do the right thing."

"But you are strong-willed also and no one can force you

into this, not if you really do not want—" Claudia broke off to stare at her. "Oh, dear. I have just realized. You truly are in love with Graystone, are you not?"

"Is it so terribly obvious?"

"Only to one who knows you well," Claudia assured her gently.

"That is indeed a relief. I am not at all certain Graystone would welcome a lovesick wife. He would probably find it quite a burden."

"So you are going to live up to the rash and reckless reputation of your side of the family and plunge yourself heedlessly into this marriage." Claudia appeared thoughtful.

Augusta poured herself another cup of tea. "Things are going to be difficult enough for a while. I just wish I did not have to follow in the footsteps of such a virtuous and noble paragon of a wife as my predecessor apparently was. I have always found comparisons of that sort quite odious and they are bound to be made in my case."

Claudia nodded in understanding. "Yes, I imagine it will be extremely difficult for you to live up to the high standards set by Graystone's first wife. From all accounts Catherine Montrose was a model of the womanly virtues. But Graystone will no doubt assist you in your efforts to improve yourself to her level."

Augusta winced. "No doubt." There was silence for a time in the library, although the sounds of trunks being shifted about overhead could be heard. "Do you know, Claudia, one of the things that concerns me most at the moment is that I shall not be able to call upon Sally for the next few weeks. She really is very ill, you know. And I am so fond of her. I shall worry a great deal about her welfare."

"You know I have never quite approved of your association with her or that club she operates," Claudia said slowly. "But I understand that you consider her a dear friend. If you like, I shall undertake to call on her once or twice a week while you are gone. I can relay news and write to you of her condition."

Augusta felt an enormous sense of relief. "You will do that for me, Claudia?"

Claudia squared her shoulders. "I fail to see why I should not do so. She might appreciate the occasional visit in your absence. And it would relieve your mind to know that I was keeping an eye on her."

"I would appreciate that more than I can say, Claudia. Why do we not go to see her this very afternoon? I can introduce you."

"Today? But you are busy preparing for your departure."

Augusta laughed. "I can make time for this call. Indeed, I would not miss it for the world. I believe you are in for a surprise, Claudia. You do not know what you have been missing."

Peter Sheldrake helped himself to the contents of Harry's claret decanter and turned to eye his host. "You want me to look into Lovejoy's background? Why the hell do you think that necessary, Graystone?"

"It is difficult to explain. Let us just say that I do not care for the man or for the way he has singled out Augusta for his unpleasant little games."

Peter shrugged. "Unpleasant they may be, but we both know they are not uncommon. Men of Lovejoy's stamp play such games with ladies all the time. Usually they are merely seeking to amuse themselves by flirting with another man's woman. Keep Augusta out of his reach and she will be safe enough."

"Incredible though it seems, my fiancée has apparently learned her lesson concerning Lovejoy. Augusta is inclined to be somewhat reckless, but she is not a fool. She will not trust him again." Harry ran one finger along the spine of a book that was resting on his desk.

The volume, titled *Observations on Livy's History of Rome*, was a slender one that he himself had written. It had only recently been published and he was quietly pleased with it, even though he knew it would never meet with the sort of popular acclaim that greeted the latest Waverley novels or an epic poem by Byron. Augusta would no doubt find the book deadly dull. Harry consoled himself with the knowledge that he was writing for a different audience.

Peter gave Harry a speculative glance and moved restlessly to the window. "If you feel your Miss Ballinger has learned her lesson, why are you concerned?"

"My instincts tell me there may be more to Lovejoy's vicious little games than a simple desire to flirt with or perhaps seduce Augusta. There is a calculated quality to the whole thing I do not like. And when I went to see him, he made a point of hinting at how unsuitable Augusta was to be my wife."

"Likely he planned to try his hand at a bit of blackmail. Mayhap he believed you would pay far more than a thousand pounds for Augusta's marker in order to keep the whole affair quiet. You have a reputation for being somewhat straitlaced, if you do not mind me saying so."

"Why should you refrain from mentioning it? Augusta flings the fact in my face at every opportunity."

Peter grinned. "Yes, she would. That, of course, is one of the reasons why she is going to be so good for you, Graystone. But about Lovejoy, just what are you hoping to discover?"

"As I said, I am not certain. See what you can find out. No one seems to know very much about him. Even Sally admits the man is a mystery."

"Sally would be the first to hear anything of him, good or ill." Peter looked thoughtful for a moment. "Perhaps I shall ask her for some help in this little investigation. She will welcome the project. It will remind her of the old days."

"Use your own judgment, but do not tire her. She has very little strength left."

"I realize that. But Sally is the kind of woman who would prefer to live every minute right up until the last rather than conserve her strength by taking to her bed."

Harry nodded, gazing out the window into the garden. "I believe you have the right of it. Very well. See if she would like a taste of old times." He slid his friend a sharp glance. "I will, naturally, expect both of you to be extremely discreet in this matter."

Peter assumed an expression of insulted innocence. "Discretion is one of my few virtues. You know that." Then he chuckled wickedly. "Unlike a certain gentleman I could name who finds himself having to procure a special license today due to a singularly indiscreet act which occurred in a closed carriage."

Harry scowled in warning. "One word of last night to anyone, Sheldrake, and you may as well set about composing your own epitaph."

"Fear not. I can be as silent as the tomb on certain subjects. But damnation, man. I wish you could have seen the expression on your face when you stepped down from that carriage with Miss Ballinger. 'Twas priceless. Absolutely priceless."

Harry swore softly. Every time he thought about last night—and he had thought about little else since—he was astounded. He still could not credit his own deplorable behavior. Never had he been so much at the mercy of his physical nature. And the worst of it was that he was not even sorry the whole thing had happened.

He reveled in the knowledge that Augusta now belonged to him as she had never belonged to any other man. Furthermore, the event had given him the excuse he had needed to push for an early marriage.

His one regret, and it was a deep one, was that his own loss of control had resulted in Augusta's failure to fully enjoy the experience. But he would soon remedy the bad impression he had left, he told himself confidently. He had never had a woman respond to him the way she had. She

had wanted him. And she had surrendered herself to him
with a gentle, eager innocence that he would remember for
the rest of his life.

Unlike that deceitful bitch Catherine.

Peter turned back toward the window. "I have been
thinking, Graystone. I wonder what the odds are of getting
the Angel alone in a closed carriage."

"I would imagine that depends on how much interest
you display in the book she is writing," Harry muttered.

"Believe me, I have done nothing but talk about *A Guide
to Useful Knowledge for Young Ladies* on every possible
occasion since you mentioned it. Damn it, Harry, why did
I have to fall for the wrong Miss Ballinger?"

"Just as well you picked the Angel. The other Miss
Ballinger is unavailable. Send me word in Dorset if you
discover anything of interest about Lovejoy."

"At once," Peter agreed. "Now, I must be on my way.
Scruggs is due to go on duty at the front door of Pompeia's
in an hour and it takes a while to get into that bloody
costume and those false whiskers."

Harry waited until Peter had left and then he opened
Observations on Livy's History of Rome and tried to read the
first few pages to see how his work looked in print. But he
did not get far. All he could think about was how he would
go about making love to his new wife in a proper bed.

After a moment Harry decided he really was not in the
mood to read a discourse on Roman history, even if he
himself had written it. He closed his own book and went to
a bookshelf to take down a copy of Ovid.

"The thing is, Claudia," Augusta said as she and her cousin
went up the steps of Lady Arbuthnott's town house.
"Pompeia's started out as a sort of salon. And then one day
it struck me that it would be much more fun to turn it into
a real club in the manner of the St. James Street establishments. You may find it a bit, well, unusual."

"I am fully prepared for Pompeia's. I assure you, I shall endeavor not to embarrass you," Claudia murmured dryly.

"Yes, I know, but occasionally you do have extremely refined notions of propriety and some of the things you see in Pompeia's may offend them."

"Such as?"

"Such as the butler," Augusta murmured as the door was opened by Scruggs.

"Well, well, Miss Ballinger," Scruggs growled as he spied Augusta on the doorstep. "Bit surprised to see you here today. Heard you were to be married with what some might call indecent haste."

"That is none of your affair, my good man," Claudia announced in quelling accents.

Scruggs's mouth fell open in astonishment as he finally noticed Claudia standing to one side. His brilliant blue eyes widened and then immediately narrowed in amazement. He recovered himself at once. "Good God. Never tell me the Angel has come calling at Pompeia's. Paying a visit to the nether regions, Miss Ballinger? What is the world coming to, pray tell?"

There was a short, charged silence as Claudia bestowed a disapproving stare on Scruggs. Then she turned to Augusta with royal disdain. "Who on earth is this odd creature?"

"This is Scruggs," Augusta explained, hiding a satisfied smile. "And you must pay him no heed. Lady Arbuthnott retains him merely to add an interesting atmosphere to the place. She is fond of eccentrics, you know."

"Obviously." Claudia looked Scruggs up and down very slowly and then swept past him into the hall. "I cannot wait to see what other bizarre things I shall find in this place. Lead on, Augusta."

Augusta swallowed her laughter. "Miss Ballinger is a new member of Pompeia's, Scruggs. She very kindly volunteered to visit Lady Arbuthnott while I am out of town and keep me informed of her condition."

"And here I was thinking things might be a bit dull without you around to liven up the place and entertain her ladyship." Scruggs's eyes never left Claudia, who stood imperiously near the drawing room door.

Augusta smiled as she removed her huge, fashionable, flower-trimmed hat. "Yes, I have no doubt things will continue to be amusing. I only regret I shall not be here to watch."

Scruggs smiled beatifically as he opened the door of Pompeia's. Augusta and Claudia stepped into Sally's drawing room.

Augusta was aware of her cousin taking in the scene around her with an observing eye as she steered her toward where Sally sat near the fire.

"How extraordinary," Claudia exclaimed softly, her gaze on the paintings of famous Greek and Roman women.

Sally closed the book on her lap, adjusted her India shawl, and looked up expectantly as Augusta and Claudia approached. "Good afternoon, Augusta. Have you brought us a new member?"

"My cousin Claudia." Augusta made the introductions quickly. "She will be calling on you in my stead during the next few weeks, Sally."

"I shall look forward to your visits, Miss Ballinger." Sally smiled at Claudia. "We shall miss Augusta, of course. She has a way of keeping things lively around here."

"Yes, I know." Claudia said.

"Do sit down." Sally waved a hand gracefully toward the nearest chair.

Augusta glanced at the book Sally had been reading. "Oh, you have a copy of Coleridge's *Kubla Khan*. I intend to read it soon. What do you think of it?"

"Extraodinary. Quite fantastical. He claims that the entire story came to him when he awoke from an opium-induced sleep, you know. I find the images of his tale fascinating. Almost familiar. I cannot explain it, but there is a certain comfort in it." She turned to Claudia and smiled. "Enough of such musings. Tell me, what do you think of our little club thus far?"

"I think," Claudia said thoughtfully, "that your butler reminds me of someone I have met."

"I expect 'tis the limp," Augusta said easily. "If you will recall, Claudia, our gardener walks in the same awkward fashion. Rheumatism, you know."

"Perhaps you are right," said Claudia.

Sally turned promptly to Augusta. "So you are to be married by special license and whisked away to Dorset, my dear."

"It is incredible how gossip swirls through the *ton*."

"And winds up here in Pompeia's," Sally concluded. "I should have known you would not do things in the usual, accepted manner."

"It was not my idea. It was Graystone's. I only hope he will not come to regret his decision." Augusta paused, tilting her head slightly to one side as she accepted a teacup. "On the other hand, it is something of a relief to see that my fiancé has an impetuous side to his nature."

"Impetuous?" Sally considered that briefly. "I do not think that is quite the right word to describe Graystone."

"What is the right word, madam?" Augusta asked, curious.

"Deceptive. Shrewd. At times rather hard, perhaps. A most unusual man, Graystone." Sally sipped her tea.

"I quite agree and I must say it can be very disturbing," Augusta said. "Do you know he has the most unnerving habit of always being aware of whatever scheme I happen to have set in motion? No matter how secretive I have been? I swear, it is rather like being pursued by Nemesis himself."

Sally sputtered on a sip of tea and dabbed quickly at her pale lips with a handkerchief. Her eyes were gleaming with laughter. "Nemesis, eh? What an odd thing to say."

* * *

Nemesis. Augusta was still mulling over that observation the next afternoon as Graystone's traveling coach bowled along the highway toward Dorset.

The wedding that morning had been quick and efficient. Graystone had appeared to be preoccupied and had taken very little note of her carefully chosen white muslin gown. He had not even complimented her on the demure ruffle that she had ordered sewn onto the low neckline. So much for her first wifely effort to impress her husband with her modesty.

Graystone had insisted on setting out immediately on the honeymoon trip to his estates. Now he lounged across from Augusta on the opposite seat of the coach. He had been sunk deep in his own thoughts since they had left London.

It was the first time they had been alone together since the night they had made love in the carriage.

Augusta fidgeted, unable to read or concentrate for long on the scenery. She plucked at the braiding of her copper-colored carriage gown and fussed with her reticule. In-between these activities she stole glances at Graystone. He looked lean and powerful in his gleaming boots, snug-fitting breeches, and elegantly cut coat. His pristine white cravet was immaculately folded, as always. A paragon.

A paragon, Augusta thought sadly. How was she ever going to live up to Harry's standards? she wondered.

"Is there something wrong, Augusta?" Harry finally inquired.

"No, my lord."

"Are you quite certain?" he asked softly.

She gave an elaborate shrug. "'Tis only that I have the oddest sensation that nothing is quite real today. I feel as if I shall awaken at any moment and discover I have been dreaming."

"I trust that is not wishful thinking, my dear. You are most definitely married now."

"Yes, my lord."

He exhaled deeply. "You are anxious, are you not?"

"Somewhat, sir." She thought of all that lay before her: a daughter she had never met, a new home, a husband whose first wife had from all accounts been a model of womanly virtue. She straightened her shoulders bravely. "I shall try to be a good wife to you, Harry."

He smiled faintly. "Will you, indeed? That should be interesting."

Her tentative smile faded. "I am well aware that I have many faults in your eyes and I realize I have a difficult task ahead of me. Naturally, it will be extremely difficult to live up to the high standards set by your first countess. But I feel certain that with time and patience I can achieve some measure of—"

"My first wife was a lying, deceitful, falsehearted bitch," Harry said calmly. "The last thing I would have you do is follow in her footsteps."

9

Augusta stared at Harry in shocked silence. "I do not understand, my lord," she finally managed to say. "I—indeed, everyone—was under the impression your first wife was a most admirable female."

"I am aware of that. I saw no reason to disabuse the world of its opinion. Prior to the marriage I, too, believed Catherine to be a model of female propriety." Harry's mouth curved bitterly. "You may be certain she was careful to allow nothing more than a few chaste kisses during our engagement. I, of course, mistook her lack of warmth for true virtue."

"I see." Augusta blushed hotly as she recalled how much she had allowed Harry before the wedding.

"It was not until I found her as cold on our wedding night as she had been during the engagement that I finally realized she did not have any affection for me at all. I also strongly suspected there had been someone else. When I confronted her she broke down in tears and explained that she did indeed love another and had given herself to him when she discovered she would be obliged to marry me."

"Why was she obliged to wed you, sir?"

"The usual practical reasons, namely my title and my fortune. Catherine's parents insisted on the match and she agreed to it. Her lover was quite penniless and Catherine was not so lost to common sense as to actually run off with him."

"How very sad. For both of you."

"You may well believe I wished she had run off with the bastard. I would gladly have paid him to take her away if I'd known my own fate. But what was done, was done." Harry shrugged. "She told me she regretted everything but that she would endeavor to be a good wife to me. I believed her. Hell, I wanted to believe her."

"And it would not have been right for you to hold her lack of virginity against her," Augusta said, frowning seriously. "Unless you yourself were, uh, untouched?"

Harry quirked a brow and did not respond to that comment. "In any event, there was little I could do about the situation except make the best of it."

"I understand. Marriage is so very permanent," Augusta murmured.

"I believe Catherine and I could have made a go of it if Catherine had not lied to me right from the start. Dishonesty is something I cannot forgive or condone."

"No, I can see where it would be very difficult for you to make allowances for a woman or anyone else who lied. You are very severe about some things, my lord."

He eyed her sharply. "Catherine, as it happens, had no intention of ever trying to be a true wife. The best I can say for her was that at least she was not carrying her lover's babe when she came to me. She did, however, become pregnant on our wedding night and was extremely angry about the fact. Apparently her lover lost interest in her as she grew big with my child. To keep him bound to her she began giving him money."

"*Harry*. How awful. Did you not notice that she was doing so?"

"Not for quite some time. Catherine could be extraordinarily convincing. Whenever she came to me for more money, she would tell me she needed the funds to further her charity work. Which was not precisely a lie, I suppose, when you think about it. Her lover was entirely without means and quite dependent on her largesse."

"Oh, dear."

"I have let the rumor stand that she died of the fever after giving birth to Meredith," Harry said without inflection. "The truth is, she was recovering quite nicely when she learned her lover was seeing someone else. She rose from childbed too soon and slipped away to confront him. When she came home she was distraught. She had also caught a chill that settled in her lungs. She went back to bed and never recovered. Toward the end she was out of her mind and she began calling for her paramour."

"That was how you discovered who he was?"

"Yes."

"What happened to him?" Augusta demanded, a sense of foreboding closing in on her.

"Cut off from his only means of reliable financial support, he was obliged to join the army. Quite soon thereafter he managed to die a hero's death on the peninsula."

"How dreadfully ironic. No one knows about all this?"

"I have kept my own counsel until now. You are the only other person I have ever told and I fully expect you to keep equally silent on the subject."

"Yes, of course," Augusta said weakly, thinking of how badly Harry's honor must have been savaged. "After such a disastrous experience, 'tis no wonder you are so concerned with the proprieties, my lord."

"It is not only my own pride that concerns me," Harry said bluntly. "I wish to maintain the fiction of Catherine's perfection for Meredith's sake. A child needs to be able to respect the memory of her parents. Meredith is nine years old and as far as she is concerned, Catherine was a loving mother and a virtuous wife."

"I comprehend completely. You need not worry that I will alter her impression of her mother."

Harry smiled faintly. "No, you would not do any such thing. You are very kind and very loyal to those for whom you feel affection, are you not? 'Tis one of the reasons I married you. I am hoping you will come to care for my daughter."

"I am certain I shall." Augusta looked down at her gloved fingers, which were laced on her lap. "I just hope she will learn to love me."

"She is an obedient child. She will do as she is told. She knows you are to be her new mother and she will show you every respect."

"Respect is not the same as love, my lord. One can force a certain amount of respect and good manners from a child, but one cannot force love from anyone, can one?" She slanted him a meaningful glance. "Not even from a wife or a husband."

"I will settle for respect and good manners from both my child and my wife," Harry said. "In addition, I shall expect loyalty from my wife. Do I make myself clear?"

"Yes, of course." Augusta went back to plucking at the braid trim on her gown. "But I have tried to tell you from the beginning, my lord, that I cannot promise to be a model of perfection."

He smiled gravely. "No one is perfect."

"I am very glad you realize that."

"I will, however, expect you to make a few earnest efforts in that general direction," Harry added, his voice quite dry.

Augusta looked up quickly. "Are you teasing me, sir?"

"Good Lord, no, Augusta. I am a dull, prosing scholar entirely lacking in the sort of lightness of spirit that would inspire me to any levity."

Augusta scowled. "You *are* teasing me. Harry, I must ask you something."

"Yes?"

"You say you cannot abide deceit in a wife, but I myself have not always been completely straightforward with you. I did not tell you about that stupid gaming debt I owed to Lovejoy, for example."

"That was not a matter of deliberate deceit. You were simply acting in your customary reckless fashion, carrying the standard of Northumberland Ballinger honor, and you quite naturally got into trouble."

"Quite naturally? Now see here, Harry—"

"If you have an ounce of common sense, madam, you will refrain from reminding me of the incident. I am trying to put it out of my head."

"It is going to be difficult to do that, sir, considering the fact that the 'incident,' as you call it, led directly to your being obliged to marry me out of hand this morning."

"I would have married you sooner or later, Augusta. I told you that."

She looked at him, perplexed. "But, why, my lord? I still do not completely comprehend why you settled on me when there were so many other more suitable candidates on your list."

Harry eyed her consideringly for a long moment. "Contrary to everyone's opinion, impeccable manners and perfection of behavior were not my chief requirements in a wife."

Augusta's eyes widened in surprise. "They were not?"

"Catherine's manners and deportment were exemplary, as it happens. Just ask anyone who knew her."

Augusta frowned. "Then, if it was not perfection of manners and behavior, what precisely were you looking for in a wife?"

"You said it yourself that night I found you sneaking about in Enfield's library. All I wanted was a truly virtuous woman."

"Yes, I know. But surely for someone such as yourself, female virtue goes hand in hand with a sound knowledge and respect for the proprieties."

"Not necessarily, although I will admit it would be convenient if it did." Harry looked rueful. "As far as I am concerned, virtue in a woman is based solely on her capacity to be loyal. From all I have observed, while you are unfortunately inclined to be impetuous and headstrong, you are also a very loyal young female. Probably the most loyal one I have ever encountered."

"*Me?*" Augusta was startled at the observation.

"Yes, you. It has not escaped my notice that you have demonstrated great loyalty toward your friends, such as Sally, and the memories of the Northumberland Ballingers."

"Rather like a spaniel, I imagine."

He smiled at her disgruntled tone. "I happen to like spaniels."

She lifted her chin, anger flaring in her. "Loyalty, my lord, is like love, at least as far as I am concerned. You cannot purchase it with a wedding ring."

"On the contrary. I did precisely that a few hours ago," he said quietly. "You would do well to remember that, Augusta. I am not concerned with the emotion you call love. But I shall expect the same degree of respect and loyalty from you that you give to the other members of your family, past and present."

Augusta drew herself up proudly. "And am I to have the same in return?"

"You may depend upon it. I shall do my duty as a husband by you." His eyes gleamed with sensual promise.

She narrowed her eyes, refusing to be drawn by the hint of teasing warmth. "Very well, my lord, loyalty it shall be. But that is all it shall be until I choose otherwise."

"What the devil is that cryptic statement supposed to mean, Augusta?"

She turned her head to gaze resolutely out the window.

"Merely that as long as you do not value love, I will not provide you with any." She would force him to realize that there had to be more to this marriage than a cold exchange of loyalties, she told herself fiercely.

"You must suit yourself," Harry replied with a shrug.

She shot him a swift, sidelong glance. "You do not mind that I do not plan to love you?"

"Not as long as you fulfill your responsibilities as my wife."

Augusta shivered. "You are very cold, my lord. I had not realized. Indeed, based upon certain recent actions of yours, I had begun to hope you might be as reckless and hot-blooded as any Northumberland Ballinger."

"No one is as reckless and hot-blooded as a Northumberland Ballinger," Harry said. "Least of all myself."

"Pity." Augusta reached into her reticule and drew out the book she had brought along to read on the journey. She opened it on her lap and gazed pointedly down at the page.

"What is that you are reading?" Harry inquired softly.

"Your newest, my lord." She did not deign to look up. "*Observations on Livy's History of Rome.*"

"Rather dull fare for you, I should imagine."

"Not at all, my lord. I have read some of your other books and I find them quite interesting."

"You do?"

"Why, yes. If one overlooks the obvious flaw in all of them, that is," she concluded smoothly.

"*Flaw?* What flaw is that, pray tell?" Harry was clearly outraged. "And who are you to point it out, may I ask? You are hardly a student of the classics, madam."

"One does not have to be a classical scholar to notice the persistent flaw in your work, my lord."

"Is that so? Why don't you tell me just what that flaw is, then, my dear?" he ground out.

Augusta raised her brows and looked straight at him. She smiled sweetly. "The chief irritation I feel in reading your historical research, sir, is that, in every single one of your volumes, you have contrived to ignore the role and contribution of females."

"*Females?*" Harry gave her a blank look. He recovered at once. "Females do not make history."

"I have decided one gains that impression chiefly because history is written by males, such as yourself," Augusta said. "For some reason male writers choose to pay no attention to female accomplishments. I noticed that particularly when I did research for the decor of Pompeia's. It was very difficult to find the information I needed."

"Good lord, I do not believe I am hearing this." Harry groaned. It was too much. He was being taken to task by an overly emotional little baggage who read Scott and Byron. And then, in spite of himself, Harry started to smile. "Something tells me you are going to be an interesting addition to my household, madam."

Graystone, the great house that reigned over Harry's Dorset estates, was as solid and forbidding as the man himself. It was an imposing structure of classical Palladian proportions that loomed above impeccably maintained gardens. The last of the late afternoon sunlight was gleaming on the windows as the traveling coach rolled up the sweeping drive.

A flurry of activity erupted as the servants rushed out to handle the horses and greet their new lady.

Augusta gazed about eagerly as Harry assisted her down from the coach. This was to be her new home, she told herself over and over again. For some reason she could not yet seem to fully comprehend the change that had taken place in her life that morning. She was now the Countess of Graystone. *Harry's wife.* These were her people.

She had a home of her own at last.

That thought was just sinking in when a small, dark-haired girl raced out of the open door and flew down the steps. She was dressed in a severely plain white muslin dress that did not boast a single flounce or ribbon.

"*Papa*. Papa, you are home. I am so glad."

Harry's expression softened into a smile of genuine affection as he bent down to greet his daughter. "I was wondering where you had got to, Meredith. Come and meet your new mother."

Augusta held her breath, wondering what sort of welcome she was about to receive. "Hello, Meredith. I am very pleased to meet you."

Meredith turned her head and looked at Augusta with intelligent, crystal gray eyes that could only have come from her father. She was a beautiful child, Augusta realized.

"You cannot be my mother," Meredith explained with unshakable logic. "My mother is in heaven."

"This is the lady who will take her place," Harry said firmly. "You must call her Mama."

Meredith studied Augusta carefully and then turned back to her father. "She is not as beautiful as Mama. I have seen the portrait in the gallery. Mama had golden hair and pretty blue eyes. I will not call this lady Mama."

Augusta's heart sank, but she summoned a smile as she saw Harry start to scowl in response to that observation. "I am sure I am not nearly as pretty as your mother, Meredith. If she was as pretty as you, she must have been very beautiful indeed. But perhaps you will find other things about me that you will like. In the meantime, why don't you call me whatever you like? There is no need to call me Mama."

Harry frowned at her. "Meredith is to show you the proper respect and she will do so."

"I am certain she will." Augusta smiled at the little girl, who was suddenly looking quite stricken. "But there are lots of respectful things she can call me, are there not, Meredith?"

"Yes, madam." The child cast an uneasy glance at her father.

Harry's brows rose repressively. "She will call you Mama and that is that. Now, then, Meredith, where is your Aunt Clarissa?"

A tall, rawboned woman dressed in a soberly cut, unadorned dress fashioned of slate-colored material appeared at the top of the steps. "I am here, Graystone. Welcome home."

Clarissa Fleming descended the steps at a stately pace. She was a handsome woman in her mid-forties who carried herself with rigid dignity. She looked out on the world with remote, watchful gray eyes, as if fortifying herself for disappointment. Her graying hair was done up in a severe bun at the back of her head.

"Augusta, this is Miss Clarissa Fleming," Harry said, completing the introductions swiftly. "I believe I may have mentioned her. She is a relative who has done me the favor of becoming Meredith's governess."

"Yes, of course." Augusta managed another smile as she greeted the older woman, but inside she heaved an unhappy sigh. There was not going to be any welcoming warmth from this quarter, either.

"We received word of the wedding by messenger only this morning," Clarissa said pointedly. "A rather hasty business, was it not? We were under the impression the date was some four months hence."

"Circumstances changed abruptly," Harry said without offering either apology or explanation. He smiled his cool, remote smile. "I am aware this all comes as something of a surprise. Nevertheless, I am certain you will make my bride welcome, will you not, Clarissa?"

Clarissa's eyes were speculative as she surveyed Augusta. "But of course," she said. "If you will follow me I will show you to your bedchamber. I imagine you will want to refresh yourself after your journey."

"Thank you." Augusta glanced at Harry and saw that he

was already busy issuing orders to his staff. Meredith was at his side, her small hand tucked in his. Neither of them paid any attention as Augusta was led away.

"We understand," Clarissa intoned as she started up the steps and into the vast marble hall, "that you are related to Lady Prudence Ballinger, the author of a number of useful schoolroom books for young ladies."

"Lady Prudence was my aunt."

"Ah, then you are one of the Hampshire Ballingers?" Clarissa asked with a touch of enthusiasm. "A fine family and one noted for its many intellectual members."

"Actually," Augusta said, tilting her chin proudly. "I am descended from a different branch of the family. The Northumberland side, to be precise."

"I see," said Clarissa. The hint of approval died in her eyes.

Much later that evening Harry sat alone in his bedchamber, a glass of brandy in one hand and a copy of Thucydides' *The Peloponnesian War* in the other. He had not read a word for quite some time. All he could think about was his new bride lying alone in her bed next door. There had been no sound from the adjoining chamber for some time now.

This was definitely not how he had envisioned spending his first night under his own roof with his new wife.

He took a sip of the brandy and tried to concentrate on the book. It was hopeless. He closed the volume with a sharp snap and tossed it onto the end table.

He had told himself during the journey that he was going to make a subtle point about his self-control to Augusta. Now he wondered if he was being a bit too subtle.

She had as good as thrown down the gauntlet when she had flung the fact of his reckless lovemaking in Sally's carriage in his face. As far as Harry was concerned, she had virtually challenged him to prove he was not a slave to his physical desire for her. He was not going to play Antony to her Cleopatra.

He could hardly blame Augusta for her assumptions, though. After the way he had seduced her in Sally's carriage, she had every right to conclude that he could not keep his hands off of her. No woman was above using that sort of power. And in the hands of a bold, daring little chit like Augusta, such power was exceedingly dangerous.

Harry had therefore decided it would be best to take a stand early on in his marriage and make it clear he was not lacking in self-control. Begin as you mean to go on, he had told himself.

Last night when they had stopped at an inn, he had booked a separate chamber for Augusta, making some excuse about her being more comfortable with her maid. The truth was, he had not trusted himself to spend his wedding night on his own side of the bed.

Tonight he had forced himself to bid his wife an excruciatingly polite good night at the door of her bedchamber. He had deliberately not given her any indication of his intentions. He wondered if she was lying awake even now, waiting to see if he would come to her.

The uncertainty would do her good, he told himself. The woman was decidedly too headstrong and far too quick to issue a challenge, as that whole damn business involving the debt to Lovejoy proved. She had gotten into that dangerous situation precisely because she had been trying to demonstrate to Harry that she was not obliged to bow to his wishes.

Harry got up from his chair and stalked across the chamber to pour himself another glass of brandy. He had been far too lenient with Augusta thus far; that was the problem. Too indulgent by half. She was, after all, one of the Northumberland Ballingers. She needed a firm hand on the reins. He owed it to their future happiness to restrain her reckless streak.

But the more he thought about it tonight, the more

Harry wondered if he was taking the right tact by staying out of his wife's bedchamber.

He swallowed more brandy and contemplated the stirring heat in his loins.

There was another way of looking at his current situation, he decided on a flash of brandy-induced wisdom. If one were to be quite logical about this—and he did pride himself on his ability to think logically—one could see that he might do better to assert his privileges as a husband right from the start.

Yes, that reasoning was much more sound than his previous thoughts on the matter. It was not, after all, his self-control he needed to demonstrate, but rather his dominant role in the marriage. He was master in his own home.

Vastly more satisfied with this new line of logic, Harry set down his glass and went across the room to open his wife's door.

He stood in the doorway and gazed into the deep shadows around the bed. "Augusta?"

There was no response.

Harry walked into the bedchamber and realized there was no one in the canopied bed. "Damnation, Augusta, where are you?"

When there was still no response, he swung around and saw that the door to the bedchamber was ajar. His insides clenched as he realized she was not in the room.

What trick was she up to tonight? he wondered as he strode toward the door and let himself out into the hall. If this was another one of her efforts to lead him in circles until he was dizzy, he would put a stop to it in no uncertain terms.

He stepped out into the hall and saw the ghostly figure. Garbed in a pale dressing gown that floated out behind her, candle in hand, Augusta was heading for the long picture gallery that fronted the house. Curious now, Harry decided to follow the wraith.

As he trailed softly behind her, Harry was aware of a sense of relief. He knew then that a part of him had secretly feared she had packed a bag and run off into the night. He should have known better, he told himself. Augusta was not the sort to run from anything.

He followed her into the long gallery and stood watching at the far end as she went slowly along the row of portraits. She paused at each picture, holding the taper high to study each face in its heavy gilt frame. Moonlight filtering in through the tall windows that lined the front of the gallery bathed her in a silvery glow, making her appear more of a ghost than ever.

Harry waited until she was examining the picture of his father before he started forward.

"I have been told I resemble him very closely," he said quietly. "I have never found it much of a compliment."

"*Harry*." The flame flickered wildly as Augusta spun around, her hand at her throat. "Good grief. I did not know you were there. You gave me a terrible start."

"My apologies. What are you doing out here in the middle of the night, madam?"

"I was curious, my lord."

"About my ancestors?"

"Yes."

"Why?"

"Well, my lord, I was just lying there in my bed thinking that they will be my ancestors, too, now, will they not? And I realized I did not know much about any of them."

Harry folded his arms across his chest and propped one shoulder against the wall beneath his father's stern face. "If I were you, I would not be in too much of a rush to claim this lot. There's not a particularly pleasant soul among them, from all I've ever heard."

"What about your father? He looks very strong and noble." She peered up at the portrait.

"Perhaps he was when he sat for that painting. I only

knew him as a bitter, angry man who was never able to deal with the fact that my mother ran off with an Italian count shortly after I was born."

"Good heavens. How terrible. What happened?"

"She died in Italy. My father locked himself in his library with several bottles for a week when he got the news. He drank himself into a stupor. When he came out, he refused to allow her name to be uttered in this house."

"I see." Augusta slanted him a searching glance. "The earls of Graystone have certainly had rather poor luck with women, have they not?"

Harry shrugged. "The various countesses of Graystone have been notorious for their lack of virtue. My grandmother had more affairs than anyone could count."

"Well, it is the fashion in Society, Harry. So many marriages are made for reasons of money and status rather than love that such things are no doubt bound to happen. People instinctively seek love, I believe. And when they do not find it in marriage, many go outside it."

"Do not even think of going outside our marriage for whatever you may feel you are missing in our alliance, Augusta."

She tossed her dark hair back over one shoulder and glowered at him. "Tell me honestly, my lord, were the various earls of Graystone any more virtuous than their countesses?"

"Probably not," Harry admitted, remembering his grandfather's string of passionate liaisons and his father's endless parade of expensive mistresses. "But one tends to notice a lack of virtue more in a woman than in a man, don't you think?"

Augusta was instantly outraged, just as he had guessed she would be. Harry watched the passionate light of battle leap into her eyes as she drew herself up for the skirmish. She held the taper in front of her as though it were a sword. The glow of the flame danced on her face, enhancing her high cheekbones and giving her an exotic allure.

She looked like a small Greek goddess, Harry thought. A young Athena garbed for war, perhaps. The thought made him smile with anticipation and the smoldering fire in his groin that had been plaguing him all evening suddenly burned hotter.

"What a perfectly odious thing to say," Augusta raged. "That is the sort of statement only an extremely arrogant, extremely obnoxious man would make. You should be ashamed of yourself, Graystone. I expected more even-handed logic and reason from you. You are supposed to be a classical scholar, after all. You will apologize for that silly, inane, totally unfair remark."

"Will I?"

"Most certainly."

"Perhaps I will do so. Later."

"Now," she retorted. "You will apologize now."

"I doubt if I will have sufficient breath left to say anything at all, let alone apologize, after I have carried you back to your bedchamber, madam."

He unfolded his arms and came away from the wall in a smooth, swift motion.

"Carried me back to my— Harry, what on earth do you think you are doing? Put me down at once."

She struggled briefly as he picked her up in his arms. But by the time he had carried her down the hall to her bedchamber and deposited her beneath the canopy, she was no longer putting up even a token resistance.

"Oh, Harry," she whispered in an aching voice. She put her arms around his neck as he came down beside her on the bed. "Are you going to make love to me?"

"Yes, my dear, I most certainly am. And this time," he told her softly, "I shall try to do a better job of it. I am going to turn you from Athena, the beautiful warrior, into Aphrodite, the goddess of passion."

10

"*Harry*. Dear God, *Harry*. Please, I cannot bear it. This is beyond anything."

Harry lifted his head to watch Augusta as she approached her first delicious, shuddering climax in his arms. Her whole body was arched, tense as a drawn bow. Her hair was fanned out against the pillow in a dark cloud. Her eyes were squeezed shut as she twisted her hands in the white sheets.

Harry was sprawled on his stomach between Augusta's raised thighs. The hot scent of her was filling his head and the indescribable taste of her was still on his tongue.

"Yes, darling. That is how I want you." He eased his finger inside her again and slowly withdrew it. He felt the tiny muscles at the entrance of her tight passage clench gently. He slid his finger back into the clinging heat while he teased the small, exquisitely sensitive little nubbin above with his thumb.

"*Harry*."

"So beautiful," he breathed. "So sweet and hot. Let it happen, darling. Give yourself up to it." Slowly, deliberately he withdrew his finger and felt everything inside her clench desperately. "Yes, darling. Squeeze a little harder once more. You're almost there. Tighten yourself, my love."

He flicked his thumb over the small nub one more time as he entered her again with his finger. And then bent his head and kissed the swollen female flesh.

"Good Lord, Harry. *Harry.*"

Augusta's hands became fists in his hair and her hips lifted up off the bed, straining fiercely against his invading finger and his teasing tongue. Her thighs shivered, her feet flexed.

Harry lifted his head. In the soft glow of the candlelight he could see that Augusta's parted lips and the slick petals that guarded her feminine secrets were both rosy pink and glistening with moisture.

Augusta shuddered and gave a high, keening cry that could surely be heard out in the hall. She convulsed in Harry's arms as ripple after ripple of reaction raced through her.

Harry felt, heard, and inhaled it all; every nuance of her response communicated itself to him. As he watched Augusta surrender to her first climax, he realized he had never seen anything so magnificently feminine, so passionate and sensual in his entire life.

Her reaction was fuel on the fires that were already burning within him. Harry knew he could not wait another second. He surged up along the length of her shuddering body and plunged himself into her tight channel before the last of the ripples had even faded.

"I do not think I shall ever tire of our midnight rendezvous, sweet wife," Harry whispered hoarsely.

His own release was upon him in an instant, a shattering explosion of sensation that whirled him away into nothingness. His hoarse, triumphant shout still echoed in the bedchamber as he collapsed against Augusta's soft, damp body.

•   •   •

A long time later Harry stirred amid the rumpled sheets and reached out for Augusta. When his groping hand encountered nothing but more bedding, he reluctantly opened his eyes.

"Augusta? Where the devil have you got to now?"

"I am over here."

He turned his head and saw her standing near the open window. She had put her nightdress back on, he noticed. The gauzy white muslin floated around her slender form, the ribbons rippling in the soft night air. Once more she looked ethereal and ghostlike. Almost untouchable. Harry had a sudden, terrible premonition that she would suddenly drift out through the window and away from him forever.

He levered himself upright to a sitting position and tossed aside the covers as an inexplicable sense of urgency overwhelmed him. He had to catch her and hold her safe. He was already starting to reach out for Augusta when he realized he was being foolish.

Augusta was no ghost. He had just touched her most intimately. He forced himself to sit calmly back against the pillows instead of lunging across the room. She was very real and very much his. She had given herself to him completely.

She was his. It had been much more than a physical thing, that moment when she had trembled and convulsed in his arms. She had bestowed the gift of herself, given him some part of her to keep safe.

He would hold her fast, Harry vowed. He would protect her, even though she did not always desire that protection. And he would make love to her as frequently as possible, strengthening and cen ing the physical bond between them.

He did not need to be told that, for Augusta, the sexual act was a commitment as deep and binding as any ancient oath of fealty.

"Come back to bed, Augusta."

"In a moment. I have been thinking about our marriage, my lord." She gazed out into the darkness, her arms wrapped tightly beneath her breasts.

"What is there to think about?" Harry eyed her warily. "It all seems quite clear to me."

"Yes, I imagine it would seem plain enough to you. You are a man."

"Ah. This is to be one of those discussions, is it?" His mouth quirked.

"I am glad you find it so amusing," she whispered.

"Not amusing so much as a waste of time. I have seen you attempt to grapple with this sort of thing before, if you will recall. Your reasoning gets muddled quickly, my dear."

She turned her head to glower at him. "Really, Harry, you can be extremely pompous and arrogant at times. Do you know that?"

He chuckled. "I shall rely on you to tell me when I become too unbearable."

"You are being unbearable now." She swung completely around to face him. The white ribbons on her nightdress fluttered. "I have something to say to you and I would appreciate it if you would give me your full attention."

"Very well, madam. You may proceed with your lecture." He folded his arms behind his head and schooled his expression into one of serious contemplation. It was not easy. Damn, but she looked alluring standing there in her nightdress. He was getting aroused all over again.

The moonlight behind her revealed the outline of her hips through the thin muslin. Harry wagered that in a mere minute he could have her back on the bed, her thighs spread wide once more. In two minutes, he was quite certain he could have the warm honey flowing between her legs. She was so amazingly responsive.

"Harry, are you paying attention?"

"Absolutely, my sweet."

"Very well, then, I am going to tell you my thoughts on the status of our relationship. We come from two different worlds, you and I. You are an old-fashioned sort of man, a man of letters, a serious scholar who has little use for frivolous things. I, on the other hand, as I have often told you, am inclined toward more modern ideas and have a rather different nature. We must face the fact that I rather enjoy the occasional frivolous amusement."

"I do not see that as a problem so long as such amusements are merely occasional." Yes, two minutes to make her damp, Harry mused, trying to be totally objective. Then another five, at the most, to bring the soft, enchanting little moans of excitement to her lips.

"There is no doubt but that in many ways we are opposites, my lord."

"Male and female. Natural opposites." After about seven to ten minutes, when she was starting to twist deliciously in his arms and arch herself for his touch, Harry decided, he would introduce her to a few variations on the basic theme.

"But we now find ourselves bound together for life. We have made a legal and moral commitment to each other."

Harry grunted an absent response to that while he considered the possibilities open to him. Perhaps he would turn Augusta over onto her stomach and draw her up on her knees. Then he would ease himself between her thighs and explore her tight, clinging feminine passage from that direction. Twenty to thirty minutes, at least, before he attempted that, he told himself. He did not want to startle her unduly. She was still very new to the erotic arts.

"I am well aware, sir, that you rushed our wedding date because you felt duty-bound to marry me after what transpired in Lady Arbuthnott's carriage. However, I would have you know . . ."

Then again, he could lie on his back and have her straddle his thighs, Harry thought. In that position, he would have an excellent view of her expressive face when she reached her climax.

Augusta took a deep breath and continued. "I would have you know that, in spite of our reputation for recklessness and daring, the Northumberland Ballingers have a sense of duty that is the equal of any noble family in the country. I daresay 'tis as great as your own. I therefore want to assure you that even though you feel you cannot love me and you do not particularly care if I love you —"

Harry scowled as her last words penetrated his erotic fantasy. "I beg your pardon, Augusta?"

"I was just about to say, my lord, that I know my duty as a wife and I will honor it, just as you intend to honor your duty as a husband. I am a Northumberland Ballinger and I will not shirk my obligations. Ours may not be a love match, but you may, nevertheless, depend upon me to fulfill my responsibilities as your wife. My sense of honor and duty is as strong as your own and I would have you know that you can rely on it."

"Are you saying you intend to be a good wife to me merely because you feel duty-bound to do so?" he asked, a wave of anger roaring through him.

"That is precisely what I am saying, my lord." She smiled tentatively. "I would like to assure you that a Northumberland Ballinger is steadfast when it comes to honoring a vow."

"Good God. How in hell did you get off on a lecture on duty and responsibility at a time like this? Come back to bed, Augusta. I have something much more interesting to discuss."

"Do you, Harry?" She did not move. Her expression was unusually grave, her eyes searching his face in the shadows.

"Most definitely." Harry threw back the covers. His bare feet hit the carpet an instant later. He took three long strides across the bedchamber and picked her up in his arms.

Augusta opened her mouth to utter some comment—a protest, perhaps. Harry covered her lips firmly with his own until she was lying flat on her back once more.

He had grossly overestimated the time it would take to maker her ready to receive him, he soon realized. Less than fifteen minutes had passed before he turned a startled Augusta over onto her stomach and drew her up into a kneeling position.

Harry stopped keeping track of the time after that, but when Augusta sang her sweet song of sensual release into the pillow, he was fairly certain she had something besides duty and responsibility on her mind.

The following morning, Augusta, dressed in a canary-colored walking dress and carrying a matching French bonnet with an enormous, gracefully curving brim, went in search of her new stepdaughter.

She found her in the schoolroom on the second floor of the big house. Meredith, primly garbed in another well-made but extremely plain white gown, sat at an old, ink-stained wooden desk. She had a book open in front of her and she glanced up in surprise as Augusta entered the room.

Clarissa Fleming, enthroned behind a large desk at the front of the room, looked up questioningly and then frowned as she saw who was interrupting the routine.

"Good morning," Augusta said cheerfully. She glanced around the schoolroom, taking in the selection of globes, maps, quills, and books that adorned it. Schoolrooms somehow always looked the same, she thought, regardless of the location or the financial means of the family.

"Good morning, madam." Clarissa nodded toward her charge. "Make your curtsy to your new mother, Meredith."

Meredith obediently got to her feet to greet Augusta. Her somber gaze held a hint of wariness and not a little uncertainty.

"Good morning, madam."

"Meredith," Clarissa said sharply. "You know his lord-ship specifically instructed you to call her ladyship *Mama*."

"Yes, Aunt Clarissa. But I cannot do that. She is not my mama."

Augusta winced and waved Clarissa Fleming to silence. "I thought we agreed you could call me whatever you like, Meredith. You may call me Augusta, if you wish. You do not need to call me Mama."

"Papa says I must."

"Yes, well, your father can be a bit autocratic at times." Clarissa's eyes sparkled in disapproval. "Really, madam."

"What does autocratic mean?" Meredith asked, genuinely curious.

"It means your father is rather overfond of giving orders," Augusta explained.

Clarissa's expression turned from disapproval to one of outrage in the blink of an eye. "Madam, I cannot allow you to criticize his lordship in front of his daughter."

"I would not dream of doing so. I was simply noting an undeniable aspect of his lordship's character. I doubt he would deny it himself, were he present." Augusta twirled her beribboned bonnet and started ambling around the room.

"Describe your curriculum to me, if you will, please, Meredith."

"Mathematics, classical studies, natural philosophy, and the use of globes in the morning," Meredith said politely. "French, Italian, and history in the afternoons."

Augusta nodded. "Certainly a well-rounded selection of studies for a nine-year-old girl. Did your father design it for you?"

"Yes, madam."

"His lordship takes a great personal interest in his daughter's curriculum," Clarissa said darkly. "He would most likely not welcome any criticism of it."

"Most likely not." Augusta paused in front of a familiar-looking volume. "Ah-hah. What have we here?"

"Lady Prudence Ballinger's *Instructions on Behavior and Deportment for Young Ladies,*" Clarissa said in forbidding tones. "Your esteemed aunt's highly instructional work is one of Meredith's favorite books, is it not, Meredith?"

"Yes, Aunt Clarissa." Meredith, however, did not look overly enthusiastic about the book.

"Personally, I found it a deadly bore," Augusta said.

"*Madam,*" Clarissa said in a strangled voice. "I must ask that you refrain from giving my charge the wrong impression."

"Nonsense. I am sure any girl with spirit would find my aunt's books exceedingly dull. All those depressing rules on how to drink one's tea and eat one's cake. And all that nonsense about appropriate conversational topics to be memorized. You must have something more interesting around here to study. What are these?" Augusta examined another set of heavy, leather-bound tomes.

"Books of ancient Greek and Roman history," Clarissa said, looking as though she were prepared to defend their presence in the schoolroom with her last breath.

"Of course. I should have expected a sizable collection of such materials, given Graystone's personal interests, hmm? And this little book?" She held up another dull-looking volume.

"Mangnall's *Historical and Miscellaneous Questions for the Use of Young People,* of course," Clarissa responded tartly. "I am certain even you will agree it is most appropriate to the schoolroom, madam. You were doubtless instructed with it yourself. Meredith can recite the answers to a great many of the questions in that book already."

"I am sure she can." Augusta smiled at Meredith. "I, on the other hand, can barely remember any of the answers, except possibly the one about where nutmeg grows. But then, I have been told I have a rather frivolous turn of mind."

"Surely not, madam," Clarissa said tightly. "His lordship would never have—" she broke off, flushing a dull red.

"His lordship would never have married a frivolous sort of female?" Augusta gave the older woman a bright, inquiring glance. "Is that what you were about to say, Miss Fleming?"

"I was not going to say any such thing. I would never dream of commenting on his lordship's personal affairs."

"Do not concern yourself with such niceties. I comment on his personal affairs all the time. And I can assure you, I am decidedly frivolous and irresponsible on occasion. As it happens, this morning is one of those occasions. I have come to collect Meredith and take her out with me on a picnic."

Meredith stared at her in astonishment. "A picnic?"

"Would you like that?" Augusta smiled at her.

Clarissa clutched a quill so tightly her knuckles turned white. "I fear that is quite impossible, madam. His lordship is most strict about Meredith's studies. They are not to be interrupted for any *frivolous* reasons."

Augusta arched her brows with gentle rebuke. "I beg your pardon, Miss Fleming. As it happens, I am in need of a guide to show me around the grounds of the estate. His lordship is locked in the library with his steward, so I have decided to ask Meredith if she will act in his stead. As we will be gone for some time, I have naturally requested that cook prepare us a picnic lunch."

Clarissa looked dubious and resentful, but she was obviously well aware there was not much she could do without the earl to back her up. And the earl, Augusta had been quick to point out, was unavailable.

"Very well, madam." Clarissa drew herself up stiffly. "Meredith may go with you to act as your guide this morning. But in future, I shall expect the routine of the schoolroom to be respected." Her eyes glittered with warning. "And I am certain his lordship will support me on this matter."

"No doubt," Augusta murmured. She looked at Meredith, whose expression was as unreadable as her father's could be on occasion. "Shall we go, Meredith?"

"Yes, madam. I mean, Augusta."

•   •   •

"Your home is very lovely, Meredith."

"Yes, I know." Meredith walked sedately down the lane beside Augusta. She was wearing a very plain, close bonnet that matched her equally plain dress.

It was difficult to tell what thoughts were going through her mind. Meredith had obviously inherited Harry's ability to keep his expression unreadable.

Thus far the child had been polite, but far from chatty. Augusta was counting on the pleasantly crisp day and the exercise to encourage conversation. If all else failed, she supposed she could always ask Meredith to recite the answers to Mangnall's *Historical and Miscellaneous Questions for the Use of Young People.*

"I used to live in a nice house in Northumberland," Augusta said, swinging the picnic basket she was carrying.

"What happened to it?"

"It was sold after my parents died."

Meredith slanted Augusta a startled, sidelong glance. "Your mama and papa are both dead?"

"Yes. I lost them when I was eighteen. I miss them very much sometimes."

"I miss Papa very much when he goes away for weeks and weeks at a time like he did during the war. I am glad he is home now."

"Yes, I imagine you are."

"I hope he stays home."

"I am certain he will for the most part. I believe your father prefers the country."

"When he went off to London at the beginning of The Season to find a wife, he said it was a *necessity*."

"Rather like taking a purge, I should imagine."

Meredith nodded soberly. "No doubt. Aunt Clarissa told me he had to find a wife so that he could get an heir."

"Your father is a man who is very conscious of his duty."

"Aunt Clarissa said he would find a *paragon of a female who would follow in my mother's illustrious footsteps*."

Augusta stifled a groan. "A difficult task. I saw the portrait of your mother in the picture gallery last night. She was, as you said, very beautiful."

"I told you so." Meredith wrinkled her brow. "Papa says beauty is not everything in a woman, though. He says there are other, more important things. He says a virtuous woman has a price beyond rubies. Is that not a pretty phrase? Papa writes very well, you know."

"I do not want to disillusion you," Augusta muttered, "but your papa did not exactly invent that phrase himself."

Meredith shrugged without apparent concern. "He could have, if he had wished to do so. Papa is very smart. He used to play the most complicated word games you have ever seen."

"Really?"

Meredith began to show some real enthusiasm at last as she warmed to her favorite topic, her papa. "When I was little I saw him working on one in the library one day and asked him what he was doing. He said he was solving a very important puzzle."

Augusta tipped her head, curious. "What was the name of the game?"

Meredith frowned. "I do not recall. It was a long time ago. I was just a child. I remember it had something to do with a spider's web."

Augusta stared down at the top of Meredith's bonnet. "A spider's web? Are you quite certain?"

"I believe so. Why?" Meredith lifted her head to peer up at her from beneath the brim of the bonnet. "Do you know the game?"

"No." Augusta shook her head slowly. "But my brother once gave me a poem named 'The Spider's Web.' I have always found the poem very strange. I never really understood it. In fact, I never even knew my brother wrote poetry until he gave that particular verse to me."

There was no need to mention the fact that the paper on which the poem had been written had been indelibly stained with her brother's blood and that the verse itself was unpleasant.

But Meredith was off on a new tangent. "You have a brother?"

"Yes. But he died two years ago."

"Oh. I am very sorry. I expect he is in heaven like my mother."

Augusta smiled wistfully. "That depends on whether the lord allows Northumberland Ballingers into heaven. Now, if Richard had been a Hampshire Ballinger, I am certain there would have been no question. But with a Northumberland Ballinger, well, it is open to speculation."

Meredith's small jaw dropped. "You do not believe your brother is in heaven?"

"Of course he is. I am merely teasing. Never mind me, Meredith. I have a very inappropriate sense of humor. Just ask anyone. Come along, now, I am quite famished and I see a perfect spot for lunch."

Meredith eyed the intended location, a grassy bank above a small stream, very warily. "Aunt Clarissa said I must be careful not to get my dress dirty. She says true ladies never get muddy."

"Nonsense. I used to get muddy all the time when I was your age. Still do, on occasion. In any event, I'll wager you have several other dresses just like that in your wardrobe, do you not?"

"Well, yes."

"Then if something dreadful happens to this one, we shall simply toss it out or give it to the poor and you may wear one of your other dresses. What is the point of having any number of dresses, if one does not use them?"

"I had not thought of it quite that way." Meredith took a renewed interest in the luncheon spot. "Perhaps you are right."

Augusta grinned and shook out the cloth that had been

packed in the basket. "That reminds me. I believe we shall send for a seamstress from the village tomorrow. You need some new dresses."

"I do?"

"Definitely."

"Aunt Clarissa said the ones I have now will do for another six months or a year at least."

"Impossible. You will outgrow them long before that. In fact, I daresay you will outgrow them by the end of the week."

"A week?" Meredith stared at her. Then she smiled hesitantly. "Oh, I see. You are joking again, are you not?"

"No, I am quite serious."

"Oh. Tell me more about your brother. I have sometimes thought I might like to have a brother."

"Have you, indeed? Well, brothers are a very interesting lot." Augusta began to talk easily of all the good times she had known with Richard as she and Meredith set out the appetizing repast of cold meat pies, sausages, fruit, and biscuits.

Augusta and Meredith had just seated themselves when a long shadow fell over the meal. A pair of glossy black boots came to a halt at the edge of the white cloth.

"Is there enough for three, do you think?" Harry asked.

"*Papa*." Meredith leaped to her feet, looking first surprised and then anxious. "Augusta said someone must show her around the grounds today and she said you were too busy to do so. She asked me to do it."

"An excellent notion." Harry smiled at his daughter. "No one knows this estate better than you do."

Meredith smiled back, clearly relieved. "Do you want a meat pie, Papa? Cook made several. And there are lots and lots of biscuits and sausages. Here, have some."

Augusta scowled ferociously. "Do not go giving away all our food, Meredith. You and I have first choice here. Your father is an uninvited guest and he only gets the leftovers."

"You are a hard-hearted woman, madam wife," Harry drawled.

Meredith's fingers froze around a pie. She looked first at Augusta with stunned eyes and then turned to her father. "There is plenty for you, Papa. Truly there is. You can have mine."

"Not at all," Harry said easily. "I shall just take Augusta's portion. I would much rather eat her share."

"But Papa—"

"Enough," Augusta said, laughing at the child's earnest expression. "Your father is teasing both of us and I am teasing him. Do not concern yourself, Meredith. There is plenty of food for everyone."

"Oh." With an uncertain glance at her father, Meredith settled back down on the cloth. She arranged the skirts of her dress very carefully so that they did not fall onto the grass. "I am glad you joined us, Papa. This is fun, is it not? I do not think I have ever been on a picnic. Augusta says she and her brother used to go on picnics all the time."

"Is that so?" Harry lounged back on one elbow and bit into a meat pie as he slanted Augusta a veiled glance.

Augusta realized with a small sense of shock that Harry was dressed in riding clothes and his throat was bare. He was not wearing his usual impeccably tied cravat. She had rarely seen him this casually garbed, except in the privacy of their bedchambers, of course. She blushed at that thought and bit into a pie.

"Yes," Meredith said, growing increasingly chatty. "Her brother was a Northumberland Ballinger, just like Augusta. They are noted for being quite bold and daring. Did you know that, Papa?"

"I believe I have heard that, yes." Harry continued munching his pie, his eyes never leaving Augusta's flushed face. "I myself can testify to the rather daring temperament of the Northumberland Ballingers. One can hardly imagine the sort of bold things Northumberland Ballingers get up to. Especially in the middle of the night."

Augusta knew she was turning a very bright shade of pink. She shot her tormentor a warning glance. "I have found the earls of Graystone can be astonishingly bold, too. One might even say overbold."

"We have our moments." Harry grinned and took another healthy bite of pie.

Meredith missed the byplay and continued chattering away to her father. "Augusta's brother was exceedingly brave. And a wonderful horseman. He was in a race once, did Augusta tell you?"

"No."

"Well, he was. And he won. He always won his races, you see."

"Astounding."

Augusta cleared her throat gently. "Would you like some fruit, Meredith?"

She managed to deflect the child's conversation until the end of the meal. Then she encouraged Meredith to try the game of floating two twigs in the stream to see which one reached a certain point first.

Meredith hesitated, but when Harry got up and showed her how the game was played, her enthusiasm for the sport grew rapidly. Harry stood on the bank watching her play upstream for a moment and then he walked back to the cloth and reseated himself beside Augusta.

"She is enjoying herself." Harry propped himself on one elbow, one leg drawn up with lazy masculine grace. "It makes me wonder if perhaps she needs more of this kind of outdoor activity."

"I am glad you agree, my lord. It is my feeling that a certain amount of frivolous pastimes are as crucial for a child as history and globes. With your permission, I should like to introduce a few additional subjects into her curriculum."

Harry frowned. "Such as?"

"Watercolors and novel reading, to start."

"Good God, most certainly not. I absolutely forbid it. I will not have Meredith exposed to such nonsense."

"You said yourself, my lord, Meredith needs a greater variety of activities."

"I said she might need a few more *outdoor* activities."

"Very well, she can paint outdoors and read novels outdoors," Augusta said cheerfully. "At least in summer."

"Damn it, Augusta—"

"Hush, my lord. You would not want Meredith to overhear us quarreling. She is having enough trouble adjusting to your marriage as it is."

Harry glowered at her. "You certainly seem to have impressed her with tales of your brave, adventurous brother."

Augusta frowned. "Richard *was* brave and adventurous."

"Mmmm." Harry's tone was noncommittal.

"Harry?"

"Yes?" Harry's eyes were on Meredith.

"Did the rumors that circulated at the time of Richard's death ever reach your ears?"

"I know of them, Augusta. I do not consider them important."

"No, of course not. They are all lies. But there is the undeniable fact that certain documents were found on him the night he was killed. I confess I have often wondered about those documents."

"Augusta, sometimes one must accept the notion that one does not always get all the answers one seeks."

"I am well aware of that, sir. But I have long had a theory about my brother's death that I would very much like to prove."

Harry was quiet for a moment. "What is your theory?"

Augusta took a deep breath. "It occurred to me that the reason Richard had those documents on him that night was because he might have been a secret military intelligence agent for the Crown."

When that comment brought no response, Augusta

turned to look at Harry. His eyes, hooded and unreadable now, were still on his daughter.

"Harry?"

"Was this the theory you wanted Lovejoy to investigate for you?"

"Yes, it was, as a matter of fact. Tell me, do you not think it very possible?"

"I think it highly unlikely," Harry said quietly.

Augusta was incensed at the casual dismissal of her long-held theory. "Never mind. I should not have mentioned the subject. After all, how would you know anything about such matters, my lord?"

Harry exhaled heavily. "I would have known, Augusta."

"Not bloody likely."

"I would have known because, one way or another, had Richard been a legitimate intelligence agent for the Crown, he would most likely have been working for me."

11

"What do you mean by saying you would have known if my brother had been secretly working for England during the war?" Augusta sat tensely, her mind reeling. "And what on earth were you doing that you would have such information in the first place?"

Harry did not move from his reclining position, but he finally took his gaze off Meredith and looked directly at Augusta. "What I was doing is no longer a matter of importance. The war is over and I am more then content to forget my role in it. Suffice it to say that I was involved in gathering intelligence for England."

"You were a spy?" Augusta was stunned.

His mouth curved faintly. "Obviously, my love, you do not see me as a man of action."

"No, it is not that." She frowned, thinking quickly. "I confess I did wonder where you learned to pick locks and you do have a habit of turning up when I least expect you. Very spylike behavior, I should imagine. Nevertheless, a career in that sort of thing is just not you, Harry."

"I could not agree with you more. In point of fact, I never saw my wartime activities as a career. I saw them as a damned nuisance. The business was a vastly annoying interruption to my real work of pursuing my classical studies and looking after my estates."

Augusta bit her lip. "It must have been very dangerous."

Harry shrugged. "Only on the odd occasion. I spent most of my time behind a desk directing the activities of others and pouring over letters written in code or sympathetic ink."

"Sympathetic ink." Augusta was momentarily diverted by that. "You mean ink that is invisible on paper?"

"Mmmm."

"How marvelous. I should love to have some invisible ink."

"I shall be happy to make you a batch sometime." Harry looked amused. "I should warn you it is not terribly useful for general correspondence. The recipient must have the chemical agent which renders the writing visible."

"One could keep one's journal in it." Augusta paused. "But perhaps code would be better. Yes, I like the idea of a code."

"I would prefer to think that my wife does not have anything so very secret to write in her journal that it requires invisible ink or a secret code."

Augusta ignored the mild warning in his tone. "Is that why you spent so much time on the continent during the war?"

"Unfortunately, yes."

"You were supposed to be furthering your research in the classics."

"I did what I could, especially when I was in Italy and Greece. But a great deal of my time was spent on Crown business." Harry selected a hothouse peach from the basket. "Now that the war is over, however, I can think about going back to the continent for more interesting purposes.

Would you like to go, Augusta? We shall take Meredith, too, of course. Travel is very educational."

Augusta arched a brow. "Is it me or your daughter you feel needs the education?"

"Meredith would no doubt profit the most from the experience. You, on the other hand, do not have to travel outside our bedchamber in order to further your education. And I must say, you are a very apt pupil."

Augusta was scandalized in spite of herself. "Harry, I vow, sometimes you say the most improper things. You should be ashamed."

"I beg your pardon, my dear. I had not realized you were such an authority on the proprieties. I bow to your greater knowledge of such matters."

"Do be quiet, Harry, or I shall dump what is left of our picnic over your head."

"As you wish, madam."

"Now, then, tell me how you can be so certain my brother was not also involved in secret work for the Crown."

"The odds are that if he had been, he would have worked for me, either directly or indirectly. I explained that a chief portion of my duties consisted of directing the activities of others in the same line of work. Those people, in turn, collected a vast amount of information from their contacts and relayed it all to me. I had to sort through the bloody stuff and try to glean the wheat from the chaff."

Augusta shook her head in amazement, still unable to envision Harry in such work. "But there must have been a great many people engaged in that sort of thing, both here and abroad."

"Too many, at times," Harry agreed dryly. "During wartime spies are rather like ants at a picnic. A great nuisance, for the most part, but it is impossible to conduct the event without them."

"If they are as common as insects, Richard could have been engaged in such activities and you might not have been aware of it," Augusta insisted.

Harry munched his peach in silence for a moment. "I considered that possibility. So I made some inquiries."

"Inquiries? What inquiries?"

"I asked some of my old friends in the business to see if Richard Ballinger had by any chance been officially involved in intelligence work. The answer was no, Augusta."

Augusta drew her knees up and wrapped her arms around them while she grappled with the finality of Harry's tone. "I still think my theory has merit."

Harry was silent.

"You must admit there is a small possibility that Richard had gotten involved in such work. Perhaps he had discovered something on his own and was going to take the information to the proper authorities."

Harry remained silent as he finished the last of his peach.

"Well?" Augusta asked, trying to conceal her anxiety over his answer. "Won't you agree that there is at least a chance that was the case?"

"Do you want me to lie to you, Augusta?"

"No, of course not." Her hands clenched into small fists. "I merely want you to agree that you could not have known everything there was to know about intelligence activities during the war."

Harry nodded brusquely. "Very well. I will agree to that. No one could have known everything. There is a great deal of fog surrounding war. Most of the actions, both on and off the battlefield, take place in a gray murk. And when the fog clears one can only count the survivors. One can never really know all of what happened while the mist was shrouding things. Perhaps it is best that way. I am convinced there is much it is better not to know."

"Such as what my brother may actually have been doing?" Augusta challenged bitterly.

"Remember your brother as you knew him, Augusta. Keep the last of the bold, daring, reckless Northumberland Ballingers alive in your memories and do not tease yourself with what may or may not have lain below the surface."

Augusta lifted her chin. "You are wrong about one thing, my lord."

"And that is?"

"My brother was not the last of the Northumberland Ballingers. I am the last one of the line."

Harry sat up slowly, his eyes cool with warning. "You have a new family now. You said as much yourself last night in the picture gallery."

"I have changed my mind." Augusta gave him a too-brilliant smile. "I have decided your ancestors are not as nice as mine."

"You are not doubt correct in that regard. No one ever called any of my ancestors *nice*. But you are now the newest Countess of Graystone and I will make certain you do not forget it."

A week later Augusta went into the sunny gallery on the second floor and seated herself on a settee directly beneath the portrait of her beautiful predecessor. Augusta glanced up at the deceptively serene image of the previous Lady Graystone.

"I'm gong to repair the damage you did around here, Catherine," she announced aloud. "I may not be perfect, but I know how to love and I do not think you ever knew the meaning of the word. You were not such a paragon, after all, were you? You wasted so much when you went chasing after false illusions. I am not such a fool," she said firmly.

Augusta wrinkled her nose at the portrait and then opened the letter from her cousin Claudia.

My Dear Augusta:

I trust all is well with you and your estimable husband. I must confess I rather miss you here in town. The Season is drawing to a close and things are not nearly so lively without you. As agreed, I have been to Pompeia's on several occasions and have much enjoyed my interesting visits with your friend, Lady Arbuthnott.

I must tell you, Lady A is a most fascinating female. I thought I would be somewhat put off by the eccentricities for which she is noted, but somehow, I am not. I find her delightful and am grieved by the severe nature of her illness.

The butler, on the other hand, is quite objectionable. Had I anything to say about the matter, I would not employ him for a single moment. He grows bolder with each visit and I fear that one of these days I shall be obliged to tell him he has overstepped himself. I still cannot escape the feeling I know him from somewhere.

To my surprise, I must admit I am rather enjoying Pompeia's. Naturally I cannot approve of such features as the club's betting book. Did you know several members placed wagers on how long your engagement would last? Nor do I approve of the rather extensive gaming activities. But I have met some interesting ladies who share my own desire to write. We have many fascinating discussions.

As to the social whirl, I can only repeat it is not as exciting without you. You always succeeded in attracting the most unusual friends and dancing partners. Without you by my side I seem to attract only the most proper sorts of people. Do you know, if it were not for Peter Sheldrake, I should find myself quite bored. Fortunately, Mr. Sheldrake is an excellent dancer. He has even persuaded me to perform the waltz with him. I only wish he were more inclined toward serious, intellectual matters. He tends to be rather frivolous by nature. And he teases me incessantly.

I would dearly love to visit with you. When will you be returning?

All my love,
Claudia

Augusta finished the letter and refolded it slowly. It was surprisingly good to hear from her cousin. Rather pleasant, too, to be told that the prim and proper Claudia actually missed her.

"Augusta, Augusta, where are you?" Meredith flew down the long hall of the gallery waving a large sheet of paper in her hand. "I finished my watercolor. What do you think of it? Aunt Clarissa said I must get your opinion, as it was your suggestion that I take up painting."

"Yes, of course. I am anxious to see it." Augusta looked up at Clarissa, who had accompanied her charge at a more stately pace. "Thank you for allowing her to try her hand at watercolors."

"His lordship informed me I was to be guided by your wishes in this matter, although he and I are agreed that watercolor painting is not a suitably serious pursuit for Meredith."

"Yes, I know, but it can quite fun, Miss Fleming."

"One is expected to apply oneself with diligence to one's studies," Clarissa pointed out. "Not have fun."

Augusta smiled at Meredith, who was shifting her gaze anxiously between the two women. "I am sure Meredith worked very hard on this particular painting because it is quite beautiful, as anyone can see."

"Do you really think so, Augusta?" Meredith hovered eagerly as Augusta examined the work.

Augusta held the child's painting out in front of her and tilted her head to one side to study it. The painting consisted largely of a great deal of pale blue wash. Some interesting slashes of green and yellow were scattered about in an apparently random fashion and in the background was a huge blob of gold.

"Those are trees," Meredith explained, pointing to the green and yellow slashes. "The brush wobbled a great deal and the paint tended to drip."

"They are wonderful trees. And I especially like your sky." Knowing the green and yellow bits were trees made it a safe guess that the wash of blue was sky. "And this is quite interesting," she added, pointing to the blob of gold.

"That's Graystone," Meredith explained proudly.

"Your father?"

"No, no, Augusta, our *house*."

Augusta chuckled. "I knew that. I was just teasing you. Well, you have done an amazing job on this, Meredith, and if you will allow me, I shall see that it is hung immediately."

Meredith's eyes grew very round. "You are going to hang it? Where?"

"Why, right here in the gallery would be a very suitable place, I believe." Augusta glanced down the row of intimidating portraits. "Perhaps right here beneath the picture of your mother."

Meredith was elated. "Do you think Papa will approve?"

"I am certain he will."

Clarissa cleared her throat. "Lady Graystone, I am not at all certain this is a wise suggestion. This gallery is reserved for family portraits that were painted by renowned artists. It is not the sort of space in which one hangs schoolroom work."

"On the contrary, I think some schoolroom work is just what this gallery needs. It is a rather somber place, is it not? We shall liven it up with Meredith's picture."

Meredith glowed. "Will it be in a frame, Augusta?"

"Most certainly. Every fine picture deserves a frame. I shall see about having someone make us a frame immediately."

Clarissa harrumphed and looked sternly down at her young charge. "Enough of this entertainment. It is time you returned to your studies, young lady. Run along, now. I shall join you in a few minutes."

"Yes, Aunt Clarissa." Eyes still bright with pleasure, Meredith bobbed a curtsy and hurried out of the gallery.

Clarissa turned to Augusta with a severe expression. "Madam, I must talk to you about the nature of the activities you are introducing to Meredith. I realize his lordship is permitting you to take a role in the education of his child, but I cannot help but feel you are pushing her into less than serious pursuits. His lordship has always been most adamant that he does not wish Meredith to grow up to be a silly, shallow female incapable of anything but idle conversation and socializing."

"I understand, Miss Fleming."

"Meredith has been accustomed to a strict course of study. She has done very well with it and I would not like to see that habit altered."

"I take your point, Miss Fleming." Augusta gave the woman a conciliatory smile. The lot of the penniless relative in a household was not a happy one. Clarissa had obviously done her best to create a niche for herself and Augusta sympathized with her. It was not easy to live in someone else's home, as she herself knew all too well. "Meredith has flourished under your capable instruction and I do not seek to change that."

"Thank you, madam."

"I do, however, feel that the child needs a few nonserious activities. Even my Aunt Prudence felt it was important that young people develop the ability to enjoy a variety of improving pastimes. And my cousin Claudia is following in her mother's footsteps. She is writing a book on the subject of useful knowledge for young ladies and she is devoting an entire chapter to the importance of sketching and water-color painting."

Clarissa blinked owlishly. "Your cousin is writing a book for the schoolroom?"

"Why, yes." Augusta suddenly realized where she had seen that look in Clarissa's eyes. It was in the gaze of quite a few members of Pompeia's, especially the ones who spent long hours at the writing tables in the club. Claudia frequently had that expression in her angelic blue eyes. "Oh, I see, Miss Fleming. You had perhaps entertained some notion of writing a book for the edification of young people?"

Surprisingly flustered by the question, Clarissa turned

an unbecoming shade of red. "I had given the subject some thought. Not that anything could ever come of it, of course. I am well aware of my limitations."

"Do not say that, Miss Fleming. We do not know our limitations until we test ourselves. Have you written anything on the subject?"

"A few notes," Clarissa mumbled, clearly embarrassed by her own presumption. "I thought of showing them to Graystone, but I fear he would find them quite paltry. His own intellectual abilities are so superior."

Augusta waved that aside. "I would not deny his intelligence, but I am not at all certain he would be a good judge of your efforts. Graystone is writing for a very small audience of academic types. You would be writing for children. Two entirely different groups."

"Yes, there is that, I suppose."

"I have a much better notion. When you have finished preparing a manuscript, bring it to me and I shall give it to my Uncle Thomas, who will send your work off to a publisher."

Clarissa took a deep breath. "Show a manuscript to Sir Thomas Ballinger? The husband of Lady Prudence Ballinger? I could not possibly impose to that extent. He would think me far too forward."

"Nonsense. It will be no imposition whatsoever. Uncle Thomas will be happy to do it. He used to attend to the matter of getting my Aunt Prudence's works published, you see."

"He did?"

"Oh, yes." Augusta smiled confidently, thinking of Sir Thomas's vague approach to the details of daily life. It would be no trick at all to persuade him to put Clarissa's manuscript in the mail to a publisher with a recommendation to print it on the grounds that it followed in Lady Prudence Ballinger's footsteps. Augusta decided she would write the letter of recommendation herself, to save Sir Thomas the trouble.

"That is most kind of you, madam." Clarissa looked and sounded dazed. "I have long been a devoted admirer of Sir Thomas's work. He has such a commendable grasp of history. Such a fine eye for the important detail and nuance. Such a scholarly style of writing. It is truly a pity he never had the inclination to write for the schoolroom. He could have done so much to mold young minds."

Augusta grinned. "I'm not so sure about that. Personally, I've always found my uncle's prose rather dry."

"How can you say that?" Clarissa demanded passionately. "It is not at all dry. It is brilliant. And to think he might look at a manuscript of mine. It is overwhelming."

"Yes, well, as I was about to say, I myself have always felt that the thing that was greatly lacking in books for the schoolroom was a work on famous women in history."

Clarissa looked at her in astonishment. "Famous women, madam?"

"There have been some very brave and noble females in the past, Miss Fleming. Famous queens, for example. And tribes of fierce Amazons. Several rather interesting Greeks and Romans. Even some female monsters. I find the notion of female monsters quite fascinating, don't you, Miss Fleming?"

"I have not given much consideration to the matter of female monsters," Clarissa admitted, looking thoughtful now.

"Only consider," Augusta said, warming to her topic, "how many famous heroes of antiquity have been absolutely terrified of female monsters like Medusa and the Sirens and such. It certainly leads one to believe women might have had a great deal of power in those days, does it not?"

"It is a most interesting notion," Clarissa said slowly.

"Imagine, Miss Fleming. Fully half of the world's history has never been written because it concerns females."

"Good Lord, what a stimulating thought. A whole new field to explore. Do you think Sir Thomas would find it an appropriate area of study?"

"My uncle is a very open-minded man when it comes to intellectual matters. I think he would find a new avenue of historical inquiry highly stimulating. And just think, Clarissa, you could be the one to point it out to him."

"I am humbled by the very notion," Clarissa breathed.

"It would take a great deal of research to even touch the surface of such a vast subject, of course," Augusta mused. "Fortunately, my husband's enormous library is available. Are you interested in undertaking such a project?"

"Extremely interested, madam. I have occasionally wondered why we do not know more about our female ancestors."

"I will strike a bargain with you, then," Augusta concluded. "I shall give Meredith instruction in watercolor painting and the reading of novels on Monday and Wednesday afternoons. You may use the time to pursue your research. Does that sound reasonable?"

"Most reasonable, madam. Most reasonable. Extremely gracious of you, if I may say so. And to have Sir Thomas's opinion and assistance, why, it is almost too much." Clarissa made an obvious effort to collect herself. "If you will excuse me, I must go back to my duties."

The dull brown skirts of Clarissa's gown swung around her with a new snap and fresh vivacity as she hurried out of the gallery.

Augusta watched her leave and then she smiled thoughtfully to herself. Clarissa was just the sort of female her uncle needed. A marriage between Clarissa and Sir Thomas would truly be a marriage of like-minded individuals. Clarissa would understand and share his intellectual passions and Sir Thomas would find Clarissa every bit as admirable as Lady Prudence had been. Definitely something to think about, Augusta decided.

She put the notion aside for the moment and reread Claudia's letter. It occurred to her, as she refolded it a second time, that as the new Countess of Graystone, it was time to start planning her debut as a hostess.

Planning parties was one of the things at which the women of the Northumberland Ballinger clan had always excelled. No doubt because of their naturally frivolous turn of mind, Augusta decided. As the last of the line, she would strive to uphold the family tradition.

She would give a house party here in the country and it would be the most spectacular event in Graystone's social history.

With any luck it would take her mind off the conversation about her brother that she had had with Harry the day of the picnic. The memory of that unpleasant discussion still rankled.

She could not and would not ever bring herself to believe that Richard had been selling secrets to the French. It was unthinkable. No Northumberland Ballinger would sink to such depths.

And most especially not her daring, dashing, honorable Richard.

It was far more difficult to believe Graystone had worked as an intelligence agent for the Crown than to believe her brother had done so, Augusta thought resentfully. Somehow Harry just did not strike one as a spy.

Of course, there was that ability of his to pick locks and he did have the most annoying habit of showing up when one least expected him.

Nevertheless, *Harry? A master spy?*

The thing about spying was that it was not considered a strictly proper career for a true gentleman. Most people held the notion that there was something rather unseemly and distasteful about the business. And Harry was such a stickler for the proprieties.

Augusta paused abruptly as the recollection of how very improper the earl could be in the privacy of their bedchamber flashed into her thoughts.

Harry was a very complex man. And she had known since the first time she had looked into his cool gray eyes that there were vast areas in him that lay in shadow.

Perhaps, just perhaps, Harry could have been an agent. The thought made Augusta strangely uneasy. She did not like to contemplate the notion of Harry taking grave risks. She pushed the possibility aside and began drawing up a list of people to invite to her house party.

After a few minutes more work on her plans she rushed off to find her husband. She discovered him in his library, pouring over a map of Caesar's campaigns.

"Yes, my dear?" he asked without glancing up from his work.

"I am thinking of giving a party here at Graystone, Harry. I wanted to ask your permission to go ahead with my plans."

He dragged his gaze reluctantly away from Egypt. "A party? A houseful of people? Here at Graystone?"

"We shall only invite close friends, Harry. My uncle and my cousin, for example. Perhaps some friends from Pompeia's. Mr. Sheldrake, of course. And anyone else you like. It is a pity Sally will be unable to travel. I would love to have her here."

"I don't know about this, Augusta. I have never bothered much with entertaining."

Augusta smiled. "Nor will you need to start bothering about it, sir. I shall take care of everything. My mother taught me a great deal about this sort of thing. A house party will provide a perfect opportunity to entertain our neighbors, too. It is high time we did so."

Harry eyed her morosely. "You are quite certain this is necessary?"

"Trust me, my lord. This is my field of expertise. We all have our talents, do we not?" She glanced meaningfully down at the old map on his desk.

"One party. That should be sufficient. I do not want to get into the habit of entertaining on a frequent basis, Augusta. 'Tis a frivolous waste of time."

"Yes, my lord. Most frivolous."

•   •   •

In spite of her instinctive feelings that Harry was a deep and mysterious man and in spite of her knowledge of his enigmatic and frequently autocratic ways, nothing prepared Augusta for the Graystone who summoned her downstairs to the library a week later.

Augusta was startled when a maid knocked on the door of the bedchamber and told her that Harry wanted her downstairs at once.

"He said at once?" Augusta looked at the maid with surprise.

"Yes, ma'am." The girl looked distinctly anxious. "Said to tell you it was most urgent."

"Good heavens, I hope nothing has happened to Meredith." Augusta put down her quill and set aside the letter she was writing to Sally.

"Oh, no, ma'am. 'Tweren't nothin' like that. Miss Meredith was with his lordship until just a few minutes ago and she is back at her studies now. I know because I just took a pot o' tea to the schoolroom."

"I see. Very well, Nan. See that his lordship is informed I shall be downstairs immediately."

"Yes, ma'am." Nan bobbed a quick curtsy and hastened off down the hall.

Curious to know the reason behind the unexpectedly urgent summons, Augusta paused only long enough to check her appearance in the looking glass. She was wearing a cream-colored muslin gown with a delicate green print. The low-cut neckline was trimmed with green ribbon and there was more green trim on the flounced hem.

Aware from the maid's nervous expression that Graystone was apparently not in a good mood, Augusta plucked a filmy green fichu from a dresser drawer and draped the scarf around her neckline. Harry had made it clear on more than one occasion that he found her taste in clothes a trifle immodest. There was no sense irritating him further this morning with the sight of a low-cut bodice if he was already annoyed about other matters.

Augusta sighed as she hurried out the door. A husband's foibles and moods were one of the many things a woman had to begin taking into consideration after she became a wife.

To be fair, however, she had to admit there was no doubt but that Harry had been obliged to make a few changes in his attitudes since their wedding. He had actually surrendered on the subject of watercolor painting and novel reading for Meredith, Augusta reminded herself.

Augusta swept into the library a few minutes later wearing a cheerful, placating smile. Harry got to his feet behind his polished desk.

Augusta took one look at him and dropped the cheery smile of greeting. The maid had had the right of it. Harry was in a dark and dangerous mood.

It struck Augusta quite forcibly that she had never seen him this coldly intent. There was something distinctly predatory about the stark, grim lines of his face.

"You asked to speak to me, my lord?"

"I did."

"If it is about the house party, sir, you may rest assured that all is under control. The invitations went out several days ago and we have already begun receiving responses in the post. I have contacted musicians and the kitchen staff has begun ordering supplies."

"I do not give a damn about your party, madam," Harry interrupted grimly. "I have just finished the most fascinating conversation with my daughter."

"Yes, my lord?"

"She tells me that the day of the picnic when you were extolling your brother's virtues, you mentioned a certain poem he left in your possession."

Augusta's mouth went dry, although she had no notion of where this was going. "That is correct, sir."

"It seems this poem was about spiders and their webs."

"My lord, it is just a simple little poem. I had not planned to show it to Meredith, if that is what you fear. I do not think it would have frightened her unduly, even if I had shown it to her. Indeed, I have often found that children rather enjoy scary verses."

Harry ignored her hasty assurances. "I am not concerned on that score. Do you still have this poem?"

"Yes, of course."

"Fetch it at once. I want to see it."

A chill went through Augusta. "I do not understand, Graystone. Why should you wish to see Richard's poem? It is not a very good poem. Rather nonsensical in many places. In fact it is a terrible verse. I only kept it because he thrust it into my hand the night he died and bid me to keep it safe." Tears burned in her eyes. "It had his blood on it, Harry. I could not throw it away."

"Go and get the poem, Augusta."

She shook her head in confusion. "Why must you see it?" Then a thought struck her. "Does this have something to do with your suspicions about him?"

"I cannot tell you that until I have seen the poem. Bring it to me at once, Augusta. I must have a look at it."

She took an uncertain step back toward the door. "I am not certain I want to show it to you. Not until I know what you think it will prove."

"It may answer some long-standing questions."

"The sort of questions that have to do with spies, sir?"

"It is just barely possible." Harry bit each word out between set teeth. "Not likely, but possible. Especially if your brother was working for the French."

"*He was not working for the French*."

"Augusta, I do not want to hear any more of the elaborate theories you have constructed to defend the circumstances in which Richard Ballinger died. Until now I have had no objection to your maintaining your illusions as long as you liked. In fact, I encouraged the process. But this matter of a poem about a spider and its web changes everything."

Augusta braced herself, her mind racing. "I will not show it to you unless you promise me you will not try to use it to prove Richard guilty of treason."

"I do not give a damn about his guilt or innocence. I have questions of my own to answer."

"But in answering them, you might very well seek to prove Richard's guilt. Is that not so, my lord?"

Harry came around from behind the desk in two long, prowling strides. "Bring the poem to me, Augusta."

"No, not unless you will give me your word that what you discover will not harm Richard's memory in any way."

"I will only give you my word to keep silent about his role in whatever was happening at the time. That is the most I can promise, Augusta."

"That is not enough."

"Damnation, woman, it is all I can give you."

"I will not let you have that poem. Not if there is the least chance it can hurt Richard's reputation. My brother was an honorable man and I must protect his honor now that he is no longer here to do it."

"Bloody hell, madam wife, you will do as you are told."

"The war is over, Graystone. No good purpose can be served by showing you that poem. It is mine and I intend to keep it. I am never going to let anyone see it, especially not someone like you who believes Richard was guilty of treason."

"Madam," Harry said in a soft, deadly voice, "you will do as I command. Bring me your brother's poem. Now."

"Never. And if you try to take it from me, I swear I shall burn it. I would rather destroy it, even though it is stained with his life's blood, than risk allowing you to use it to further tarnish his memory." Augusta whirled and fled from the library.

She heard the muffled crash of shattering glass just as she slammed the door shut behind her.

Harry had thrown something very heavy and very fragile against the library wall.

12

*S*tunned at his loss of control, Harry gazed in fury at the sparkling shards of broken glass. They glittered in the sunlight like the paste jewels Augusta wore with such pride.

He could not believe he had allowed her to drive him to this.

The woman had bewitched him. One moment he lusted for her with an outrageous passion; the next he was consumed with gratitude as he watched her slowly but surely befriend his daughter. In yet another instant she would make him laugh or drive him to distraction with her unpredictable actions.

And now she had finally brought him to the jagged edge of a seething jealousy that was unlike anything he had ever experienced.

And the worst of it was that Harry knew he was jealous of a dead man. *Richard Ballinger.* Bold, daring, reckless, very likely traitorous Richard.

Augusta's brother, a man who, even if he were still alive, would not be a sexual rival. But a man who, emtombed and enshrined as the last male issue of the dashing Northumberland Ballingers, occupied a place in Augusta's heart that Harry knew was forever closed to him.

Locked in the safe, untouchable realm of the beyond, Richard would live forever in Augusta's imagination as the ideal Northumberland Ballinger, the glorious older brother whose honor and reputation she would defend to the last.

"Goddamn you to hell, you damn Northumberland bastard." Harry stalked back to his chair and threw himself down into it. "Were you still alive, you son of a bitch, I believe I would call you out."

And thereby sever whatever fragile bond I do have with my new wife and cause her to hate me forever, Harry reminded himself bitterly. He might as well confront the logic of the matter. There was no doubt but that if the situation were put to the test, Augusta would side with her brother against her husband.

As she had proven only a few minutes ago.

"Bastard," Harry said again, unable to think of any other word to describe his ghostly rival for Augusta's affections. *How does one fight a ghost?*

Harry sprawled in the chair behind the desk and forced himself to contemplate the disastrous situation from every angle.

He had to admit that he had handled the thing wrong right from the start. He should never had summoned Augusta to the library with such urgency. Nor should he have ordered her to turn over the poem. If he had kept his wits about him, he would have done it all much differently.

But the truth was he had not been thinking all that clearly. After Meredith had casually dropped a mention of Richard Ballinger's poem about webs and spiders, Harry had been swamped with a violent need to get his hands on it.

Harry thought he had convinced both himself and Sheldrake that he had put the war and all its horror behind him. But he acknowledged now that he would never be able to forget the man called the Spider. Too many men had died because of the bastard. Too many risks had been taken by good men such as Peter Sheldrake. Too many battlefield losses had been caused by the traitor.

And the knowledge that the Spider had very likely been English had only made the frustration and anger all the more searing for Harry.

Harry knew he had had a reputation for going about his intelligence work with cold blood and even icier logic. But the truth was that it had been the only way he had been able to perform his grim tasks. If he had allowed his emotions to interfere, he would have been paralyzed. Each move and countermove, each decision, each estimate or analysis would have been skewed by the gut-destroying fear of making a mistake.

Cold, clear logic had been the only way to carry on. But beneath the veneer of ice, the anger and frustration had raged. And for Harry, because of the role he had been obliged to play, most of that dark fury and desire for revenge had been focused on his opposite number in the field, the Spider.

Harry's talent for logic and a desire to get on with his life had enabled him to put aside his desire for revenge in the months since Waterloo. Knowing that there would most likely never be answers to the tormenting questions he had often lain awake asking, Harry had accepted the inevitable. In the haze of war, many facts were forever buried, as he had explained to Augusta on the day of the picnic. The true identity of the Spider had appeared to be one of those lost facts.

But now, because of a chance remark from his daughter, a fresh clue to the Spider's identity might have been unearthed. Richard Ballinger's poem about the spider and its web might mean everything or nothing. Either way, Harry knew he had to examine it. He could not rest until he had seen the damned thing.

But he should have approached the matter more cautiously, he chided himself. The present unpleasant situation was entirely his own fault. He had been so bloody anxious to see the poem, so certain that Augusta would obey him in the matter, that he had not stopped to think about where her true loyalty might lie.

He considered his options.

If he were to go upstairs and force Augusta to turn the poem over to him, Harry knew he would surely lose whatever tender feelings she had for him. She might never forgive him.

On the other hand, the knowledge that her loyalty toward her brother's memory was stronger than her new loyalties as a wife was eating at Harry's insides.

He slammed his fist against the arm of his chair and got to his feet. He had told Augusta on the journey down from London that he did not particularly care about love. Loyalty was the thing he demanded from a wife. She had agreed to give it to him. She had agreed to fulfill her duties as a wife.

She could bloody well do precisely that.

Harry made his decision. Augusta had issued enough challenges of her own. It was time he issued one to her.

He strode across the Oriental carpet, opened the library door, and went out into the tiled hall. He stalked up the red-carpeted staircase to the next floor and went down the corridor to the door of Augusta's bedchamber.

He opened the door without bothering to knock and walked into the room.

Augusta, seated at her small gilt escritoire, was busy sniffling into a lacy handkerchief. She started when the door opened and looked up immediately. Her eyes flashed with fear and fury and unshed tears.

The Northumberland Ballingers are a bloody damn emotional lot, Harry thought with an inner sigh.

"What are you doing here, Graystone? If you have come to wrest Richard's poem from me by force, you can forget it. I have hidden it very carefully."

"I assure you, madam, it is highly unlikely you could

think of a hiding place that I would not find, were I to try." Harry closed the bedchamber door very softly and stood facing her. His booted feet were braced slightly apart as he prepared to do battle with his wife.

"Are you threatening me, my lord?"

"Not at all." She looked so thoroughly miserable, so tremulously proud, so very hurt, that Harry momentarily felt himself weaken. "It need not be like this between us, my love."

"Do not call me your love," she spat. "You do not believe in love, if you will recall."

Harry exhaled heavily and walked across the bedchamber to Augusta's dressing table. He stood gazing meditatively at the array of crystal containers, silver-backed brushes, and other delightfully frivolous, delightfully feminine items arranged on it.

He thought briefly of how much he enjoyed walking into this bedchamber unannounced through the connecting door and catching Augusta seated in front of the looking glass. He liked finding her dressed in one of her frilly wrappers with a nonsensical little lace cap perched on her chestnut curls. He took pleasure in the intimacy of the situation and in the blush his arrival always brought to her cheeks.

Now she had gone from thinking of him as a lover to believing him to be her enemy.

Harry turned away from the dressing table and looked at Augusta, who watched him with a deep wariness.

"I do not believe this is a good time to discuss your notion of love," Harry said.

"Really, my lord? What shall we discuss, then?"

"Your notion of loyalty will do."

She blinked uncertainly and looked even more wary. "What are you talking about, Graystone?"

"You vowed your loyalty to me on our wedding day, Augusta. Or have you forgotten so soon?"

"No, my lord, but—"

"And on our first night together in this very bedchamber, you stood over there by the window and swore that you
would fulfill your duty as a wife."

"Harry, that is not fair."

"What is not fair? To remind you of your vows? I will
admit, I did not think it would be necessary to do so. I
believed you would honor them, you see."

"But this is a different matter entirely," she protested.
"This involves my brother. Surely you can understand
that."

Harry nodded sympathetically. "I understand that you
are torn between your loyalty to your brother's memory and
your loyalty to your husband. It is a difficult situation for
you and I am more sorry than I can say that I have caused
your dilemma. Life is rarely simple or evenhanded in a
moment of crisis."

"Damn you, Harry." She clenched her fists in her lap and
looked at him with eyes that glistened.

"I know how you must feel. And you have every right.
For my part, I apologize for having sprung my demand
upon you with so little consideration. I ask your forgiveness
for the summary fashion in which I ordered you to produce
the poem. I can only say on my own behalf that the matter
is of some import to me."

"It is a matter of some import to me, also," she tossed
back furiously.

"Obviously. And you have apparently made your decision. You have made it very plain that protecting your
brother's memory is more important than doing your duty
as a wife. Your loyalty goes first to the last of the
Northumberland Ballingers. Your lawful husband will only
get what is left over."

"My God, Graystone, you are cruel." Augusta got to her
feet clutching the handkerchief. She turned her back to him
and dabbed at her eyes.

"Because I ask that you obey me in this matter? Because

as your husband I ask for your full loyalty, not just some small portion of it?"

"Are duty and loyalty all you can think about, Graystone?"

"Not entirely, but right now they appear to be paramount."

"And what about your duty and loyalty to your wife?"

"I have given you my word not to discuss your brother's wartime activities, whatever they may have been, with anyone. That is all I can promise, Augusta."

"But if there is something about that poem that seems to indicate my brother was a . . . a traitor, then you will very likely interpret it that way."

"It will not matter, Augusta. The man is dead. One does not pursue the dead. He is beyond the reach of the law or my own personal revenge."

"But his honor and reputation are not dead."

"Be honest with yourself, Augusta. It is you who are afraid of what may be concealed in that poem. You are fearful of having the brother you have placed on a pedestal knocked down to the ground."

"Why is the poem so important now that the war is over?" She glanced back over her shoulder, searching his face.

Harry met her gaze. "For the last three or four years of the war there was a mysterious man called the Spider who worked for the French doing very much what I did for the Crown. We believed him to be an Englishman partly because his information was so accurate and partly because of the way he operated. He cost the lives of many good men and if he is still alive I would have him pay for his treason."

"You want revenge on this man?"

"Yes."

"And you will ruin our relationship as husband and wife to get it."

Harry went still. "I do not see that our relationship

should be affected by this business. If it is, 'tis only because you allow it to happen."

"Aye, my lord," she muttered. "That is the way to go about it. How very clever of you. Blame me for whatever ill feelings arise because of your cruelty."

Harry's anger flared once more. "What about your cruelty to me? How do you think it makes me feel to know that you have chosen to defend your brother's memory rather than give your loyalty to your husband?"

"It seems a great chasm has opened up between us, my lord." She turned around to confront him fully. "Whatever happens, nothing can be the same between us again."

"There is a bridge across that abyss, madam. You may stand forever on your side, the side of the brave, dashing Northumberland Ballingers, or you may cross over to my side, where your future lies. I leave the decision entirely up to you. Rest assured I will not take the poem from you by force."

Without waiting for a response, Harry turned and let himself out of the bedchamber.

A polite, frozen calm settled over the household during the next two days. The grim atmosphere was all the more noticeable to Harry because it contrasted so sharply with the weeks of flowering warmth that had preceded it.

It was the marked change in the mood of everyone at Graystone that brought home to Harry just how much of a transformation the household had undergone during the time Augusta had been its mistress.

The servants, always a punctilious, well-trained lot, had, since Augusta's arrival, begun to go about their duties with a cheerfulness that Harry had never before noticed. It had brought to mind Sheldrake's comment on Augusta's habit of being kind to staff.

Meredith, that miniature scholar of serious mien and

obedient temperament, was suddenly painting pictures and going on picnics. Her simple muslin dresses all seemed to have grown flounces and ribbons lately. And she had begun to wax enthusiastic on the subject of the characters in the novels Augusta was reading to her.

Even Clarissa, that dour, sober-minded female of irreproachable character who had once devoted herself to her duties as a governess, had altered. Harry was not precisely certain what had happened during the few weeks of his marriage, but there was no doubt that Clarissa had definitely thawed toward Augusta. Not only had she thawed, she had been showing definite signs of having developed some passionate enthusiasm that, in another woman, might have signaled a romance.

Lately Clarissa frequently excused herself from some planned outing or from joining the family in the drawing room after dinner to rush upstairs to her own bedchamber. Harry got the impression she was working on a project of some sort, but he hesitated to inquire. Clarissa had always been an intensely self-contained, unapproachable female and he had always respected her privacy. It was, after all, something of a Fleming trait.

Harry was quite certain there was no romance in Clarissa's narrow, constrained world of the schoolroom, but the unfamiliar sparkle in her eyes had made him exceedingly curious. He had attributed that change, along with all the others, to Augusta.

But during the two days following the outbreak of hostilities with Augusta, the household visibly altered once more. A frigid, correct atmosphere reigned. Everyone was painstakingly polite and formal, but it was obvious to Harry that the inhabitants of Graystone were collectively blaming him for the chill.

That knowledge was vastly annoying. He contemplated it as he went up the staircase to the schoolroom on the third day. If the various members of the household were inclined to take sides in the silent battle of wills going on between himself and Augusta, it was patently obvious they should have taken his side.

He was in command here at Graystone and everyone's livelihood on the estate depended on him. One would have thought the servants and Clarissa, at least, would have been acutely aware of that fact.

One would have thought Augusta would have been aware of it.

But it was becoming increasingly clear that Augusta gave her loyalty where she gave her heart and her heart had been given to the memories of the past.

Harry had spent the past two nights alone in his bed contemplating the closed door of Augusta's bedchamber. He had told himself it was his wife who must open that door and he had been certain she would eventually. Now, as he faced the prospect of a third night alone, however, he was beginning to question his assumption.

At the top of the stairs Harry turned and walked down the hall to the schoolroom door. He opened it quietly.

Clarissa glanced up, frowning. "Good afternoon, my lord. I did not realize you would be visiting today."

Harry heard the distinct lack of welcome in her tone and decided to ignore it. He knew he was not particularly welcome anywhere in the house lately. "I had a spare moment and decided to see how the painting lessons are going."

"I see. Meredith has started early today. Her ladyship will be along in a moment to take over instruction, as usual."

Meredith looked up from her watercolors. Her eyes brightened for an instant and then she looked away. "Hello, Papa."

"Continue with your work, Meredith. I only want to observe for a while."

"Yes, Papa."

Harry watched her select a new color for her brush.

Meredith moistened the bristles carefully and put down a great wash of black paint on the pristine white paper.

Harry realized it was the first time he had ever seen his daughter select such a dark backdrop for her work. The paintings that showed up regularly now in the picture gallery were generally bright, energetic creations that glowed with sunny colors.

"Is that going to be a picture of Graystone at night, Meredith?" Harry went forward to examine the painting in more detail.

"Yes, Papa."

"I see. It will be rather dark, will it not?"

"Yes, Papa. Augusta says I must paint whatever I feel like painting."

"And you feel like painting a dark picture today, even though it is sunny outside?"

"Yes, Papa."

Harry's jaw tightened. Even Meredith was being affected by the silent warfare in the household. *And it was all Augusta's fault.* "Perhaps we should take advantage of the beautiful day outside. I shall send around to the stables to have your pony saddled. We shall ride to the stream this afternoon. Would you like that?"

Meredith glanced up quickly, her eyes uncertain. "Can Augusta come with us?"

"We can ask her," Harry said, wincing inwardly. He had no doubt about Augusta's response. She would politely decline, of course. She had somehow managed to ensure that she spent no time in Harry's company during the past two days except at the dining table. "She may have other plans for the afternoon, Meredith."

"As it happens," Augusta said calmly from the doorway, "I have no other plans. I should very much enjoy riding to the stream."

Meredith brightened at once. "That will be fun. I shall go and change into my new riding habit." She glanced quickly at Clarissa. "May I be excused, Aunt Clarissa?"

Clarissa nodded with regal approval. "Yes, of course, Meredith."

Harry turned slowly to meet Augusta's eyes. She inclined her head politely.

"If you will excuse me, my lord, I, too, must change. Meredith and I shall join you downstairs shortly."

Now, what the devil is this all about? Harry wondered as he watched her disappear after Meredith. On the other hand, perhaps he should not inquire too closely.

"I do hope you enjoy your ride with her ladyship and Miss Meredith, sir," Clarissa said very primly.

"Thank you, Clarissa. I am sure I shall."

Just as soon as I find out what Augusta is up to now, Harry added silently as he left the schoolroom.

Half an hour later Harry was still waiting for an answer to his silent questions. Meredith's mood, at least, had lightened into one of childish enthusiasm. She looked adorable in her small hunter-green riding habit, which was identical to the one Augusta was wearing, right down to the jaunty little plumed hat perched atop her gleaming curls.

Harry watched his daughter urge her dappled gray pony ahead down the lane and then he gave Augusta a considering glance.

"I am pleased you were able to accompany us this afternoon, madam," he said, determined to break the silence.

Augusta sat gracefully in the sidesaddle, her gloved hands elegant on the reins. "I thought it would be good for your daughter to get some fresh air. The house has become rather stifling of late, has it not?"

Harry cocked a brow. "Yes, it has."

Augusta bit her lip and flicked him a quick, questioning glance. "Oh, devil take it, my lord, you must know why I agreed to come along today."

"No, madam, I do not. Do not mistake me, I am pleased you chose to accompany us, but I certainly do not pretend to understand why you did so."

She sighed. "I have decided to turn Richard's poem over to you."

A surging sense of relief swept over Harry. He very nearly reached out and pulled Augusta off her horse and onto his lap. But he managed to resist the urge. He really was becoming far too prone to act on impulse lately. He must watch the tendency.

"Thank you, Augusta. May I ask what changed your mind?" He waited tensely for the response.

"I have done a great deal of thinking about the matter and I realize I have very little choice. As you have pointed out on numerous occasions, it is my duty as your wife to obey you."

"I see." Harry was silent for a long moment, much of his relief turning sour. "I am sorry you are guided only by duty, madam."

She frowned. "What else would you have me guided by, if not duty?"

"A sense of trust, perhaps?"

She inclined her head politely. "There is that. I have concluded that you will keep your word. You said you would not expose my brother's secrets to the world and I believe you."

Harry, who was not accustomed to having his word questioned in the first place, not even for a moment, could not quite squelch his irritation. "It took you nearly three full days to conclude you could trust my oath, madam?"

She sighed. "No, Harry. I trusted your word from the start. If you must have the truth, that was never really the problem. You are a very honorable man. Everyone knows that."

"Then what was the problem?" he demanded roughly.

Augusta kept her eyes focused between her mare's ears. "I was afraid, my lord."

"Afraid of what, for God's sake? Of what you might learn about your brother?" It took all his willpower to keep his voice low so that Meredith would not overhear.

"Not precisely. I do not doubt my brother's innocence for a moment. But I was anxious about what you would think of me if, after reading that poem, you somehow conclude that Richard was guilty of treason."

Harry stared at her. "Damnation, Augusta. You believed I would think less of you because of something I concluded your brother might have done?"

"I am a Northumberland Ballinger, too, my lord," she pointed out in a strained voice. "If you believed one of us was capable of treason, you might very well question the integrity of others in my family."

"You thought I might question *your* integrity?" He was appalled at the workings of her mind.

She sat very straight in the saddle. "I am aware that you already believe me to be sadly frivolous and inclined toward mischief as it is. I did not want you to question my honor, as well. We are bound together for life, my lord. It will be a very long and difficult road ahead for both of us if you think all Northumberland Ballingers lacking in honor."

"Devil take it, madam, 'tis not honor you lack, but intellect." Harry halted his horse and reached out to sweep Augusta off the sidesaddle.

"*Harry*."

"Were all the members of the Northumberland side of the family so singularly obtuse? I can only hope it does not run in the blood."

He pulled her across his thighs and kissed her soundly. The heavy skirts of her riding habit swung against his stallion's sides, causing the animal to prance. Harry tightened his hand on the reins without lifting his mouth from Augusta's.

"Harry, my horse," Augusta gasped when she could. She clutched at her outrageous little green hat. "She will wander off."

"Papa? Papa, what are you doing to Augusta?" Meredith's voice was thin with anxiety as she jogged back toward her father.

"I am kissing your mother, Meredith. See to her mare, will you? We do not want her to run off."

"Kissing her?" Meredith's eyes widened. "Oh, I see. Do not worry about Augusta's mare, Papa. I will catch her."

Harry was not in the least concerned about the mare, which had only wandered as far as the nearest clump of grass. All he really cared about at the moment was getting Augusta into bed. The battle had only lasted two nights and three days, but that was definitely two nights and three days too long.

"Harry, really. You must put me down at once. Whatever will Meredith think?" Augusta glowered up at him as she lay cradled in his arms.

"Since when did you become so concerned with the proprieties, madam wife?"

"They have been increasingly on my mind since I became the mother of a daughter," Augusta grumbled.

Harry roared with laughter.

Harry opened the door to Augusta's bedchamber later that night and found her sitting at her dressing table. Her maid had just finished preparing her mistress for bed.

"That will be all, Betsy," Augusta said, her eyes riveted to Harry's in the mirror.

"Yes, ma'am. Good night, sir." Betsy's eyes held a pleased, knowing expression as she made her curtsy and let herself out the door.

Augusta got to her feet with a tentative smile. Her wrapper fell open and Harry saw that her nightdress was made of sheerest muslin. He could see her soft breasts swelling against the gossamer fabric. When he allowed his gaze to wander lower, he saw the dark, triangular shadow that crowned her thighs. Suddenly he was achingly aware of his arousal.

"I suppose you have come for the poem?" Augusta said.

Harry shook his head and smiled slowly. "The poem can wait, madam. I have come for you."

13

Augusta rose from the bed a long time later, her body still warm from Harry's lovemaking. She relit a taper and carried it across the bedchamber to her dressing table. Harry stirred in the bed behind her.

"Augusta? What are you doing?"

"I am getting Richard's poem." She opened the small chest which contained her mother's necklace and the folded sheet of paper she had saved for two years.

"It can wait until morning." Harry propped himself on his elbow and watched her with narrowed eyes.

"No. I want to finish this now." She carried the folded sheet back to him. "Here. Read it."

Harry took the paper from her hand. His dark brows drew together in a frown. "'Tis doubtful I can tell anything about it with only a quick glance. It will need study."

"It is nonsense, Harry. Not an affair of state at all. Just nonsense. He was dying when he bid me take it and keep it. In his agony he may have been suffering from some strange inner visions."

Harry looked up at her and Augusta abruptly ceased talking. She sighed, sank down on the edge of the bed, and looked at the terrible brown stains on the paper. She had memorized the words by heart.

THE SPIDER'S WEB

Behold the brave young men who play upon the glistening web,
    See how their silver sabers shimmer.
They meet for tea at number three and return again to serve their master's dinner.
He dines amid the silken strands and drinks the careless young men's blood.
He bides his time at three and nine until the light grows dimmer.
    Now many are few and few are none.
The spider plays a hand of cards and finds he is the winner.
Count twenty as three and three as one until you see the glimmer.

Augusta waited tensely as Harry reread the poem in silence. When he was finished he looked at her again, this time with a cool, searching intensity.

"Did you show this to anyone after your brother's death, Augusta?"

Augusta nodded. "A man came to talk to Uncle Thomas a few days after my brother was killed. He asked to see my brother's effects and Uncle Thomas said I should show him everything. He read the poem."

"What did he say?"

"That it was nonsense. He was not interested in it. Only in the documents that had been found on Richard's body. And then he started hinting that Richard had been selling information to the French. He and Uncle Thomas agreed the matter should be kept quiet."

"Do you remember the man's name?"

"Crawley, I believe."

Harry closed his eyes briefly in disgust. "Crawley. Yes, of course. That stupid, blundering buffoon. No wonder there were no further inquiries made."

"Why do you say that?"

"Crawley was a fool."

"Was?" Augusta frowned.

"He died over a year ago. He was not only an idiot, he had some rather antiquated notions about the propriety of gathering military intelligence. He found that sort of task highly improper and far beneath the touch of a true gentleman. As a result, he knew very little about the process and would not have recognized a coded message if it had bitten him on the ass. Damn the man."

Augusta set down her taper and rested her chin on her updrawn knees. "You think that poem is in code?"

"I think it very likely. I shall have to study it more in the morning." Harry carefully refolded the paper.

"Even if it is a coded message, it might have been one Richard was carrying to an English agent, rather than a French agent."

Harry put the poem on the nightstand. "The important thing is that it does not matter, Augusta. Not to us. I do not care what your brother was doing two years ago. I would never judge you by his actions. Do you believe me?"

She nodded slowly, her eyes locked with his. "I believe you." She realized with a sense of relief that Harry would be scrupulously fair in that regard. His wife would not be held accountable for the actions of other members of her family.

"You are cold, Augusta. Come here and get back beneath the quilt." Harry put out the candle flame and pulled Augusta into his arms.

She knew he lay awake for a long while as he held her in the darkness. She knew it because she was unable to sleep for a long time herself. The question of whether or not she had done the right thing by giving Harry the poem spun endlessly in her mind.

Shortly before dawn, Augusta stirred from an uneasy state that was midway between sleep and wakefulness. She did not turn her head on the pillow or open her eyes as she felt Harry steal softly out of bed.

She heard the faint crackle of paper as Harry picked up the bloodstained poem that lay on the nightstand. And then she heard the door to his bedchamber open and close quietly.

Augusta forced herself to stay in bed until there was a hint of light in the sky and then she, too, got out of bed and prepared for the long day ahead.

A glance out the window told Augusta that the new dawn had arrived beneath a dark, leaden canopy that promised rain.

Harry appeared briefly at the breakfast table, stayed just long enough to help himself to servings from the various egg and meat dishes on the sideboard, and then vanished into his library. He barely spoke a word to either Augusta or Meredith. His mood was one of intense preoccupation which the entire household appeared to take in its stride. It was obviously a mood everyone had witnessed on previous occasions.

"Papa gets like this when he is working on one of his manuscripts," Meredith explained to Augusta. Her clear gray eyes were earnest as she gazed anxiously at her stepmother. "You must not think he is still angry with you."

"I see." Augusta smiled in spite of herself. "I shall bear that in mind."

"Our guests will be arriving in three days' time, will they not?" Meredith asked, her grave gaze betraying a hint of genuine excitement.

"They certainly will. And Miss Appley will no doubt be by this afternoon to finish fitting the last of your new dresses. Remind your aunt that lessons much be cut short today. We will all three be busy with the seamstress."

"I will, Augusta." Meredith got up from the table and hurried off to the schoolroom.

Alone in the breakfast room, Augusta sipped her coffee in silence. She went through the letters that had arrived earlier and then she read one of the London newspapers that had been delivered along with the post.

When she was finished she consulted with the butler and the housekeeper concerning the necessity of hiring extra staff for the house party.

The door to the library remained solidly shut all morning. Augusta's eyes were drawn to it every time she went through the downstairs hall. The continued silence from within Harry's sanctum grew intolerable. She could not stop herself from speculating on what he was concluding about Richard from the terrible poem.

When Augusta could stand it no longer she ordered her mare to be saddled and brought around. Then she went upstairs to change into her riding habit. When she returned to the front hall, the butler gave her a worried glance.

"It appears as though we might have rain later this afternoon, madam."

"Perhaps." Augusta smiled wanly. "Do not concern yourself, Steeples. A little rain will not hurt me."

"Are you certain you do not wish a groom to accompany you, madam?" Every dour line in Steeples's long face was turned down in an expression of deep concern. "I know his lordship would no doubt prefer you to ride with one."

"No, I do not want a groom. This is the country, Steeples. We need not worry about the sort of problems a woman alone might encounter in Town. If anyone inquires, you may say I shall be back late this afternoon."

Steeples inclined his head in a stiff, disapproving manner. "As you wish, madam."

Augusta sighed as she went down the steps and mounted

her horse. Even the butler was difficult to please here at Graystone.

She rode for nearly an hour beneath the ominous sky and felt her spirits begin to lift slightly. It was impossible to stay melancholy in the face of a gathering storm, Augusta decided. She raised her face to the brisk, snapping breeze and felt the first hints of rain. It refreshed and revitalized her as nothing else could have done on that dreary day.

Although she'd had plenty of warning, the first roll of thunder caught Augusta by surprise. She knew it was too late to get back to Graystone before the storm broke. When she spotted a tumbledown cottage in the distance, she headed for it at once. It was vacant.

Augusta found shelter for her mare in the small shed behind the cottage. Then she let herself into the single empty room and stood in the open doorway to watch the rain sweep over the landscape.

She was still standing there twenty minutes later when a horse and rider appeared from the heart of the storm. The stallion's hoofbeats blended with a clap of thunder and lightning arced across the sky just as the beast was brought to a shuddering halt in front of the door.

Harry scowled down at her from atop the horse. His many-tiered greatcoat swirled around him like a black cloak. Rain dripped from his black beaver hat.

"What the devil do you think you're doing out here in the middle of a storm, Augusta?" The stallion danced as more lightning crackled in the distance. Harry soothed the nervous animal with a gloved hand. "Good God, woman, you lack the common sense of a schoolgirl. Where is your horse?"

"Inside the shed at the back."

"I shall see to my animal and join you in a moment. Do shut the door, madam. You are going to get soaked."

"Yes, Harry." Augusta's muttered response was lost beneath the noise of the pounding rain.

A few minutes later the door promptly slammed open

again and Harry strode into the room, dripping water onto the earthern floor. He was carrying kindling he must have found in the shed. He kicked the door shut behind himself, dropped the kindling on the hearth, and began removing his coat and hat.

"I trust you have an explanation for this nonsense?"

Augusta shrugged. She wrapped her arms around herself defensively, aware that the cottage seemed considerably smaller now that Harry was in it with her. "I was in the mood for a ride."

"In weather like this?" Harry stripped off his gloves. He stamped his feet to get the water off his beautifully polished boots. "And why did you not take along a groom?"

"I did not feel the need of one. How did you find me, my lord?"

"Steeples had the presence of mind to note the direction in which you were headed when you left the house. I had little difficulty following you. A few of the tenants had noticed you as you went past their cottages and one of them remembered this place and suggested you might have taken shelter here. 'Tis the only vacant cottage for miles."

"How very logical of you, my lord. As you can see I was perfectly safe at all times."

"That is not the point, madam. Common sense or the lack of it is the point. Whatever possessed you to go riding on a day like this?" Harry went down on one knee in front of the hearth and with quick, practiced movements, began to build a fire. "If you have no thought of yourself, what about my daughter?"

That comment surprised Augusta. A small bubble of happiness rose in her. "Meredith was concerned?"

"Meredith does not know you are gone. She is still busy in the schoolroom."

"Oh." The tiny bubble of happiness collapsed in on itself.

"What I meant was, what sort of example do you think this kind of behavior sets for my daughter?"

"But if she does not even know I am gone, Harry, I cannot see a problem."

"It is just chance she was not aware of your having left the house alone."

"Yes, of course. I see what you mean." Augusta felt some of her initial defiance crumple. "You are quite right, of course. I have set a very poor example. I shall very likely set more such examples in the future, my lord. I am, after all, a Northumberland Ballinger, not a Hampshire Ballinger."

Harry came to his feet in a swift, dangerous motion that made Augusta take a hasty step back.

"*Damn it to hell, Augusta, you will cease using the reputation of your family as an excuse for your own behavior, do you comprehend me?*"

A chill went through her. Harry was very angry indeed and Augusta knew it was not just because she had gone out riding in the face of an oncoming storm. "Yes, my lord. You make yourself quite clear."

He drove his fingers through his damp hair in a gesture of frustrated fury. "Stop looking at me as though you are the last Northumberland Ballinger standing on the castle ramparts preparing to fight the enemy. I am not your enemy, Augusta."

"You sound like one at the moment. Do you think you will feel obliged to lecture me during the whole of our married life, Graystone? It presents an unhappy prospect, does it not?"

He turned back to survey the blaze he had started. "I have some small confidence that you will eventually develop the ability to control your impulsive inclinations, madam."

"How very reassuring. I regret you were forced to come after me this afternoon, my lord."

"So do I."

Augusta studied the strong set of his broad shoulders. "You had best tell me the worst of it straightaway, Harry. I know 'tis not solely my riding off unescorted this afternoon that has you in this mood. What did you discover in Richard's poem?"

He turned around slowly and gave her a hooded, brooding glance. "We have agreed that you are in no way responsible for your brother's actions, have we not?"

A coldness clutched at her insides. *No, Richard. You were no traitor. I do not care what they say.* Augusta forced herself to lift one shoulder in a negligent gesture. "As you wish. What was in the poem, my lord?"

"It appears to be a message to the effect that the man we called the Spider was a member of a club called the Saber."

Augusta frowned. "I do not believe I have ever heard of it."

"That is hardly surprising. It was a small gentleman's club that catered to military types. The premises were off St. James Street. It did not last long." Harry paused. "There was a fire, I believe. Some two years ago, as I recall. The building was destroyed and the club was never revived by its members, to the best of my knowledge."

"I do not recall Richard ever mentioning that he was a member of this Saber Club."

"He may not have been. But somehow he found out that the Spider was. Unfortunately, he does not tell me the identity of the bastard in that damned poem. Only that he was a member of the club."

Augusta considered that. "But if you had a list of the members you might be able to figure out which one was the Spider? Is that what you are thinking?"

"'Tis precisely what I was thinking." Harry's brow rose. "You are very shrewd, my dear."

"Perhaps I missed my calling. I might have made you an excellent intelligence agent, my lord."

"Do you even mention the possibility, Augusta. The very thought of you working for me as an agent is enough to keep me awake nights."

"What will you do now?"

"I shall make some inquiries, see if the proprietor of the

club can be found. He might still have a list of the members or be able to recall their names. It might be possible to track down some of them."

"You are very determined to find this creature you call the Spider, are you not?"

"Yes."

Augusta heard the frightening lack of emotion in his words and felt cold again. She gazed into the fire behind Harry. "Now that you have studied Richard's poem, you are more convinced than ever that he was a traitor, are you not?"

"The matter is not yet resolved and probably never will be, Augusta. As you said, there is the possibility your brother was trying to get the information to the authorities."

"But not very likely."

"No."

"As usual, you are depressingly honest, my lord." Augusta summoned a weary smile. "I shall, of course, form my own opinion."

Harry inclined his head gravely. "Of course. You must continue to believe as you wish on the matter. Whether or not Richard was a traitor is no longer of great consequence to anyone."

"Except to me." Augusta drew herself up bravely. "I shall continue to believe in his innocence, my lord. Just as he would have continued to believe in mine were the situation reversed. We Northumberland Ballingers always stuck together, you know. We would have trusted each other to hell and back. I shall not turn my back on my family, even though all I have left are the memories."

"You have a new family now, Augusta." Harry's voice was harsh in the small room.

"Do I? I think not, my lord. I have a daughter who cannot bring herself to call me Mama because I am not as pretty as her real mother. And I have a husband who cannot bring himself to risk loving me because I might turn out to be too much like the other Lady Graystones who have gone before me."

"For God's sake, Augusta. Meredith is but a child and she has only known you for a few brief weeks. You must give her time."

"And you, Harry? How much time will you require to decide that I am not like my predecessors? How long will I go about feeling as though I am being constantly tested and judged and perhaps found wanting?"

Harry was suddenly behind her, his hand on her shoulder. He turned her around to face him and Augusta looked up into his stark face.

"Damnation, Augusta, what do you want from me?"

"I want what I had when I was growing up. I want to be part of a real family again. I want the love and the laughter and the trust." From out of nowhere the tears came, burning in her eyes and spilling down her cheeks.

Harry groaned and pulled her into his arms. "Please, Augusta. Do not cry. All will be well. You will see. 'Tis only that you are overwrought today because of the matter of the poem. But nothing has altered between us because of it."

"Yes, my lord." She sniffed into the warm wool of his jacket.

"But it would be best, my dear, if you did not go on making comparisons between your dashing Northumberland Ballinger ancestors and the members of your new family. You must accustom yourself to the realization that the earls of Graystone have always tended to be a rather dull, unemotional lot. But that does not mean that I do not care about you or that Meredith is not learning to accept you as her mother."

Augusta sniffed one last time and raised her head. She managed to summon a smile. "Yes, of course. You must forgive my stupid tears. I do not know what came over me. My spirits have been very low today. The weather, no doubt."

Harry smiled quizzically as he handed her a snowy white handkerchief. "No doubt. Why do you not come over to the fire and warm yourself? It will be a while before this storm passes. You can spend the time telling me your plans for the house party."

"Just the sort of topic to distract a woman of frivolous temperament, my lord. By all means, let us discuss my plans for the house party."

"Augusta . . ." Harry broke off, scowling.

"I am sorry, my lord. I was teasing you. Not at all fair of me when I knew you were only trying to comfort me." She stood on tiptoe and brushed her lips across his jaw. "Let me tell you first about the menu I have drawn up for late supper on the night of the ball."

Harry smiled slowly, his eyes still watchful. "It has been a long time since a ball was held at Graystone. Somehow I cannot quite imagine the place done up for one."

The guests began arriving early in the afternoon on the appointed day. Augusta plunged herself into the role of hostess, directing the traffic on the stairs, consulting with the kitchens, and making last-minute arrangements for sleeping accommodations.

Meredith was constantly at her side, her serious gaze absorbing everything from the proper preparation of the bedchambers to the way one organized food for large numbers of people who would not be keeping regular hours.

"It is very complicated, is it not?" Meredith asked at one point. "This business of entertaining, I mean."

"Oh, yes," Augusta assured her. "It is quite a task to make everything come off in such a way that nothing looks as though it was difficult to organize. My mother was very good at this kind of thing. Northumberland Ballingers enjoy entertaining."

"Papa does not enjoy it," Meredith observed.

"I expect he will grow accustomed to it."

Late that afternoon Augusta was standing on the top of the steps, Meredith and the housekeeper, Mrs. Gibbons, at her side, when a sleek green phaeton pulled by a matched set of grays bowled down the drive.

"I do believe, Mrs. Gibbons," Augusta said as she watched Peter Sheldrake alight from the racy phaeton and toss the reins to a groom, "that we shall put Mr. Sheldrake in the yellow bedchamber."

"That will be next door to Miss Claudia Ballinger, then, madam?" Mrs. Gibbons made a note on a piece of paper.

"Yes, exactly." Augusta smiled and went down the steps to greet Peter. "How good of you to come, Mr. Sheldrake. I do hope you will not be too bored here in the country. Graystone has been telling me for days that country parties are not really your thing."

Peter's brilliant blue eyes danced with laughter as he bent his head over her hand. "Madam, I assure you, I do not expect to expire of boredom in your drawing room. I understand your cousin will be here?"

"She arrived but half an hour ago with Uncle Thomas and is presently refreshing himself." Augusta smiled down at Meredith. "You have been acquainted with Graystone's daughter, I believe?"

"I have seen her once or twice. But I had definitely forgotten how very pretty she is. What a charming gown, Lady Meredith." Peter turned the full force of his smile on the girl.

"Thank you." Meredith appeared unaware of Peter's charm. She was staring past him at the bright green phaeton with its high springs and elegant, daring lines. There was a sparkle of something that might have been longing in her eyes. "That is a most wonderful carriage, Mr. Sheldrake."

"I am rather proud of it," Peter admitted. "Won a race in it just last weekend. Would you care for a ride in it later?"

"Oh, yes," Meredith breathed. "I should enjoy that more than anything."

"Then we shall plan on it," Peter said.

Augusta grinned. "Actually, I would not be adverse to a ride in your phaeton myself, sir. Graystone, as you no doubt know, does not precisely approve of such dashing conveyances. He thinks them unnecessarily dangerous."

"You shall both be safe enough in my hands, I assure you, Lady Graystone. We shall go quite slowly and take no chances."

Augusta laughed up at him. "Do not make it sound too safe, sir, or you will take all the sport out of the thing. What is the point of driving about in a phaeton if one does not go fast?"

"Do not let your husband hear you say that," Peter warned, "or he will probably forbid you and Lady Meredith to go about in it with me. Graystone's notion of having an exciting time of it is to uncover an old Latin text featuring Cicero or Tacitus."

Meredith began to look worried. "Is a phaeton quite dangerous, then, Mr. Sheldrake?"

"It certainly can be if it is driven recklessly." Peter winked at her. "Are you afraid to ride in mine?"

"Oh, no," Meredith assured him gravely. "It is only that Papa does not like me to do dangerous things."

Augusta looked down at Meredith. "I have an idea, Meredith. We will simply not tell your father how fast we go in Mr. Sheldrake's phaeton. What do you think about that?"

Meredith blinked at the novel notion of deliberately not telling her father a fact. Then she said in a serious voice, "Very well. But if he asks me about it directly, I shall have to tell him all. I could not possibly lie to Papa."

Augusta wrinkled her nose. "Yes, of course. I understand. You must blame me entirely if we happen to land in a ditch during our drive."

"What's this? A conspiracy?" Harry asked, sounding

amused as he came down the steps. "If Sheldrake lands anyone other than himself in a ditch, he shall have a great deal of explaining to do. To me."

"A dreadful notion," Peter drawled. "You were never very understanding or sympathetic about mistakes and miscalculations, Graystone."

"Keep that in mind." Harry glanced down the drive as another carriage approached. "I am certain Mrs. Gibbons is about to show you to your bedchamber, Sheldrake. When you have refreshed yourself, I would like for you to join me in the library. There is something I wish to discuss with you."

"Of course." Peter gave Augusta another of his laughing smiles and went on up the steps behind the housekeeper.

Meredith looked anxiously up at her father. "Is it truly all right for me to go for a ride in Mr. Sheldrake's beautiful phaeton?"

Harry gave Augusta a smiling glance over the top of his daughter's head. "I believe it will be safe enough. Sheldrake has more brains than to take undue risks with the two people in the world who happen to be most important to me."

Augusta felt herself warmed by the expression in her husband's eyes. Flustered by the look, she smiled at Meredith. "There, now, it is settled. We shall not have to sneak about in order to ride in Mr. Sheldrake's phaeton, after all."

Meredith smiled her father's slow smile. "Perhaps Papa will buy us our very own phaeton."

"Don't be ridiculous," Harry muttered. "I am not about to spend good money on such a frivolous conveyance. In any event, I am nearly bankrupt already due to the excessive expenditures Augusta seems to have made lately on her wardrobe and your own."

Meredith was instantly appalled. She glanced down at the pretty pink ribbons on her dress. "Oh, Papa. I am sorry.

I did not realize we were spending too much money on my gowns."

Augusta glowered at Harry. "Meredith, your father is teasing us most shamelessly. We have not even begun to put a dent in his income and in any event, I believe he rather likes our new clothes. Is that not so, Graystone?"

"They are worth every penny, even if it puts me in dun territory," Harry said gallantly.

Meredith smiled in relief and her hand stole into Augusta's as her attention went back to the green phaeton. "It really is a most beautiful phaeton."

"So it is," Augusta agreed. She squeezed Meredith's hand gently.

Harry looked down at his daughter. "I perceive a taste for adventure developing here. It appears my daughter is beginning to take after her new mother."

For some reason Augusta felt quite ridiculously pleased by that notion.

14

"*I* must say, Graystone, you are surviving married life very nicely." Peter helped himself to claret from the decanter that had been set out in the library.

"Thank you, Sheldrake. I flatter myself that not every man could survive being married to Augusta."

"Takes a certain degree of stamina, I would imagine. But it appears you are thriving. In fact, I would go so far as to say you have undergone a distinct change in your temperament. Who would have imagined you bothering with a house party in the past?"

Harry's mouth curved wryly as he took a swallow of his own claret. "Who, indeed? But Augusta seems to enjoy that sort of thing."

"So you enjoy indulging her? Amazing. You have never been the indulgent type." Peter grinned mockingly. "I told you she would be good for you, Graystone."

"So you did. And how are you doing with the other Miss Ballinger?"

"I have succeeded in getting her attention, I will say that

much for my efforts. The Angel is proving the very devil to woo, however. But Scruggs has supplied me with a great deal of useful information about her tastes and opinions. You would not believe the sort of books I have been reading lately in order to make conversation on the dance floor. Even had to plow through one of yours."

"I'm honored. Speaking of Scruggs and related matters, how is Sally?"

The amusement vanished from Peter's expression. "Physically, she is growing extremely frail. She really will not last much longer. But she has taken a keen interest in tracking down details of Lovejoy's background for you."

"I got your letter last week saying there was very little information available," Harry said.

"The man has an unexceptional past, to be sure. Last of his line, apparently. At least there are no close relatives that Sally or I could discover. Estates in Norfolk seem profitable, although Lovejoy does not appear to pay much attention to them. Some investments in mining, too. Excellent record as a soldier, good at cards, popular with the ladies, no close friends, and that is about it."

Harry swirled the claret in his glass and considered the matter. "Just another bored ex-soldier seeking to amuse himself with an innocent lady of the *ton,* is that it?"

"I fear so. Do you think he was attempting to provoke a challenge? Some men enjoy the sport of the dueling field." Peter grimaced in disgust.

Harry shook his head. "I don't know. 'Tis possible. But I had the feeling his goal was to put me off the notion of marrying Augusta altogether rather than provoke a challenge. It was as if he wanted to discredit her in my eyes."

Peter shrugged. "Probably wanted her for himself."

"Sally told me Lovejoy did not start paying any marked attention to Augusta until her engagement to me was announced."

"I told you once that some men enjoy the challenge of seducing another man's woman," Peter reminded him.

Harry mulled that over in his mind, unwilling to let the puzzle drop. But there were other, more pressing riddles. "Very well. My thanks, Sheldrake. Now I have a far more interesting task to set you. I believe I have found a clue that may point us in the direction of the Spider."

"*The devil you have.*" The glass in Peter's hand made a sharp cracking sound as he set it down on the desk. His blue eyes were riveted on Harry. "What have you got on that bastard?"

"He may have been a member of the old Saber Club. Do you recall it?"

"Gone. Burned down a couple of years ago, did it not? It was not around long."

"Correct. What we need," Harry said as he opened the desk drawer and removed the bloodstained poem, "is a list of the members."

"Ah, Graystone," Peter murmured as he took the small sheet of paper from Harry's hand. "You never cease to amaze me. May I ask how you came by this?"

"No," said Harry. "You may not. Suffice it to say we would have had our hands on it two years ago if Crawley had not been the one sent to make inquiries after a certain suspicious incident."

Peter swore. "*Crawley*. That bumbling idiot?"

"Unfortunately, yes."

"Ah well, what is done is done. Tell me what this means."

Harry leaned forward and started to talk.

Betsy was fastening the clasp of the ruby necklace around Augusta's throat when the urgent knock came on the door of the bedchamber. She went to answer it and frowned when she saw the young maid hovering anxiously in the hall.

"Well, what is it, then, Melly?" Betsy demanded

imperiously. "Her ladyship's busy gettin' ready to greet her
guests downstairs."

"I'm sorry to bother her. It's Miss Fleming. I'm 'avin' a
terrible time. Her ladyship told me I must help her get
ready for the evenin', but Miss Fleming don't want 'elp.
She's in a frightful takin', she is."

Augusta got up from the dressing table, the skirts of her
deep golden gown swirling about her golden satin slippers.
"What on earth is the matter, Melly?"

The young maid looked at her. "Miss Fleming won't
wear the new gown you ordered, ma'am. Says it's the wrong
color."

"I will speak to her. Betsy, come with me. Melly, run
along and see if any of the other maids need help tonight."

"Yes, ma'am." Melly scurried off down the hall.

"Come along, Betsy." With her maid at her heels,
Augusta swept along the corridor and flew up the staircase
to the next floor, where Clarissa's bedchamber was located.

At the top of the stairs she nearly collided with an
unfamiliar young man wearing Graystone's black and silver
livery. "Who are you? I've never seen you around here
before."

"Beg pardon, your ladyship." The young man looked
flustered and embarrassed at having nearly run down his
mistress. He was heavily muscled and the livery strained
across his shoulders. "The name's Robbie. Got taken on two
days ago as a footman to help out with the house party."

"Oh, I see. Well, run along, then. They'll be needing
help in the kitchens," Augusta said.

"Yes, your ladyship." Robbie hastened off.

Augusta continued on down the hall and came to a stop
in front of Clarissa's door. She pounded loudly on it.
"Clarissa? What is going on in there? Open the door at
once. We have very little time."

The door opened slowly to reveal a besieged-looking
Clarissa who was still wearing her wrapper. Her graying
hair was tucked into an old muslin cap. Her mouth was set

in militant lines. "I shall not be coming down, madam. Do not concern yourself."

"Nonsense, Clarissa. You must come down. I am going to introduce you to my uncle tonight, remember?"

"I cannot possibly come down to join your guests."

"It is the gowns, isn't it? When they arrived late this afternoon, I was afraid you would be concerned about the colors."

At that an astonishing glimmer of tears appeared in Clarissa's handsome eyes. *"They are all wrong,"* she wailed.

"Let me see them." Augusta marched to the wardrobe and opened the door. An array of gowns hung there, all in deep jewel tones. There was not a slate gray or dull brown one in the lot. Augusta nodded in satisfaction. "Just what I ordered."

"What *you* ordered?" Clarissa was astounded. "Madam, I allowed you to talk me into new clothes for your house party, although as you know I held strong opinions on the impropriety of a governess attending such an event. But I distinctly told that silly dressmaker that I wanted everything done in dark, subdued shades."

"These are dark shades, Clarissa." Augusta fingered a deep amethyst silk and smiled. "And they will look divine on you. You must trust me on this. Now hurry and get dressed. Betsy will help you."

"But I cannot possibly wear such brightly colored gowns," Clarissa said, looking frantic.

Augusta fixed her with a stern expression. "You must remember two things here, Miss Fleming. The first is that you are a member of his lordship's family and he will expect you to dress appropriately for this evening. You would not want to embarrass him."

"Oh, good heavens, no, but . . ." Clarissa broke off, her expression hunted.

"The second is that my uncle, even though a scholarly sort, has been living for some years now in London and has grown accustomed to a certain style among the women of his acquaintance, if you see what I mean." Augusta crossed her fingers on that last bit.

She had a hunch Sir Thomas would not notice whether a woman wore sackcloth or silk, but it would not hurt to have Clarissa make a good impression. And she knew how badly Clarissa wanted to impress Sir Thomas. At this point Clarissa no doubt had only intellectual passions in mind, but Augusta had hopes for a more fundamental relationship developing between the two. Getting Clarissa into a flattering gown was only prudent.

"I see." Clarissa drew herself up, her eyes going to the array of new gowns in her closet. "I had not realized your uncle held opinions on female style."

"Well, the thing is," Augusta said in a confidential tone, "he has spent his whole life studying the lives of the ancients. And I fear that most of those women of antiquity were noted for their stylishness. Only think of Cleopatra and the fine draping on all those Greek statues."

"Oh, dear. I see what you mean. Sir Thomas has no doubt absorbed a certain classical ideal of how a female should appear, is that what you are saying?"

Augusta smiled. "Precisely. As it happens, the gowns we have ordered for you will give you a classical silhouette and Betsy will arrange your hair in the Greek style. You shall look exactly like a goddess of antiquity when you descend the stairs tonight."

"I shall?" Clarissa was clearly awestruck by that image.

"Betsy will see to it, won't you, Betsy?"

Betsy bobbed a curtsy. "I'll do my best, ma'am."

Augusta's brows rose. "I shall depend upon you, Betsy. Put Miss Fleming in the amethyst tonight, will you? Now, then, I must be off. His lordship will no doubt be pacing the floor, wondering where I am."

Augusta rushed back downstairs to her bedchamber and threw open the door, only to discover Harry. He paused in midstride and scowled ferociously. He glanced meaningfully at the clock.

"Where the devil have you been?"

"I am very sorry, Harry." Augusta gazed at him in deep appreciation. Harry looked elegant and powerful in his black and white evening clothes. "Clarissa balked at the notion of wearing something besides gray or brown. I had to convince her that she would severely embarrass you if she did not wear one of her new gowns."

"I do not care in the least what Clarissa wears."

"Yes, well, that is somewhat beside the point, my lord. Where is Meredith? I distinctly told her to be down here by half past so that we could all walk downstairs together."

"I still feel Meredith is much too young to be allowed to attend this sort of thing," Harry said.

"Nonsense. She has been extremely helpful in the preparations and she deserves to be allowed to participate for at least a short while. My parents always allowed me to come downstairs long enough to be introduced to their friends. Do not concern yourself, Harry. Meredith will be off to bed before you know it."

Harry looked doubtful, but he apparently decided not to do battle over the issue. Instead he allowed his gaze to skim over Augusta's golden gown. "I was under the impression, madam, that you were going to start ordering your gowns cut a bit higher at the neckline."

"The dressmaker made a slight miscalculation, my lord," Augusta said breezily. "No time to repair it now."

"A miscalculation?" Harry took two strides forward and inserted his finger just inside the low bodice. He slid the finger slowly, tantalizingly over one nipple.

Augusta sucked in her breath, partly in shock and partly because she always reacted fiercely to his touch. "Good grief, Harry. Stop that at once."

He slowly removed his finger, his gray eyes gleaming. "Do you know what I think, Augusta? I think the miscalculation was yours. As you will no doubt discover later this evening when I come to your room with a measuring tape."

Augusta blinked and then laughter bubbled up inside her. "You are going to measure me, sir?"

"Most carefully."

A knock on the door spared Augusta the necessity of answering that. She opened it and found Meredith in the hall looking very serious indeed. Augusta examined the charming little frock of white muslin which was trimmed with lace and ribbons.

"My goodness, Meredith, you look exquisite." Augusta turned to Harry. "Does she not look wonderful, my lord?"

Harry smiled. "A diamond of the first water. In fact, I do believe both of my ladies will put all the other ladies in the shade this evening."

Meredith's anxious expression dissolved into a smile as she basked under her father's approval. "You look very nice tonight, too, Papa. And so does Augusta."

"Then let us be off to greet this houseful of people we seem to have acquired," Harry said.

At the top of the stairs Harry took his wife's arm and his daughter's hand. And as the three of them descended into the hall Augusta felt a little surge of contentment.

"I vow, we look quite like a real family tonight, Harry," she whispered as they entered the drawing room, where everyone was gathering for the evening.

He shot her a strange glance, but Augusta ignored it. She was much too busy with her duties as a hostess.

With a wide-eyed Meredith at her side, Augusta floated among the guests. She introduced her stepdaughter proudly to those who did not know her, made certain everyone was involved in a conversational group, and kept an eye on the flow of beverages.

Satisfied that all was going smoothly on this, her first social occasion as mistress in her own home, Augusta paused at a small cluster of people that consisted of Harry, Sir Thomas, Claudia, and Peter Sheldrake.

Peter grinned with relief when he saw her. "Thank God you are here, madam. I am being overwhelmed with the details of some very ancient battles. I vow, I have lost track of which famous Greek or Roman hero did what to whom and when."

Claudia, angelic as ever tonight in an elegant gown of palest blue trimmed with silver, smiled archly. "I fear Uncle Thomas and Graystone are off on one of their favorite topics. Mr. Sheldrake has apparently grown bored."

Peter was aggrieved. "Not bored, Miss Ballinger. Never that. Not as long as you are near. But history is not my favorite subject and even you must admit the endless details of some very old battles do become a bit tedious after a while."

Augusta grinned as her cousin blushed a lovely shade of pink. "Actually, Meredith and I were having a most interesting discussion about historical matters ourselves just the other day. Is that not so, Meredith?"

Meredith brightened. Her serious eyes were lit with a familiar gleam that was not unlike the expression in her father's gaze when he was involved in a discussion of this sort.

"Oh, yes," Meredith said quickly. "Augusta pointed out the most astonishing fact to me, one I had never noticed before. It has made me think a great deal about the ancient heroes of Greek and Roman legend."

Sir Thomas flicked a slightly startled glance at Augusta, cleared his throat, and looked down at the girl. "And what fact is that, my dear?"

"Why, how often the heroes in the old legends were obliged to prove they could outfight or outwit a female. Augusta says that fact demonstrates that the ancients knew that women can be very strong and fierce. Just as strong and fierce as men. She says we do not know nearly enough about the ladies of the classics. Aunt Clarissa agrees with her."

A startled silence greeted this unexpected remark.

"Good Lord," Sir Thomas muttered. "I had not thought about that. What a singular notion."

Harry's brow rose as his eyes rested on Augusta. "I must

admit, I had never put the facts in quite that light," he murmured.

Meredith nodded seriously. "Only think, Papa, about the famous female monsters the ancient heroes had to overcome. There was Medusa and Circe and the Sirens and a great many others."

"Amazons," Claudia said, looking quite thoughtful. "The old Greeks and Romans were always exceedingly concerned about fighting off Amazons, were they not? It does give one pause. We are always being told that women are the weaker sex."

Peter chuckled, a rueful expression in his eyes. "I, for one, have never underestimated the ability of the female of the species to make herself a most wily adversary."

"Nor I," Harry said softly. "But I much prefer the ladies when they are in a friendlier frame of mind."

"Yes, well, a man would, would he not?" Augusta said blithely. "So much easier for him that way."

Sir Thomas was scowling in grave consideration. "I say, Graystone, this is an interesting notion. Outlandish, but interesting. It makes one realize that we do not know a great deal about the women of the Greek and Roman cultures. Just the name of the occasional queen. And there are bits and bobs of poetry that have survived, of course."

"Such as the beautiful love poems by Sappho," Augusta put in cheerfully.

Harry gave her a sharp glance. "I did not know you read that sort of thing, my dear."

"Yes, well, you know my frivolous nature, sir."

"Yes, but *Sappho?*"

"She wrote most charmingly of the feelings love produces in a person."

"Damn it, as far as we know she wrote most of those poems to other women——" Harry broke off, aware of Meredith's fascinated gaze.

"I suspect the feelings engendered by true love are

universal," Augusta said thoughtfully. "Both men and women can succumb to them. Don't you agree, my lord?"

Harry scowled. "I think," he said grimly, "that is quite enough on the subject for now."

"Of course, my lord." Augusta's attention was diverted by the sight of a newcomer in the doorway. "Oh, look, there is Miss Fleming. Does she not appear quite stunning this evening?"

Everyone automatically glanced around to where Clarissa stood gazing uneasily into the crowded drawing room. She was wearing the deep amethyst satin gown that Augusta had chosen for her and her hair was done in a classical chignon secured by a fillet. She held herself proudly, shoulders back, chin outthrust, as she prepared to face the uncomfortable social situation.

"Good God," Harry muttered, and took a swallow of his claret. "Never saw Aunt Clarissa looking quite like that before."

Sir Thomas was riveted. He stared at the figure in the doorway. "I say, Augusta, who did you say this was?"

"One of Graystone's relations. A most intelligent female, Uncle. You will find her extremely interesting. She has been doing some research on the very subject we were just discussing."

"Has she, indeed? I say, I should like to talk more about the matter with her."

Augusta smiled, satisfied with the reaction. "Yes. Now, if you will excuse me, I shall go and fetch her."

"By all means," Sir Thomas said hastily.

Augusta detached herself from the group and headed toward the door to catch hold of Clarissa before the older woman lost her nerve and dashed back up the stairs.

"I must say, Augusta, this is turning out to be a most entertaining house party," Claudia declared the following evening as she and Augusta stepped out of the crowded ballroom for some fresh air and privacy. "The trip to the seaside at Weymouth today was great fun."

"Thank you."

Back in the ballroom the musicians struck up a country dance and the guests took the floor enthusiastically. In addition to the elegantly dressed visitors from London, the colorfully garbed local gentry were out in full force. Every Graystone neighbor for miles around had been invited to the ball. Augusta had laid on a lavish buffet, including plenty of champagne.

Well aware that it was the first time in many years that such an event had been held at the great house, Augusta had wanted everything to be perfect and she was secretly delighted with the results. It was obvious that a talent for entertaining ran in the blood of her branch of the Ballinger family.

"I am delighted you and Uncle Thomas were able to come down to Dorset." Augusta paused beside a circular stone fountain and took a deep breath of the cool night air. "For so long I have wanted to be able to thank you properly for all you have done for me since Richard was killed."

"Really, Augusta. No thanks are necessary."

"You and your father were very good to me in London, Claudia. I fear I sometimes did not always express my gratitude properly, nor was I able to repay you."

Claudia gazed into the shadowed pool of the fountain. "You repaid us in ways that you did not even guess, Augusta. I realize that now."

Augusta looked up quickly. "That is very kind of you, cousin, but we both know I was something of a nuisance in your household."

"Never that." Claudia smiled gently. "Unconventional and unpredictable and sometimes extremely unsettling, but never a nuisance. You rather brightened things up, you know. I would never have gone out into Society if it had not been for you. I would never have experienced Pompeia's or had an opportunity to get to know Lady Arbuthnott." She paused. "I would never have met Peter Sheldrake."

"Ah, yes, Mr. Sheldrake. I must say he appears quite enchanted by you, Claudia. How do you feel about him?"

Claudia studied the satin tips of her dancing slippers and then raised her eyes to meet Augusta's inquiring gaze. "I fear I find him most charming, Augusta, although I do not understand why. His compliments are frequently too warm to be quite proper and he sometimes infuriates me with his teasing. But I am convinced that beneath that devil-may-care exterior that he presents to the world, he is really quite intelligent. I sense a serious side to his nature that he is careful to conceal."

"I do not doubt it. He is, after all, a close friend of Graystone's. I like Mr. Sheldrake, Claudia. Indeed, I have always liked him. I feel he would be good for you. And you would be good for him. He needs a stable and calming influence."

Claudia's mouth curved in a rueful smile. "Are you going on the theory that opposites may attract?"

"Certainly. Only consider my own situation." Augusta wrinkled her nose. "No two people could be as opposite as Graystone and I."

"It would appear so on the surface." Claudia shot her a quick searching glance. "Are you happy in your marriage, cousin?"

Augusta hesitated, unwilling to launch into a detailed discussion of how she actually felt about Harry and her marriage. It was all still too complex, still too new, and there was still so much she longed for in the dark hours before dawn. She did not know if she would ever have everything she desired from Harry. She did not know if he could learn to love her the way she loved him.

She did not know how long he would silently watch and wait to see if she was going to prove as lacking in virtue as the other countesses of Graystone.

"Augusta?"

"I have everything a woman could hope for in a marriage, Claudia." Augusta smiled brightly. "What more could I possibly want?"

Claudia frowned intently. "That is quite true, of course. The earl is all that one could wish for in a husband." She paused, cleared her throat delicately, and then added in a tentative tone, "I wonder, cousin, if you have had an opportunity to make any observations yet about husbands in general."

"Observations about husbands? Good grief, Claudia. Does this mean you are seriously interested in Sheldrake? Is marriage in the offing?"

In the shadows it was impossible to see Claudia blush, but there was no doubt she was doing so. Her normally cool, calm tone of voice was clearly strained. "There has been no mention of marriage and I would naturally expect Mr. Sheldrake to approach Papa first if he intended to make an offer."

"The way Graystone did when he offered for me? I would not count on that." Augusta laughed softly. "Mr. Sheldrake is not nearly so given to old-fashioned proprieties. My guess is he will ask you first. Then he will go to Papa."

"Do you think so?"

"Definitely. Now, then, you want to know my observations on managing a husband, is that the question?"

"Well, yes, I suppose that is what I am asking," Claudia admitted.

"The first thing one must learn about the proper management of husbands," Augusta said in her best lecturing tone, "is that they prefer to think themselves in command of the household. They quite enjoy the illusion that they are the field marshals and that their wives are the captains who carry out orders, if you see what I mean."

"I see. Is it not rather annoying?"

"On occasion, yes. Without doubt. However, men are a bit slow-witted in some things and that rather makes up for the problems caused by their tendency to believe they are in charge."

"Slow-witted." Claudia was shocked. "Surely you cannot be talking about Graystone? He is very intelligent and very scholarly. Everyone knows that."

Augusta waved a hand with airy dismissal. "Most certainly he is intelligent enough when it comes to knowing the odd historical fact such as the date of the Battle of Actium. But I must tell you it is no great task to let a husband go on believing he is in command of the household whilst one goes about organizing things precisely as one wishes. Does that not imply they are a bit slow in some respects?"

"You may have a point. Now that I consider the matter, I must admit I have always known one could manage Father in that fashion. He is always so preoccupied with his studies, he pays no attention to household matters. Yet he believes himself to be in command."

"I rather think we can say the tendency is a common trait of men in general. And I have come to the conclusion that women do not disabuse their men of the notion because men appear to be more accommodating when they believe themselves to be in charge of even small matters."

"Quite a fascinating observation, Augusta."

"Yes, it is, is it not?" Augusta was warming to her topic now. "Another trait I have discovered in husbands is that they have a rather limited notion of what constitutes proper female behavior. They tend to worry excessively about the cut of a neckline or whether one has gone riding without a groom or how much one has spent on even bare essentials such as new bonnets."

"Augusta—"

"Furthermore, I would advise any female considering marriage to give careful thought to the matter of another common masculine characteristic I have discovered. That is their inclination to be astonishingly stubborn once they have formed an opinion. And that is another thing: Men are never loath to form opinions very quickly. Then one must—"

"Uh, Augusta—"

Augusta ignored the interruption. "Then one must set about the annoying business of getting them to see reason. Do you know, Claudia, were I to be in a position of advising a woman on what to look for in a husband, I would ask her to consider the qualities she would look for were she to be in the mood to purchase a horse, instead."

"*Augusta.*"

Augusta held up her gloved hand and began to ennumerate crisply. "Look for good blood, strong teeth, and sound limbs. Avoid the creature that shows any inclination to kick or bite. Pass up one which exhibits a tendency toward laziness. Avoid the beast which displays excessive stubbornness. Some thickheadedness is unavoidable and no doubt to be expected, but too much probably indicates genuine stupidity. In short, search out a willing specimen who is amenable to training."

Claudia clapped her hands over her mouth, her eyes brimming with something that might have been either shock or laughter. "Augusta, for heaven's sake, look behind you."

An ominous sense of impending disaster settled on Augusta. She turned slowly around and saw Harry and Peter Sheldrake standing less than five feet away from her. Peter appeared to be having a great deal of difficulty swallowing his amusement.

Harry, one hand braced negligently against a tree limb, wore an expression of polite curiosity. There was, however, a suspicious glint in his eyes.

"Good evening, my dear," Harry said softly. "Please feel free to carry on. Do not let us interrupt your conversation with your cousin."

"Not at all," Augusta said with an aplomb she felt would have done credit to Cleopatra greeting Caesar. "We were just conversing about the qualities one looks for in a good horse, were we not, Claudia?"

"Yes," Claudia agreed quickly. "Horses. We were talking about horses. Augusta has become quite an authority on the subject. She was telling me the most fascinating details about managing them."

Harry nodded. "Augusta never ceases to amaze me with the breadth and scope of her knowledge about the most unusual subjects." He extended his arm to his wife. "I understand they are just about to play a waltz, madam. I trust you will honor me with a dance?"

It was a command, not a request, and Augusta had no difficulty recognizing it as such. Wordlessly she tucked her hand under Harry's arm and allowed him to lead her back into the house.

15

"*Forgive* me, my dear, but I had no idea you were such an expert on horses." Harry fitted his hand to the small of Augusta's back and swung her into the waltz.

It occurred to him in a flash of insight that she came to him here on the dance floor with the same sweet, willing sensuality that she displayed when she came to him in bed. She was light and graceful and enticingly feminine here, just as she was in the bedchamber. And he experienced a surge of desire that was very much akin to the feeling he got when he saw her lying against white pillows with her hair loose and her eyes full of womanly welcome.

Harry suddenly realized that until lately he had never particularly enjoyed dancing. It had simply been one more necessary accomplishment a man was obliged to learn in order to go about in society. But with Augusta, it was different.

So much was different with Augusta.

"Harry, you are a beast to tease me. How much did you overhear?" Augusta looked up at him through her lashes, a deep rosy blush staining her cheeks. The lights of the chandelier danced on her pretty paste necklace.

"A great deal, and all of it most interesting. Are you perhaps intending to write a book on the subject of managing a husband?" Harry inquired.

"I only wish I had a talent for writing," she grumbled. "Everyone else around me appears to be producing a manuscript of some sort. Only think of how practical a book on husband management would be, Harry."

"I do not doubt the practicality of your subject, madam, but I have serious reservations about your qualifications for writing about it."

The gleam of rebellion shone immediately in her lovely eyes. "I would have you know, sir, that I have learned a great deal in the course of the few weeks we have been married."

"Not nearly enough to write a book," Harry told her in his most pedantic tone. "No, not nearly enough. Judging from what I overheard, there are several glaring errors in your theories and vast confusion in your logic. But never fear, it will be my pleasure to continue your instruction until such time as you have got it right, even if it takes years and years of effort on my part."

She stared up at him, clearly uncertain how to take his outrageous comment. And then, to Harry's surprise, she tipped back her head and laughed with delight. "That is most gracious of you, my lord. I vow, few other teachers would have such patience with their students."

"Ah, my sweet, I am a very patient man. About most things." Pleasure shot through him and his hand tightened against the small of her back. He wished he could drag her upstairs to the bedchamber right now, this very minute. He longed to turn the laughter into passion and then change it back again.

"Speaking of educators," Augusta said, catching her breath as Harry drew her into a particularly daring whirl, "have you noticed how well your aunt is getting along with my uncle? They have been inseparable since they met."

Harry glanced across the room to where Clarissa, resplendent in a claret-red gown and a matching toque, was once more holding forth on the subject of teaching history to young ladies. Sir Thomas was listening intently and nodded appreciatively. Harry thought the gleam in the older man's eyes had a distinctly nonacademic sparkle.

"I do believe you have managed to unite two kindred spirits, my dear," Harry said, smiling down at Augusta.

"Yes, I rather thought they would suit each other. Now, if only my other little project will come to fruition, I shall be quite satisfied with this house party."

"Other little project? What else are you working on, madam?"

"I have a feeling you will learn all about it soon enough, my lord." Augusta gave him a distinctly superior sort of smile.

"Augusta, if you are plotting something, I would have you tell me about it at once. The thought of you carrying out another one of your rash schemes is quite alarming."

"Rest assured this scheme is quite harmless, sir."

"Nothing you attempt is ever *quite harmless*."

"How very gratifying of you to say so, my lord."

Harry groaned and swung her out through the open French doors onto the terrace.

"Harry? Where are we going?"

"I must talk to you, my dear, and now is as good a time as any." He stopped dancing, although the last strains of the music were still drifting through the doors.

"What is it, Graystone? Is something wrong?"

"No, no, there is nothing wrong," he assured her gently. He took her hand and led her deeper into the shadowed garden. He was not looking forward to what he had to say next. "It is just that I have decided to accompany Sheldrake back to London in the morning and I wanted to let you know tonight."

"Go back to London in the morning? Without me?" Augusta's voice rose with sudden outrage. "Whatever do you mean by that, Graystone? You cannot be intending to abandon me here in the country. We have only been married less than a month."

He had known this was going to be difficult. "I have been talking to Sheldrake about that poem of your brother's. We have drawn up a plan of action that might enable us to track down some members of the Saber Club."

"I knew it had something to do with that damn poem. I just *knew* it. Did you tell him Richard wrote that verse?" Her eyes widened in anger and pain. "Harry, you swore to me you would not do so. You gave me your word."

"Damnation, Augusta, I assure you I have kept my word. Sheldrake does not know who wrote that poem or how I obtained it. He is accustomed to working for me and he knows better than to pry when I tell him a subject is closed."

"He is accustomed to working for you?" she gasped. "Are you telling me that Peter Sheldrake was one of your intelligence agents?"

Harry winced, wishing he had waited until later to bring up the subject. The trouble with that notion was that if she had started shouting at him in the privacy of her bedchamber, all the guests in the neighboring rooms would have overheard. He had chosen the garden as the best site for what he had known would be a heated discussion.

"Yes, and I would very much appreciate it if you would keep your voice down, madam. There may be others out here in the garden. Furthermore, this is a private matter. I do not want it bandied about that Sheldrake once worked for me. Is that quite clear?"

"Yes, of course." She glowered at him. "Do you swear to me you did not tell him where you got the verse?"

"I have already given you my word on that matter, madam, and I do not care for your obvious lack of faith in my honor," he said coldly.

"You do not care for it? How very unfortunate for you, my lord. But it seems to me we are even on that score. You do not appear to have a great deal of faith in my honor, either. You are forever hovering about like Nemesis."

"Like *what*?" He was startled, in spite of himself. Sometimes his wife was more perceptive than she realized.

"You heard me. Like Nemesis. It's as if you're waiting for me to display some indication of a lack of virtue. I feel I must always worry about someday having to *prove* myself."

"Augusta, that is not true."

"Not true? Then why do I find myself living constantly with the notion that I am being watched for indications of impropriety? Why is it that every time I go into the picture gallery and see my predecessors, I grow uneasy for fear of being seen in the same light? Why do I feel like Pompeia waiting for Caesar to denounce her because she was not quite above suspicion even though there was no real evidence against her?"

Harry stared at his wife, shocked at the rage and anguish in her voice. He caught hold of her bare shoulders. "Augusta, I had no idea you were thinking such thoughts."

"How could I think otherwise? You go on incessantly about the cut of my gowns. You chide me for riding without a groom. You make me afraid that I will set a bad example for your daughter—"

"That is quite enough, Augusta. You have allowed your imagination to run wild. This is what comes of reading all those novels, my dear. I did warn you about their influence. Now, you will calm yourself at once. You are on the verge of hysteria."

"*No.*" Her hands clenched into fists at her sides as she took a deep, shuddering breath. "No, I am not on the verge of hysteria. I am not so missish as to have a fit of the vapors or lose my self-control in such a fashion over such a trivial matter. I am quite all right, Harry. It is just that I am very angry."

"That much is obvious. And I would not say the matter

was trivial. But you have certainly blown it out of all proportion. How long have you been fretting over this? How long have you visualized me as Caesar waiting to denounce Pompeia?"

"I have felt like that from the beginning, my lord," she whispered. "I knew then that in marrying you I was taking a grave risk. I was aware I might never be able to earn your love."

His hands tightened on her. "Augusta, we are talking about trust, not love."

"The kind of trust I want from you, Harry, must spring from love."

Harry eased her a small distance away and raised her chin with his forefinger. He studied her shadowed, shimmering eyes, wanting to comfort her and at the same time annoyed that it should be necessary. He had already given her all he had to give to a woman. If he had anything left that she might term love, it was behind a locked door somewhere deep inside and he knew that door would never be opened.

"Augusta, I care for you, I desire you, and I trust you more than I have ever trusted any other woman. You possess everything I have to give to a wife. Is that not enough?"

"No." She freed herself, stepped back, and snatched a small lace hanky out of her tiny, beaded reticule. She blew briskly and dropped the scrap of lace back into the little bag. "But obviously it is all I am going to get. When all is said and done, I have no real grounds for complaint, have I? I knew I was being very reckless when I agreed to let our engagement stand. I knew I was taking an enormous chance."

"Augusta, you are very emotional tonight, my dear. It cannot be healthy."

"Just because you do not care for strong emotions, my lord, does not mean they are unhealthy. The Northumberland Ballingers have always thrived on strong emotions."

At the mention of those ghostly figures he could never equal in her memory, a raw anger flared in Harry. He reached out, clamped a hand over her bare shoulder again, and swung her around to face him.

"Augusta, if you dare throw your damned Ballinger ancestors in my face one more time, I believe I shall do something extremely drastic and unpleasant. Do I make myself clear?"

Her mouth fell open in astonishment as she gazed up at him. She closed it quickly and gave him a mutinous look. "Yes, my lord."

Harry pulled violently on the reins of his temper, more annoyed with himself for losing it than with Augusta for being the cause. "You must indulge me, my dear," he said dryly. "Something about knowing I can never live up to the standards of your illustrious forebears makes me exceedingly short-tempered at times."

"Harry, I had no notion you were thinking along such lines."

"Most of the time I do not," he assured her bluntly. "It is only on the odd occasion when you point out my deficiencies. But that is neither here nor there at the moment. Let us get back to the matter at hand. Do you believe me when I tell you that Sheldrake does not know the source of the poem?"

She continued to study him for a long moment and then her lashes settled wearily on her cheeks. "Of course I believe you, my lord. I do not doubt your word. Truly, I do not. 'Tis just that the subject of Richard makes me very unsettled. I do not always think clearly when it is raised."

"I am well aware of that, my dear." He pulled her back against him and pressed her face into his shoulder. "I am sorry, Augusta, but I must be blunt. It would be best if you could leave your brother in the past where he belongs and not concern yourself with what he may or may not have been doing two years ago."

"I believe you have already read me this lecture once or twice before," she muttered into his coat. "It has become quite dull."

"Very well," he said gently. "The fact remains that I wish to find the answers to the questions raised by that poem.. Sheldrake and I can accomplish more working together than one of us on his own. There is a great deal of territory to be covered in Town. It is a question of efficiency, Augusta. That is why I am returning to London in the morning."

"Very well. I can understand the importance of efficiency." She raised her head. "Return to London if you must."

Relief soared through him. She was going to accept the inevitable after all. Harry smiled slowly with deep approval. "That is the way a good wife should answer her lord. I commend you, my sweet."

"Oh, rubbish. You did not allow me to finish, Harry. You may indeed return to London in the morning. But be warned, Meredith and I shall accompany you."

"The devil you will." He thought quickly. "The Season is over. You will be quite bored."

"Nonsense. It will a most educational trip for your daughter," Augusta said, unfazed. "I shall take her about the Town and show her the sights. We shall go to the bookshops and Vauxhall Gardens and the museum. It will be great fun."

"Augusta, this is a business trip."

"There is no logical reason it cannot be combined with an educational experience for your daughter, Graystone. In the interests of efficiency, of course."

"Damnation, Augusta, I will not have time to dance attendance on you and Meredith in Town."

Augusta smiled a very determined smile. "We shall not expect you to do so, my lord. I am certain Meredith and I are fully capable of entertaining ourselves."

"The mind reels at the thought of you turned loose on London with a nine-year-old child who has never been out of the country. I will not have it and that is final. Now we should be getting back to your guests."

Without waiting for a response and more than a little uneasy about the one he would get if he did wait for it, Harry took hold of Augusta's arm and started back toward the house.

Augusta said nothing as he guided her toward the lights and music and laughter that spilled through the open windows. In fact, she was unnaturally quiet. He had expected more protests and tears and a series of arguments couched in the emotional style of a Northumberland Ballinger. But all he was getting was a suspicious silence.

Harry told himself Augusta had finally realized he was quite serious. He comforted himself with the thought that she was coming to grips with the realization that when he gave orders in his own home, he intended them to be obeyed. It was no doubt something of a shock to her because he had indulged her so liberally in recent weeks.

It was unfortunate that she was unhappy with the present situation, but it was for the best. Harry knew he was going to be extremely busy in London. He would not have time to accompany Augusta or Meredith on their outings and he did not like the thought of Augusta going to a series of entertainments alone. Especially *evening* entertainments.

Augusta was at her most dangerous at night, from what Harry had observed. His brain quickly summoned up a multitude of all-too-vivid scenes: Augusta paying midnight visits to gentlemen's libraries; Augusta dressed in breeches while she attempted to break into a locked desk that was not her own; Augusta dancing with rakehells like Lovejoy; Augusta playing too deep at cards; Augusta in a darkened carriage, shivering with passion.

It was enough to make any intelligent, cautious husband extremely wary.

Harry was in the process of reassuring himself on that point when the toe of his boot struck something soft in the grass. He glanced down and saw that it was a man's glove.

"What the devil? I believe one of our guests will be

looking for this, Augusta." Harry scooped up the glove and then he saw the gleam of a boot in the bushes. A pale blue satin slipper was right next to it. "Then again, perhaps he knows precisely where he dropped it."

"What is it, Harry?" Augusta turned to see what he was doing and then she closed her mouth on a soft little giggle as she saw the boot and the blue slipper. She started to smile.

Peter Sheldrake swore calmly and stepped out of the bushes, his arm still wrapped firmly around a furiously blushing Claudia. Claudia was frantically struggling to push the tiny sleeve of her blue gown back up onto her shoulder.

"I do believe that is my glove you have found, Graystone." Sheldrake held out his hand with a rueful smile.

"I rather thought so." Harry handed over the glove.

"You may as well be the first to know," Sheldrake said easily, his eyes on Claudia's embarrassed face as he put on his glove. "Miss Ballinger has just consented to become engaged to me. I shall be speaking to her father before we leave for London in the morning."

Augusta shrieked with delight and threw her arms around her cousin. "Oh, Claudia, how wonderful."

"Thank you," Claudia managed, still struggling to straighten her sleeve. "I only hope Papa will approve."

"Of course he will." Augusta stepped back, smiling with supreme satisfaction. "I know Mr. Sheldrake will be perfect for you. I have been certain of it all along."

Harry stared at her and suddenly remembered something she had said earlier during the waltz. "Was this the second project you mentioned, my dear?"

"Yes, of course. I knew Mr. Sheldrake and Claudia would do famously together. And only think how practical the marriage is from my cousin's point of view, sir."

"Practical?" Harry's brow rose inquiringly.

"Certainly." Augusta smiled a bit too sweetly. "Claudia

will be gaining not only an extremely handsome and gallant husband, but a highly trained butler, too."

There was a frozen instant of silence and then Harry heard Sheldrake groan as realization sunk in. Harry shook his head in rueful acknowledgment of his wife's perceptive qualities.

"I congratulate you, my dear," he said dryly. "Sheldrake, here, has fooled a great many observant people with that butler role."

Claudia's eyes widened. "*Scruggs*." She whirled around and confronted her intended. "You are Scruggs at Pompeia's. I knew I recognized you from somewhere. How dare you fool me like that, Peter Sheldrake! Of all the conniving, underhanded tricks. You should be ashamed of yourself, sir."

Peter winced and shot Augusta a sour look. "Now, Claudia, my dear, I was only playing the part of Scruggs in order to help out an old friend."

"You could have told me who you were. Why, when I think of all the times you were rude to me as Scruggs, I could throttle you." Claudia drew herself up proudly. "Let me tell you, sir, I am not at all certain I wish to remain engaged to such an ill-mannered gentleman."

"Claudia, be reasonable. It was just a little game I was playing."

"You owe me an abject apology, Mr. Sheldrake," Claudia snapped fiercely. "I will expect you to get down on your knees for that apology. *On your knees,* do you hear me?"

Claudia picked up her skirts and fled back toward the lights of the great house.

Peter turned on Augusta, who was choking on her laughter. "Well, madam, I trust you are satisfied with this night's mischief. You seem to have put an end to my engagement before it was even begun."

"Not at all, Mr. Sheldrake. You shall just have to work a bit harder at the task of wooing my cousin. She deserves that apology, by the way. I am not particularly pleased with you, either, I might add. When I think of how sympathetic I was toward you whenever you complained of your rheumatism, I get vastly annoyed."

Peter bit back another oath. "Well, you have certainly had your revenge."

Harry folded his arms across his chest, amused by the wrangling.

"May I ask when you first realized I was playing the role of Scruggs?" Peter growled.

Augusta smiled wickedly. "Why, 'twas that night when you drove Graystone and me about London for an hour or so before taking us back to Lady Arbuthnott's. I recognized your real voice when you tried to tell Harry that the drive might not be such an excellent notion."

"As you are happily married now, madam, it seems to me you should be thanking me for playing the role of coachman that night," Sheldrake retorted. "You should be feeling gratitude, not a desire for a paltry vengeance."

"That," Augusta said, "is a matter of opinion."

"Is that so? Well, allow me to point out—"

"*Enough*." Harry hastily interrupted as he realized he did not care for the direction in which the sparring was headed. The last thing he wanted tonight was for Augusta to recall how she had been coerced into a hasty marriage because of what had occurred in Sally's darkened carriage that night. He had enough problems on his hands without dredging up that bit of ammunition for her to use against him. "The two of you are beginning to remind me of a pair of small children and we do have guests to see to."

Peter muttered grimly under his breath. "I suppose I had better see about making that apology. Do you really think Claudia meant that part about me getting down on my knees?"

"Yes, I do," Augusta assured him.

Peter grinned suddenly. "I always knew she had spirit beneath that prim, angelic facade."

"Naturally," Augusta said. "Claudia may be not a Northumberland Ballinger, but she is still a Ballinger."

A long while later, when the great house was dark and silent at last, Harry sprawled in a chair in his bedchamber and considered the real reason he did not want to take Augusta to London.

He was afraid.

Afraid that in London she would once again find friends of a kindred spirit who would encourage her in her inclination toward recklessness.

Afraid that even though The Season was over she would still find ways to plunge herself into the whirl of activities and pleasures that she had enjoyed so much before her marriage.

Afraid that in Town she might just possibly encounter the kind of man who would appear to be a far more appropriate mate for a passionate female of the dashing Northumberland Ballinger clan than the man she had married.

Afraid that in London she might encounter the man to whom she could truly give her heart.

And yet he knew that even if that should occur, Augusta would honor her wedding vows, come what may. She was a woman of honor.

It struck Harry that he had everything that he thought he had wanted from the start. He had a woman who would be faithful as a matter of honor, even though her heart might be given to another.

Yes, he possessed her loyalty and her sweetly responsive body and they were no longer enough.

No longer enough.

Harry looked out into the night while he carefully opened the locked door deep inside himself. For an instant he peered very briefly into that hungry, desperate, smoldering darkness. He slammed the door shut at once but not before he had understood something he had not wanted to face until now.

For the first time he admitted that he longed to have Augusta's wild, passionate Northumberland Ballinger heart as well as her vow of faithfulness.

"Harry?"

He turned his head as the connecting door between Augusta's bedchamber and his own opened. Augusta stood there, soft and sweet and alluring in her white muslin nightdress.

"What is it, Augusta?"

"I am sorry I made such a fuss earlier tonight when you told me you must go to London." She trailed slowly into the room, the white muslin floating around her. "I understand that you fear Meredith and I will tie you down in Town. Perhaps you are right. If we would be a constant source of concern for you, then we would hamper your efficiency. I would not want that. I know finding the Spider is very important to you."

He smiled slowly and held out his hand. "Not as important as one or two other things in my life. Come here, Augusta."

She put her hand in his and he pulled her down onto his lap, cradling her against him. She smelled warm and womanly and very, very inviting. He felt his manhood stir and begin to throb against her thigh.

Augusta wriggled against him. "You had best forget about that sort of thing if you are to leave first thing in the morning," she said with a soft little laugh.

"I have changed my mind."

"You are not going to London tomorrow?"

"No." He nuzzled the curve of her shoulder, delighting in the sweet vulnerability of that particular spot. "I shall let Sheldrake go on ahead and get started on the investigation. You and I and Meredith will follow the day after tomorrow. I believe it will take at least a day to get you two ladies packed and ready."

Augusta leaned away to study his face. "Harry, you are going to take us with you, after all?"

"You were right, my sweet. You have a claim on Richard's poem and you deserve to be near while Sheldrake and I pursue our investigations. And, quite frankly, I do not want to spend a great many nights alone. I have grown accustomed to having you in my bed."

"So you are bringing me along to serve as a bed-warmer?" Her eyes were brilliant in the shadows.

"Among other things."

She hugged him jubilantly. "Oh, Harry, you will not be sorry, I swear it. I will be a model of perfection, a paragon of wifely behavior. I will be terribly conscious at all times of the proprieties. I will take good care of Meredith and make certain she does not get into any trouble. We shall attend only educational entertainments. I will—"

"Hush, love. Do not go making rash promises." Harry wrapped his hand around the nape of Augusta's neck and brought her lips down to his, effectively silencing her.

Augusta sighed softly and nestled warmly against him, her hand stealing inside the opening of his dressing gown.

He slid his palm up along her leg under the hem of her gown and when he felt her shiver in response, he let his fingers roam higher, coaxing, teasing, probing gently. After a very short time he could feel the hot honey.

"So sweet," he said against her breast. He felt her shudder again as he tested her gently with his finger. She closed around him, tight and eager. Slowly he eased his finger out of her silken sheath. He pushed the muslin gown to Augusta's waist.

Then he opened his own gown and his aroused manhood sprang free. He eased Augusta's legs apart and arranged her so that she straddled his thighs.

"Harry? What are you doing?" Augusta caught her breath. "Oh, my goodness. *Harry*. Here?"

"That's it, darling. Take me inside. Oh, God, *yes*." He reveled in the soft, clinging heat of her as he brought her down onto his fiercely erect shaft. His hands cupped her buttocks, squeezing softly.

Augusta's fingers bit into his shoulders as she found the rhythm of the mating dance. Her head fell back and her hair streamed down behind her.

And then Harry felt the first tiny shudders deep within her and he was once more caught up in the sweet fire he had ignited. He let himself be whirled away into the flames and gloried in the knowledge that in this, at least, he was as wild and free as any Northumberland Ballinger.

16

*L*ady Arbuthnott's housekeeper was attending the door at Pompeia's four days later when Augusta and Meredith, preceded by a footman, went up the steps. There was no sign of Scruggs.

"Mr. Scruggs is indisposed, madam," the housekeeper explained when Augusta questioned the absence. "Or so I'm told. And likely to be for some time."

Augusta hid a smile. She was well aware that between Harry's demands on Peter's time these days and Claudia's distinct disapproval of her new fiancé's habit of amusing himself by playing at butler, poor Peter was unlikely to ever don his makeup and whiskers again.

The housekeeper closed the door behind Augusta and Meredith. "But as he was rather unreliable in the first place, I don't suppose it will make much difference around here." She eyed Meredith with some misgivings. "Will you both be wanting to visit Lady Arbuthnott, then? Or shall I take the young lady down to the kitchens for a bite to eat?"

Meredith looked anxiously at Augusta, silently asking if

she was going to be deprived of the promised visit to the club, after all.

"Meredith will be staying with me," Augusta said as the drawing room door was opened.

"As you wish, madam."

Augusta led the way into the drawing room. "Here we are, Meredith. Welcome to my club."

Pompeia's was quite lively this afternoon, even though The Season was over. Augusta greeted her friends and paused to speak to several of them as she made her way down the long room to Lady Arbuthnott's chair.

Rosalind Morrissey paused in the middle of a conversation and smiled at Meredith. "I see the members of Pompeia's are becoming younger by the day."

Meredith blushed and looked at Augusta for guidance.

"One should never overlook an opportunity to expand an intelligent young lady's education," Augusta declared. "Allow me to introduce my new daughter. She is my guest today."

After a moment's chat, she and Meredith continued on their way.

Meredith was wide-eyed, taking in every detail of the club, from the paintings on the walls to the newspapers on the tables. "Is this really what Papa's clubs are like?"

"Very similar, so far as we were able to establish," Augusta whispered. "Except that they are filled with gentlemen instead of ladies. The stakes are not as high at our tables as they are in the gaming rooms of the St. James Street establishments, of course, but other than a few details such as that, I think we did an excellent job of providing the proper atmosphere."

"I like the paintings very much," Meredith confided. "Especially that one."

Augusta followed her gaze. "That is a picture of Hypatia, a famous scholar in Alexandria. She wrote books on mathematics and astronomy."

Meredith absorbed that information. "Perhaps I shall write a book someday."

"Perhaps you shall."

At that moment, Augusta glanced down the length of the room and saw Sally's head turn toward her. A wave of dismay crushed the enthusiasm she had been experiencing at the thought of seeing her old friend again.

There was no denying that Sally's health had deteriorated a great deal during the past month. She had taken great care with her attire, as usual. But the elegant gown could not conceal the pale, translucent skin, the air of extreme frailty, and the stoic acceptance of never-ending pain in Sally's eyes. It was almost more than Augusta could bear. She wanted to cry and knew she would only upset Sally.

Instead, she rushed forward and leaned down to hug her friend gently. "Oh, Sally, it is good to see you again. I have worried about you so."

"I am still here, as you can see," Sally said in a surprisingly firm voice. "And more busy than ever assisting that tryant you married. Graystone always was a severe taskmaster."

"Assisting Graystone? Not you, too?" Augusta groaned as she realized the implications. "I should have guessed. You were part of his—" She broke off, remembering Meredith's presence.

"Of course, my dear. You knew I had a rather sordid past, did you not?" Sally's chuckle was weak, but it contained real amusement. "Now, introduce me to this young lady. Graystone's daughter, if I am not mistaken?"

"Just so." Augusta made the introductions and Meredith made her curtsy.

"The resemblance is unmistakable," Sally said affectionately. "Same intelligent eyes. Same slow smile. How lovely. Run along, Meredith. You may help yourself to some cakes from the buffet."

"Thank you, Lady Arbuthnott."

Sally watched Meredith hurry toward the array of food

on the other side of the room. Then she turned slowly back to face Augusta. "A most charming child."

"And every bit as scholarly as her father. She tells me she might write a book." Augusta seated herself in a nearby chair.

"She probably will. Knowing Graystone, I imagine she is being taught a very comprehensive curriculum. One shudders to think of it."

Augusta laughed. "Never fear, Sally. I have taken care to make up for the lack of certain frivolous subjects in Meredith's curriculum. I have started her on an intense program of watercolor painting and novels. In addition, I have enlisted the assistance of her governess in exposing Meredith to a view of history she will never get from her father's books."

Sally laughed. "Oh, my irrepressible Augusta. I knew you would be good for Graystone. Some part of him must have known it, too, or he would never have put your name at the top of his list."

"At the top of the list, did you say? I always assumed I was at the bottom. A sort of afterthought." Augusta helped herself to tea and replenished Sally's cup. As she set the pot back down she noticed the small jar of tonic that sat on the table near Sally's chair.

When Augusta had left Town, Sally had been in the habit of only calling for her tonic when she needed it. Now she apparently kept the bottle beside her all the time.

"You were never an afterthought. Quite the opposite. Graystone was never able to get you out of his mind after he met you."

"Rather like a case of hives or an itch he longed to scratch?"

Sally laughed again. "You underestimate yourself, my dear. By the way, I have a complaint to lodge with you. You have cost me an excellent butler."

"Do not blame me. 'Tis my cousin who obliged poor Scruggs to quit his post."

Sally smiled. "So I am given to understand. I saw the announcement of the engagement in the *Post* yesterday morning. I believe it will be an excellent match."

"Uncle Thomas was pleased."

"Yes. Sheldrake is a bit of a rake, but I have always believed he longs to be reformed. He has been racketing about London since returning from the continent, searching for a mission. Getting married and attending to his father's estates will give him the direction he has been seeking."

"I formed the same opinion," Augusta agreed.

"You are very perceptive, my dear Augusta." Sally reached for the tonic. She opened the jar and added two drops of the medication to her tea. She noticed Augusta watching sadly and smiled. "Forgive me, Augusta. As you no doubt have guessed, I am having more difficulty these days."

Augusta reached out and touched her hand. "Sally, is there anything I can do? Anything at all?"

"No, dear. This is something I shall be obliged to handle on my own." Sally's eyes drifted thoughtfully to the jar of tonic.

"Sally?"

"Calm yourself, my dear. I am not going to do anything drastic just yet. I am much too busy at the moment seeking information for Graystone on the Saber Club. Heaven knows I always adored this sort of work. I have been in touch with old contacts I have not heard from in nearly two years. Amazing how many are still around and looking for employment."

Augusta sat back slowly in her chair. She glanced at Meredith, who had paused beside the writing desk to observe something Cassandra Padbury was showing her. Probably Cassandra's latest effort at an epic poem, Augusta thought.

"My husband is very determined to track down the information he seeks," Augusta murmured to Sally.

"Yes. Graystone has always been a very determined man.

And he wants the Spider very much. The connection to the old Saber Club is an interesting one. It makes a great deal of sense when you think about it."

"What do you know of the club?"

Sally shrugged elegantly. "Not a great deal. It did not last long. Attracted young military officers who thought themselves quite daring and dashing and in need of a club that catered to their image of themselves. But the place burned down within a year after it had been established and that was the end of it. I have not been able to discover any of the members as yet, but I believe I may have tracked down one of the former employees. He may well remember some names."

Augusta was fascinated in spite of her misgivings about what might eventually be discovered in the course of this investigation. "How exciting. Have you spoken to this person?"

"Not yet. But I expect to do so soon. Arrangements are being made." Sally's shrewd gaze settled on Augusta for a long moment. "You are personally concerned with this project of Graystone's, are you not?"

"I am interested in the outcome, yes. I know it is important to him," Augusta said evasively.

"I see." Sally was silent for a moment and then she appeared to come to a decision. "Augusta, my dear, you are aware that Pompeia's betting book is always left open to the current page?"

"Yes. What of it?"

"If you were ever to find it closed, I would have you take the book to Graystone. Make certain it is opened."

Augusta stared at her. "Sally, what are you talking about?"

"I know this must all sound quite mysterious and melodramatic, my dear, when in reality it is not. 'Tis merely a precaution. Just promise me that you will see that the book gets to Graystone in the event something unexpected should happen."

"I promise. But Sally, will you tell me what this is all about?"

"Not yet, my dear. Not yet. Graystone knows I always prefer to verify my information before I turn it over to him. Harry can be the very devil about unverified information. Your husband has very little tolerance for mistakes." Sally smiled at some private memories. "Just ask our old friend Scruggs. I shall never forget the time he got into trouble with a French officer's wife and . . . ah, but that is an old story."

"I see." Augusta sipped her tea in silence, aware once more of the familiar sense of being on the outside looking into a warm room. She knew that she held no place in the intimate circle of friendship that bound Harry, Sally, and Peter together.

She knew this feeling well. It was the wistful sense of longing that she had often experienced since her brother's death. She supposed she should be accustomed to it by now.

At times during the short weeks of her marriage, Augusta had thought the feelings of not belonging to a real family had finally begun to fade once and for all. It had seemed that Meredith was beginning to accept her, and Harry's passion had made Augusta feel desired, at least physically.

But Augusta knew she wanted much more than what she had. She wanted to be an important part of Harry's life in the way that Sally and Peter were. She wanted to be her husband's intimate friend, as well as his wife.

"The three of you were rather like a family in some ways, were you not?" Augusta asked quietly after a moment.

Sally opened her eyes in surprise. "I had not thought of it before, but perhaps we were. We were all quite different, Graystone, Peter, and I, but we were obliged to share some very dangerous adventures. We needed each other. And we were frequently dependent upon each other for our very lives. That sort of thing binds people together, does it not?"

"Yes, I would imagine so."

• • •

Harry was seated at his desk in the library when he at last heard the commotion in the hall that heralded the return of his wife and daughter. *It is about time,* he thought grimly.

Augusta had only been back in Town two days and already she was dashing about the city with Meredith in tow. When he had arrived home an hour ago no one had seemed precisely certain just where the pair had gone. Craddock, the butler, was under the vague impression Augusta had taken Meredith to the British Museum.

But Harry knew better. There was no telling what sort of amusements Augusta would deem suitable for a child of nine. Harry did not believe for one minute that his wife and daughter had spent the day at the museum.

He got to his feet and went to the door. Meredith, still wearing her new pink bonnet, saw him at once. She rushed toward him across the hall, bonnet strings flying. Her eyes were alight with rare excitement.

"Papa, Papa, you will never guess where we have been."

Harry glanced sharply at Augusta, who was removing a seductively brimmed hat trimmed with huge red and gold flowers. She smiled innocently. He looked down at Meredith again. "If I shall never guess, then you must tell me."

"To a gentlemen's club, Papa."

"A *what?*"

"Augusta explained that it was just like yours, Papa. Except that it was for ladies. It was so interesting. Everyone was very nice and talked to me about a great many things. Some of the ladies there are writing books. One of them was writing a story about Amazons. Is that not fascinating?"

"Very." Harry gave his wife a quelling glance which she ignored.

Meredith missed the byplay and continued with her summary of the afternoon's events. "And there were pictures of famous classical ladies on the wall. Even Cleopatra. Augusta says they are excellent examples for me. And I met

Lady Arbuthnott, who said I could eat as many cakes as I liked."

"It sounds as though you have had quite an adventure, Meredith. You must be exhausted."

"Oh, no, Papa. I am not in the least exhausted."

"Nevertheless, Mrs. Biggsley will take you upstairs to your bedchamber now. I would like to talk to your mother."

"Yes, Papa."

Obedient as ever, but clearly still bubbling over with enthusiasm, Meredith was taken away by the patient housekeeper.

Harry frowned at Augusta. "Please come into the library, madam. I would have a word with you."

"Yes, my lord. Is something wrong?"

"We will discuss this in private, madam."

"Oh, dear. You are annoyed with me again, are you not?"

Augusta dutifully went past him and sat down on the other side of the desk. Harry seated himself. He folded his hands in front of him on the polished wooden surface of the desk and said nothing for a long moment. Deliberately he let Augusta feel the silent, heavy weight of his displeasure.

"Really, my lord, I do not like it when you glower at me like that. It makes me exceedingly uncomfortable. Why do you not just say what is on your mind?" Augusta started to strip off her gloves.

"What is on my mind, madam, is that you had no business taking a child to Pompeia's."

She rallied to the battle instantly. "Surely you can have no objection to us visiting Lady Arbuthnott."

"That is not the issue and I believe you know it. I have no objection whatsoever to Meredith meeting Sally. But I object very strong, indeed, to exposing my daughter to the atmosphere of that damned club. We both know that women of a certain stamp tend to congregate there."

"*A certain stamp?*" Augusta's eyes sparkled with anger.

"Whatever do you mean by that, my lord? You make us all sound like professional courtesans. Do you think I will tolerate such an insult?"

Harry felt his temper begin to slip its leash. "I did not imply the club members were courtesans. By a *certain stamp*, I merely meant that the sort of females who frequent the place tend to turn a blind eye toward many of the proprieties. They pride themselves on being Originals. From my own personal experience, I can truthfully say that the ladies of the club are inclined to be somewhat reckless and outrageous. Not the sort of females who would set good examples for my daughter."

"I would remind you, sir, that you married one of the members of Pompeia's."

"Precisely. A fact which qualifies me to judge the character of the women who become members, does it not? Let us be clear on this point, Augusta. When I gave you permission to accompany me to London, I told you I would not be able to dance attendance on you or supervise your outings. You gave me your word you would exercise good sense when taking Meredith about the Town."

"I am exercising good sense. She was in absolutely no danger of any kind."

"I did not mean physical danger."

Augusta glowered at him. "Are we talking about moral danger, perhaps, my lord? You see the club members as bad influences on the morals of your daughter? If that is the case, you certainly should not have gone out of your way to marry one of the founders of Pompeia's. That 'damned club,' as you call it, was my idea from the start."

"Damnation, Augusta, you are deliberately putting the wrong construction on my words." Harry was furious with himself for having allowed what should have been a simple husbandly lecture on female decorum to turn into a full-blown quarrel. He made a heroic bid for his self-control and his temper. "It is not the morals of the ladies of the club which alarm me."

"I am very glad to hear that."

"'Tis, rather, a certain streak of recklessness I find in them."

"How many of them do you know, my lord? Or are you, perhaps, generalizing on the basis of what you have learned about me?"

Harry narrowed his gaze. "Do not play me for the fool, madam. I am well acquainted with the names on the membership list of Pompeia's."

That set her back. "You are?"

"Of course. I examined it most carefully once I realized I would very likely be marrying you," Harry admitted.

"This is an outrage." Augusta leaped to her feet and began striding angrily back and forth across the room. "You conducted an investigation of Pompeia's? Just wait until I inform Sally of this. She will be furious with you."

"Who do you think gave me the membership list to examine?" Harry asked dryly. "Between what I knew of the backgrounds of the ladies on that list and what Sheldrake and Sally were able to tell me, I concluded that you were in no serious moral danger. That does not mean that I approve of the place or of you taking my daughter there."

"I see."

"I would order you to withdraw your membership were it not for the fact that Sally is so ill and has so little time left. I am well aware that she enjoys both the club and your visits. Therefore, I will not deny you permission to go to Pompeia's."

"How very kind of you, my lord."

"But henceforth, you will not take Meredith with you. Is that clear?"

"Quite clear," she said through set teeth.

"You will also, in future, leave me a detailed schedule of all the activities you have planned for each day. I did not like coming home this afternoon only to be informed you were simply *out* with no exact information as to where you had gone."

"A schedule. Yes, my lord. You shall most certainly have a *schedule*. Will there be anything else, Graystone?" Augusta paced furiously. Her anger was palpable.

Harry sighed and sat back in his chair. He drummed his fingers on the desk and eyed Augusta broodingly. He very much wished he had never initiated this confrontation. On the other hand, a man had to take a firm stand when dealing with a woman like this. "No, I believe that will be all, madam."

She came to an abrupt halt and swung around to confront him. "If you have quite finished, my lord, I have a favor to ask you."

Having mentally braced himself for more outrage and another impassioned defense of Pompeia's, Harry was speechless for a few seconds. When he finally found his voice, he reacted quickly, anxious to find a way to be generous now that he had played the heavy-handed husband yet again.

"Yes, my dear?" He put as much warm encouragement as he could into his tone. *Hell*, he told himself, feeling suddenly magnanimous, *what is another new bonnet or a gown if I can restore her good temper?*

Augusta came back across the carpet and planted both hands on the edge of the desk. Leaning forward, she fixed him with an intent gaze. "Harry, will you allow me to assist you in your investigations?"

Dumbfounded, he stared at her. "Good God, no."

"Please, Harry. I know I do not know much about that sort of thing, but I believe I could learn quickly. I realize that I would not be of much use to you or Peter, but I could function as an assistant to Sally, could I not?"

"You are quite right, Augusta," he said coldly. "You know nothing about this sort of thing." *And as God is my witness, you will never learn*, he thought. *I will protect you from that kind of knowledge if it is the last thing I do.*

"But Harry—"

"Your offer is appreciated, my dear, but I assure you, you would be more hindrance than help."

"But my lord, there are elements of your investigation that concern me as much as they do you and your friends. I want to be a part of your efforts. I have a right to be involved. I want to help."

"No, Augusta, and that is absolutely the last word." Harry picked up his quill and pulled a journal toward him across the desk. "Now, I must bid you good day. I have much to do this afternoon and I will be out for most of the evening. I shall be dining at my club with Sheldrake."

Augusta straightened slowly, her eyes bright with unshed tears. "Yes, my lord." She turned and went toward the door.

It was all Harry could do not to go after her, take her into his arms, and relent. He forced himself to remain where he was. He had to be firm. "By the way, Augusta."

"Yes, my lord?"

"Do not forget to give me the schedule of your plans for tomorrow."

"If I can think of anything sufficiently boring and therefore unobjectionable to your lordship, I will definitely put it down on the schedule."

Harry winced as she slammed the door on her way out of the room.

He sat quietly for a long while contemplating the gardens outside his window. There was no way he could tell her the real reason he could not give her even a token role in the investigation.

It was bad enough that she was angry about being excluded. But he could deal with her anger better than he could the pain he knew would come if she were to get involved in this situation and thereby learn too much.

Once he had deciphered Richard Ballinger's encoded poem, Harry had known that the rumors that had circulated at the time of the young man's death were founded in fact. The last male in the Northumberland Ballinger line had in all likelihood been a traitor.

Later that night Harry, accompanied by Peter, stepped down from the cab of a hired carriage and into the very heart of one of London's grimiest stews. It had started raining an hour ago and the paving stones underfoot had become slick. Moonlight gleamed dully on the greasy surfaces.

"Do you know, Sheldrake, it concerns me somewhat that you know your way so well around this part of Town." Harry saw a pair of beady red eyes glinting in the shadows and casually used his ebony walking stick to discourage the rat, which was the size of a large cat. The creature vanished into a vast pile of offal that marked the entrance to a narrow alley.

Peter chuckled softly. "In the old days your sensibilities were rarely offended by the notion of how and where I acquired my information."

"You will have to learn to refrain from amusing yourself in places such as this now that you are about to become a married man. I cannot see Claudia Ballinger approving of this sort of outing."

"True. But once I have married Miss Ballinger I expect to have far more interesting things to do in the evenings than dive into the stews." Peter paused to get his bearings. "There's the lane we want. The man we are seeking has arranged to meet us in the tavern at the end of this filthy little street."

"You trust your information?"

Peter shrugged. "No, but 'tis a starting point. I was told this man Bleeker witnessed the fire the night the Saber Club burned down. We shall no doubt discover the truth of that claim soon enough."

The lights of the dingy tavern shone with an evil yellow glow through the small windows. Harry and Peter pushed their way inside and found the interior smoky and over-heated by a fierce fire on the hearth. There was a sullen atmosphere about the place. A handful of patrons was sprinkled about the long wooden tables. Several of them glanced up as the door opened.

Each pair of ratlike eyes took note of the shabby cut of the coats and the worn boots Harry and Peter had donned for the occasion. Harry could almost hear the collective sigh of regret as the would-be predators decided the new prey did not look promising.

"There's our man," Peter said, leading the way toward the back of the tavern. "Near the door at the rear. I was told he would be wearing a red scarf around his neck."

Bleeker had the look of a man who had downed far too many bottles of gin in his time. He had small, restless eyes that darted about constantly, never staying focused for more than a few seconds on any one object.

In addition to a red scarf, Bleeker was also wearing a filthy cap pulled down low over his sweating brow. His heavily veined nose was his most prominent feature. When Bleeker opened his mouth to growl a short greeting, Harry saw huge gaps between the man's yellowed, rotten teeth.

"You be the coves what's wantin' to know about the fire at the old Saber Club?"

"You have the right of it," Harry said, sliding down onto the wooden bench across from Bleeker. He was aware that Peter remained on his feet, his gaze moving with deceptive casualness around the stifling room. "What can you tell us about that night?"

"It'll cost ye," Bleeker warned with a foul grin.

"I'm prepared to pay. Assuming the information is good."

"Good enough." Bleeker leaned forward with a conspiratorial air. "I saw the cove what set that fire, I did. I was in the alley across the street from the club waitin' for a likely cully to come along. Just mindin' me own business, ye

know. Then I hears this sudden roarin' noise. I looks up and
there's flames in all the windows of the club."

"Go on," Harry said calmly.

"How do I know ye'll come across with the blunt?"
Bleeker whined.

Harry put a few coins on the table. "You will get the rest
if I find the information sufficiently interesting."

"Bloody 'ell, you're a mean 'un, ain't ye?" Bleeker leaned
closer, his poisonous breath wafting across the table. "All
right, then, 'ere's the rest of it. There was two men come
runnin' out the front door o' the Saber that night. The first
is clutchin' his stomach and bleedin' like a pig. 'E makes it
across the street and falls down at the entrance o' the alley
where I was standin'."

"Convenient," Harry murmured.

Bleeker ignored the remark. He was growing increasingly enthusiastic about his own tale. "I stays in the
shadows and the next thing I know, this second cove comes
rushin' out. Searches the street until 'e finds the poor
bleedin' cully, 'e does. Then he goes up to 'im and stands
there lookin' down. I could see 'e's got a knife in 'is 'and."

"Fascinating. Pray continue."

"Then the poor dyin' cully says to 'im, *You've killed me,
Ballinger. You've killed me. Why'd ye do it? I'd never 'ave told
a bloody soul who ye really was. I'd never 'ave said nothin' about
you bein' no Spider.*" Bleeker sat back, satisfied. "Then the
poor sod dies and the other 'un takes off. I got outta there,
I can tell ye that."

Harry was silent for a moment as Bleeker came to the
end of his story and sat waiting expectantly. Then he got
slowly to his feet. "Let us be off, friend," he murmured to
Peter. "We have wasted our time this night."

Bleeker scowled in alarm. "'Ere, now, what about me
blunt? You promised to pay me for tellin' you what
'appened that night."

Harry shrugged and tossed a few more coins on the
table. "That will have to suffice. It is all your lies are worth.

Collect the rest of your pay from whoever told you to feed me that tale."

"Lies? What lies?" Bleeker blustered furiously. "I was tellin' ye the bloody damn truth."

Harry ignored him, aware that there was a stir of interest occurring among the tavern patrons as they turned to eye the commotion at the back of the room.

"The back door, I think," Harry said to Peter. "It suddenly looks like a very long way to the front door."

"Excellent observation. I have always been a great believer in the virtue of a strategic retreat." Peter flashed a brief grin and quickly opened the rear door. "After you, sir." He waved Harry politely ahead of him.

Harry stepped out into the alley. Peter was right behind him, slamming the door shut on the angry shouts of Bleeker and the restless horde of tavern patrons.

"Damn," said Harry as he saw the man with the knife looming up out of the reeking shadows.

Moonlight glinted on the blade as the man leaped for Harry's throat.

17

Harry swept his ebony walking stick up in a slashing arc. The cane struck his assailant's outstretched arm in a savage blow that sent the knife flying off into the shadows.

Harry rotated the stick's handle a quarter turn with a practiced one-handed movement. The hidden blade inside the walking stick leaped out, pressing against the assailant's neck.

"*Bloody 'ell.*" The man jumped back and promptly stumbled over a heap of garbage. He lost his footing on the greasy stones and fell to the pavement. He flailed wildly and began screaming curses.

"Best be on our way," Peter said cheerfully with only a passing glance at Harry's victim. "I expect our friends will be coming through that door any minute."

"I had no intention of delaying our departure." Harry flicked the walking stick handle back a quarter turn and the blade disappeared as silently as it had emerged.

Peter led the way out of the alley. Harry followed

quickly. They raced out into the lane where Peter unhesitatingly turned to the right.

"It occurs to me," Peter growled as they dashed up the lane, "that I have found myself in this sort of situation more than once with you, Graystone. I am beginning to think these things come about because you never leave a decent tip."

"Very likely."

"Cheeseparing, that's you, Graystone."

"I, on the other hand," Harry said as he pounded down the street beside his friend, "have noticed that I only seem to find myself in these circumstances when I have you along as a guide. One does tend to wonder if there is not some logical connection."

"Nonsense. Simply your imagination."

Thanks to Peter's intimate knowledge of the underbelly of the city and the general reluctance of the denizens of the stews to get involved in what looked like trouble, both men soon found themselves standing in relative safety on a busy street.

Harry used his walking stick to hail a hackney carriage which had just set down a group of drunken young dandies. Apparently the hackney's previous passengers intended to sample the darker side of London's nightlife.

For his part, Harry had seen more than enough. He bounded up into the cab and dropped down on the seat across from Peter.

A thoughtful silence descended. Harry idly studied the dark streets outside the window as the hackney headed toward a better part of Town. Peter watched him from the shadows, saying nothing for several minutes. Then he spoke.

"An interesting story, was it not?" Peter finally asked.

"Yes."

"What do you make of it?"

Harry went over Bleeker's tale again in his mind, searching for possibilities. "I am not yet certain."

"The timing fits," Peter said slowly. "Ballinger was

killed the night after the fire at the Saber Club. He could have set the fire to muddy his own trail and killed that witness. And then gotten himself shot by that highwayman the next night."

"Yes."

"So far as we know, the Spider became inactive shortly before Napoléon abdicated in April of 1814. That would fit with the time of Ballinger's death, too. He was shot in late March of that year. There was no sign of the Spider having resumed his work during the short time between Napoléon's escape from Elba and the final defeat at Waterloo."

"The Spider was too shrewd to have cast his lot with Napoléon a second time. The attempt to regain the throne of France in 1815 was a lost cause from the start and everyone but Napoléon knew it. Defeat was inevitable the second time and the Spider would have realized it. He would have stayed out of the affair."

Peter's mouth twisted wryly. "You may be correct. You always did have a talent for second-guessing the bastard. But the end result is the same. The Spider vanished from the scene in the spring of 1814. Perhaps the reason we never heard from him again was simply because he had the bad luck to fall victim to a highwayman's bullet. Richard Ballinger could have been the Spider."

"Hmmm."

"Even brilliant spymasters must occasionally find themselves on the wrong road at the wrong time of night. They are no more immune to the odd highwayman than anyone else, I should imagine," Peter said.

"Hmmmm."

Peter groaned. "I detest it when you get into this mood, Graystone. You are not an entertaining conversationalist at such times."

Harry finally turned his head and met his friend's eyes. "I am certain there is no need to mention that I would not want any of these speculations of yours to get back to Augusta, Sheldrake."

Peter grinned briefly. "Credit me with some sense, Graystone. I have every intention of living to see my wedding night. I am not about to overset Augusta and thereby risk your wrath." His smile faded. "In any event, I count Augusta a good friend, as well as a member of my future wife's family. I have no more wish to see her suffer because of her brother's dishonorable actions than you do."

"Precisely."

Half an hour later, after the hackney had made its way through the clogged streets of the more fashionable part of town, Harry alighted at the door of his town house. He bid Peter a good night and went up the steps.

Craddock, stifling a yawn, opened the door and informed his master that everyone else, including Lady Graystone, had retired for the evening.

Harry nodded and went into the library. He poured himself a small glass of brandy and went to the window. He stood gazing out into the shadowed garden for a long while, mulling over the evening's events.

When he had finished the brandy he crossed to the desk and frowned as he glanced down and saw a sheet of foolscap lying squarely in the center. It had obviously been placed where he could not fail to see it. The plump, curving handwriting was Augusta's.

SCHEDULE FOR THURSDAY:

1. *Morning:* Visit Hatchards and other booksellers to purchase books.
2. *Afternoon:* Observe Mr. Mitford's balloon ascent in park.

There was a brief note scrawled beneath the short list of activities. *I trust the above schedule meets with your approval.*

Harry wondered glumly if the paper would singe his fingers if he were to pick it up. The thing about his volatile Augusta, he reflected, was that one always knew what sort of mood she was in, even when she communicated in writing.

A large crowd had turned out in the park to observe Mr. Mitford's hot air balloon ascend into a cloudless blue summer sky. Meredith was enthralled from the moment she and Augusta arrived. She began asking questions at once and did not cease, although Augusta was hard put to answer most of them. That did not stop Meredith.

"What makes the balloon go up into the sky?"

"Well, sometimes hydrogen is used, but it is rather dangerous, I understand. Mr. Mitford is apparently using hot air today. The air inside the balloon is being heated by that big fire you see. The hot air will cause the balloon to rise. See those sacks of sand they are loading into the basket? Mr. Mitford will toss them overboard to make the craft lighter as the air in the balloon cools. That way he can keep traveling for an enormous distance."

"Will the people who go up in the balloon get hot as they get closer to the sun?"

"Actually," Augusta said, frowning slightly, "I have heard that they get quite chilled."

"How very odd. Why is that?"

"I have no notion, Meredith. You must ask your father that question."

"Can I go up in the balloon with Mr. Mitford and his crew?"

"No, dear, I fear Graystone would object very strongly to that plan." Augusta smiled wistfully. "Although it would be a very fine adventure indeed, would it not?"

"Oh, yes. Lovely." Meredith gazed rapturously at the brightly colored silk balloon.

Excitement mounted steadily around the basket as the huge balloon was filled with hot air. Ropes trailed everywhere, tethering the craft to the earth until it was time for the ascent. Mr. Mitford, a thin, energetic man, leaped about, shouting orders and giving directions to several sturdy young boys who were assisting him.

"Stand back, everyone," Mr. Mitford finally yelled in a commanding voice. He stood with two other people in the basket and waved the crowd away from the ropes. "Back, I say. Ho, lads, release the ropes."

The colorful balloon began to rise. The crowd roared approval and shouted encouragement.

Meredith was thrilled. "Look, Augusta. There it goes. Oh, how I would love to be going with them."

"So would I." Augusta tipped her head back and clung to the brim of her yellow straw bonnet as she watched the balloon rise.

When she first felt the tug on her skirts, she thought someone had bumped into her in the packed crowd. When the tug came a second time, however, she glanced down and saw a small urchin gazing up at her. He extended a grimy hand and offered her a small piece of folded paper.

"You be Lady Graystone?"

"Why, yes."

"This is for you." The lad shoved the paper into her fingers and dashed off through the throng.

"What on earth?" Augusta gazed down at the slip of paper. Meredith had noticed nothing. She was too busy cheering Mr. Mitford's bold crew.

Augusta opened the folded paper with a gathering sense of dread. The message inside was short and unsigned.

If you would learn the truth about your brother be in the lane behind your house at midnight tonight. Tell no one or you will never have the proof you seek.

"Augusta, this is truly the most wonderful thing I have ever seen," Meredith confided, her eyes still focused intently on the rising balloon. "Where are we going tomorrow?"

"Astley's Amphiteatre," Augusta murmured absently as

she dropped the note into her reticule. "According to the advertisement in the *Times*, we shall see astounding feats of horsemanship and some fireworks."

"That will be nice, but I do not think it will be as wonderful as this balloon ascent." Meredith turned to look at her at last as Mr. Mitford's balloon began to move off over the city. "Will Papa be able to come with us to Astley's?"

"I doubt it, Meredith. You know he has a great deal of business to attend to while we are in town. Remember, we are supposed to amuse ourselves."

Meredith smiled her slow, thoughtful smile. "We are doing that famously, are we not?"

"Famously."

Harry opened the door of his library as Augusta and Meredith swept into the hall of the town house. His eyes snagged Augusta's and he smiled slightly.

"Did you enjoy the balloon ascent?"

"It was most interesting and very educational," Augusta said coolly. All she could think about was the note in her reticule. She longed to rush upstairs and study it again in the privacy of her bedchamber.

"Oh, Papa, it was the most amazing thing," Meredith enthused. "Augusta bought me a beautiful souvenir handkerchief with a picture of Mr. Mitford's balloon on it. And she said you would explain why it is that the people sometimes get quite cold when they go up in a balloon, even though they are actually closer to the sun."

Harry cocked a brow and slanted an amused glance at Augusta while he replied to his daughter. "She said I would explain it, did she? What made her think I would know the answer to that?"

"Come, now, Graystone," Augusta chided. "You usually have all the answers, do you not?"

"Augusta—"

"Will you be going out again this evening, my lord?"

"Unfortunately, yes. I shall not be back until quite late."

"We will, of course, not wait up for you." Without waiting for a response, she started sedately up the stairs to her bedchamber. She glanced back over her shoulder and saw Meredith tug at her father's sleeve.

"Papa?"

"Come into the library for a few minutes, Meredith. I will attempt to answer your question."

Augusta heard the library door close. She picked up her skirts and ran the rest of the way to her bedchamber. As soon as she reached her sanctum, she sank down onto the chair behind the escritoire and yanked open her reticule. *If you would learn the truth about your brother . . .*

Perhaps, just this once, Graystone did not know all the answers. She would show him, Augusta vowed. She would produce the proof of her brother's innocence and confound Harry with her cleverness.

After careful consideration, Augusta decided the safest way out of the town house and into the night-shrouded garden was through the window of her husband's library.

The only other option was the back door, but that route would take her through the kitchens near the servants' quarters. There was too much chance she might awaken someone.

It was no trick to open the window of the darkened library and slip out into the garden. She had, after all, explored the route in reverse on the fateful evening when she had paid her midnight call on Harry.

Looking back, she was still amazed that Graystone had wanted to marry her after that hoydenish act. His sense of honor had no doubt tipped the balance when it came to making his decision.

Augusta dropped down onto the ground, leaving the window open behind her for a quick return. She gathered her dark cloak around her, pulled up the hood, and stood listening for a moment.

When she heard no sound she went cautiously toward the garden gate. One had to be careful about this sort of thing, she warned herself. She must keep her wits about her. She would question whoever was waiting in the lane very thoroughly. And she would make certain he kept his distance. She could always yell for help if necessary. The servants or the neighbors would hear.

She paused before opening the gate, straining to detect any sounds out in the lane. There was not even a whisper or footstep to be heard.

Augusta unlatched the gate and opened it carefully. The hinges squeaked in protest.

"Hello? Is anyone out there?"

There was no response. Down at the end of the lane the lights were shining in all of Lady Arbuthnott's windows, but the other nearby residences were in darkness. Carriage wheels clattered out in the street and moved off into the night.

"Hello?" Augusta peered anxiously into the deep shadows for a few minutes. "Please, are you there? I got your note, whoever you are. I want to talk to you."

She took a step out of the safety of the garden and her toe collided with a hard object on the ground.

"What in the world?" Automatically Augusta glanced down and saw a square shape lying on the paving stones. She started to step over the object and then realized it was a book of some sort. She bent down and picked it up.

As her hand closed around the leather-bound volume she heard the sudden ring of hooves on stone at the far end of the lane. She whirled about in time to see a horse and rider disappear around the corner.

Someone had been watching her from the shadows, she realized with a chill. Someone had hovered there in the darkness, waiting until she had retrieved the book, and then he had vanished.

For some reason, Augusta was suddenly very afraid, far more afraid than when she had set out on this adventure. She jumped back into the garden and hastily closed and latched the gate. Clutching the thin volume in one hand, she flew toward the safety of the house. The dark cloak swirled around her and as she ran her hair came loose from its pins.

By the time she reached the library window, she was breathing quickly. She tossed the volume over the sill onto the carpet, planted both hands on the stone wall, and hauled herself into a sitting position. Then she threw one leg over the sill and started to drop down onto the floor.

She froze as the lamp on the desk flared into life. "Oh, no."

Harry sat back in his chair and regarded her with hooded eyes and an unreadable expression. "Good evening, Augusta. I see you are paying another of your unconventional calls."

"*Harry.* Good God, I did not realize you were home. I thought you would be out late again tonight."

"Obviously. Why do you not come all the way into the library, madam? It cannot be terribly comfortable sitting in the window in that manner."

"I know what you must be thinking, my lord, but I can explain everything."

"And you most certainly will do precisely that. From inside the library."

Augusta eyed him warily as she slowly swung her other leg over the sill, arranged her skirts, and jumped down onto the carpet. She looked at the volume lying at her feet as she slowly removed her cloak. "I fear 'tis a rather unusual story, my lord."

"With you, it always is."

"Oh, Harry, are you very angry?"

"Very."

Her heart sank. "I was afraid of that." She stooped down and picked up the book.

"Sit down, Augusta."

"Yes, my lord." Dragging the cloak behind her in one hand, she went across the room to sit down on the other side of the desk. Her chin lifted as she prepared to defend herself. "I know this looks very bad, Graystone."

"It does, indeed. It would be amazingly easy, for example, for me to jump to the obvious conclusion that you are returning from some illicit midnight rendezvous with another man."

Augusta's eyes widened in horror. "Good heavens, Harry, 'tis nothing of that sort at all."

"I am, of course, relieved to hear it."

"Honestly, Harry, that would be a perfectly ridiculous assumption."

"It would?"

Augusta straightened her shoulders. "The thing is, my lord, I was conducting my own investigations."

"Into what?"

She frowned at his obtuseness. "My brother's death, of course."

"*The hell you were, madam.*" Harry sat forward swiftly, looking vastly more dangerous than he had a minute ago.

Augusta pressed herself back into the depths of her chair, alarmed by the sudden show of anger. "Well, yes. I was, as it happens."

"Damnation. I should have known. You are surely going to be the death of me, madam wife. Innocent fool that I am, I assumed you were merely taking a shortcut back through the gardens after a late visit to Pompeia's."

"Oh, no, it had nothing at all to do with Pompeia's. I went to meet a man, you see. Only he was not there. Rather, he was, but he did not show himself until—"

"You just told me this did not involve a man," Harry reminded her grimly.

"Not in the way I assumed you meant," she explained, trying to be patient. "There was no romantic rendezvous, you see. Let me tell you the whole story and then you will understand."

"I sincerely doubt that I will ever understand you, Augusta, but by all means, tell me this story. Please tell it quickly and succinctly, as my patience is hanging by a thread. That fact makes your situation extremely precarious, my dear."

"I see." She bit her lip, collecting her thoughts hurriedly. "Well, today at the balloon ascent a small boy thrust a note into my hand. The note said that if I would come out into the lane behind the house at midnight tonight I should have the truth about my brother. That is all there was to it."

" 'All there was to it.' Dear God in heaven." Harry closed his eyes and briefly lowered his head into his hands. "I am going to end up in Bedlam. I know I am going to end up there."

"Harry? Are you all right?"

"No, I am not all right. I just explained to you that I am in imminent danger of going mad." Harry shot to his feet and came around to the front of the desk. He stood there towering over Augusta, folded his arms across his chest, and fixed her with a cold stare. "We will take this one step at a time. Who had the note sent to you?"

"I do not know. As I said, whoever it was did not show himself out in the lane. But he was watching and waiting for me to pick up this book. As soon as I noticed it, he rode out of the lane and went down the street. I never got a close look at him."

"Let me see that book." Harry plucked it out of her lap and began leafing through it.

Augusta jumped up and craned her neck to get a glimpse of what had been written inside. She saw at once that it was filled with handwriting. " 'Tis a private journal of some sort."

"Yes, it is."

"Slow down, you are turning the pages too fast. I cannot read it."

"I doubt if you would understand the meaning, even if you could read it. 'Tis in code. An old one that was broken a long time ago."

"Really? Can you read it? What does it have to do with my brother? What do you think it means, Harry?"

"Please be quiet, Augusta. Sit down and give me a few minutes to examine it. I have not dealt with this particular code for quite some time."

Augusta obeyed, sitting very still, her hands laced tightly together in her lap as she eagerly awaited the results of her investigations.

Harry went back around behind his desk and sat down. He opened the volume to the first page and studied it with an intent expression. He turned the page and then he turned another. Finally he glanced at a few pages toward the end of the book.

After an excruciatingly long time, he closed the journal and raised his eyes to meet Augusta's. There was a new coldness in his gaze, an icy chill that went beyond anything she had ever seen in those crystal gray eyes.

"Well, my lord?" she whispered.

"It appears to be a record of coded dispatches sent with various couriers during the war. I recognize some of the dispatches mentioned because my agents intercepted them and I decoded them."

Augusta frowned. "But how does that relate to my brother?"

"This is a very personal journal, Augusta." Harry fingered the volume gently. "A private record meant for no one's eyes except the one who wrote in it."

"But who would that have been? Can you tell?"

"Only one man could have known about all of these dispatches and only one man could have known the names of all these couriers and French agents listed at the beginning. This journal must have once belonged to the Spider himself."

Augusta began to panic. "But, Harry *what does that have to do with my brother?*"

"It would appear, Augusta, based on this and some other evidence, that someone is trying to tell us that your brother was the Spider."

"*No, that is impossible.*" Augusta shot to her feet. "What you say is a lie."

"Please sit down, Augusta," Harry said quietly.

"I will not sit down." She took one step forward, planted her hands on the desk, and leaned toward him, willing him to believe her. "I do not care how much proof you produce. Do you hear me? My brother was no traitor. My lord, you must believe me. No Northumberland Ballinger would ever betray his country. Richard was not the Spider."

"As it happens, I am inclined to agree with you."

Dazed by his ready acceptance of Richard's innocence after all the damning evidence, Augusta sat down abruptly. "You agree with me? You do not believe that journal belonged to Richard? For it most certainly did not, my lord. It is not in his handwriting. I swear it is not."

"The handwriting proves nothing. An intelligent man would most certainly have developed a unique style of writing for the purposes of keeping a dangerous journal such as this."

"But Harry—"

"As it happens," Harry interrupted gently, "there are other reasons which make it difficult if not downright impossible to believe your brother was the Spider."

Augusta smiled slowly, aware of a deep surge of glorious relief. "I am glad, my lord. Thank you for believing in his honor. I cannot tell you how much this means to me. I shall never forget your kindness in this matter, and rest assured you shall have my everlasting gratitude and appreciation."

Harry regarded her silently for a moment, his fingers drumming absently on the leather-bound volume. "Naturally, I am pleased to hear you say that, madam." He put the journal into his desk drawer and turned the key in the lock as he spoke.

"'Tis true, Harry." Augusta's smile grew brilliant. Then she cleared her throat delicately. "Given the evidence of that horrid poem and this journal, plus your tendency to prefer logic to blind faith, however, I do have a question."

"Yes?"

"May I ask precisely why you are so ready to believe Richard was not the Spider?" She waited in unbearable suspense to see if Harry would admit that it was his affection for her that had swayed his opinion.

"The answer is obvious, Augusta."

"Yes, my lord?" She beamed at him.

"I have been living with a Northumberland Ballinger for some weeks now and I have come to know the habits and characteristics of the breed rather well. And as I have been assured that all Northumberland Ballingers share a number of traits—" He broke off with a shrug.

Augusta was beginning to get confused. "Yes, Harry? Pray continue."

"Allow me to be blunt, madam. No Northumberland Ballinger would be at all likely to have the temperament suited to a brilliant spymaster who managed to escape detection for years and whose identity is still unknown."

"Temperament, Harry? Whatever does that mean?"

"It means," Harry said, "that the average Northumberland Ballinger, which your brother evidently was from all accounts, is *too damned emotional, too rash, too indiscreet, too impetuous, and too bloody idiotic* to make a halfway decent spy, let alone a master of spies."

"Oh," said Augusta, blinking as she absorbed the unexpected response. And then the depths of the insult struck home. She leaped to her feet again, incensed. "How dare you say such things? How dare you? Apologize at once, sir."

"Do not be ridiculous. One does not apologize for the truth."

Augusta stared at him in mounting fury. "Then you leave me no option, my lord. You have insulted my family one too many times. As the last of the Northumberland Ballingers, I demand satisfaction for your slanderous remarks."

Harry stared at her in amazement. Then he got slowly to his feet behind his desk. When he spoke his voice was lethally soft. "I beg your pardon?"

"You heard me, sir." Augusta was trembling with her outrage, but she kept her chin high. "I hereby challenge you to a duel. Your choice of weapons, of course." She scowled as Harry continued to fix her with a stunned look. "You are allowed the choice in this instance, are you not? I understand that is how it is done. I issue the challenge, you choose the weapons. Is that not correct?"

"Correct, madam?" Harry started around the desk. "Yes, that is definitely the correct form for a duel. In fact, as the one who is being challenged, I demand the right to choose not only the weapons, but the location of this appointment."

"Harry?" Alarmed by the unrelenting expression in his eyes as he came toward her, Augusta began to edge backward. "My lord, what do you think you are doing?"

Harry reached her just as Augusta was thinking it might be very smart to turn and run for the door. She took another step backward, but she was too late.

Harry scooped her up as though she were a sack of flour and tossed her over his shoulder. He stalked toward the door, opened it, and carried Augusta out into the hall.

"Good grief, Harry. Stop this at once." Augusta pounded on his broad back. She kicked out wildly, but he clamped his arm around her thighs, anchoring her.

"You wanted a duel, madam; you shall have one. We shall use the weapons with which nature has already endowed each of us and the field of honor shall be my bed.

I assure you there will be no quarter given until you beg for it."

"Damnation, Harry. This is not what I intended at all."

"That is unfortunate for you."

Harry was halfway up the stairs with Augusta when Craddock emerged from the direction of the servants' hall. The butler was struggling hastily into his jacket. His shirt still hung open and he was carrying his shoes. He stared at his master and mistress in astonishment.

"I heard a commotion, your lordship," Craddock stammered, looking distinctly uncomfortable. "Is aught amiss?"

"Not a thing, Craddock," Harry assured him as he stalked on up the stairs with Augusta over his shoulder. "Lady Graystone and I are merely on our way to bed. See to the lamps."

"Of course, your lordship."

Augusta caught a glimpse of Craddock's face as Harry carried her around the corner at the top of the stairs. The butler was struggling valiantly to stifle a great shout of laughter. She groaned in disgust.

Harry dismissed his valet with a single word as he strode into his bedroom. "Out."

The man vanished, closing the door behind him, but not before Augusta had seen the grin on his face. She shot Harry a withering glance as he dumped her lightly down onto the bed.

When he sat down next to her and began removing his boots, Augusta sat up hurriedly. Her fury had already begun to fade and common sense was returning quickly. She was well aware that what she had said downstairs in the library had been utterly beyond the pale.

"Harry, I am sorry I made that wild challenge. I realize it truly was outside the limit for a wife to do such a thing, but you do have a way of infuriating me."

"That is nothing compared to the effect you have on my temper, madam." The second boot hit the floor. Harry stood up and started to strip off the remainder of his clothing.

Augusta saw that he was already fully aroused. She felt the familiar warmth begin to twist and curl in her lower body. *I love him so,* she thought resentfully. It really was most unfair that he had such power over her.

"Now, madam wife, we shall begin the duel." Harry came down onto the bed and pushed the skirts of her gown and petticoats up to her waist with one swift motion. His hand clamped boldly on her thigh and his eyes gleamed as he bent over her.

"And will you apologize if I win?" she whispered as her skin warmed under his touch.

"There will be no apologies from me, madam. But you demanded satisfaction and I swear you shall have it. Of course, I shall also have mine."

His mouth covered hers as he crushed her beneath him.

18

Augusta stirred in the big bed, aware of the hard, solid, disturbingly masculine body beside her. The heavy scent of the recent lovemaking hovered in the air and her body was still damp.

She opened her eyes and saw a pale moon outside the window. Slowly she stretched out her legs, wincing at the slight soreness in her thigh muscles. It was always this way after Harry had made love to her. She felt as though she had ridden a blooded stallion long and hard. *Or perhaps it was she who had been ridden*. She smiled to herself.

"Augusta?"

"Yes, Harry?" She turned on her side and propped her elbows on his bare chest.

"There is something I would know about this night's work."

"And what is that, my lord?" She twined her fingers in the crisp mat of hair on his chest. It was amazing how what they shared together in bed could affect both their moods, she reflected. For example, she was no longer feeling at all belligerent and defensive.

"Why did you not come to me immediately with that note the lad handed you this afternoon? Why did you try to keep such a dangerous rendezvous on your own?"

Augusta sighed. "I doubt that you would understand, Harry."

"Try me."

"Even if you do understand, you will doubtless not approve."

"You have the right of it on that point. But tell me why you did not come to me with that note, Augusta," he ordered gently. "Was it because you feared the information you would be given would be evidence against your brother?"

"Oh, no," she said quickly. "Just the opposite, in fact. I assumed from the note that it would be the proof I needed to remove the cloud of suspicion that hangs over Richard's name."

"Then why did you not confide in me? You knew I would be interested in whatever transpired tonight."

She stopped toying with his chest hair. "I wanted to show you that I could be as useful and helpful in your investigations as your close friends."

"Sally and Sheldrake?" Harry frowned. "That was most foolish, Augusta. They have had a great deal of experience at this kind of thing. They know how to take care of themselves. You know nothing about conducting an investigation."

"But that is just it." She sat up beside him. "I want to learn. I want to be part of your circle of truly close friends, the ones with whom you share your deepest thoughts. I want to have the kind of bond with you that Sally and Peter do."

"Hell, Augusta, you are my wife," Harry muttered, exasperated. "Our bond is far more intimate than any I share with Sally or Peter Sheldrake, I assure you."

"The only time I feel truly close to you is when we are in bed together as we are now. And that is not enough, because even then there is a distance between us."

"There is no distance at all between us at such times, madam." He smiled as he stroked a hand down over her hip. "Or need I remind you?"

She wriggled away from his touch. "But there is a kind of distance because you do not love me. You only feel some physical passion for me. It is not at all the same thing."

His brow rose. "You are an expert on the difference?"

"I expect every woman is an expert on the difference between passion and love," Augusta retorted. "'Tis no doubt an instinct."

"Are we going to get ourselves mired again in that useless argument with all its confounded feminine logic?"

"No." Augusta leaned forward eagerly. "'Tis just that I have decided if I cannot have your love, Harry, I would have your friendship. Your *close* friendship. I want to be a part of your inner circle of companions. The ones with whom you share everything. Do you not understand, my lord?"

"No, I do not understand. You are not making sense."

"I want to feel as though I belong to your special circle of intimates. Do you not see, my lord? It would be like being part of your real family."

"Damnation, Augusta, you are talking a lot of emotional nonsense. Hear me well, wife, you are most certainly a part of this family." He caught hold of her chin, his eyes intent. "And do not ever forget that fact, madam. You are not, however, a trained intelligence agent and I will not have you playing dangerous games the way you did tonight. Is that quite clear?"

"But I did a good job, Harry. Admit it. I brought you some very interesting evidence. Only think, my lord. Someone went to all that trouble just to make us think that the Spider was my brother and has therefore been dead for two whole years. That raises some interesting possibilities, does it not?"

His mouth twisted wryly. "Indeed it does. The most interesting of which is that the Spider is no doubt very much alive and wants everyone to think him dead. Which leads us to the conclusion that he may presently be enjoying a position as an accepted member of Society and wants to continue living his new life. He clearly has a great deal to lose now if the truth about his past should emerge. And that makes him more dangerous than ever."

Augusta considered that closely. "Yes, I see what you mean."

"The more I reflect on tonight's event's, my dear, the more I believe you had a very close brush with disaster. I have only myself to blame."

Augusta grew alarmed. She was learning that whenever Harry got that tone in his voice, he usually started issuing orders. "Oh, pray, do not blame yourself, my lord. It was an accident and will most certainly not happen again. The next time I receive a strange note I shall come straight to you with it, I swear."

He eyed her morosely. "We shall take steps to ensure that you do so, Augusta. You and Meredith are not to leave this house without either myself as an escort or at least two footmen in attendance. I shall choose the servants I wish to accompany you and I shall inform Craddock you are not to go anywhere without them."

"Very well, my lord." Augusta heaved a sigh of relief. It was not as bad as it could have been, she told herself. He could have gone so far as forbidding her to leave the house without him. As he was rarely available these days, that would have meant virtual imprisonment for herself and Meredith. She congratulated herself on a narrow escape.

"Do I make myself clear, madam?"

Augusta inclined her head acquiescently, as a dutiful wife should. "Very clear, my lord."

"And furthermore," Harry added deliberately, "you are not to go out at night, with or without the footmen, unless I am with you."

That was too much. Augusta promptly fought back. "Harry, you go too far. I assure you Meredith and I will take an entire brigade of footmen with us at all times if that is your wish, but you cannot confine us to the house every evening."

"I am sorry, Augusta," he said, not ungently. "But I will not be able to concentrate on my investigations if I am not assured you are safe at home."

"Then you can be the one to tell your daughter that she cannot go to Astley's Amphitheatre tomorrow night," Augusta announced.

"You were planning to take her to Astley's?" Harry frowned. "I am not at all certain that would have been a particularly sound choice of entertainment. Astley's is famous for its silly spectacles and melodrama. Women flying about on horseback and that sort of thing. Not particularly elevating or educational for a young child, do you think?"

"I think," Augusta said bluntly, "that Meredith will enjoy it immensely. *And so will I.*"

"Well, in that case, I believe I can adjust my schedule to allow me to escort the two of you to Astley's tomorrow evening," Harry said smoothly.

Augusta was caught completely off balance by the unexpected capitulation. "You will?"

"Pray do not look so astounded, my dear. As the victor in our duel tonight, I can afford to be generous to the loser."

"Victor? Who named you the victor?" Augusta grabbed the pillow and began pummeling him unmercifully with it.

Harry's laughter was husky and liberally laced with masculine passion.

The entertainment at Astley's was not nearly as dull as Harry had feared. It was not, however, the ladies dashing about on horseback, the music, or the inane melodrama with its fireworks and singing heroes that held his serious attention. What held Harry's gaze was the sight of his wife and daughter leaning precariously out of the box to watch the proceedings below.

Augusta had been right about one thing. Meredith was enjoying herself to the hilt. It struck Harry again just how much his overly serious daughter had blossomed during the past few weeks. It was as if she were discovering the pleasures of childhood for the first time.

The sight made him do something he rarely did, and that was to doubt the wisdom of one of his own carefully considered decisions. It occurred to Harry that the strict educational curriculum he had ordained for Meredith during the past few years might have been a bit severe. Perhaps he had not allowed for enough harmless fun and play in the schedule.

Harry watched Meredith gasp with amazement as a young lady in the ring below vaulted over a barrier of several scarves and landed safely on the rump of a galloping pony. It was obvious his daughter was thriving under the new regime, he thought ruefully. He would be lucky indeed if she did not develop aspirations to take a balloon voyage or join Astley's troop of daring bareback riders.

His gaze shifted to his wife, who was pointing out the villain of the piece to Meredith. The brilliant glow from the huge chandelier suspended over the center of the stage caught the rich highlights in Augusta's hair. The words she had spoken to him so beseechingly last night rang in his ears. *I want to feel as though I belong* . . .

He knew she was still struggling with the feeling of not being part of a family like the one she had once known. She was the last of the Northumberland Ballingers and she had been feeling very much alone since her brother's death. He understood that now.

But how could Augusta not realize just how much a part of his small family she had become? Harry wondered. Surely she saw how Meredith was becoming increasingly dependent on her. True, the child did not yet seem inclined to call Augusta Mother, but that no longer seemed quite so important to Harry.

Augusta's tendency to agitate herself because her husband did not get down on his knees and proclaim his everlasting love was ridiculous. A typical example of her overly emotional nature. As far as Harry was concerned he had more than amply demonstrated his affections. And his trust. Harry scowled, thinking of just how indulgent he had been with his new countess.

Any other man who had witnessed a wife climbing back into the house through a window at midnight would have assumed he had just been cuckolded.

Last night Augusta should have been begging for forgiveness and vowing to never again pursue adventure. Instead, she had lost her temper and challenged her husband to a duel.

The woman had been reading too many novels, that was the problem.

I want to have the kind of bond with you that Sally and Peter do.

Naturally he had excluded her from the investigations, Harry thought. Not only because she lacked experience, which was reason enough, but because he had not wanted her troubled by further indications of her brother's connection to the case.

Now Harry wondered if he had a right to keep Augusta out of the investigation. Like it or not, she was involved because her brother had apparently been involved. Perhaps the last of the Northumberland Ballingers had a right to know the truth.

Harry listened to the music swell as the performance below came to a conclusion. Horses and actors both took their bows to several rounds of enthusiastic applause.

Meredith talked nonstop in the carriage on the way back to the town house.

"Papa, do you think I could learn to ride a horse the way the lady in pink did?"

"I do not think you would find the skill particularly useful," Harry said, his eyes flicking to Augusta's amused face. "One rarely is called upon to ride standing up on top of a horse."

Meredith frowned at that logic. "I suppose not." Then she brightened again. "Was it not exciting when the pony rescued the lady?"

"Very."

"What part did you like best, Papa?"

Harry smiled slowly, his eyes again on Augusta. "The scenery."

As the carriage came to a halt in front of the town house, Harry touched Augusta's arm. "Stay a moment, if you please." He glanced at Meredith. "Go on inside, Meredith. Augusta will be along in a moment."

"Yes, Papa." Meredith hopped down from the carriage and started to regale the footman with details of the thrilling performance she had just witnessed.

Augusta gave Harry an inquiring glance. "Yes, my lord?"

He hesitated and then took the plunge. "I am going on to meet Sheldrake at one of my clubs."

"More investigations, I suppose."

"Yes. However, the three of us—Sally, Sheldrake, and myself—have arranged to hold a conference much later tonight. We are going to discuss everything we know about the investigation so far and see if we can find some answers. You may join us if you like."

Augusta's eyes widened. "Oh, Harry. Truly?"

"You have some rights in this matter, my dear. Perhaps I have been wrong to exclude you."

"My lord, how can I ever thank you?"

"Well, I—umph." Harry was taken by surprise as Augusta threw her arms around him.

She hugged him ecstatically even though the door of the

carriage stood wide open and at least one groom and a footman had a full view of the interior.

"What time shall I expect you back here, Harry?"

"Uh, somewhere around three o'clock this morning." He gently untwined her arms from around his neck, aware that his body was already reacting to the soft, round contours of hers. "Be in the library. We shall take the shortcut through the garden."

"I will be there." Her smile was more brilliant than the lights over the stage at Astley's.

Harry waited until she was safely inside the house and then he signaled his coachman to drive on to the club, where he was to meet Peter. As the vehicle moved off, Harry tried to assure himself that he was doing the right thing by allowing Augusta into the heart of the small group involved in the investigation.

He might be doing the right thing, but he was definitely going against his own better judgment. Harry gazed thoughtfully out the window, aware of a deep sense of unease.

Peter Sheldrake, stylish as always in trousers and an elaborately ruffled shirt, was just coming out of the card room when Harry walked into the club. He was carrying a bottle of claret, which he waved cheerfully at Harry.

"Oh-ho. I see you have survived the evening's frivolity. Come join me in a glass or two and tell me all about the wondrous sights you must have seen at Astley's. Took a couple of nephews there once a few years back. It was all I could do to keep them from signing on with the bareback riding troop."

Harry smiled reluctantly as he followed Peter to a private corner of the room and sat down. "I was concerned I might face a similar problem myself. And it was not just Meredith I feared losing to the stage. I have a suspicion that Augusta was entertaining dreams of glory, too."

"Well, look at it from her point of view," Peter said with a mocking grin. "Being the Countess of Graystone probably seems rather dull compared to the notion of performing daring feats of horsemanship in front of a cheering crowd. Think of the applause. Think of the cheers. Think of the gentlemen leering down from the upper boxes."

Harry grimaced. "Don't remind me. As it happens, however, Augusta's life is about to become a bit more exciting."

"Oh?" Peter took a swallow of claret. "How is that? Are you going to allow her to go about without a fichu to fill in the neckline of her gowns? What a thrill that will be for her."

Harry shot Peter a brief, quelling glare and wondered glumly if perhaps he had been something of a tyrant about Augusta's gowns. "We shall see how you feel about the subject of your wife's choice of necklines after you are married."

"So we shall." Peter chuckled.

"What I was going to tell you about Augusta's exciting new life is that she will be joining you and me and Sally later tonight when we have our meeting."

Sheldrake sputtered and frantically swallowed claret. He stared at Harry. "Bloody hell. You're going to allow her to get involved in this thing? Do you think that's wise, Graystone?"

"Probably not."

"With everything pointing toward her brother, it's bound to be painful for her."

"It's obvious Ballinger was involved in this mess somehow. But trust me, Sheldrake, when I tell you that there's no way he could have been the Spider."

"If you say so." Peter looked sceptical.

"I do. What we have now are strong indications that someone very much wants us to believe the Spider died two years ago." Harry quickly ran through a description of the journal Augusta had found in the lane behind the town house.

"Good God," Sheldrake breathed. "The journal is real? Not a fake that someone fixed up to trick us?"

"I am certain it is real. I will tell you truthfully, Sheldrake, it gives me a cold chill to think about who may have been watching Augusta in that lane last night."

"I see what you mean."

Harry was about to discuss the details of what he had discovered in the journal when he realized that Lovejoy was crossing the room to join them. The man's green eyes glittered with bored menace.

So many bored and dangerous men floating about London like so much flotsam after the storm of war, Harry thought.

"Good evening, Graystone. Sheldrake. I am surprised to find you both here tonight. Would have thought you'd have been dancing attendance on your ladies. Congratulations on your engagement, by the way, Sheldrake. Although, I must say, it was rather unsporting of you to remove one of the few viable heiresses from the scene. Not much left for the rest of us to choose from, hmmm?"

"I am certain you will find one to your taste," Peter murmured.

Harry turned the half-empty glass of claret in his hand, studying the ruby highlights. "Was there something you wanted, Lovejoy?"

"As a matter of fact, there was. Thought I'd warn you both that there's a master cracksman operating in Town these days. Broke into my library a few weeks ago."

Harry looked at him without expression. "Is that so? Did you report the loss to the magistrate?"

"Nothing was taken that cannot easily be replaced." Lovejoy smiled coldly, turned, and left.

Harry and Peter sat in meditative silence for a few minutes.

"You may have to do something about Lovejoy," Peter finally observed.

"Yes, it would appear so." Harry shook his head. "The only thing I do not understand is why he has settled on me as his target."

"In the beginning, he was probably simply intent on seducing Augusta for the hell of it. But now he has no doubt reasoned out that you ruined his little game by breaking into his library to get Augusta's vowels. He would no doubt like to even the score. He has not had the opportunity because you have been out of town for the past few weeks."

"I shall keep an eye on him."

"Do that. I would assume from his not-so-veiled threats that he will try to use Augusta to gain his revenge."

Harry thought about that as he finished his claret. "I still believe there is more in this Lovejoy business than meets the eye. Perhaps it is time I paid another late-night visit to his library."

"I shall go with you. It might prove interesting." Peter grinned slowly. "But surely you do not intend to try anything like that tonight. Your schedule is already rather crowded this evening."

"You are quite right. Some other evening when I am free. We have other important business tonight."

Augusta was pacing the library when Harry and Peter arrived. She had dressed appropriately for the adventure. She was wearing a black velvet cloak over her black gown, a pair of matching black gloves, and black velvet half boots. She had chosen the boots because she thought they would stand up to a tramp through the garden and down the lane better than her pumps or slippers.

She had sent the staff to bed hours ago and had been fidgeting with excitement ever since. The significance of being invited to join Harry and his friends tonight nearly overwhelmed her. *She had gained admission to his special circle at last.*

Augusta realized she was at last going to share with Harry that wonderful close friendship he shared with Sally and Peter. Together they would solve a mystery and Harry would see that Augusta could do her part. He would learn to respect her cleverness, she promised herself. He would start to see her as one of his true friends, a woman he could trust and with whom he shared the secret aspect of himself.

The soft sound of the door opening and closing in the hall brought Augusta to a halt. There was a murmur of men's voices and the sound of booted feet on the tile. She whirled around quickly and ran to the library door. When she opened it she found a dour-looking Harry and a grinning Peter Sheldrake.

Peter sketched a gallant bow. "Good evening, madam. May I be allowed to tell you how perfectly attired you are for this evening's event? The black velvet cloak and boots are extremely dashing. Does she not look splendidly dressed for this sort of thing, Graystone?"

Harry scowled. "She looks like a damn highwayman. Let us be off." He motioned both of them out the door with his ebony cane. "I want to get this over as quickly as possible."

"Are we not going to go out through the library window?" Augusta asked.

"No, we are not. We are going to go out through the kitchens in a normal, reasonably civilized manner."

Augusta wrinkled her nose at Peter as they followed Harry out of the library. "Does he always get like this when he is involved in an investigation?"

"Always," Peter assured her. "Quite a killjoy, our Graystone. No sense of adventure."

Harry threw his companions a quelling glance over his shoulder. "Be still, both of you. I do not want to waken the staff."

"Yes, sir," Peter murmured.

"Yes, sir," Augusta whispered.

The trio made their way safely out into the garden without incident and found they did not need a lamp to light the route down the lane. There was enough moonlight to reveal the paving stones, and the warm glow from the upstairs windows of Lady Arbuthnott's house served as a beacon.

As they drew closer to their goal, Augusta noticed that the downstairs of the big house was dark. "Will Sally be waiting for us at the kitchen door, then?"

"Yes," Peter said softly. "She'll take us into her library and we will talk there."

When they reached the gate of Lady Arbuthnott's garden, Harry paused. "It's open."

"No doubt she sent a servant out earlier to unlatch it for us," Peter said, pushing at the heavy gate. "I do not think she has the strength to walk this far on her own anymore, poor dear."

"I am amazed she can continue to operate Pompeia's," Augusta whispered.

"'Tis all that keeps her going. That and the pleasure of being involved in one last investigation for Graystone, of course," Peter confided.

"Silence," Harry ordered.

Augusta clutched the folds of her cloak around her and followed Harry in dutiful silence. Peter brought up the rear of the short column.

Because she was directly behind him, Augusta nearly collided with Harry when he came to an abrupt halt.

"Ooomph." She caught her balance. "Harry? What is it?"

"Something is wrong." There was a deadly flat quality in Harry's voice which alarmed Augusta as nothing else could have done. She realized he was grasping his ebony walking stick in a rather odd manner.

"Trouble?" Peter spoke softly in the shadows, all trace of banter gone from his voice.

"The back door is standing open. There is no light and no sign of Sally. Take Augusta back to the house. Rejoin me once you have seen her safely inside."

"Understood." Peter reached out to take Augusta's arm.

Augusta sidestepped him hurriedly. "Harry, no, please let me come with you. Sally might have become gravely ill. Perhaps that is why—" Augusta cried out as her toe tangled in the hem of a woman's gown that had drifted out from beneath a clump of bushes. "Oh, dear God, no. *Sally*."

"Augusta? What the hell—" Harry spun around and started toward her.

Augusta was already on her knees, crawling frantically beneath the heavy foliage. "'Tis Sally. Oh, Harry, I know 'tis her. She must have collapsed out here. *Sally*."

Augusta touched her friend's body, fumbling with Sally's expensive silk gown. Her black gloves were instantly soaked in warm blood. A shaft of starlight gleamed dully on the hilt of the dagger that was still buried in Sally's breast.

"Goddamn his bloody soul." Harry's voice was savage as he tore his way through the bushes and dropped down beside his old friend. He groped for Sally's wrist and felt for a pulse. "She lives."

"Christ." Peter found his way to Sally's side. He stared at the dagger and swore again. "The goddamned son of a bitch."

"Sally?" Augusta grasped the limp hand and was horrified by the cold feel of it. Sally was dying. That was a certainty.

"Augusta? Is that you, dear?" Sally's voice was barely a whisper of sound. "I am glad. Glad you are here. 'Tis not pleasant to die alone, you know. 'Tis the one thing I feared."

"We are all here, Sally," Harry said quietly. "Peter and Augusta and I. You are not alone."

"My friends." Sally's eyes closed. "'Tis better this way. The pain was getting so bad. So bad. I did not think I could go on much longer, you know. Still, I would have preferred to do the thing myself."

Tears started in Augusta's eyes. She gripped Sally's hand

fiercely, as if she could hold on to her through sheer physical strength.

"Sally, who did this?" Harry asked. "The Spider?"

"Oh, yes. It must have been him. Never saw his face. But he knew about the list. Knew I had it. Got it from the cook."

"What cook?" Peter asked gently.

"Cook at the old Saber Club. Got it this morning from him."

"Damn the Spider's bloody soul to hell," Harry whispered. "I will see that he pays for this, Sally."

"Yes, I know, Graystone. This time you shall have him. Always knew that one day you would settle accounts with the Spider." Sally started to cough dreadfully.

Augusta held on to the frail hand more tightly, the tears spilling down her face to mingle with her friend's blood. Once before she had held someone like this and watched helplessly as the life within dwindled to a tiny flame and then flickered and went out. There was no more terrible task in the world than this kind of vigil.

"Augusta?"

"Sally, I shall miss you so," Augusta said through her tears. "You have truly been my friend."

"And you have been a true friend to me, my dearest Augusta. You have given me more than you will ever know. Now you must let me go. 'Tis past time."

"Sally?"

"Do not forget to open the book, Augusta."

"No. I will not forget."

And then Sally was gone.

19

*H*arry held Augusta as she sobbed in his arms. He could think of no way to comfort her and nothing hurt as much as not being able to alleviate her pain. This overflowing emotion was no doubt the way a Northumberland Ballinger dealt with grief and he envied Augusta the release of tears. For himself, he could do nothing but plot revenge.

Unable to do anything else, Harry closed his arms tightly around Augusta there in the hall of the big, silent Arbuthnott mansion and willed the storm to pass.

And he forced himself to think only of vengeance.

Augusta was calming slightly when Harry looked over her head and spotted Peter coming through the back door.

"It looks like he had time to search her bedroom and the library," Peter said. "Both rooms are a shambles. But the other rooms are still in good order. He must have heard someone or something and left before he had time to finish the job. Probably decided that with Sally dead, no one else would be able to find the list, either."

"It's a big house. Difficult to search thoroughly. Have you taken care of everything else?" Harry asked quietly.

Peter nodded, his blue eyes chips of ice. "Yes. One of the servants has gone to summon the magistrate. I've had Sally's body taken to one of the bedrooms. God, she was frail, Graystone. There was nothing left of her. She must have been living on spirit and willpower alone for the past few weeks."

Augusta stirred in Harry's arms and raised her head. "I shall miss her so."

"We all will." Harry stroked Augusta's back soothingly. "I shall always be extremely grateful to her."

"Because she was so brave during the war?" Augusta blinked back the tears and dabbed her eyes with Harry's handkerchief.

"No, although I have always admired her courage. The reason I shall forever be grateful to her is that it was she who suggested I arrange to meet you by contacting Sir Thomas. Sally said you should be added to my list of potential wives," Harry said candidly.

Augusta looked up, startled. "She did? How very odd. Why on earth would she think I would make you a good wife?"

Harry smiled faintly. "I asked her that question myself, as I recall. She said I would do better with a wife who was not in the classical style."

Peter closed the door. "Sally understood you very well, Graystone."

"Yes, I rather believe she did." Harry gently put Augusta a little away from him. "My friends, we must do our grieving later. The authorities will assume Sally's murder was perpetrated by thieves who attempted to break into the house. There is no point in letting them think otherwise."

"Agreed," Peter said. "Nothing they could do in any event."

"We must find the list Sally mentioned." Harry glanced

down the hall, thinking how huge the house was and how long it was going to take to go through it properly. "I know something of Sally's methods for hiding items she did not want discovered. She tended to choose the obvious places, on the grounds that no one would think to look in them."

Augusta sniffed into the handkerchief. "The book."

Harry glanced at her. "What book is that?"

"Pompeia's betting book." Augusta bravely thrust the wet handkerchief deep into a pocket in her cloak and started down the hall to the drawing room. "Sally told me that if I ever found it closed, I must make certain you open it. And you heard her a few minutes ago just before she . . . she died. She said I must not forget the book."

Harry exchanged a glance with Peter, who simply shrugged and prepared to follow Augusta.

The door to Pompeia's was closed. Harry heard Augusta start to weep again as she opened it, but she did not hesitate. She walked into the dark, silent room and lit a lamp.

Harry glanced around, curious in spite of himself. He had visited Sally frequently, but she had never entertained him here in the drawing room after it had been turned into Pompeia's. The club was for women only, she had said. She could not violate the rules, even after hours.

"Gives a man an odd feeling, doesn't it?" Peter kept his voice down as he came to a halt next to Harry. "I was never allowed past the threshold, you know. But I always felt a little uncomfortable when I got a good look inside from the door."

"I see what you mean." Harry studied the shadowed pictures on the wall. He recognized many of them at once. They were all women who had managed to survive in myth and legend in spite of what Augusta called the general historical bias against females. Harry was beginning to wonder just how much history had been lost because it had pertained to women and had therefore been deemed unimportant.

"Makes a man curious about what females get up to and what they actually talk about when they are on their own together with no men around," Peter observed quietly. "Sally always said I'd be surprised if I knew."

"She used to tell me I'd be shocked," Harry admitted wryly.

He watched the black velvet cloak swirl around Augusta as she walked over to a Greek pedestal. There was a large, leather-bound volume lying on top.

"This is the notorious betting book?" Harry walked across the room to join Augusta.

"Yes. And it is closed. Just as she said I might someday find it." Augusta opened the volume slowly and started turning the pages. "I do not know what I am searching for."

Harry glanced at some of the entries, all in feminine handwriting.

Miss L.B. wagers Miss R.M. ten pounds that the latter will not get her journal returned in time to avert disaster.

Miss B.R. wagers Miss D.N. five pounds that Lord G will ask for the Angel's hand within the month.

Miss F.O. wagers Miss C.P. ten pounds that Miss A.B. will cry off her engagement to Lord G. within two months.

"Good God," Harry muttered. "So much for a man thinking he has some privacy."

"The ladies of Pompeia's are very fond of wagers, my lord." Augusta sniffed again. "The club will close now, I suppose. I shall miss it. It was a home to me. Nothing will ever be the same here."

Harry was about to remind Augusta that she did not need Pompeia's because she had a home of her own when a piece of notepaper fluttered between two pages of the book.

"Let me see that." He snatched it up and examined the list of names.

Peter came forward to peer over his shoulder while Augusta craned her head to get a peek.

"Well?" Peter demanded.

"It's a list of names, all right. No doubt a partial membership list of the Saber Club. This is Sally's writing."

Peter scowled at the list. "I do not recognize any of those names."

"Hardly surprising." Harry pulled the lamp closer and studied the list more closely. "It's in the old code Sally was accustomed to use for her messages to me."

"How long will it take you to decode all those names?" Peter asked. "There must be at least ten there."

"Not long. But after we know who the members were, it will take some time to determine which ones could possibly be the Spider." Harry folded the paper and stuck it safely into his pocket. "Let us be off. We have much to do before dawn."

"What do you want me to do?" Augusta asked quickly.

Harry smiled grimly and readied himself for the battle ahead. "You must go home and awaken the household. Then you will see that you and Meredith are packed and ready to leave for Dorset by seven o'clock."

She stared up at him. "Seven o'clock this morning? But Harry, I do not want to leave town now that we are so close to finding Sally's killer and the identity of the Spider. You must let me stay."

"There is not a chance of me allowing you to stay. Not now that the Spider is aware of this list and will stop at nothing to get it." Harry took her arm and hauled her toward the door. "Peter, perhaps your fiancée would enjoy a short stay in Dorset?"

"I think that would be an excellent notion," Peter replied. "God knows I would just as soon she was out of town until we find the Spider, and I am certain Augusta would like the company."

"I do wish the two of you would cease making plans for me as though I were not able to think for myself," Augusta said loudly. "I do not want to go to Dorset."

"But you will," Harry said calmly.

"Harry, please—"

He thought fast, searching for the most effective lever to use in this argument. When he found it, he applied it mercilessly. "It is not just your own pretty neck I am worried about, Augusta. There is Meredith to consider. I must be certain my daughter is safe. We are dealing with a monster and we do not know to what depths he will sink."

Augusta was clearly thunderstruck by the implications. "You believe he might threaten Meredith? But why would he do that, my lord?"

"Is it not obvious? If the Spider reasons I am the one trying to find him, he could use Meredith to get at me."

"Oh, yes. I see what you mean. Your daughter is your one great weakness. He might know that."

You are wrong about that, Augusta. I have two great weaknesses. You are the other, Harry thought. He said nothing aloud, however. Let her think his chief concern was Meredith and that he was depending on her to take care of his daughter. It was her nature to go to the rescue and defend the innocent. "Please, Augusta. I need your help. I must know Meredith is safely out of the city before I can concentrate on finding the Spider."

"Yes, of course." She looked at him, her eyes grave with the acknowledgment of her responsibility. "I will guard her with my life, Harry."

Harry touched her cheek gently. "And you will take excellent care of yourself, too, hmmm?"

"Certainly."

"You and Meredith shall have a little help," Harry said. "I am sending you down to Dorset with an armed escort. The men will stay with you at Graystone until I get down there myself."

"An armed escort. Whatever does that mean, Harry?" Augusta was clearly startled.

"Less exciting than it sounds. I shall send a couple of grooms with you who have been in my service a long while. They both will be armed and they will know what to do if there is any trouble."

"She'll be safe enough at Graystone," Peter said. "In the country everyone knows everyone else and a stranger in the district will be noticed immediately. And then there are the dogs. No stranger will be able to get into the house without the dogs sounding an alarm."

"Exactly." Harry looked at Augusta. "And you will have Claudia for company."

Augusta smiled slightly. "I would not count on that. I seriously doubt that my cousin can be ready to travel by seven o'clock this morning."

"She will be ready," Peter vowed softly. "I want her out of Town as badly as Harry wants you out."

Augusta eyed him thoughtfully. "I see. I am certain Claudia will find the experience of being sent off at a moment's notice extremely interesting."

Peter shrugged, apparently unconcerned by the notion of a recalcitrant Claudia.

By seven o'clock the next morning, all was in readiness. Harry stood on the steps of the town house and said good-bye first to his daughter. Meredith was disappointed at having to leave the city and all its entertainments, but her father had explained there were matters at the estate which required Augusta's attention. She accepted that explanation, but nevertheless reminded him that she had not yet seen Vauxhall Gardens.

"You shall return shortly and I will take you there myself," he promised her.

Meredith nodded, satisfied. She hugged him fiercely. "That will be nice, Papa. Good-bye."

"Good-bye, Meredith."

Harry put his daughter into the big black traveling coach and then turned to meet Augusta, who was just coming down the steps. He smiled at her elegant dark green carriage dress and frivolous high-crowned bonnet. Trust Augusta to look stylish even when she was being hurriedly packed off to the country at seven in the morning.

"Is all well, then?" she asked as she came to a halt in front of him. She fixed him with a steady look, her eyes serious in the shadow of the bonnet.

"Yes. Your cousin will be waiting for you at her house. You shall all be on your way shortly. You will spend the night at an inn and be at Graystone tomorrow afternoon." Harry paused. "I shall miss you, Augusta."

She smiled tremulously. "And I shall miss you, my lord. We shall be awaiting your arrival down in Dorset. Please be very, very careful, Harry."

"I will."

She nodded and then, without any warning, she stood on tiptoe and kissed him full on the mouth right there in front of Meredith and the cluster of servants milling about the carriage. Harry started to fold her close, but it was too late. She was already pulling away.

"I love you, Harry," Augusta said.

"*Augusta*." Harry instinctively reached out for her, but she had already turned and stepped into the waiting coach.

Harry stood watching as the black and silver coach rumbled out into the street. For a long while he simply stood there, repeating Augusta's parting words over and over again in his mind. *I love you, Harry.*

It was, he realized, the first time she had ever actually said the words aloud. He knew now that a part of him had been waiting to hear them for a very long while.

I love you, Harry. The locked door hidden deep inside him opened wide and what lay behind it no longer appeared so bleak.

Dear God, but I love you, too, Augusta. I had not realized until this moment how much a part of me you have become.

Harry waited until the black coach was out of sight and then he went on up the steps and into his library. He sat down behind his desk and unfolded the list of names Sally had found. It did not take him long to decode them.

When he was done, he studied the eleven names. Some of the men on the list he knew had died in the war. Some he knew simply did not have the intelligence or temperament to have been the Spider. A few of the names he did not know at all. Peter no doubt would recognize them.

But it was the last name on the list that caught and held his attention.

He was still sitting there, staring at the last name, when Peter was shown into the library.

"Well, they're off, safe and sound," Peter announced as he sprawled in a chair. "I just came from putting Claudia into your coach. Meredith said to say good-bye to you again and to remember that in addition to Vauxhall, she would very much like to go back to Astley's."

"And Augusta?" Harry tried to keep his tone cool and restrained. "Did she have any further words for me?"

"Said to tell you again that she would take care of your daughter for you."

"She is very loyal," Harry said softly. "She is a woman a man can trust with his life or his honor or his child."

"Yes, she certainly is," Peter said with a knowing look. He leaned forward. "What have you found? Anyone interesting on that list?"

Without a word, Harry turned the decoded list of names around so that Peter could read them. He saw Peter's mouth thin as he reached the last one.

"*Lovejoy.*" Peter looked up quickly. "Good God. It fits, doesn't it? No family, no past, no close friends. He has realized we are making inquiries. He tried to deflect us by making it appear Richard Ballinger was the Spider."

"Yes. He must have discovered that the list of members of the Saber Club had fallen into Sally's hands."

"He went to search for it. She was awake, waiting for us, and no doubt surprised him. So he killed her." Peter's hand closed into a fist. "The bastard." Peter sat back. "Well, sir? What is our first step?"

"It is past time I paid that second late-night visit to Lovejoy's library."

Peter cocked a brow. "I shall go with you. Tonight?"

"If possible."

But it was not possible. Lovejoy spent the evening entertaining male friends at home. Harry and Peter kept watch from a darkened carriage as the lights in Lovejoy's library stayed on until nearly dawn.

The next night, however, Lovejoy went out to his club. Harry and Peter entered the library through the window shortly before midnight.

"Ah, there is the globe safe you mentioned," Peter murmured, starting toward it.

"I think we can forget the globe." Harry peeled back the edge of the carpet. "Lovejoy made no secret of it when I came here to speak to him the morning after Augusta and I discovered her vowels in it. He probably uses it chiefly as a convenient storage place for minor valuables and perhaps as a decoy. The Spider will doubtless have a second, better-hidden treasure chest."

"I see what you mean. Nothing much in here." Peter had gotten the globe open and was peering inside. He closed it again and began systematically going over the paneling at the far end of the room.

Twenty minutes later, Harry found what he was searching for when he tripped the hidden lock mechanism in a floorboard.

"I think this is what we want, Sheldrake." Harry lifted a small metal box out of the flooring. He went still, as a footstep in the hall announced a servant who was probably sneaking in late after a visit to a tavern. "We had best examine this elsewhere."

"Agreed." Peter was already halfway out the window.

An hour later, sitting comfortably in his own library, Harry got the metal box open. The first thing that caught his eye when he looked inside was the glitter of gems.

"The Spider appears to have taken his traitor's pay in jewels," Peter mused.

"Yes." Harry fished impatiently through the heap of precious stones that littered the bottom of the box. His fingers closed around a packet of papers and he lifted it out.

He flipped through them quickly and paused when a small notebook fell into his hand. He opened it and saw that for the most part there were only a few short, cryptic entries for dates and times that could have meant anything or nothing. The last note, however, was far more interesting. And far more disturbing.

"What have you got there?" Peter leaned forward for a closer look.

Harry read the note aloud. " 'Lucy Ann. Weymouth. Five hundred pounds for month of July.' "

Peter looked up. "What the devil does that mean? Is the bastard keeping a ladybird in Weymouth?"

"I doubt it. Not to the tune of five hundred pounds per month." Harry was silent for a moment as he followed the logic of the situation. "Weymouth is not above eight miles from Graystone and it has an active harbor."

"Well, of course. Everyone knows that. So?"

Harry looked up slowly. "So the *Lucy Ann* is undoubtedly a vessel, not a wench. And the Spider appears to have paid someone, perhaps the ship's captain, the enormous sum of five hundred pounds for the month of July."

"That's this month. Why on earth would he have laid out that kind of blunt on a ship?"

"To assure that it be kept in readiness for an immediate departure, perhaps? The Spider was always fond of slipping away via a water route, if you will recall."

"Yes. He was, was he not?"

Harry closed the notebook, a cold feeling in his gut. "We must find him. Now. Tonight."

"I could not agree more, Graystone."

But Lovejoy had covered his tracks well. It took Harry and Peter most of the following day to discover that the Spider had already left London.

The first night back at Graystone, Augusta lay awake for hours, staring at the ceiling. She was conscious of every creak and squeak in the great house.

Earlier she had followed the footman around and watched closely as he locked every door and every window. She had checked to be certain the dogs had been bedded down for the night in the kitchens. The butler had assured her the house was secure.

"His lordship ordered special locks years ago, madam," Steeples had told her. "Very stout locks."

Nevertheless, Augusta could not sleep.

She finally shoved back the covers and reached for her wrapper. Picking up a taper, she lit it, slid her feet into a pair of slippers, and went out into the hall. She would just look in on Meredith one last time, she decided.

Halfway down the hall, she saw that the door to Meredith's room was open. Augusta broke into a run, shielding the fragile flame with one hand.

"Meredith?"

Meredith's bed was empty. Augusta forced herself to remain calm. She would not panic. Meredith's window was still securely locked. There were several logical explanations for the child's absence. She might have gotten up to get a drink of water. Or perhaps she had gone downstairs to get something to eat from the kitchens.

Augusta flew toward the staircase. She was halfway down when she glanced over the railing and saw a crack of light under the library door. She closed her eyes and took a deep breath. Then she hurried on down the stairs.

When she opened the library door, Augusta spotted Meredith instantly. The child was curled up in her father's big chair. She looked very tiny and fragile there. She had lit a lamp and there was a book in her lap. She glanced up when Augusta came into the room.

"Hello, Augusta. Did you have trouble sleeping, too?"

"Yes. As a matter of fact, I did." Augusta smiled to hide her enormous relief at finding the girl safe. "What are you reading?"

"I am trying to read the *The Antiquary*. It is rather difficult. There are a great many words."

"So there are." Augusta put her taper down on the desk. "Shall I read it to you?"

"Yes, please. I should like that very much."

"Let's go over to the settee. That way we can both sit together and you can follow along as I read."

"All right." Meredith slid out of Harry's massive leather chair and followed Augusta to the settee.

"First," Augusta said as she knelt briefly in front of the hearth, "I shall light the fire. It is rather chilly in here."

A few minutes later they were both comfortably settled in front of a roaring blaze. Augusta picked up the new novel that was being attributed to Walter Scott and began to read softly of missing heirs, treasure hunts, and perilous adventures.

After a while Meredith yawned and nestled her head on Augusta's shoulder. Several moments went past. Augusta eventually looked down and saw that her stepdaughter was asleep.

For a long time Augusta sat there watching the fire and thinking that she felt almost like Meredith's real mother tonight. She certainly felt as protective as a real mother.

She also felt very much like a real wife tonight, Augusta reflected. Surely only a wife could know this dreadful sense of uncertainty while she waited for her husband to return to her.

The library door opened softly and Claudia, dressed in a chintz wrapper, came into the room. She smiled when she saw Augusta curled up on the settee with Meredith asleep beside her.

"It seems we all had a problem getting to sleep tonight," Claudia whispered as she sat down near the settee.

"It appears so. Are you worried about Peter?"

"Yes. I fear he is inclined to be somewhat reckless. I pray he will not take any chances. He was terribly angry because of Sally's death."

"There was a great rage in Harry, too. He tried to conceal it, but I saw it burning in his eyes. He is really a very emotional man under that calm, controlled facade he shows to the world."

Claudia smiled. "I must take your word for that. Peter, on the other hand, conceals his emotions behind a cheerful, teasing mask. But he, too, feels deeply. I wonder why it took me so long to see the underlying seriousness of his nature."

"Probably because he is skilled at concealing his true feelings. Just as Harry is. Each, in his own way, has learned to be cautious about exposing his deepest thoughts and emotions. I suppose they both had far too much practice doing so during the war." *And Harry had learned a great deal about self-control even before he had faced the dangers of intelligence work,* Augusta thought, remembering the faithless women in the picture gallery.

"It must have been a terrible ordeal for them."

"The war?" Augusta nodded, her heart aching for Harry and Peter both. "They are good men and good men must suffer enormously in war."

"Oh, Augusta, I love Peter so." Claudia rested her chin in her hand and gazed into the fire. "I am so dreadfully worried about him."

"I know, Claudia." Augusta realized that she felt closer

to her cousin tonight than she ever had in the past. It was a good feeling. "Do you ever think about the fact that even though we both descend from different branches of the Ballinger family, we do share a common ancestry, Claudia?"

"I have thought about it frequently in recent days," Claudia admitted wryly.

Augusta laughed softly.

The two women sat quietly in front of the flames for a long time. Meredith slept peacefully beside them.

The following night Augusta's sense of uneasiness grew steadily into a great anxiety that threatened to overwhelm her. She eventually managed to get to sleep only to fall into a vague nightmare.

She woke with a start. Her palms were damp and her heart was pounding. She felt as though she were being buried alive under the bedding.

Fighting panic, she shoved the covers aside and leaped out of the bed. Then she stood breathing quickly, trying to calm the strange fear that still held her in its grip. When she could tolerate it no longer, she gave in to it.

Snatching up her wrapper, she hurried out of the bedchamber and rushed down the hall to Meredith's room. Augusta told herself she would be able to calm down after she had seen that Meredith was safe.

But Meredith was not tucked up safely in her bed. Once again she was gone and this time the window stood wide. The night breeze stirred the curtains and chilled the bedchamber.

There was just enough moonlight to see the stout rope that had been secured to the windowsill. It hung all the way to the ground.

Meredith had been kidnapped.

20

Augusta had the entire household assembled before her in the front hall within ten minutes. She paced up and down in front of them as the last straggling chambermaid stumbled from a warm bed and took up her position at the end of the line. Even the dogs were in attendance. Aroused by the commotion, they had padded out of the kitchens to see what was happening. No one had thought to lock them up or put them outside.

Claudia stood tensely nearby, her gaze riveted on Augusta. Steeples, the butler, and Mrs. Gibbons, the housekeeper, waited anxiously for instructions. The servants were still in shock, as was Clarissa Fleming. Everyone had instinctively turned to Augusta for leadership in the crisis.

Foremost in Augusta's mind was the crushing knowledge that she had failed to keep Meredith safe. *I will guard her with my life, Harry.*

She had failed to keep her vow. She must not fail to get Meredith safely back. For once in her life she must be cool and logical and she must act swiftly. She told herself firmly she must put aside emotion and think as clearly as Harry would think if he were here.

"If I may have your attention, please," she said to the assembled crowd. An instant silence descended. "You all know what has happened. Lady Meredith has been stolen from her bed."

Some of the maids started to weep.

"Quiet, please," Augusta snapped. "There is no time for emotion. Now, I have been thinking about what has happened. The window was not forced. It was obviously opened from the inside. The dogs were not alerted. Steeples and I and Mrs. Gibbons have been through the house and there is absolutely no sign of forced entry. There is, I believe, only one conclusion."

Everyone drew in a breath and stared at Augusta.

Augusta searched the faces of the staff. "My daughter has been kidnapped by someone from inside Graystone. You are a large group. Who is missing among you?"

A collective gasp greeted this observation. Instantly everyone was looking at everyone else. And then a shriek went up from the back row.

"Robbie's gone," the cook yelled loudly. "Robbie, the new footman."

At this news, the young chambermaid at the end of the row burst into fresh tears.

Augusta eyed the girl while she spoke quietly to Steeples. "When was this Robbie taken on?"

"I believe it was a couple of weeks after his lordship's marriage, madam. About the time we were taking on extra staff for the house party. Decided to keep Robbie on after the affair. Said he had relatives in the village. Said he'd been working until recently at an important house in London and now wanted to find a permanent post in the country." Steeples looked distraught. "He had an excellent reference, madam."

Augusta met Claudia's eyes. "An excellent reference from the Spider, no doubt."

Clarissa's mouth tightened. "Do you think it possible?"

"The timing of it seems to fit." Augusta broke off as the chambermaid on the end fell to her knees sobbing. "What is it, Lily?"

Lily looked up at her with streaming eyes. "I was afeared he had some wicked intentions in mind, ma'am. But I thought he only meant to pinch some silver. I never thought he'd do anythin' like this, I swear I didn't."

Augusta beckoned to her. "Come into the library. I wish to speak with you in private." She glanced at the butler. "Start the search immediately. So far as we know, Robbie must have been on foot. Is that correct?"

"There be no horse missin' from the stables," a groom volunteered. "But he may 'ave 'ad one o' 'is own waitin' on the grounds."

Augusta nodded. "True. Very well. Here is how you will proceed, Steeples. Have all the available horses saddled at once, including my mare. Mount those who can ride. Send everyone else out on foot with torches and the dogs. Send someone into the village to rouse the people there and dispatch a messenger to London to inform his lordship of what has happened. We must move quickly."

"Yes, madam."

"Miss Fleming will help you organize the search, won't you, Miss Fleming?"

Clarissa took on a militant expression. "Indeed I will, madam."

"Very well. We shall begin." Steeples turned to take command of the troops.

Claudia followed Augusta into the library and stood listening intently as Lily spilled her tale.

"I thought he liked me, ma'am. He was always bringing me a flower or a little present. I thought he was courtin' me, I did. But I wondered at some o' the things he done."

"What made you think he was up to something wicked?" Augusta pressed.

Lily sniffed. "Robbie said he would be comin' into a lot

of the ready soon. Said it would be enough to set him up for life and he would buy a little house and live like a lord. I laughed at him, but he seemed so serious that I almost believed him at times."

"Was there anything else he said that alarmed you?" Augusta asked quickly. "Think, girl. My daughter's life is at stake."

Lily looked at her and then dropped her forlorn gaze to the floor. "Not exactly somethin' he said, ma'am. More like things he did when he didn't think anyone was watchin', I used to see him lookin' the house over real careful like. That's when I wondered if he might be thinkin' of helpin' himself to some silver. I was going to tell Mrs. Gibbons, honest I was, but I wasn't sure like, if you know what I mean. And I didn't want to see Robbie dismissed if he wasn't plannin' anything wrong."

Augusta went to the window and stood gazing out into the darkness. It would be dawn soon. Steeples had moved quickly to follow her orders. She could see horses being led around to the front of the house. The dogs were barking excitedly. Even as she watched, several people carrying torches started off into the woods. *Oh, Meredith, my dear little Meredith. Do not fear, I shall find you.*

Augusta pushed aside the frantic desperation that threatened to well up inside her. She forced herself to think logically once more. "He cannot get far before morning, even on horseback. He has Meredith with him and that means he cannot make good time. Her weight will slow him down. In daylight he will be easily noticed by people who will ask questions and wonder what is going on. Therefore we will assume he intends to hide Meredith by day and travel at night."

"He can hardly stop at an inn carrying Graystone's daughter," Claudia said. "It will be questioned. And Meredith is not likely to stay silent."

"Precisely. Very well, we shall assume he has set out for a place where he can conceal Meredith until he makes contact with the Spider. There cannot be too many places around here where Robbie could hide with Meredith for any length of time."

Lily's head came up abruptly, her eyes clearing. "The old Dodwell cottage, ma'am. 'Tis vacant now on account of needin' repairs. Robbie took me there a while back." She started crying again. "I thought he was goin' to propose to me, fool that I was. But he said he just fancied the stroll."

"A long stroll," Augusta said, remembering the cottage where she had taken shelter during a storm. Graystone had been annoyed at having to come after her that day. She remembered that very well. She also recalled that he had told her the place was the only vacant cottage on the estate.

"Too long. That's what I told him. We walked for nearly two hours to get to the place. Then all he did was have a look around. Said he'd seen enough and that we should start back. My feet was hurtin' somethin' terrible by the time we returned."

"Is this cottage isolated?" Claudia asked. "Would it make a likely hiding place?"

"Yes, it would, for a short time. It is definitely worth checking." Augusta came to a decision. "Everyone else has already left to begin the search, including those two armed men Graystone sent down here to Dorset with us. I shall get dressed and ride over to the Dodwell cottage myself."

Claudia started for the door. "I shall come with you. It will not take me long to dress."

"I had best see if Steeples can secure us a pistol," Augusta said.

"Will you know how to use it if it becomes necessary?" Claudia asked in surprise.

"Of course. Richard taught me."

Half an hour later, with dawn just breaking, Augusta and Claudia brought their horses to a halt in the woods behind the Dodwell cottage. They saw a horse tethered in the old shed.

"Dear God," Claudia said softly. "I believe he really is here with Meredith. We must go back and get help."

"We may not have time to return for assistance." Augusta dismounted and handed the reins to her cousin. "And we do not know for certain that Robbie brought Meredith here. It could be a vagrant or some traveler who got caught by nightfall and found this cottage. I am going to see if I can get a look at who is inside."

"Augusta, I am not at all certain we should attempt this on our own."

"Do not fret. I have the pistol. Wait here. If something goes wrong, make for the nearest cottage. Anyone in the district will come to the aid of Graystone's family."

Augusta removed the pistol from the pocket of her riding habit and held it tightly as she went forward through the trees.

It was easy enough to make her way to the back of the cottage without calling attention to herself. There were no windows in the back wall of the crumbling structure and the old shed provided additional cover.

The horse tethered in the shed looked at Augusta without much interest as she started to slip past. Augusta eyed the animal thoughtfully and then went into the shed and untied the old mare.

The swaybacked old horse clomped obediently along when Augusta took hold of the halter and started around the side of the cottage. Near the front of the cottage Augusta paused and smacked the mare soundly on the rump.

Startled, the horse moved into a brisk trot that took it straight past the front door and down the lane.

A bellow of alarm sounded from inside the cottage. Augusta heard the door slam open and a young man still wearing Graystone's livery charged out.

"What in bloody hell? Come back here, you damned nag." Robbie whistled frantically at the disappearing horse.

Augusta raised the pistol and hugged the shelter of the side wall.

"Damn and blast. Goddamned nag. Damn it to bloody hell." Robbie was clearly torn about what to do next. He evidently decided he could not afford to lose the horse.

Augusta heard the front door being closed and then came the sound of Robbie's footsteps as he ran, cursing mightily, after the old mare.

Augusta waited until Robbie was out of sight and then she rushed to the front door of the cottage and pushed it open. Holding the pistol firmly in front of her, she stepped into the small room.

Meredith, gagged, bound, and lying helpless on the floor, stared toward the door with frightened eyes. And then she recognized Augusta. There was a muffled exclamation from behind the gag.

"'Tis all right, Meredith. I am here, darling. You are safe now." Augusta ran across the room and yanked off the gag. Then she set to work on the ropes that bound the girl's wrists.

Meredith threw her arms tightly around Augusta's neck as soon as she was free. "*Mama*. I knew you would come, Mama. I knew it. I was so scared of him."

"I know, darling. But now we must hurry."

Augusta took her hand and hauled her out of the cottage and around the corner of the house.

Claudia saw what was happening at once and started forward, leading Augusta's horse. "Hurry," she called. "We must get out of here at once. I hear a horse coming toward us in the lane. Robbie must have caught the mare."

Augusta listened to the strong, rhythmic hoofbeats of a swiftly cantering horse and knew it was not the old farm horse she had just set free. This was blooded stock, the kind of animal only a gentleman would ride. There was no way to know if whoever was on his way toward them would be friend or foe.

Augusta was filled with a desperate need to get Meredith out of the way.

"Here, darling. Get up in front of Miss Ballinger. Hurry." She pushed Meredith up into the saddle and Claudia caught hold of her. Augusta stepped back quickly. "Be off, Claudia. Now."

"Augusta, what are you doing?"

"You must see to Meredith. I must be free to use the pistol if it becomes necessary. We have no way of knowing who is coming up the lane. Go, Claudia. I shall be right behind you."

Claudia wheeled her horse about, her eyes filled with worry. "Very well, but do not delay." She sent her horse flying off through the trees.

"Be careful, Mama," Meredith called softly.

Augusta mounted her own mare and prepared to follow. She could still not see whoever was approaching. He was hidden by the bulk of the cottage.

Augusta leaned forward, pistol still firmly clutched in one hand, and urged her mare into a gallop.

At that instant a shot crashed through the woods, sending up a cloud of leaves and dirt beneath the mare's hooves.

The animal reared in panic, thrashing wildly at the air with its hooves. Augusta dropped the pistol in a desperate effort to steady the creature. But one rear hoof skidded on dead leaves and the beast started to twist to one side.

Augusta leaped off the sidesaddle just as the horse stumbled and fell. She landed in a heap on the ground, winded, unarmed, and trapped by the skirts of her habit. The mare scrambled to her feet and fled through the trees, heading for home.

By the time she had caught her breath a man with heavy whiskers and hair that had been powdered to the color of steel was standing over her. He had a pistol pointed straight at her heart.

Augusta knew at once that the whiskers and gray hair were a disguise. She would have recognized Lovejoy's fox-green eyes anywhere.

"You got here a bit early, my dear," Lovejoy grunted. He motioned her to her feet. "I did not think you would miss Graystone's offspring so quickly, nor rouse your staff and start the search so soon. But I see the stupid little maid said exactly what she was supposed to say. That dolt Robbie was sure she would. And I was certain you would make the obvious assumptions."

"You wanted me, Lovejoy? Not Meredith?"

"I wanted both of you," Lovejoy snapped. "But you have deprived me of Meredith, so I shall just have to make do with you. Let us hope Graystone is as fond of his new wife as he should be; otherwise you will be quite useless to me. And I don't have any patience with things that are useless to me. Your brother learned that soon enough."

"*Richard*. You killed him. Just like you killed Sally." Augusta leaped at him, her hands bunched into small fists.

Lovejoy slammed her aside with a powerful backhanded slap that sent Augusta sprawling once more in the dirt. "Get up, you little bitch. We must move quickly now. I do not know how long Graystone will bumble around London before he realizes who I am and that I have left the city."

"He will kill you, Lovejoy. You know that, do you not? He will kill you for this."

"He has wanted to kill me for a long time and as you can see, he has failed thus far. Graystone has always been clever, I'll give him that, but I have always had luck on my side."

"Until recently, perhaps. Your luck has run out, Lovejoy."

"Not at all. You are my good luck charm, madam. And I think you will be a very amusing one indeed. It will be a pleasure to take what belongs to that damned Graystone. I did try to warn him that you were not good wife material."

Lovejoy reached down and grabbed Augusta's arm. He hauled her to her feet.

Heedless of the pistol, Augusta whirled, scooped up her heavy skirts, and tried to flee. Lovejoy caught her in two strides and slapped her viciously. His arm circled her throat and the nose of the pistol rested against her temple.

"One more such attempt to run and I will put a bullet through your brain here and now. Do you understand?"

Augusta did not bother to answer. Her head was reeling from the violent blow. She sensed she must bide her time now.

Holding her cautiously, Lovejoy started toward the stallion that he had left in front of the cottage.

"What do you mean, you tried to warn Graystone that I would not make him a good wife?" Augusta demanded as he forced her to mount the prancing stallion.

"I really did not want the two of you getting together, Augusta. I was afraid that living in close proximity to you, Graystone might just possibly stumble across some clue from your brother's past the would lead him to me. It was not very likely, but it was always a worrisome possibility. I tried to avoid any such potential problem by heading off the marriage."

"That was what you were about when you lured me into that game of cards."

"Precisely." Lovejoy got up behind her, the mouth of the pistol pressed firmly into her ribs. "The idea was to compromise you when you came for your vowels, but that did not work. And the next thing I knew, the son of a bitch had married you out of hand."

"Where are you taking me?"

"Not far." He picked up the reins and spurred the stallion forward. "We are going to take a pleasant sea voyage, you and I. And then we shall seclude ourselves in a remote location in France while frustration and rage eat Graystone alive."

"I do not understand. Why do you need me?"

"You are my bargaining piece, my dear. With you as hostage, I shall get safely across the Channel and into seclusion in France. Graystone will pay dearly for you. His sense of honor, if not his affection, will see to that. And when he eventually is permitted to purchase your freedom, I shall lure him into a trap and kill him."

"And then what?" Augusta challenged. "Everyone will know who you are at last. My husband has friends."

"So he does. But as far as your husband's friends are concerned, I shall also be dead. Killed by a valiant Graystone who died in the attempt to free his poor wife. Who was also unfortunately killed. Very tragic. 'Twill be something of a nuisance to assume a new identity afterward, but I have done it before."

Augusta closed her eyes as the stallion pounded down the lane. "Why did you kill Richard?"

"Your foolish brother tried to play a dangerous game, Augusta. One he did not even begin to comprehend. He joined the Saber Club because it was just the dashing sort of club that appealed to men like him. Then he somehow stumbled onto the fact that a master spy called the Spider was also a member. He reasoned I was doubtless using the place to collect valuable information. Those dashing young officers talked very freely when they were in their cups. A pretty girl, a few bottles of wine, and whatever information the members of the club had was mine for the asking."

"They talked freely because they thought you were one of them."

"Indeed. It worked very well until your brother somehow figured out what was going on. Although I did not think he knew which of the members was the Spider, I decided not to take any chances. I knew that he planned to seek out the authorities and turn his information over to them. I followed him home one night."

"And shot him in the back before you planted incriminating documents on his person."

"It was easier that way. I burned the Saber down and

made certain that all the club's records and membership rolls were consumed in the blaze. The place was soon forgotten. Now, then, enough of such pleasant reminiscences. We have a journey ahead of us."

Lovejoy brought the stallion to a halt near a small bridge. He dismounted and jerked Augusta off the horse. She stumbled as she found her footing and when she pushed the hair back out of her eyes she saw the sleek, closed carriage hidden in the trees. It was horsed with two powerful-looking bays that were secured to a tree.

"You must forgive me for what will no doubt be a most uncomfortable journey, madam." Lovejoy deftly bound Augusta's hands and gagged her with a twisted cravat. "But rest assured there is worse to come. The Channel can be very rough."

He tossed her into the small carriage, pulled down the curtains on the windows, and slammed the door shut. A moment later Augusta heard him climb onto the box and pick up the reins.

The horses set off at a furious pace. Lost in the darkness of the carriage, Augusta had no way of knowing which direction they were headed. Lovejoy had said something about a sea voyage.

The nearest harbor was Weymouth. Surely he would not be so bold as to try to get her aboard a vessel in such a public place, Augusta thought.

Then she reminded herself that, whatever else could be said of him, no one would deny that the Spider was as bold as he was vicious.

She could only bide her time and wait for an opportunity to escape or draw attention to herself. In the meantime, she must fight the despair that threatened to seize her. At least Meredith was safe. But the thought of never seeing Harry again was too much to bear.

•   •   •

The smell of the sea, the clatter of wagon traffic, and the creak of timber roused Augusta a long time later. She listened carefully, trying to pinpoint their location. It was unmistakably a harbor, and that meant Lovejoy had indeed driven to Weymouth.

Augusta straightened uncomfortably in the seat, wincing as the bindings cut into her wrists. She had managed to loosen the gag without Lovejoy taking notice by catching the twisted cravat on a brass fitting near the door and tugging against it.

The carriage came to a halt. Augusta heard voices and then the door was opened. Lovejoy, still in disguise, leaned inside. He was holding a large cloak and a black, heavily veiled bonnet.

"A moment, my good man," he said to someone over his shoulder. "I must see to my poor wife. She is not feeling at all well."

Augusta tried to evade the bonnet, but Lovejoy gave her a glimpse of the knife in his hand and she went still as she realized he would have no compunction about slipping it between her ribs.

In a remarkably short time, veiled and securely wrapped in the hooded cloak, Augusta was lifted out of the carriage. Lovejoy must have appeared very much the solicitous husband as he carried her along the stone quay to where a small ship was tied. No one could see the knife concealed in his hand because of the folds of the cloak.

Augusta peered through the thick black veil, watching for whatever opportunity might present itself.

"I'll fetch yer luggage for ye, sir," a familiar, rasping voice volunteered from close at hand.

"My luggage should already be on board," Lovejoy snapped. He stepped onto the gangplank. "Tell your scoundrel of a captain that I wish to sail immediately. We have the tide."

"Aye, sir," said the rasping voice. " 'E's just been waitin' fer ye, 'e 'as. I'll tell 'im yer 'ere."

"Be quick about it. I have paid him a great deal of money for his services and I expect satisfaction."

"Aye, sir. But first I'll point out yer cabin. Yer lady wife looks like she'll be wantin' to take to 'er bunk directly, eh?"

"Yes, yes, point out the cabin. Then notify the captain to get under way. And watch what you are doing with that line, man."

"It's in the way, ain't it? Cap'n don't like that. 'E runs a nice tight ship, 'e does. 'E'll have me arse for that. I'd best get the blasted thing outta the way."

"What the bloody hell?" Lovejoy staggered, trying to catch his balance as the line looped around his boot like a snake. His grip on Augusta slipped.

Augusta saw her chance. She screamed and threw herself forward out of Lovejoy's arms as he fought to keep his feet.

Augusta heard a bellow of rage from her captor as he lost his grip on her. Through the veil she saw the grizzled seaman with the rasping voice reach out to catch her, but he fell back under the impact, enveloped by her cloak.

"Damnation," Peter Sheldrake muttered as he and Augusta both toppled over the edge of the gangplank and plummeted into the cold water of the harbor.

Harry saw his friend go over the edge with Augusta and realized that his wife was safe. Peter would take care of her.

Harry had his own hands full with an enraged Lovejoy, who was already back on his feet, a knife in his fist.

"Goddamn you," Lovejoy hissed. "You were well named, *Nemesis*, but the Spider always drinks his victim's blood in the end."

"There will be no more blood for you, Spider."

Lovejoy hurtled forward, his arm extended for a gut-slashing thrust. Harry sidestepped the attack and managed to catch hold of Lovejoy's arm as he tried to shift direction at the last instant.

Both men were thrown off balance. Lovejoy went down and Harry went with him, still clutching the arm that held the knife. They landed heavily and rolled nearly to the edge of the gangplank.

"You went too far this time, Spider." Still grappling with Lovejoy's knife arm, Harry tried to force back his assailant's hand. The point of the blade hovered just over Harry's eye. "But then, that was always your problem, was it not? You always took things one step too far. Too many deaths, too much blood, too clever for your own good. That was why you lost in the end."

"Bastard." The goading words had lit more wild, uncontrolled fires in Lovejoy's glittering eyes. His teeth were bared in a savage grimace as he fought to sink the blade into Harry's eye. "I shall not lose this time."

Harry felt the surge of maniacal power in Lovejoy's arm. He heaved frantically to the side to avoid the thrust. At the same time his fingers slid down to Lovejoy's wrist.

Harry twisted the wrist with every ounce of strength at his command. Something snapped. The blade altered direction, pointing upward.

Lovejoy screamed as he came down on top of his own knife. He spasmed and rolled to the side, then seized the handle of the knife and jerked it out of his chest.

Blood spurted, the bright red blood of death.

"The Spider never loses," Lovejoy muttered hoarsely as he stared at Harry with disbelieving eyes. "He cannot lose."

Harry sucked in air, tried to catch his breath. "You are wrong. You and I were fated to meet, Lovejoy. The final rendezvous has been kept."

Lovejoy did not answer. His eyes glazed as he died the death he had meted out to so many others. He toppled over the edge of the gangplank and fell into the sea.

Harry heard Augusta calling to him, but he could not seem to gather the energy to get to his feet. He simply lay there on the gangplank, utterly exhausted, and listened to the sound of her footsteps as she ran toward him.

"*Harry.*"

When he felt water dripping onto his face, he opened his

eyes and smiled up at her. She was drenched. The skirts of
her gown were soaked and her hair was plastered to her
head. Love and anguished concern blazed in her eyes. She
had never looked more beautiful.

"Harry. Harry, are you all right? Tell me you are all
right." She crouched beside him, cradling him against her
damp bodice.

"I am all right, love." He caught her fast, heedless of her
wet clothing. "I am all right now that I know you are safe."

Augusta clutched at him. "Dear heaven, I was so
terrified. How did you realize what was happening? How
did you know he was bringing me to Weymouth? How did
you know which vessel he had planned to take?"

It was Peter who answered her questions as he came up
behind her. "The Spider always did have the devil's own
luck. But Graystone, on the other hand, was known for
being able to second-guess old Lucifer himself."

Augusta shivered and glanced over the edge of the
gangplank. Lovejoy was floating facedown in the water.

"You are cold, darling," Harry said quietly. He got to
his feet and turned her away from the sight of Lovejoy's
body. "We must get you into some warm clothes."

He led her toward the warmth of a nearby tavern.

Augusta, Harry, and Peter arrived back at Graystone late in
the afternoon and the entire household rushed out to greet
them. The servants grinned broadly and told each other
they had all known their master would rescue the mistress.

Clarissa Fleming beamed in relief from the top of the
steps as Meredith went running toward her parents.

"*Mama,* you are safe. I knew Papa would save you. He
told me so." Meredith wrapped her arms around Augusta
and hugged her fiercely. "Oh, Mama, you are so brave."

"So are you, Meredith." Augusta smiled down at her. "I
shall never forget what a brave little girl you were when I
found you in that cottage. You didn't even cry, did you?"

Meredith shook her head violently, her face still concealed by the skirts of Augusta's gown. "Not then. But I cried later when Miss Ballinger took me away and we realized you had not been able to follow us."

"I did not know what to do then," Claudia said, standing to the side with her hand in Peter's. "I heard the pistol shot and was absolutely frantic. I realized I could not risk Meredith's life by turning back. So I kept going. Graystone and Peter were just arriving at the house when Meredith and I got there. They guessed immediately Lovejoy was heading for Weymouth."

"Once we knew we were too late to keep you out of his clutches, Weymouth was the next logical place to look," Harry explained. "The Spider was always fond of the sea as an escape route. Sheldrake and I rode straight for Weymouth and got there ahead of Lovejoy's carriage. Then we went looking for a ship called the *Lucy Ann.*"

"It turned out to be an old smuggler's craft," Peter said. "The captain had apparently worked for the Spider occasionally during the war. We persuaded him to let us take over his vessel for a time this morning."

"You persuaded him?" Claudia smiled skeptically.

"Let us say the man soon saw the light of sweet reason when Graystone used a bit of cold, clear logic on him," Peter said blandly. "Graystone is very good at logic, you know. It is obvious your cousin Richard had concealed information about the Spider in that coded poem. He was trying to get word to the British authorities the night he was killed."

"Peter was right," Harry said much later. "I am very good with logic."

Augusta smiled. She was lying in his arms in the deep shadows of his bed. She felt warm and safe and wanted. She felt she had finally come home. "Yes, Harry, everyone knows that."

"But I am not particularly clever about a few other

things." He tightened his arm around her and drew her close. "I did not, for instance, recognize love when I fell straight into it."

"*Harry.*" Augusta raised herself up on one elbow so that she could look down into his eyes. "Are you telling me that you fell in love with me right from the start?"

His mouth slanted in a slow, wicked smile that sent delicious shivers through her. "Obviously that must have been what happened, madam. Otherwise, there really is no accounting for my totally irrational behavior during our courtship and marriage."

Augusta pursed her lips. "I suppose that is one view of the situation. Oh, Harry, I am so happy tonight."

"That delights me more than I can say, my love. I have discovered that my happiness is forever linked with yours." He brushed his mouth across hers and then grew more serious as he watched her through narrowed eyes. "You risked your life to save Meredith today."

"She is my daughter."

"And you are fiercely loyal to the members of your family, are you not?" He smiled slightly as he ran his fingers through her hair. "A little tigress."

"It is very good to have a family again, Harry."

"You told me just before I sent you out of London that you knew Meredith was my greatest weakness. But you were wrong. You are my greatest weakness. I love you, Augusta."

"And I love you, Harry. With all my heart."

Harry's hand wrapped around the back of her head. Augusta's hair tumbled over his arm as he dragged her mouth down to his once more.

Harry came awake abruptly the next morning as his wife leaped from the bed and grabbed the chamber pot.

"Excuse me," Augusta gasped as she bent over the pot. "I believe I am going to be very ill."

Harry got up and went to hold her head. "Nerves, no doubt," he announced as she finished being sick. "Too much excitement yesterday, I imagine. You must spend the day in bed, my dear."

"'Tis not nerves." Augusta glowered at him as she used a damp cloth to wipe her face. "No Northumberland Ballinger was ever ill from nerves."

"Well, then," said Harry quite calmly, "in that case, you must be pregnant."

"Good Lord." Augusta sat down abruptly on the edge of the bed. She stared at him in shock. "Do you really believe it possible?"

"I would say it was a distinct possibility," Harry assured her with satisfaction.

Augusta thought about that for a moment. And then she smiled gleefully. "I would think that the combination of the Northumberland Ballinger bloodlines and those of the earls of Graystone should prove very interesting. What do you think, my lord?"

Harry laughed. "Very interesting indeed, my love."

21

*T*hree months later Augusta was entertaining Claudia, who had recently returned to Town after her wedding trip, when Harry stalked into the drawing room. She saw at once that he was scowling ferociously over a document he held in one hand.

Augusta arched a brow. "What on earth is the matter, my lord? Did your publisher reject your manuscript on Caesar's military campaigns?"

" 'Tis far worse news than that." Harry handed her the document. "That is from the solicitors who have just finished settling Sally's estate."

"Is something wrong with the way it was handled?" She scanned the legal paper quickly.

"You will notice," Harry said evenly, "that you are named in her will."

Augusta was delighted. "How thoughtful of Sally. I would so love to have something of hers as a keepsake. I wonder what she left me. One of the pictures in Pompeia's, perhaps? We could hang it in the schoolroom. Meredith and Clarissa would enjoy it."

"That is an excellent notion," Claudia agreed, eagerly looking over her cousin's shoulder. "I was wondering what would happen to all those wonderful paintings."

Harry's scowl deepened. "Sally did not leave you a painting, Augusta."

"No? Then what was it? A silver bowl or one of the statues, perhaps?"

"Not exactly," Harry said. He laced his fingers behind his back. "She has left you the whole damn club."

"What?" Augusta raised her head to stare at him in astonishment. "She left Pompeia's to me?"

"She has left you her entire town house to be run as a private club for the benefit of ladies such as yourself *who share a certain similarity of outlook and temperament.* I believe that is how it is expressed in the will. She hopes that your cousin will be one of the patronesses."

"Me?" Claudia appeared shocked and then she started to smile. "What a wonderful thought. We could turn it into the most fashionable salon in town again. I shall so enjoy that. Miss Fleming will love Pompeia's, too."

"Sir Thomas may have something to say about that, seeing as he intends to marry Clarissa next month," Harry warned.

"Oh, I am certain Papa will not mind." Claudia smiled. "Wait until I tell Peter."

"Yes, it will be interesting to see how Sheldrake reacts to the notion, will it not?" Harry observed grimly. "After all, he is now a married man and as such I believe he has recently discovered a whole new sense of the proprieties."

"Yes, he has become something of a prig lately, has he not?" Claudia shrugged. "But I expect I can convince him that reopening Pompeia's will be a wonderful notion."

Desperate now, Harry turned back to Augusta. "I do not care for the expression on your face, my dear. 'Tis obvious your brain is already churning forth ideas of how Pompeia's could be reopened immediately."

"Graystone, just think," Augusta said encouragingly. "It would not take long to get everything ready. We shall have to take on staff, of course, but many of the old servants may still be available. Clarissa can help us manage things. We can notify all the ladies who were once members and they can tell their friends. This is so exciting. I cannot wait to get started. Pompeia's will be bigger and better than ever."

Harry held up a hand and infused his voice with dark, masculine authority. "If there is to be a new Pompeia's, there will also be a few new rules."

"Now, Harry," Augusta began coaxingly. "You need not concern yourself with the petty details of Pompeia's management, my dear."

He ignored that. "First, there will not be any gaming allowed in the new version of Pompeia's."

"Graystone, really, you are much too straitlaced about some things."

"Second, the place shall be run strictly as a genteel salon for ladies, *not* as a parody of a gentlemen's club."

"Honestly, Harry, you are positively old-fashioned," Augusta muttered.

"Third, Pompeia's will not be reopened until after my son and heir is born. Is that quite clear?"

Augusta lowered her eyes, the very picture of the demure, virtuous wife. "Yes, my lord."

Harry groaned. "I am lost."

Harry's son, a healthy babe with a lusty wail that could only have come from the Northumberland Ballinger side of the family, was born five months later.

Harry took one look at the infant and then smiled at his tired but happy wife. He was almost as exhausted as she was this morning. Last night had been harrowing, although the midwife had assured him everything was proceeding quite routinely.

Harry had spent every moment at his wife's bedside during her labor. He had vowed eternal celibacy every time he had put a cool washcloth on Augusta's sweating brow or felt her nails dig into his palm. Now she was safe and he realized he had never been more grateful for anything in his life.

"I believe we shall call him Richard, if that suits you, Augusta."

She glowed up at him from the pillows. Harry thought she had never looked more beautiful.

"I should like that very much. Thank you, Harry."

"I have a small surprise for you." He sat down on the edge of the bed and opened the velvet pouch he had brought upstairs with him. "Your mother's necklace was returned from the jeweler's this morning. As you can see, the man did an excellent job of cleaning and polishing it. I, uh, thought you might like to see it for yourself."

"Oh, yes. I am glad it is back." Augusta watched as the ruby necklace spilled onto the quilt. The brilliant red stones burned with a fiery light in the morning sun. She smiled, clearly pleased. "They did an excellent job indeed. It looks lovely." Then she frowned.

"Is something wrong, sweetheart?"

Augusta picked up the gleaming necklace. "There is something different about my necklace, Harry." She sucked in her breath. "Good heavens, my lord, I believe we have been cheated."

Harry narrowed his eyes. "Cheated?"

"Yes." Augusta cradled her son in one arm and examined the necklace very closely. "These are not my mother's rubies. They are darker. More brilliant." She looked up with a grim expression. "Harry, the jeweler has switched stones."

"Calm yourself, Augusta."

"No, I am certain of it," she said. "I have heard of this sort of thing happening."

"Augusta—"

"One sends a perfectly good necklace out to be cleaned or repaired and the jeweler replaces the genuine stones with cut glass. Harry, you must go back to the jeweler's at once. You must make him return our rubies."

Harry started to laugh. He could not help it. The whole thing was too ludicrous for words.

Augusta scowled at him. "Pray tell, what is so amusing, my lord?"

"Augusta, I assure you those rubies are quite real."

"Impossible. I shall go to the jeweler myself and demand he return my mother's rubies."

Harry laughed harder. "I would like to see the look on his face when you complain that he switched the stones. He will think you have gone mad, my love."

Augusta eyed him uncertainly. "Harry, are you trying to tell me something?"

"I wasn't going to tell you anything at all, but since you are determined to make an issue of this matter, you had better know the truth. One of your illustrious ancestors pawned the Northumberland Ballinger rubies years ago, my love. It was Sally who realized your rubies were actually nicely cut glass."

Augusta's eyes widened in shock. "Are you certain?"

"Positive. Just to be sure, I had the necklace appraised before I did anything rash. I'm sorry, sweetheart. I thought I could carry off the switch, but obviously you have found me out."

Augusta stared at him in wonder. "Harry, if you replaced all of the rubies in my necklace, you must have spent a fortune."

"Mmmm, yes, one could say that." He grinned. "But it was worth it, my dear. After all, I have got myself a most virtuous wife and her value is infinitely far above rubies. Indeed, there is no way I could ever put a price on her. But the least I can do is see that when she wears rubies, she wears the real thing."

Augusta started to smile. "Oh, Harry, I do love you so."

"I know, my sweet." He kissed her gently. "Just as you must know that you are my heart and soul."

She held his hand very tightly. "Harry, I want you to know that with you I have found my home and my heart."

"And I am the luckiest of men," he told her softly. "I have found that treasure beyond price that I was seeking."

"A virtuous woman?"

"No, my darling. It turns out that was not quite what I was searching for, after all, although I have most certainly got myself a virtuous wife."

She regarded him curiously. "Then what was it you were seeking, my lord?"

"I did not know it in the beginning, but what I really wanted was a loving wife."

"Oh, yes, Harry." She smiled up at him with a lifetime of love in her eyes. "You most definitely have got yourself a loving wife."

ABOUT THE AUTHOR

AMANDA QUICK, who also writes as Jayne Ann Krentz, is a bestselling, award-winning author of contemporary and historical romance. There are over fifteen million copies of her books in print. She feels that the romance novel is a vital and compelling element in the world of women's fiction. She adds that something about historical romance, in particular, defines the very word "romance."

Amanda Quick makes her home in the Northwest with her husband, Frank, and a bird named Ferd.

Amanda Quick has done it again! Here's a tempting sneak preview of her new romantic novel, Ravished, *coming soon from Bantam Books.*

The thick gray fog that had rolled in from the seas during the night still clung tenaciously to the shore at ten o'clock the next morning. Harriet could not see more than a few feet in front of her as she made her way down the cliff path to the beach. She wondered if St. Justin would keep the appointment she had set up for them to view the thieves' cavern.

Harriet also wondered uneasily if she truly wanted him to keep the appointment. She had lain awake most of the night worrying she had made a dreadful mistake in sending the fateful letter to the notorious viscount.

Her sturdy leather half boots skidded on some pebbles as she hurried down the steep path. Harriet took a firmer grip on her small bag of tools and reached out with her free hand to balance herself against a boulder.

The path down the cliffs was safe enough if one was familiar with it, but there were some tricky patches. Harriet wished she could wear breeches when she went out to hunt fossils, but she knew Aunt Effie would collapse in shock if the notion was even casually put forth. Harriet tried to humor her aunt insofar as it was possible.

She knew Aunt Effie was opposed to the whole matter of fossil hunting in the first place. Effie considered it an unseemly occupation for a young woman and could not comprehend why Harriet was so passionately devoted to her interest. Harriet did not want to alarm the older woman any further by pursuing her fossils in a pair of breeches.

Heavy tendrils of mist coiled around Harriet as she reached the bottom of the path and paused to adjust the weight of the bag she carried. She could hear the waves lapping at the shore but she could not see them through the dense fog. The damp chill seeped through the heavy wool of her old dark green pelisse.

Even if Gideon did put in an appearance this morning, he probably would not be able to find her in this fog, Harriet thought. She turned and started along the beach at the base of the cliffs. The tide was out but the sand was still damp. When the tide was in, there was no beach visible along this stretch at all. The seawaters lapped against the cliffs at high tide, flooding some of the lower caves and passageways.

Once or twice Harriet had made the mistake of lingering too long in her explorations inside the caves and had very nearly been trapped by the incoming tide. Memories of those occasions still haunted her and caused her to time her trips into the caverns with great care.

She walked slowly along the base of the cliffs, searching for footprints in the sand. If Gideon had come this way a few minutes ahead of her she would surely be able to distinguish the imprint his huge boots would leave. Again she questioned the wisdom of what she had done. In summoning St. Justin back to Upper Biddleton she had obviously gotten more than she had bargained for.

On the other hand, Harriet told herself bracingly, something had to be done about the ring of thieves using her precious caves as a storage facility. She could not allow them to continue on as they were now. She simply had to be free to explore that particular cavern.

There was no telling what excellent fossils were waiting to be discovered in that underground chamber. Furthermore, Harriet reminded herself, the longer she allowed the villains to use the cave, the graver the risk grew that one of them might be shrewd enough to start digging for fossils himself. Or worse yet, he might tell someone else who might just mention it to another collector. Upper Biddleton might be overrun with fossil hunters.

It was unthinkable. The bones waiting to be discovered in these caves belonged to her.

No, there was no choice but to proceed along her present course, Harriet decided. She needed someone powerful and clever to help her get rid of the thieves. What did it matter if Gideon was a dangerous rogue and a blackguard? What better way to handle the thieves than to sic the infamous Beast of Blackthorne Hall on them? It would serve them right.

At that moment the fog seemed to swirl around her in a slightly altered pattern. Harriet halted abruptly, aware that she was no longer alone on the beach. Something was making her hair on the nape of her neck stir. She whirled around and saw Gideon materialize out of the mist. He walked toward her.

"Good morning, Miss Pomeroy. I had a hunch you would not be deterred by the fog."

"Good morning, my lord." Harriet steadied her nerves as she watched St. Justin stride forward across the damp, packed sand. It seemed to her overwrought imagination that he was emerging from the mist like a demon beast moving through the smoke of hell. He was even larger than she remembered.

He was wearing black boots, black gloves, and a dark gray, heavily caped greatcoat with a high collar that framed his scarred face. His black hair was uncovered and it glistened with morning mist.

"As you can see, I have obeyed your command yet again." Gideon smiled with faint irony as he came to a halt and stood looking down at her. "I must watch this tendency to jump to do your bidding, Miss Pomeroy. I would not want it to become a habit."

Harriet drew herself up and managed a polite smile. "Have no fear, my lord. I am certain you are not likely to get in the habit of obeying others unless you happen to feel like doing so for your own purposes."

He dismissed that with a slight shrug of one large shoulder.

"Who knows what a man will do when he is dealing with an interesting female?" His cold smile twisted his ruined face into a dangerous mask. "I await your next order, Miss Pomeroy."

Harriet swallowed and busied herself adjusting the weight of her cumbersome bag. "I have brought along two lamps, my lord," she said quickly. "We shall need them inside the passageway."

"Allow me." Gideon took the bag from her fingers. It dangled from his huge hand, seemingly weightless. "I shall deal with the equipment. Lead on, Miss Pomeroy. I am curious to see your cavern full of stolen goods."

"Yes. Of course. Right this way." She turned and hurried forward through the mist.

"You do not seem quite so certain of yourself this morning, Miss Pomeroy." Gideon sounded amused as he stalked silently along behind her. "I suspect someone, probably the good Mrs. Stone, has given you a few lurid details about my past history here in Upper Biddleton?"

"Nonsense. I am not interested in your past, sir." Harriet made a desperate effort to keep her voice very cool and extremely firm. She did not dare look back over her shoulder as she hastened across the sand. "It is no concern of mine."

"In that case, I must warn you that you should never have summoned me in the first place," he murmured with silky menace. "I fear I cannot be separated from my past. Where I go, it goes. The fact that I am in line for an earldom is extremely useful in getting people to overlook my past on occasion, but there is no denying I cannot shake it entirely. Especially here in Upper Biddleton."

Harriet glanced quickly over her shoulder, frowning intently at the veiled emotion she sense in his voice. "Does it bother you, my lord?"

"My past? Not particularly. I long ago learned to live with the fact that I am perceived as a fiend from the nether regions. To be perfectly frank, my reputation has its uses."

"Good heavens. What uses?" Harriet demanded.

His expression hardened. "It serves to keep me from being pestered by marriage-minded mamas, for one thing. They are extremely cautious about throwing their daughters in my path. They are terrified that I will shamelessly seduce their fledglings, have my wicked way with them, and then cast the poor things aside as soiled goods."

"Oh." Harriet swallowed.

"Which they would most certainly be," Gideon continued evenly. "Soiled, that is. It would be quite impossible to put a young girl back on the marriage mart after it got around that she had ruined herself with me."

"I see." Harriet coughed a bit to clear her throat and hurried forward a little faster. She could feel Gideon behind her, although she could not hear his footsteps on the packed sand. The very silence of his movement was unnerving because she was so vividly conscious of his size and presence. It was, indeed, like having a great beast on her heels.

"In addition to not pestering me with their young innocents," Gideon continued relentlessly, "not a single parent in recent memory has attempted to force me to make an offer by employing the old trick of accusing me of having compromised his daughter. Everyone knows such a ploy is highly unlikely to work."

"My lord, if this is your unsubtle way of warning me not to get any such notions, you may rest assured you are quite safe."

"I am well aware that I am safe enough, Miss Pomeroy. It is you who should exercise some caution."

Harriet had had enough. She came to a sudden halt and whirled around to confront him. She discovered he was almost on top of her and she took a quick step back. She scowled up at him. "Is it true, then? Did you cast aside the previous rector's daughter after getting her with child?"

Gideon studied her with grave interest. "You are very curious for someone who professes no interest in my past."

"You are the one who insisted on bringing it up."

"So I did. I fear I could not resist. Not after it became obvious you had already heard the tale."

"Well?" she challenged after a taut moment. "Did you?"

Gideon quirked one heavy black brow and appeared to give the matter serious consideration. His eyes burned with a cold fire as he gazed down at Harriet. "The facts are exactly as they were no doubt related to you, Miss Pomeroy. My fiancée was with child. I knew it when I ended the engagement. She apparently went home and shot herself."

Harriet gasped and recoiled another step. She forgot all about the cavern full of stolen goods. "I do not believe it."

"Thank you, Miss Pomeroy." He inclined his head with mocking politeness. "But I assure you that everyone else certainly does."

"Oh." Harriet recovered herself. "Yes. Well, as I said, it is no concern of mine." She spun about to hasten toward the cave entrance. Her face was flaming. She should have kept her mouth shut, she told herself furiously. The whole situation was unbelievably embarrassing.

A few minutes later Harriet breathed a sigh of relief as she reached her goal. The dark opening in the cliff wall loomed dimly in the mist. If she had not known precisely where it was located she would have missed it in the fog.

"This is the entrance, my lord." Harriet halted and turned once more to face him. "The cavern the thieves are using lies some distance inside this passageway."

Gideon gazed at the opening in the cliff for a moment and then set down the bag he had carried. "I believe we will need the lamps now."

"Yes. One cannot see a thing once one is more than a few steps inside the entrance."

Harriet watched Gideon remove the lamps from the bag and light them. For all their size and power, his hands moved with an unexpected grace and deftness. When he held one of the lamps out to her, his eyes caught hers studying him. He smiled coolly and the scar on his face twisted again.

"Have you started to have a few second thoughts about going into the caves alone with me, Miss Pomeroy?"

She glowered at him and practically snatched the lamp from his hand. "Of course not. Let us get on with it."

Harriet stepped through the narrow entrance and held the lamp aloft. Tendrils of fog had drifted into the cave and caused the lamp to throw strange shadows against the damp rock walls. She shivered and wondered why this passage seemed so extraordinarily eerie and forbidding this morning. She reminded herself that this was certainly not the first time she had been alone in it.

It was the viscount's presence that was making her nervous, she decided. She really must get a firm grasp on her imagination. *Stick to the business at hand,* she lectured herself silently.

Gideon came up behind her, moving with his noiseless, gliding tread. The glow of his lamp added to the bizarre shadows on the walls. He looked around, his face set in disapproving lines. "Have you been in the habit of entering these caves alone, Miss Pomeroy, or do you generally have someone accompany you?"

"When my father was alive, he was usually my companion. But since his death I have always gone exploring alone."

"I do not think it a particularly sound notion."

She slanted him a wary glance. "So you have said. This way, my lord." She walked deeper into the cave, chillingly aware of Gideon hard on her heels. "The passage is actually quite comfortably wide, as you can see. It does not get much narrower than this even at its smallest point."

"Your notion of comfort is somewhat different than my own, Miss Pomeroy." Gideon's tone was dry.

Harriet glanced back over her shoulder and saw that he was having to stoop and angle his massive shoulders in order to get through the passage. "You are rather large, are you not?"

"A good deal larger than you, Miss Pomeroy."

She bit her lip. "Well, do try not to get stuck. It would be very awkward."

"Yes, it would. Especially given the fact that this portion of the cave is obviously flooded when the tide is in." Gideon examined the dripping rock walls. A small, pale crab scurried out of the glare of the lamplight and darted into the shadows.

"All the lower portions of these caverns along the base of the cliffs are filled with seawater during high tide," Harriet said, moving forward again. "That should be extremely useful information for you to utilize when you plan how you will apprehend the thieves. The villains are, after all, only around late at night and only when the tide is out. Any scheme constructed for catching them will need to be based on those facts."

"Thank you, Miss Pomeroy, I shall bear that in mind."

She frowned at his wryly sarcastic words. "I was merely trying to assist you in this matter."

"Ummm."

"Need I remind you, my lord, that I am the one who has been observing the villains? It seems to me you should be glad of the opportunity to consult with me on how best to go about laying a trap for them."

"And I would remind you, Miss Pomeroy, that I used to live in this district. I am well aware of the terrain."

"Yes, I know, but you have no doubt forgotten a great many small details. And due to my extensive explorations I am something of an expert on these caves."

"I promise you, Miss Pomeroy, that should I need your advice, I will request it."

Irritation overcame Harriet's wariness. "You would no doubt enjoy somewhat broader social acceptance, sir, if you could contrive to be more polite."

"I have no particular interest in expanding my social life."

"Apparently not," she muttered. She was about to say something more on the subject when one of her half boots skidded on a stray bit of seaweed that had been left behind by the departing waters. She slipped and reached out to catch herself. Her gloved hand slid along the slimy wall without finding purchase. "Bloody hell."

"I have you," Gideon said calmly. His arm circled her waist and pulled her securely back against his broad chest.

"Excuse me." Harriet was suddenly breathless as she found herself locked to Gideon. His arm was like a bond of steel, hard and utterly unyielding.

She could feel the solid, muscled outlines of his chest against her back. The toe of one of his massive boots had somehow wedged itself intimately between her feet. She was acutely conscious of the pressure of his thigh against her buttocks.

When she took a deep breath she caught the warm, masculine scent of his body. It was richly laced with the smell of damp wool and leather. She tensed instinctively at the unaccustomed sensation of being held so close by a man.

"You must exercise more care, Miss Pomeroy." Gideon released her. "Or you will surely come to a bad end in these caves."

"I assure you, I have never been in the least bit of danger in these caves."

"Until now?" He gave her a bland look of inquiry.

Harriet decided to ignore that. "This way, my lord. It is only a little farther now." She straightened her pelisse and the skirts of her gown. Then she took a firmer grip on the lamp, held it boldly aloft, and strode forward into the bowels of the cave.

Gideon followed in silence, only the play of light and shadows on wet stone giving any indication of his presence. Harriet did not venture to say another word about plans and schemes for apprehending thieves. She led him along the gradual upward incline of the sloping passageway until they reached the point where the seawaters did not lap during high tide.

The cave walls and floor were dry here, although a bone-chilling cold permeated the atmosphere. Harriet automatically studied the rocky surfaces as the lamplight struck them. Her customary enthusiasm for fossils got the better of her.

"Do you know, I found a wonderful fossil leaf embedded in a stone here in this portion of the cave." She glanced back over her shoulder. "Have you by any chance read Mr. Parkinson's articles on the importance of relating fossil plants to the stratum in which they are found?"

"No, Miss Pomeroy, I have not."

"Well, it is the most amazing thing, you know. Similar fossil plants are found in exactly the same strata throughout England, no matter how deep the strata happen to be. It appears to be true on the continent as well."

"Fascinating." Gideon sounded amused rather than fascinated, however. "You appear to be quite passionate on the subject."

"I can see the subject of fossils is of little interest to you, but I assure you, sir, that there is much about the past to be learned from them. I myself have great hopes of someday discovering something of great importance here in these caves. I have made several intriguing finds already."

"So have I," Gideon murmured.

Unable to decide just what he meant by that remark and not at all certain she wished to know, Harriet lapsed back into silence. She was well aware that she tended to bore people who did not share her enthusiasm for her favorite subject.

A few minutes later she turned a corner in the passageway ahead and halted at the entrance to a large cavern. Harriet stepped through the opening and held the lamp higher to throw light on the array of canvas bags that sat in the center of the rocky floor. She looked at Gideon as he followed her into the cavern.

"This it is, my lord." She waited with a sense of expectation for him to appear properly astounded by the sight of the stolen goods stacked in the chamber.

Gideon said nothing as he moved farther into the room. But his expression was satisfyingly grave as he stopped near a canvas bag. He crouched beside it and untied the leather thong that closed it.

Harriet watched as he held his lamp higher to peer inside the sack. He studied the contents for a moment and then plunged his gloved hand inside. He withdrew a beautifully chased silver candlestick.

"Very interesting." Gideon watched the light gleam on the silver. "Do you know, when you told me the tale of this cavern yesterday, Miss Pomeroy, I confess I had a few doubts. I wondered if you were perhaps indulging an overambitious imagination. But now I have to agree there is something serious going on here."

"You see what I mean when I say the items must be from some other locale, my lord? If something very fine such as that candlestick had gone missing around Upper Biddleton, we would have heard about it."

"I take your point." Gideon retied the thong and rose to his feet. His heavy greatcoat flowed around him like a cloak as he moved to another sack.

Harriet watched him for a moment longer and then lost interest. She had already given the goods a cursory examination when she had first discovered them.

Her main interest, as always, was the cave itself. Something deep within her was certain that untold treasures lay in wait here in this place, treasures that had nothing to do with stolen jewelry or silver candlesticks.

Harriet wandered over to take a closer look at an interesting outcropping of rock. "I trust you will deal with the villains quickly, St. Justin," she remarked as she ran her gloved fingers over a faint outline embedded in the stone. "I am very eager to explore this cavern properly."

"I can see that."

Harriet frowned intently as she bent closer to view the outline. "I can tell from your tone of voice that you think I am ordering you about again. I am sorry to annoy you, my lord, but I really am getting most impatient. I have been forced to wait several days already for you to arrive and now I suppose I shall have to wait a bit longer until the villains are apprehended."

"No doubt."

She glanced back at where he was hunkered down beside another sack. "How long will it take you to act?"

"I cannot give you an answer just yet. You must allow me to deal with the matter as I see fit."

"I trust you will not be long about it."

"Miss Pomeroy, if you will recall, you summoned me here to Upper Biddleton because you wanted to turn the problem over to me. Very well. You have done so. I am now in charge of clearing the villains out of your precious cavern. I will keep you informed of my progress." Gideon spoke absently, his attention on a fistful of glittering stones that he was removing from the sack.

"Yes, but—" Harriet broke off. "What have you got there?"

"A necklace. A rather valuable one, I should say. Assuming these stones are genuine."

"They probably are." Harriet shrugged the matter aside. She had no particular interest in the necklace except insofar as she wanted it out of her cavern. "I doubt anyone would go to the trouble of hiding a fake necklace in here." She turned back to her examination of the fossil outline and peered intently at it. "Good heavens."

"What is it?"

"There is something very interesting here, my lord." She held the lamp closer to the surface of the stone. "I am not precisely certain, but it may well be a tooth." Harriet studied the outline in the rock with mounting excitement. "And it appears to be still attached to a portion of the jaw."

"A great thrill for you, apparently."

"Well, of course it is. A tooth that is still embedded in a jaw is ever so much more easy to identify than one that is not. If only I could use my mallet and chisel to get it out of this rock today." She whipped around anxiously, willing him to understand the importance of retrieving the fossil for study. "I do not suppose I dare—"

"No." Gideon dropped the glittering necklace back into the sack and rose to his feet. "You are not to use your tools in here until we have cleaned out this nest of thieves. You were quite right to hold off on your work in this cavern, Miss Pomeroy. We do not wish to alarm this ring of cutthroats."

"You think they might move their stolen goods elsewhere if they thought they had been discovered?"

"I am far more concerned that if anyone saw evidence of fossil collecting in here, the trail would lead straight back to you. There cannot be that many collectors in the district."

Harriet eyed the rocky outcropping in frustration. The thought of leaving this new discovery behind was very upsetting. "But what if someone else finds my tooth?"

"I doubt anyone will notice your precious tooth. Not when there is a fortune in gems and silver sitting in the middle of this chamber."

Harriet scowled thoughtfully and tapped the toe of her half boot. "I am not so certain my tooth will be safe here. I have told you before that there are a great many unscrupulous fossil collectors. Perhaps I should just chisel this one little bit out of the rock and trust that no one will notice—*oh*."

Gideon had set down his lamp and taken two long strides forward. He was suddenly looming over her, one huge hand planted against the cave wall behind her head. She was caged between his solid body and the equally solid rock. Her eyes widened.

"Miss Pomeroy," Gideon said very softly, each word spaced for maximum emphasis, "I will say this once more and once more only. You are going to stay out of this cavern until further notice. Indeed, you will not come anywhere near this place until I say it is safe to do so. In fact, you will stay out of all the cliff caves until I have taken care of matters."

"Really, St. Justin, you go too far."

He leaned closer. The yellow glare from the lamp in Harriet's hand cast his harsh features into demonic relief. For a moment he truly looked like the beast he was reputed to be.

"You will not," Gideon said through his teeth, "hunt fossils anywhere on this beach until I have given you express permission to do so."

"Now, see here, sir. If you think I will tolerate this sort of behavior from you, you may think again. I have no intention of giving up all fossil hunting along this beach until such time as you see fit to allow it. I have certain rights in this matter."

"You have no rights in this, Miss Pomeroy. You have clearly come to think of these caves as your personal property, but I would like to remind you that my family happens to own every square inch of the land that is presently over your head," Gideon bit out. "If I catch you anywhere near these caves I shall consider it trespassing."

She eyed him furiously, trying to determine if he was actually serious. "Is that so? And what will you do, sir? Have me clapped into prison or transported? Don't be ridiculous."

"Perhaps I shall find another way to punish you for disobeying me, Miss Pomeroy. I am St. Justin, remember? The Beast of Blackthorne Hall." His eyes gleamed in the golden light. The scar on his face was a vivid, savage slash of old pain and mortal danger. "The local people think I am a man totally lacking in honor when it comes to dealing with women. Ask anyone around here and he will you tell you I am the devil himself where innocent young ladies are concerned."

"Rubbish." Harriet's fingers were trembling on the lamp,

but she held her ground. "I believe you are deliberately trying to frighten me, sir."

"Damn right." His hand closed around the nape of her neck. The leather of his glove was rough against her skin.

Harriet abruptly read the intent in him, but it was too late to run. Gideon's fierce, leonine eyes flamed behind his hooded dark lashes. He brought his mouth heavily down on hers in a crushing kiss.

Harriet stood transfixed for a timeless instant. She could not move, could not even think. Nothing she had ever experienced in her entire twenty-four and a half years had prepared her for Gideon's embrace.

He groaned heavily, the sound reverberating deep in his chest. His big hand flexed with startling gentleness around her throat, his thumb tracing the line of her jaw. And then he was urging her closer to the fierce warmth of his own body. The heavy greatcoat brushed against Harriet's legs.

She could not seem to catch her breath. After the initial shock, a shimmering, glittering excitement roared through her. When Gideon removed the lamp from her limp, unresisting fingers, she scarcely noticed. Without conscious volition, Harriet raised her hands to his shoulders and sank her fingers into the heavy wool of his coat. She did not know whether she was trying to push him away or pull him closer.

"Bloody hell." Gideon's voice was husky now, betraying some new emotion that Harriet could not identify. "If you had any sense you would run from me as fast as you possibly can."

"I do not think I could run a single step," Harriet whispered in bemused wonder. She looked up at him through her lashes and gently touched his scarred cheek.

Gideon flinched at the feel of her fingers. Then his eyes narrowed. "Just as well. I am suddenly not in the mood to let you escape me."

He lowered his head again and his mouth moved on hers, easing apart her lips until she realized with shock that he wanted inside. Hesitantly, she obeyed the silent command.

When his tongue surged into her warmth with stunning intimacy, she moaned softly and sagged against him. Never had a man kissed her in this manner.

"You are very delicate," he finally said against her lips. "Very soft. But there is strength in you." Gideon slid his hands around Harriet's waist.

She shivered as he grasped her firmly and lifted her up high against his chest. He held her effortlessly off the stone floor. Her booted feet dangled helplessly in midair. She was forced to steady herself by clinging to his broad shoulders.

"Kiss me," he ordered in a deep, dark voice that sent a delicious chill down Harriet's spine.

Without stopping to think, she wrapped her arms around his neck and brushed her mouth shyly across his. Was this what it meant to be ravished? she wondered. Perhaps it was just this heady mix of emotion and desire that had encouraged poor Deirdre Rushton to surrender to Gideon all those years ago. If so, Harriet decided, she could now understand that young woman's recklessness.

"Ah, my sweet Miss Pomeroy," Gideon muttered, "can it be that you do not find my features any more offensive than those of your precious fossil skulls?"

"There is nothing in the least offensive about you, my lord, as I am certain you are well aware." Harriet moistened her lips with the tip of her tongue. She felt dazed with the emotions that were surging within her. She touched his ravaged face lightly and smiled tremulously. "You are magnificent."

Gideon looked startled for an instant. His eyes blazed. And then his expression hardened. He set her slowly on her feet. "Well, then, Miss Harriet Pomeroy?" There was an unmistakable challenge in the words.

"Well, what, my lord?" Harriet managed with a coolness she was far from feeling. It was true she had virtually no experience in this sort of thing, but all her womanly instincts were assuring her that Gideon had been as powerfully affected by that kiss as she had been. She did not understand why he had suddenly gone all cold and dangerous.

"You have a decision to make. You may either take off your gown and lie down on the stone floor of this cave so that we can finish what we have started or you may run back toward the beach and safety. I suggest you make your choice quickly, as my own mood is somewhat unpredictable at the moment. I must tell you that I find you a very tempting little morsel."

Harriet felt as if he had thrown a bucket of cold seawater over her head. She stared at Gideon, her sensual euphoria vanishing in the face of the obvious threat. *He is serious,* she thought. He was actually warning her that if she did not get out of this cavern right now he might ravish her on the spot.

It was her own fault, she realized in belated dismay. She had responded much too readily to his kiss. He was bound to think the worst of her.

Harriet's face flamed with humiliation and not a little primitive female fear. She scooped up her lamp and fled toward the safety of the passage that led to the beach.

Gideon followed, but Harriet did not once look back. She was too afraid that she would see the taunting laughter of the beast in his golden eyes.